THE

SERIAL KILLER SERIES

BOOKS 6-10

DAN PADAVONA

Copyright Information

Published by Dan Padavona

Visit our website at www.danpadavona.com

Cover Design by eBookLaunch

Although some of the locations in this book are actual places, the characters and setting are wholly of the author's imagination. Any resemblance between the people in this book and people in the real world is purely coincidental and unintended.

Scarlett Bell Books 6-10

Scarlett Bell Books 6-10

CHASING THE DEVIL

CHAPTER ONE

He's in the fog behind her.

Closer.

To one side, the creek giggles like the souls of lost children. To the other, gangling weeds turn devilish in the dark.

The distant bicycle appears in the mist, and Scarlett Bell hurries. Chest tight with lost breath and terror.

It's dangerous to look back, yet she does.

For a moment, he appears. She holds back a scream, for there is no face on her pursuer. Only a smooth patch of skin where the eyes, nose, and mouth should be. He is more monster than man.

Her legs pump harder. Sprint for the bike. For safety. His footsteps keep pace. Gain on her. The man is too strong, too fast for a child to outrun.

Cold, slithery fingers touch her neck. Like the undead appendages of a nameless beast rising out of the creek bed.

The scream inside her dream pulled Bell awake. She was stunned by her surroundings at first, not the stifling darkness of her bedroom's blackout curtains but the dim, soothing light of Dr Morford's office. A ticking clock kept beat with the daylight, which slipped around the curtains and reminded her that night is not forever, and slowly her heartbeat conformed to that of the clock. Her hands ceased trembling. Breathing slowed.

"Sorry. Did I scream?"

Balding and almost a foot taller than Bell, Dr Morford stroked his goatee and examined her over his glasses. These moments often made Bell feel like a lab rat, or maybe a strange animal on display at the zoo.

"No, you were quiet as a mouse."

Bell rubbed her temples. A thin sheen of dampness coated her hair. A cold sweat.

"Did you see him this time, Scarlett?"

A tremor of fear rolled through her body as she recalled the faceless man in the fog.

"Just a shapeless face."

"No mouth or eyes again?"

"None."

Bell's hands curled into fists, nails dug at her pant legs.

"You did well, Scarlett. Don't expect answers overnight."

"Overnight? We've been at this for over a year, and I still don't know who he is or if any of this happened. For all I know, this is just my imagination convincing me a nightmare I had when I was nine actually occurred."

"Tell me what you saw when the man appeared. What time of day was it?"

Bell recounted the hypnosis-induced nightmare. The darkness suggested it was well after sunset, but that made no sense. In the past, she'd dreamed her childhood friend's killer chased her during the early morning before most of the neighborhood rose from bed.

Morford slid his glasses atop his head and crossed one leg over the other. Leaning to one side of a lounge chair, he chewed the end of his pen in thought.

"I'm curious, Scarlett. Have you discussed your dreams with your parents?"

"God, no."

"No?"

"Why would I drag my parents through that again? You have to understand what it was like for them. For all of us. After the killer murdered Jillian, the neighborhood... changed. We weren't allowed to play without supervision, and our parents aged twenty years overnight. Especially Mom and Dad."

"Because you were Jillian Rossi's closest friend."

"Yes. We played together and followed the creek to-and-from our homes. It could have been me he caught." Bell bit her lower lip. "I wish it had been."

Morford wrote something on a notepad.

"Why do you wish it had been you who died?"

Bell looked at the dust motes dancing before the curtained window, seeing another place and time.

"If you had seen Jillian's parents...after her death, it was as if they weren't alive anymore. Like they were husks. I wouldn't wish that on anyone."

"And yet if it had been you who died, the same fate would have befallen your parents."

She gave a meaningless nod. She understood this on a conscious level. Understanding didn't lend her relief. As a BAU criminal profiler with the FBI she faced monsters daily and was equipped with the ability to process darkness better than an adult Jillian would. Maybe that wasn't fair. Bell envisioned Jillian as an adult and wondered if she would have taken up the sword as Bell had and become a field agent, sworn to avenge her best friend's death.

"My parents haven't spoken about what happened to Jillian in a long time. Why open the closet and release the skeletons again?"

Morford wore an ironic smile.

"You're a profiler, Scarlett. You know better than anyone that your parents never stopped thinking about Jillian or worrying over what happened. Are you certain you never told them the killer tried to catch you?"

"Or that I dreamed it happened."

"The descriptions you give are unusually vivid for a dream."

Bell laughed without mirth, a dry, dead-leaf sound.

"I'm told I have an overactive imagination."

"It serves you well. Your record is exemplary."

And yet serial killer Logan Wolf eluded Bell and managed to stalk Bell to California, Kansas, and to her oceanside Virginia home without her knowing. It took her months before she learned Gavin Hayward, the lead reporter for the nation's largest tabloid, *The Informer*, followed her from case-to-case and photographed Bell.

Pain caught her attention. She'd dug her fingernails into her thighs again.

"Is it possible I'll never know if the killer chased me or if it was a nightmare? I was nine, halfway through grade school. I have sharp memories from when I was younger, so I should remember."

Morford crossed the other leg and glanced at the clock. To a new patient, it might appear Morford was disinterested, even rude. After a year of therapy, she recognized this mannerism as deep thought, consideration. For goodness sake, she was interpreting her psychologist's actions and playing the role of profiler.

"Whether it was real or dream, fight or flight could explain why you don't recall what happened. Jillian's murder is an open wound, so imagine how it feels to a child—too much to process. Naturally, the mind chooses flight and builds protective walls. Otherwise, the damage is too much for a nine-year-old to handle. Whether it was a dream or an actual experience, your mind strives to suppress the memory." Morford clicked the pen off and placed it in his lap. "But physical proof is irrefutable. If Jillian's murderer attempted to abduct you, surely you told your parents. I trust a police report exists."

When she failed to reply, Morford set the notepad on the table.

"I believed we could determine the truth through hypnosis. It's time for a different approach. Speak to your parents, Scarlett. The truth cannot be more terrifying than your nightmares."

Bell closed her eyes and fell back against the couch.

This wasn't the answer she wanted.

CHAPTER TWO

The last leg of the drive home took Bell down the coast. With the calendar having changed to March, the sun was noticeably stronger and baked the car's interior, even on cool days. The Atlantic sparkled and crashed behind grassy dunes, the off-season beach sparsely populated but beginning to fill with fishers and boaters. Temperatures climbed into the sixties, and the osprey were back and nesting near the shoreline atop dead trees, telephone poles, and docks. By mid-June the seasonal restaurants would reopen, heralding the influx of vacationers.

Bell navigated the car around a bend and saw the roof of Lucas's beach house peek over a dune. She caught herself gripping the steering wheel too tight and inhaled. Slow and deep, ballooning her stomach before she exhaled as Dr Morford taught her. Though no reason existed for Lucas to incite anger or anxiety—they'd talked out their differences, and Lucas assured Bell he wasn't jealous she shared the same room with Gardy during cases—a barrier existed between them. A glass wall that allowed sight and prevented touch. Conversations felt forced and awkward. She'd believed nearly two months would be sufficient to break the ice coating their relationship..

She contemplated swinging into his driveway, then

continued down the road until the beach house vanished from the mirrors. A black Explorer idled near the back of the lot when she brought her vehicle to a stop in front of her apartment. She locked the car and waved. Though it was impossible to see beyond the tinted windows on a sunny day, she perceived movement and knew he'd waved back. She didn't know who was inside the vehicle. Different FBI agents watched her building on a 24-hour rotation and would protect her until they captured Logan Wolf. A horrendous waste of resources, Bell thought. Wolf hadn't contacted her since she refused to develop a profile of his wife's killer. The evidence pointed to Wolf, and logic told her the FBI was correct in targeting the former BAU agent, but she wasn't sure he'd killed his wife. Unlike most killers who murdered their spouses, he seemed broken by her loss. Dying inside.

The key slipped into the lock, and the door opened to a shadowed apartment and the cool breath of air conditioning. It took a while for her eyes to adjust as she squinted at the mountain of mail, most of it junk from apparel stores she never frequented. She removed a postcard from the pile and grinned. Her parents lived only three hours away, and her mother routinely sent texts and emails, but Tammy Bell had an affinity for postcards and sent one to Bell monthly. This card featured a green palm tree leaning over impossibly blue waters, and Bell smirked. This was a postcard you sent from a vacation in the Bahamas, not from your cozy house in Bealton, Virginia while Dad oiled the door hinges. Bell read it over and tucked it away with a silent promise to call her parents later.

Bell aimed the remote at the television and turned on the news, background noise to keep her company while she finished the morning chores. In her bedroom, she checked the news aggregator on her laptop and typed the search terms she used every day: missing, child, abduction, murder, river, creek. The search results always yielded noise and false alarms, but a new headline filled her body with ice.

Missing Child's Body Discovered at Lutzke Creek.

Opening the story, she scanned the text until she determined the location of Lutzke Creek. A small Georgia town called Erwin. In a separate window, she typed the town's name into Google Earth. It took a long time to load, then a three-dimensional image filled the window. She zoomed in, taking note of Erwin's proximity to the coast. Fifteen miles. Now she viewed Erwin from street level. Erwin could have been any small town in America, including Bealton, except the swampy terrain and tropical foliage choking out competing flora marked the area as southeastern. A chill crawled down her back.

An unbidden view came to her. The killer's perspective. So much seclusion offered by the jungle-like environs. Here, dumping a body without being seen would be easy, especially if done in the dead of night.

She clicked the article and brought the window to the forefront. Bregan Dane, age ten. Too close to Jillian's age.

The girl, last seen playing near the creek, went missing five days ago. Search crews combed the town and surrounding wilderness and found no sign of Dane as though someone plucked the girl from the earth. A group of teenagers discovered the girl's body along the creek bed last night. The teens likely partied by the creek, Bell reasoned. The location was remote enough to avoid prying eyes, and in the dark, no one would see them drinking unless they slogged across a hundred feet of boggy field.

Automatically, she reached for her phone and typed in Gardy's number. She stopped herself before pressing send. Technically, she was on administrative leave, a fancy way of saying Bell couldn't return to work until the psychology evaluation came back clean. In less than a year, she'd killed three men: serial killer Alan Hodge, sniper William Meeks, and William Schuler, who murdered three women over several horrifying days. The rapid escalation of

Schuler's killing spree still shocked Bell.

She didn't blame the FBI. Don Weber, the Deputy Director of CIRG and Bell's immediate supervisor, needed to be certain she was fit for field work, and the lack of progress with Dr Morford and constant nightmares weren't helping her case.

Bell copied the article into a Google document. She'd saved several others over the last year, a few promising leads, most dead ends. Bregan Dane's murder cut closest to the bone. The anxious intensity which overcame her at the onset of a new hunt returned to her now. Logan Wolf had told Bell Jillian's killer was still loose. Active again. How Wolf obtained this information she could only guess. Strangely, she trusted the madman's judgment.

Bell sat back in her chair, fingers steepled against her chin. Her heart raced, skin clammy. She instinctively reached for the Glock-22 and remembered the FBI confiscated the weapon, pending the psychological evaluation.

Bell needed to convince Weber to reinstate her and send a team to Erwin. If only he would listen.

CHAPTER THREE

The tabloid lies open on the passenger seat of his car. Like the wings of an ancient beast.

Though the focus of the article is Scarlett Bell, the young profiler for the FBI's Behavioral Analysis Unit, he is the story's antagonist. Emotions quiver through him—excitement over his stardom, anger at the woman's insistence she will solve Jillian Rossi's murder and put the cold case to rest.

The decades between his first kill and present day dulled his memory as though it bobbed at the bottom of a swamp, concealed by oily waters. Jillian Rossi. He'd almost forgotten her name, though the girl's face remained permanently etched in his memory. They say the first time is best. Drug users call it chasing ghosts. The hunger never abates.

His eyes fix on Bell's picture. Follow the supple curves of her body. Mature women do little for him, yet she draws him for reasons he doesn't understand. He rubs his thumb across her face, imagining the soft warmth of her flesh and how it would feel to touch the profiler.

A child's yell pulls his attention back to the park. Two young girls, one blonde, one redhead, both in skirts. And a boy. He estimates their ages between eleven and fourteen. The redhead shoves the blonde toward the boy, a flirtatious game that results in laughter and the blonde twisting away before she falls into the boy's arms.

Their coquettish game draws him. Flies to carrion. Three children are too many to contain, and the boy may prove to be a problem.

A black dog patrols along the fence. Tail wagging, it darts after a small animal in the underbrush.

The man is content to observe from hiding. An old elm extends moss-covered branches and throws a dark cloak over the car. Spanish moss hangs like wizards' beards, adds a sense of mystery and wonder as though the scene takes place on an alien planet. The March sun is bright, strong, and previews the coming summer heat, but the shade keeps the vehicle cool. He opens the window and invites the earthy, damp scents into the car. Insects hum behind the car somewhere in the gloomy nether regions of tropical foliage. A darting dragonfly announces a pond is nearby.

A fence girds the park, a baseball field with a freshly lined diamond at the far end, playground equipment erected close to the parking lot.

The girls race to the swing set. The redhead wins the race, the blonde out of breath and lagging behind. Vulnerable.

As he scans the parking lot for intruders, the girls climb onto the swings. Their legs pump, pale flesh revealed to the upper thighs, and drive the girls higher—into the depthless blue where birds fly—while the boy pushes each from behind.

This is the moment which excites him. Tantalizes. Though the chance of a successful hunt is low, the possibilities are endless. Most times, all he does is watch, and today may end in disappointment. The boy needs to leave. That is step one. But the boy appears smitten with the blonde, perhaps with the redhead as well. If the boy departs, he still needs to get one of the girls alone. The blonde is the optimal target. The race proved the other girl to be faster, stronger, and if the chase became a footrace, he'd have a better chance to catch the blonde.

Their laughter carries to the car like the cries of gulls.

While his mind wanders, they climb down from the swings. The boy tries to kiss the blonde, and she runs in a circle to avoid him. Finally, the redhead catches her, holds the blonde's arms behind her back until the boy leans in and plants a kiss on the girl's cheek. Playfully, the blonde rubs the remnants of the kiss on her shirt as though it is an infectious disease.

When the man was young, he perceived his classmates as much larger than him. Not physically, for he stood a hair taller than average. They were more mature somehow, confident, and he submissively cowered in their presence, girls included. He never considered slipping a love note into a locker let alone kissing a girl on the cheek. Then he outgrew his trepidation, became stronger. The alpha. And developed a taste for blood.

When he decided to take one of the girls, they would be powerless to stop him. If he strode across the park now and caught the blonde, he'd risk the other two escaping.

No witnesses. No police. Better he exists as a ghost, a legend. A boogeyman tale they whisper of at midnight.

The dog is on its belly near the back of the park, pawing at its quarry. The man's patience wanes when the boy, still laughing from the awkward kiss, waves and backs away.

Then the boy turns as if embarrassed and runs across the outfield toward a break in the fence. It isn't until now the man recognizes the path arrowing into a neighborhood of old southern homes. He needs to remain watchful of adults sneaking into the park. The boy repeatedly stops and yells back to the girls. The words echo off the trees, incomprehensible from inside the car. He vanishes into the neighborhood, his red backpack visible through a stand of bushes, then he disappears completely.

Only the two girls remain.

The man's courage builds. He dreams of capturing the blonde. An incredible risk should he fail.

One last glance around the park. Then he opens the door.

CHAPTER FOUR

"For the last time, the answer is no."

Bell hid clenched fists behind Weber's desk. She battled not to squirm. Silver-haired, a nose and jaw cut to sharp and dangerous edges, Weber intimidated with an unwavering glare and a baritone voice that suggested a much larger man.

The door stood closed, muffling her co-workers' voices. Now-and-then she saw a shape pass by the window and wondered if it was Gardy checking on her, but the partially drawn blinds prevented her from recognizing faces.

"The murder is an exact replica of Jillian Rossi's. Same age range, body dumped along the creek for the neighbors to find."

Weber removed his glasses and set them down with a bang. His forefinger and thumb worked along the bridge of his nose, eyes clamped shut.

"What's it been, Agent Bell? Twenty years?"

"Twenty-three." She paused, then sheepishly added, "Sir."

"Twenty-three years is too long to chase a ghost. I fear your therapy has stalled. Your friend's killer is either incarcerated or dead." Weber held up a hand to thwart

Bell's next point. "Right now, there are over 100,000 open cases involving missing children in the U.S., and in any given year, half-a-million disappear. While I concede similarity exists between the Erwin murder and what happened to your friend, it's hardly unusual for a killer to dump a body in a rural location along a body of water."

Bell's eyes wandered to the plaques, university degrees, and letters of commendation covering the walls. Expertise in profiling wasn't necessary to realize Weber always set the tone—he was the alpha dog, superior. He was impenetrable, refused to budge.

"Even if it's not the same killer, the BAU should provide assistance on the case."

Weber swiveled casually in his chair. He glanced at his watch, a sign he'd tired of this discussion.

"Unless the local authorities request our presence, the BAU has no jurisdiction in Erwin. And until the psychological evaluation demonstrates you're fit to work again, you're officially on administrative leave."

Bell clamped her tongue against the roof of her mouth to stop herself from arguing. Weber's eyes held the gleam of victory, and he'd relish firing Bell if she became insubordinate. The only female field agent with the BAU, Bell often wondered if Weber was chauvinistic against women or simply prejudiced. Sometimes men in power supported women's rights but didn't consider women capable of handling dangerous, male-dominated careers. A quiet form of oppression.

"At least put me back on desk work. Let me provide assistance to the field agents."

"Absolutely. As soon as the evaluation shows you're ready."

"So now what?"

"Go home, Agent Bell. Most people in America relish a paid vacation."

"It's not a vacation when an agent watches you day

and night."

Bell jammed her sunglasses onto her face and stomped down the concrete steps into the parking lot. A part of her wanted to spin around and throw a lewd gesture toward the building, knowing full well the deputy director watched her from the window. Instead, she cut between two rows of vehicles, temporarily confused until she remembered she'd parked her new Rogue two spaces from Gardy's minivan.

She snickered when she saw Gardy's ride, and was tempted to write *Soccer Mom* on a piece of paper and attach it to his window. Then she remembered the strain between them. It had only grown since he interrogated Bell about William Schuler's knife wounds. She couldn't explain how she'd come upon the knife or why her prints didn't register on the hilt. Because it wasn't her weapon. Logan Wolf had murdered Schuler while Gardy lay unconscious downstairs.

Muscle-draining heat lunged out of the SUV when Bell opened the door, and although the heat of summer was a long way off, she couldn't help but question the intelligence of purchasing a black SUV south of the Mason-Dixon line. When she reached Route 1, she automatically checked her mirrors for an FBI trail. There wasn't one, of course. The FBI staked out her apartment in the hope of catching Logan Wolf but left her alone otherwise. It made no sense. If Wolf wanted to kill Bell, he could stalk her to the supermarket.

The roads were unusually clear along the coastal route, and she could see the Atlantic waves sparkle under the noonday sun. Bell was five minutes from her apartment when she decided. To hell with Weber, Gardy, and the BAU. Erwin, Georgia was a nine-hour drive from Arkendale, quicker if Richmond traffic didn't slow her.

The FBI vehicle sat near the back of the lot as Bell rolled past. Unable to see past the tinted glass, she stopped beside the vehicle and lowered her window. A heartbeat later, the other vehicle's window came down. Flanagan. A dark-haired junior agent with the FBI. Sharp instincts but inexperienced. He appeared annoyed.

"Enjoying the weather?"

"Move along, Agent Bell."

The window ascended. It was obvious Flanagan didn't appreciate Bell risking his cover. Bell gunned the motor and brought the Rogue to a stop in front of her apartment.

It took her ten minutes to pack. Bell always had an overnight bag ready to go. She instinctively reached for her badge and gun, and anger jetted into her throat.

A quick peek out the window verified Flanagan hadn't moved. Then she got down on all fours inside the bedroom closet and removed the pair of t-shirts cloaking her safe. After she entered the passcode, the latch clicked and she reached inside. Bell had evaluated several firearms which mimicked the feel of her FBI-issued Glock-22. None felt quite right, so she'd opted to purchase her own. She slipped the Glock into her holster and donned a baggy sweatshirt to cover the weapon.

Halfway out the door, Bell spied Flanagan's vehicle. Nobody asked questions when she left the apartment, though an understanding existed between Bell and Weber that she notify the assigned agent when she planned to leave for an hour or more. Always observant, Flanagan would notice the overnight bag.

The bag dangled off Bell's arm as she stood with the apartment door cracked open. No way she'd make it to the Rogue. Another idea occurred to her, and she backtracked to the kitchen and grabbed the garbage. Keeping the overnight bag hidden behind the garbage, she locked the door and descended the stairs. With her SUV shielding her, she dropped the overnight bag in front of the bumper and circled around to the dumpster. The garbage deposited, she walked empty-handed to the Rogue, opened the back door to provide herself another shield, then slid the overnight bag below the seat.

The dark and empty eyes of the FBI vehicle's windshield reflected the sun as she turned out of the lot. She checked her mirrors and confirmed Flanagan hadn't followed.

Bell reached I-95 before the agent realized she'd ditched him.

CHAPTER FIVE

The dry warmth of early spring along the Georgia coast should have brought a smile to Officer Elle Lason's lips. It didn't. A sickness gurgled at the bottom of her stomach as she leaned against the cruiser, radio in hand, outside the St. Clair residence. The St. Clair's thirteen-year-old daughter, Rebecca, hadn't returned from the town park. The girl had left with her friend, Nat LaFey, a little after ten. Lason checked her phone. It was two now, and though only four hours had passed, the missing St. Clair girl came on the heels of Bregan Dane's murder. For God's sake, teenagers had discovered the girl's body less than twenty-four hours ago. Dane was probably on the ME's autopsy table right now, and already another girl vanished.

So much for the quiet of rural Georgia. Thirty-six and as fit as she was during her days as Erwin High School's star defender on the varsity soccer team, Lason once set her sight on a career with the FBI. Her application never caught the bureau's eye, or perhaps she didn't own the right connections. Lason slid into the cruiser and caught her reflection in the mirror. A few insurgent grays sprouted from her straight brunette hair. A cut under her eye marked the errant left hook thrown by Kenny Abbott during a bar fight at Kelsey's last weekend. It took Lason and three other officers to subdue the drunk and the out-of-towner Abbott had picked a fight with.

Except for the good ole boy antics, there were advantages to working in her hometown. Most of Lason's family lived here, and with her great aunts and uncles pushing into their eighties, she took comfort knowing they weren't alone and abandoned. Her parents were both dead from early heart attacks, but Lason's brother lived on the east side of town near the coast and regularly invited Lason over for dinner and a Netflix binge.

Little had changed in Erwin over the years. The corner cafe offered WIFI, and a Target slowly consumed the Ma and Pa businesses, but otherwise, a postcard photo taken today looked the same as one taken twenty years ago. The high school was exactly as she remembered, except for the all-glass addition to the library where she'd spoken to female students last year about safety and self-defense. Though the students thought the presentation overkill and unnecessary,

Lason knew hormones affected overzealous boys. Sexual situations spun out of control, and before the girl realized what was happening, the boy forced himself upon her. Rape, though the majority of boys didn't realize what they did was wrong, let alone prosecutable.

But Lason never dreamed of a child murderer running amok in Erwin. A serial killer? She kept the thought to herself.

One whisper of *serial killer* would be a lit match on a bed of hay.

She pulled the car off the shoulder and started down the tree-lined road. Monstrous oaks with interwoven branches blocked much of the light, a tunnel effect. Spanish moss dripped overhead, and a diverse birdsong played in the trees. The radio crackled every several seconds as Chief Haggens directed cruisers toward the town's four corners. The chief tasked her with searching the park. If the

St. Clair girl was in Erwin, they'd find her, and a second nightmare would be averted. But if they didn't find her…

Lason saw her distressed reflection in the windshield. Was it too soon to call the FBI? She'd suggest it to Haggens after she finished her investigation, not that the chief was likely to agree. A good cop, Haggens was a southern boy at heart and harbored mistrust of federal law enforcement. Give them an inch, and they'd take a mile. True, Quantico resided in the south, but anything related to DC reeked of the north as much as Philly and Boston.

She turned down Elm Street. Larger homes, more money. At the dead end, she parked in front of a powder-blue Greek Revival with multiple white columns, a slice of southern Americana. On a low traffic road such as Elm, every kid in the neighborhood played outdoors. Not today. A curtain parted behind one of the Revival's many windows, and an elderly face peeked out.

Following the path into the park, Lason radioed her position to dispatch. The baseball field was rich green, the infield arced in deep browns which ended with pearl-white foul lines. Beyond the outfield rested playground equipment —a swing set, merry-go-round, and monkey bars—and that's where Lason headed.

A coat of fresh red paint glimmered on the equipment. It seemed impossible a murderer had walked these fields this morning. Officer Schenk had interviewed the missing girl's friend, Nat. The redhead said the two girls split up before eleven with a nebulous plan to meet at the park later. After Schenk prodded her, Nat admitted a boy had joined them. Justin Cary, a fair-haired fourteen-year-old and member of the junior varsity football team, was apparently interested in the St. Clair girl.

The two had flirted in the park. Nat claimed Justin departed before she left, but that didn't mean the boy hadn't secretly come back to the park afterward. Justin and Rebecca might be at a friend's house or one of the many secluded make-out points common to all small towns.

Long skid marks below the swing set indicated where kids dragged sneakers to halt their momentum. Lason scanned the ground for evidence and found nothing but an old lollipop stick, one end tinged purple by candy. No matted grass or unusual scuff marks to indicate a struggle. But the field stretched a long way back to the parking lot, too much ground to cover for one officer.

It was more than a whim which drew her to the lot. A pair of shade trees hung over the fence and dropped a veil-like shadow over the parking spaces. A good place to hide and observe, Lason thought with a sick stomach. Recent rains had left oily puddles, and when she scanned the blacktop, a gray streak caught her eye. A tire track. Shielded from the wind, the muddy print was partially intact but drying. She pulled out her phone and snapped pictures from multiple angles, noticing the track came from a car, not a truck. The car could have belonged to anyone. A jogger, a parent. The severe hook the track followed before fading to dirt speckles suggested the driver had been in a hurry.

A second track followed parallel to the first. The passenger side tire, she thought, though the print looked too faded to be of use. She started to turn away when she noted two additional tracks. The width between the new prints was different from the others, not drawn by the rear tires. Another vehicle? It was possible, but each set of tracks followed the same arc out of the parking spot.

"Carradine, come in."

The dispatcher answered her radio call after a moment.

"I have multiple tire tracks near where the St. Clair girl disappeared."

Carradine passed the information to the chief who promised crime scene assistance from Savannah. Lason sent the photographs to the station for further evaluation and sighed as she looked over the sprawling park. She might as well be searching for the proverbial needle in a haystack. The midday sun burned as she returned to the field and swept the area between the lot and playground.

CHAPTER SIX

Bell intended to drive straight through to Erwin before her hunger grew teeth. Pulling off I-95 at the Florence, SC exit, she dragged herself into a diner situated in a tractor trailer-friendly lot across the road from a chain hotel. The waiter looked a little older than college age, a scruffy red beard shielding a face full of acne. He was tall and skinny, tattooed along the arms. He suggested the Paradise Cheeseburger, and Bell gave her approval.

Two texts waited on her phone. One from Gardy asking where she was. Bell assumed Flanagan raised the red flag when Bell didn't return to the apartment, and soon the FBI would come looking if she didn't call off the dogs. She responded with a lie about visiting friends out of town.

The second message was from Lucas. Her thumb paused over the message, then she opened the text. He'd invited her for dinner and included a picture of him proudly dangling a fish from a line. Immediately, she questioned her decision to drive south on a wild goose chase. Weber was right. She was following a ghost, a killer who'd probably been dead for years.

Except she kept hearing Logan Wolf's warning in her head when doubts arose.

The scruffy waiter set a glass of water on the table. Lost in thought, Bell ripped the paper off the straw and rolled it around in her hand.

She called up Lucas's message again and replied.

Geez, I wish you'd asked earlier. I'm out of town for the day visiting friends.

The same lie she'd told Gardy. She'd woven herself into a tangled web.

Bell's phone buzzed in her hand and surprised her. Lucas again.

You're missing a brilliant sunset. And I got key lime pie from Antonia's.

Regret clawed at Bell's heart. What was she doing in Florence? She could be home before midnight if she reversed course after dinner.

Sounds amazing. Can I take a rain check?

No promises I don't eat the entire pie tonight.

Bell grinned, the most she'd smiled in weeks.

You'll turn into a tub-o-lard.

A moment's pause, then…

I eat too much when I'm lonely.

And there it was. The dagger to the heart. Feeling more foolish by the second, she glanced toward the kitchen and saw her plate ready for pickup.

Sorry. I would have come if you'd asked earlier.

When will you be home?

Bell chewed on her answer for a moment.

Two days. Maybe tomorrow. Convince me to leave now. Please.

That doesn't sound like you. Enjoy hanging out with your friends. I'll be here when you get back. At least you aren't away on some grisly murder case.

Bell stood from her chair and surveyed the parking lot. She half-expected to see Lucas, laughing because he'd caught her in a fib. Instead, a mixed bag of rusty southern license plates colored the travel stop. A lonely sight, Bell thought.

She thanked Lucas for understanding. She missed him, wished to bridge the chasm between them when she returned to Virginia.

The burger wasn't good, gristly and dripping with a king's ransom of condiments, but it hit the spot the way all comfort foods do when one is starving and morose. She finished the burger and ate a plate of fries, silently issuing a promise to hit the gym.

While Bell waited for the waiter to return with change —not wanting the FBI to track her credit card usage, she brought enough cash to pay for gas, food, and a hotel—she checked her phone for updates on the Bregan Dane murder.

And saw the front-page article about another missing girl on the *Erwin Standard* website.
Rebecca St. Clair, age thirteen, older than Dane and Jillian but young enough for a child killer. The girl's picture accompanied the lead story. Blonde, gaunt yet pretty. She couldn't imagine the parents' panic.

Bell sensed the case getting away from her. A semi truck hurtling down the highway at seventy mph with Bell chasing on foot. Waiting impatiently for the waiter to return, Bell stuffed the phone into her pocket and watched the last light of day seep beneath a horizon of southern pines. Finally, she told him to keep the change and rushed to her SUV.

Bell was two hours from Erwin when Officer Lason got the first break in the search for Rebecca St. Clair.

CHAPTER SEVEN

Twilight colored the town of Erwin as Officer Lason leaned over Walt Schenk's shoulder. The crew cut junior officer looked like a teenager to Lason despite being twenty-eight, his forehead and neck blemished by a few stray acne dots. A vehicle database displayed on the younger officer's computer screen.

"What you need to understand is there are over 15,000 identifiable tire tracks and nearly as many vehicle types on the road. Furthermore, any given vehicle can accept a multitude of tires."

Lason choked on the lukewarm coffee and placed the Styrofoam cup on Schenk's desk. She was aware tire models fit multiple vehicles, but the situation seemed hopeless. Though she hadn't expected immediate identification of the tire from her photographs, the reality of sifting through 15,000 track patterns gave her a headache.

"I might as well throw darts blindfolded."

"Not at all. You did good work. The crime techs couldn't make track impressions, but they figured out why the two tracks were different widths."

"Two different vehicles?"

"Not likely. The paths were too similar to be a

coincidence as you noted. It came from the same vehicle."

The truth slammed Lason.

"Oh, God. It's a trailer."

"You got it."

"Why didn't I figure it out at the scene? Of course. That's a good way to stash someone. If we were uncertain somebody abducted St. Clair..."

"Yeah, it's obvious now. Otherwise, why would he drive a trailer to a playground?"

Lason picked up the coffee and took a long sip. This new information gave her a jolt, energized her after a long, fruitless search.

"So we're looking for a car dragging a trailer. That narrows the search considerably. We can rule out most sports cars. They don't play well with trailer hitches."

"Technically, a sports car can pull a trailer, but it's not a good idea. We can do even better. By measuring the distances between the tires and the wheel base, the techs ruled out most of the remaining possibilities and fed the information to the FBI. The working theory is our suspect drives a Buick LaCrosse."

"Wow. All this from a pair of tire tracks."

"Crazy, isn't it? Now we know what we're looking for."

The jittery buzz coursing through Officer Lason during the drive home might have been from the coffee—Schenk always made the strong stuff—but she didn't think so. They had their first break in the case. Still, the clock ticked against them. Every second lost decreased the odds of finding St. Clair alive. After a fourteen hour workday, exhaustion claimed Lason's body with an iron grip. She needed sleep, but her brain didn't get the message. How could she sleep when she could return a teenage girl to her parents?

Unable to bear the thought of rest, Lason circled and crisscrossed Erwin, hyper-vigilant for a LaCrosse or similar sedan dragging a trailer. The killer might not be inside Erwin anymore, and if he was smart, he would unhitch the trailer and conceal it well. Something kept him in Erwin. Many predators acted territorial in the wild, some sharks known to scope out a section of ocean and hunt until it depleted the food source.

Erwin took on an air of menace at night. Shadowy. Hidden secrets. The houses appeared haunted, and every unlit window hid a killer's face.

Buoyed by the light of the town center, Lason parked her car on Main Street and crossed the road to the Renaissance Cafe. The last thing she needed was caffeine, but a cup of hot decaf in a well-lit eatery was just what the doctor ordered.

Per the establishment's name, the Renaissance Cafe was designed to look like a castle, complete with a gray brick exterior and pink, flowery curtains over the windows that might have adorned a princess's room. Thankfully, modern alternative was the music of choice instead of lutes and cornetts. Lason enjoyed a Renaissance fair as much as anyone, but there were limits.

A college age boy in horn-rimmed glasses brought the decaf to Lason. As she sat in the rear of the cafe, her uniform drew notice from the patrons. A middle-aged couple leaned close and spoke of Erwin's imminent demise in stage whispers certainly meant for Lason to hear. Everyone was upset and frightened. So was Lason. This was the time to pull together, not point fingers.

Officer Lason finished her coffee when she spied the stranger watching her.

CHAPTER EIGHT

A rundown, seedy motel by the name of The Erwin Inn represented the town's only accommodations. A neon sign flashed NO VACANCY with half the letters unlit so it read NO CAN. Bell checked her phone and found a bounty of hotel options in Savannah, a forty-mile trip. Coming to Erwin seemed more foolish by the moment, and now she faced the potential of sleeping in the Rogue.

On her way through town, Bell spotted an odd cafe adorned in sixteenth century decor. A strange beast in this sleepy southern town.

Too tired to drive another hour, she pulled the Rogue into one of a dozen empty parking spots bordering a tree-lined sidewalk. Redbrick sidewalks cut down Main Street. Forest green lamp posts sprouted at regular intervals and kept the walkways brightly lit. Four residential streets branched off Main, all reminding Bell of the small Virginia villages of her youth where everyone knew their neighbors, and the post offices, barber shops, and corner markets were only a few blocks from your house. Nostalgic memories shifted to anger. The Erwin murder became personal to her as if the killer stalked Bealton.

And maybe he had a long time ago. When he butchered Jillian and left her corpse by the creek for everyone to see.

Bell sensed the paranoia drifting like a toxic haze through the town. On second thought, it wasn't a haze at all, but a void. The void lived in the absence of music thumping out of the bars, on the empty sidewalks beneath a picturesque southern evening, among the empty parking spaces, and through the monument park erected on an island in the middle of Main Street where a leaf crawled centipede-like past a lonely statue. Bell hurried across the street as though the void might take shape and rush out of the darkness.

A chime sounded when Bell pushed the door open. Coffee aromas wafted to her as did the sweet scents of confectionery delights. The young man behind the glass counter eyed her curiously as he took her order. She didn't care about flavor as long as the coffee was an extra-large.

The sidelong looks continued when Bell sat down with her coffee. The patrons ranged from young adult to elderly, and each seemed as interested in Bell as she was with the case. Her eyes moved over the room and stopped on a female police officer. The dark haired woman wore her uniform, a police radio laid upon the table. The other customers sat away from the officer. To Bell, the patrons seemed wary of the officer rather than respectful of her space. Probably angry a murderer was at-large and wondering if the police were competent enough to catch him.

This was the first moment Bell contemplated her plan. Along the drive from Virginia, determining if Jillian's killer murdered the Dane girl had become her sole focus. Scoping out the murder scene would raise suspicion, and interjecting herself into an ongoing investigation seemed a horrible idea.

Bell swallowed when the officer rose from her chair and walked in her direction. Dammit. She'd stared at the woman too long and evoked suspicion. Bell trained her eyes back to the coffee, but it was too late. The female officer stood before Bell's table.

"Do I know you?"

Bell shook her head.

"Sorry if I was staring. I had a long trip, and I'm exhausted."

The woman's hand dangled close to her nightstick, the radio squawking gibberish where she'd left it on the table. As though they expected a Renaissance version of a barroom brawl to break out, several customers grabbed their coffees and left.

"Long trip, huh? Where you from?"

Except for Bell and the officer, whose badge identified her as Lason, only the man behind the counter remained, and he busied himself wiping the glass, lest he draw the perturbed officer's attention.

"I'll save you the interrogation, Officer. My name is Scarlett Bell, and I'm law enforcement like you. FBI."

Bell motioned to the empty chair across the table. The woman squinted at Bell, dubious and apprehensive.

"No thank you, ma'am. May I see your ID?"

Bell's heart fluttered when she remembered Weber took her FBI badge. She'd locked the Glock-22 in the glove compartment, thank goodness. If the officer noticed a gun on Bell, there was no telling how she'd react. She fished her wallet out of her sweatshirt pocket and handed the license to the officer.

"FBI, you said? This isn't an FBI badge. What's your business in Erwin, Ms Bell?"

"Is there somewhere we could speak privately?"

"Why should I trust you?"

"Because I may be of assistance if you will give me the chance. It's about your murder and abduction cases."

Lason's eyes narrowed.

"You know something about Bregan Dane's murder?"

"I work with the Behavior Analysis Unit. I build profiles of serial killers."

"That's a little hard to swallow without FBI identification."

Bell looked over her shoulder at the worker boxing desserts. He was eavesdropping.

"I'm on administrative leave."

Lason raised an eyebrow.

"That could mean anything from getting injured on the job to punching out your supervisor."

Bell pictured Weber unconscious and snorted. She was starting to like Lason. Then Bell remembered *The Informer* articles. Though humiliating, they verified Bell's FBI credentials. She swiped her phone to the Internet browser and loaded the article.

"This should prove I'm with the BAU," Bell said, handing the phone to Lason. "Try not to laugh. It's embarrassing enough."

Lason glanced between Bell and her picture in the article. The officer waved a finger at Bell.

"I was sure I recognized you from somewhere. Sure, Agent Scarlett Bell. The serial killer's worst nightmare. I read about you in *The Times*. Now I'm intrigued about this administrative leave business."

"Just to lay all the cards on the table, officially, I'm not supposed to be here. Care to take a walk?"

Officer Lason sneaked a glance out the window. Two men in Carhartt overalls talked in front of the cafe.

"Hard to keep a secret in this town. How about you follow me back to my place? We'll sit on the deck and drown our sorrows."

Bell groaned and stretched the small of her back.

"Lead the way, Officer Lason."

CHAPTER NINE

A scratching at the window brought Rebecca St. Clair awake. Her head ached, felt light and clouded, flu-stricken. The bedroom was too dark, and her inability to see moonlight filtering through the window confused her.

The aching extended through her body, down her spine and into her legs. As though someone hollowed out her insides and filled Rebecca with mud. Mouth dry and lips parched, she needed a glass of water, but when she tried to stand something snagged her hips and held her fast. The bed covers? No, it grasped like a rope. And why was she seated?

Finding her wrists bound, panic rippled through Rebecca. The fog lifted from her brain, and suddenly she remembered being alone in the park after Nat left.

And a man.

A stranger she hadn't recognized.

He'd spoken to her. What was it? Something about a lost kitten…and would she help him look…and she agreed, though Mom warned her to never trust a stranger…

…and then he…

…he…

The memory rushed back to her. The man grabbing

Rebecca from behind, powerful arms snaked around her chin and head, forearm dug against her neck. Putting her to sleep as she flailed and tried to scream for help...but his grip cut her voice, sapped her strength, turned her into a rag doll. Then she thought of the little girl dumped beside the creek, and the likelihood her kidnapper was the murderer sent her into hysterics.

The scratching sound came again, and this time the scream bellowed out of her like the fire engine sirens that rolled past her window when Mr Elgin's house caught fire last summer. The scream continued for a split second after she stopped. Not an echo, but an odd, tinny reverberation. As though someone stuffed her into a metal box.

Dark. So dark. All that black strained her eyes and rang in her ears.

"Hello? Please help me."

Scratch scratch.

The noise was closer now. Inside the room? She instinctively drew in her legs, lifted them so her feet rested on the chair.

Then a louder scratching. An animal clawing at the walls.

"Mommy! Daddy! I'm in here!"

Her pleas brought no help, but the animal sounds stopped. Rebecca called again and listened. No rumbles of nearby traffic, nothing to gauge her location.

She tugged harder at the bindings. The ropes dug into her wrists and burned. She recalled tug-of-war games at camp a few summers ago and how the ropes left red welts across her palms after the stronger girls pulled Rebecca across the boundary. Itchy pain that lingered. Little match flares beneath the skin.

A disturbing thought. The kidnapper might be inside the room with her. Watching her from the dark. Sweat left a sheen on her skin, made her clothes stick and clutch.

The wind whistled over the roof. The little room

trembled like a living thing.

Rebecca took deep breaths as her father taught her until her heart slowed. She wasn't good at sports, not as fast or strong as her friends, but she'd played youth softball for a year. The breathing trick settled her nerves when she was afraid of the ball and helped her arrange her thoughts during school tests. She needed it now more than ever.

She lowered her feet to the floor and stomped. Not concrete or floorboards, but a sheet of wood. The stomp shook the room and caused the tinny reverberation to return.

Wood floor, metal roof and walls.

An oily scent came to her nostrils, the smell familiar. Yes, Uncle Steve's trailer. She'd climbed inside when her family helped him pack the trailer for a Grand Canyon vacation. Was that where she was? Inside a trailer?

She kicked the floor a second time, a deafening bang. Someone should have heard. Unless she was in the middle of nowhere.

The banging attracted unwanted attention. She held her breath as something big lumbered outside the trailer. Or was it inside the trailer? Sniffing. Breathing. It caught her scent. Then a guttural growl, and the monster raked its claws along the walls.

Rebecca shivered in the dark.

CHAPTER TEN

Bell's head swam when she lowered the beer to her lap. She'd only drank two bottles, but Lason's beer inventory came exclusively from a local brewer, and as the officer warned, the little beasts had kick to them.

Lason's deck overlooked a bog. Bell couldn't see the water, but a symphony of peepers, nature's woodwinds, sang out from the dark. Now and again, something large splashed into the water like a dead body falling out of the trees. Bell gave silent thanks alligators didn't call Virginia home.

"The next thing I need to figure out is how to involve you in the case without the department finding out," Lason said, taking a swig from her bottle. For the officer's part, she was one bottle ahead of Bell but looked no worse for wear. "Schenk's cool. He'll keep his mouth shut if I explain the situation. But Chief Haggens is strictly by the book. If Haggens catches you snooping around, he'll call your supervisor, and we'll both have hell to pay."

"How did the killer abduct Bregan Dane?"

"Girl left school at three. These days schools worry parents will sue, so the buses pick up and drop off right in front of the kids' houses. Not like when we went to school. I walked almost two miles each way whether it was pouring or ninety-five degrees. Dane lived just inside the radius. One neighborhood over and she'd have taken the bus."

"And she never made it home."

Lason set her beer down and fixed her eyes on a scuff mark on the table.

"Let's go over the case one more time," Bell said, pulling a notepad from her bag.

Though the Erwin Police Department held the official case files, Lason recreated the evidence from memory, everything from where the teenagers found the Dane girl's body to the tire tracks and trailer theory. Bell recorded her personal thoughts, including a rough profile of the unknown subject. After they'd gone over the case from start-to-finish a second time, Lason closed her eyes and leaned back in her chair.

"So if the FBI and Savannah crime techs know what they're talking about, he's hauling a trailer behind a Buick LaCrosse. Other than that, we haven't learned the first thing about the guy."

"Typically, abductors drive dull-colored vehicles. White, gray. Something that doesn't stand out in traffic," Bell said, checking her phone. No messages from Lucas or Gardy.

"To avoid attracting attention."

"And to inspire confidence. Bold colors are more likely to unsettle a child."

Lason leaned forward, elbows on knees and hands clasped.

"Why use a trailer? Seems a van is more convenient and inconspicuous."

"Think of the trailer as his refuge, a safe place he can take the girls without risk of being seen. He's not from around here, or he'd take the girls to his home. He...works out of his trailer."

"I think I'm going to be sick."

"You and me, both. Have your department check rural

locations, places he could take the girls without drawing attention."

Lason issued a dark laugh.

"You just described a hundred-mile radius surrounding Erwin. We had an FBI agent come speak when I was in the police academy. Sharp guy. Taught us who the most likely suspects were when someone got abducted. When Bregan Dane vanished, we focused our investigation on men who knew her. The girl's father, teachers, clergy. And when that well ran dry, we looked at neighbors. People who saw her daily." Lason jiggled her head as if shaking away cobwebs. "Either I misinterpreted the agent's message, or I watch too many serial killer shows on TV."

"On the contrary, your line of reasoning was perfectly logical. That's where I begin every abduction case, and statistics prove victims almost always know their abductors."

"Losing Rebecca St. Clair this morning changed our opinion. St. Clair and Dane attended separate churches and schools and lived on opposite sides of town. Erwin is small, but we can't find anything in common between the two girls."

"Except that they were available to be taken."

Lason drew her sweatshirt hood tighter and rubbed her legs together.

"Makes you want to lock every kid inside and never let them out of your sight."

A look of disgust twisted Lason's face. Bell glanced up.

"What?"

"Aren't abductions sexually motivated?"

"Yes," Bell said, tapping the pen on the notepad. "And in the case of child killers, the act of murder is a replacement for sex."

"God. Hey, you truly believe the Erwin killer is the same man who murdered your friend? It's been over twenty years."

Bell opened her mouth to reply and closed it, unsure how to proceed. She'd told Lason she believed the Erwin killer was the same man who killed Jillian. The theory sounded ludicrous even to her own ears, but she'd learned to trust her intuition hunting serial killers for the BAU, and her gut screamed the elusive killer of her nightmares was close. Just imagining the murderer holed up in Erwin raised goosebumps on Bell's arms. Finally, she worked up the fortitude to answer.

"It's him."

"For both our sakes I hope you're wrong. At least tell me this is more than a gut feeling."

As if afraid someone would hear, Bell's eyes followed the outline of the trees bordering Lason's yard, a black and craggy wall holding back the dangers of the swamp.

"It's something a former BAU agent who had information about Jillian Rossi's killer told me after the Schuler case," said Bell, unwilling to admit she'd corresponded with Logan Wolf. "He's active again, and he knows my identity now."

Lason looked confused. Her expression lit with understanding, and she snapped her fingers.

"Because he saw your article in *The Informer*."

"That's what I'm afraid of."

A darker possibility ate at Bell and drove guilt into her stomach. A moment of quiet lingered before Lason picked up on Bell's thoughts.

"Oh, no you don't. You aren't going to blame yourself over a psychopath's actions. He murdered Bregan Dane and kidnapped Rebecca St. Clair because he's a sick sociopath. The minute you allow yourself to internalize a criminal's actions, you become the victim. Don't martyr yourself."

Lason's words stunned Bell and left her speechless. The cricket songs became louder, and a ground fog slithered through the trees and made the yard appear mystical. A smile quirked Bell's lips.

"Who stole Officer Lason and replaced her with my mom?"

They shared laughter, a welcome relief after the dark conversation. Bell leaned her head back, and the deck appeared to undulate like a fun house.

"That's it," Lason said, snatching Bell's keys off the table. "You've had too many to drive tonight."

Bell supported herself with her palms on her thighs and waited for the nausea to pass.

"I think you're right."

The bottles clinked together as Lason gathered them in her arms.

"Where are you staying anyhow?"

Too embarrassed to admit she had nowhere to stay, Bell tried to remember the name of the motel in town. Watching Bell closely, Lason ascertained the truth.

"Jesus, Bell. What exactly was the plan? Drive from Virginia to Georgia with nowhere to stay so you could secretly hunt a serial killer while avoiding the police?"

"Face it, I'm no Jodie Foster."

"No, you're not. You're more Hannibal Lecter." Bell grabbed her bottles and followed Lason into the kitchen. The officer ran the water, flicking a finger through the stream until satisfied it was hot enough. "There's a guest room at the end of the hall. You're welcome to stay as long as it takes to catch this guy. You don't snore, do you?"

Bell couldn't answer. When was the last time she shared a bedroom with anyone? Then she thought of Gardy.

"Not that I know of."

"Good, because I'll be two doors down." The sink

blossomed with soap suds. A bubble perched on the end of Lason's nose. The officer noticed Bell staring and put her hands on her hips. "What?"

"Nothing. Here, let me help you."

Bell sponged off a dirty plate and rinsed the soap away.

"You don't need to wash the dishes, Bell. You're a guest."

"The last thing I need is for you to pen an expose' for *The Informer* about Scarlett Bell being a no good freeloader."

Bell lay awake a long time listening to the swamp songs through the open window. A light breeze set the translucent curtains in motion, and they danced like specters over the bed. The mattress felt hard against her back, the twin bed small enough for her feet to extend off the end. When sleep finally claimed her, Bell's nightmares were of dark trailers and screaming children.

CHAPTER ELEVEN

The little house lifted and crashed down as though a great wind hauled the home from its foundation and dropped it in another world.

The impact brought Rebecca awake. Her teeth clicked together. Neck whipped back and shot forward like a slingshot.

She wasn't in a house, she remembered. A trailer. And it was moving.

The chair didn't topple, and Rebecca felt lucky she hadn't cracked her head open on the wooden floor. But when she wiggled against her bindings, she realized the chair was fixed to the floor somehow. Bolted or nailed.

Glancing around the black belly of the trailer, she saw slivers of light crawling through the door. Daylight. The brightness assaulted her eyes, yet she didn't look away. Knowing the sun shone buoyed Rebecca and lent her hope.

The trailer hit another bump, and this time she tumbled sideways. The ropes supported Rebecca, prevented her from falling. For an excruciatingly long time, she dangled marionette-like, the cruel rope fibers cutting and burning. She pulled herself up to her seat and panted in the dark.

He'd come to her during the night. Late, when the only sounds were the crickets and peepers. The door had opened and admitted a cool whoosh of night air, and then he circled the chair to face her, shoes heavy and loud on the trailer floor. He was a big man. Had to slump over to avoid knocking his head on the roof.

It was too dark to see his face, only the rough outline of long, uncombed hair. Something about its wild shape appeared savage.

"There's no need to worry. I'm an angel of God. I've come to save you."

Then the rough, scratchy texture of his thumb and fingers as he lifted her head, which insisted on slumping over in exhaustion. He studied her the way someone might a new exotic pet, and all the while she prayed he'd go back to the vehicle. After several minutes of prodding—he hadn't *touched* her, had he?—the man released her face with a tired grunt and let her chin fall to her chest.

Now as she fought to free her wrists, the trailer took several sharp turns. Each roiled her stomach, gave her motion sickness the way riding in the backseat of a car had when she was younger. Yet she didn't wish the ride to end, for as long as the vehicle moved, her kidnapper couldn't hurt her.

After she acclimated to the light, it no longer seared her eyes. The light was weaker than she'd first thought, gray and dingy like daybreak on an overcast morning. A fantasy came to her, one in which superhero strength infused her, allowing her to snap the ropes, leap from the chair and batter the door open with her fists and feet. But this wasn't a comic book, and Erwin's real heroes had no idea where the kidnapper had taken her.

The vehicle moved at a snail's pace. The constant jostling of the trailer meant the road was slow going. And that frightened her, for she realized they weren't anywhere near the paved streets of Erwin. How far away from home was she? She'd been unconscious for most of the time since the kidnapper captured her in the park, and a car could travel a long way in a day.

Another sharp turn forced Rebecca to strain her arms against the chair back, and the light sifting along the door took on an ethereal quality. Dust. She sneezed, eyes burning as the dust melted through the opening like a malevolent fog.

Then the trailer slowed and swung left. Just as quickly, the vehicle reversed course, and the trailer moved backward.

Another turn. The kidnapper was backing up the trailer.

The engine cut off. Now the beating of her heart grew loud. Breaths fast and sharp.

In a moment, he'd whip open the trailer and flood the inside with blinding light. She'd see his hideous, monster face and know her fate was the same as young Bregan Dane's.

Rebecca lowered her head and clamped her eyes shut in prayer as the vehicle door opened and slammed shut. The force sent a tremor through the trailer.

Footsteps swished through grass and approached the trailer door.

Her hands curled into fists.

And the footsteps passed the trailer and continued into an unseen wilderness where tree branches snapped like firecrackers and the wind rattled the leaves. They were in the countryside. Somewhere a bullfrog croaked, and Rebecca remembered her father's warning to stay close to home and avoid the creek, because the police found little Bregan's body beside the water.

Panic flared white-hot. Rebecca yanked on the ropes, pulled and pulled, ignoring the agony her bindings caused. She heard voices. A man's voice followed by another.

Rebecca tried to listen over the wind, but it was hard to make out the conversation. More branches snapped, the sound of one man walking toward the other. Friendly conversation, welcoming voices.

Rebecca screamed and nothing came out. Her throat felt parched as though scraped by a razor blade. Trembling, she worked up enough spittle to swallow. She repeated until she had one good, loud scream left.

The men's indistinct voices carried over the nature sounds when Rebecca's cry pierced the morning. The scream came from a deep place inside her, a place of desperation and last chances. It hurt her own ears and summoned blood from the back of her throat, yet she kept yelling until she became hoarse.

A moment of quiet. Then the voices began again, and one sounded closer to the trailer than it had before.

"What the hell was that?"

"Sounded like a hawk."

"You insane, man? That was a girl screaming."

Trees rustled, and the bullfrog bellowed again. One of the men fought through the brush toward the trailer, the other protesting.

Then a loud thud and a pig's squeal of frantic pain. With her hands trapped behind her back, Rebecca couldn't plug her ears to the sound of the kidnapper beating the man to death. She pictured the maniac, eyes crazed, face splattered with blood droplets, a thick branch held above his head. He brought it down again and again until the shrill screeches became whimpers, the sound of a crippled animal dragging itself across the ground. Another horrid thud, and the dying man went quiet.

A long moment passed in which she imagined the killer quietly stalking toward the trailer. Instead, the man grunted as he lifted the body. Through labored breaths, he hauled the broken man into his arms. The footsteps, Rebecca realized, headed away from the trailer and into the dark unknown. She listened until she didn't hear him anymore, only the birds and frogs and an incessant wind that whistled over the trailer's roof. There were things in the woods and water that could kill a man in Georgia, and though she'd never wished death upon anyone, she did so now.

A noise caught her attention. Something outside the trailer.

Claws scraped at the door.

The monster was back.

CHAPTER TWELVE

Bleary-eyed and battling an upset stomach, Bell hit the road before dawn. Lason had just plated a breakfast of eggs and toast, the officer's hair wrapped in a towel, when Bell left the house. The radio on Bell's hip allowed her to monitor police activity, but she couldn't communicate with Lason over the radio. Instead, Bell and Lason agreed to keep in touch with their phones, Bell promising to text her position once she ventured onto rural back roads. The Glock-22 she hadn't disclosed to Lason rested beside the radio.

CR-5 bisected Centerville Road, and after she got her bearings from Google, Bell swung a right onto Centerville and drove deeper into the untamed countryside. One ear tied to the police band, Bell circled through the forested countryside she'd targeted. The occasional farm broke miles of nothingness, and a manure scent clung to the air. This countryside seemed perfect for anyone who wanted to hide from the law. Or dump a body.

The milky sky darkened by midmorning, and as Bell pulled the Rogue onto a soft shoulder, the air through the open window thickened. She wasn't on Centerville Road anymore, and the dusty route she'd chosen lacked a road sign.

Confused, Bell grabbed her phone and discovered the map wouldn't load. No service. This wasn't good.

Pulling herself up, Bell sat on the hood and paged through a dogeared road atlas. She was one of the few people she knew who still carried a paper map in the current age of GPS and digital connectivity. As Dad often told her, technology gave you all the answers until the power failed. Or in this case when you ventured outside the cell tower's range.

She estimated her position several miles outside of Erwin. The killer required privacy but would stay close to town, his hunting ground. What drew him to this particular location? The body dump along the creek shore drew similarities to Bealton, but creeks, rivers, and oceans covered the world.

Making an educated guess, Bell figured she was on an unlabeled route cutting between a network of farm-to-market roads just west of Erwin. She ran her forefinger along the undulating line and stopped on an area of swampland surrounded by forest. Identical areas of wilderness sprouted to the north, but they were too far from Erwin or under county or state park jurisdictions.

Tossing the map on the passenger seat, Bell fired the engine and followed a series of turns, certain she knew her location now. Her phone connected. The digital map sprang to life and verified her position, and she utilized Bluetooth to call Lason. The officer answered on the second ring.

Lason was quiet and covert when she spoke, a sign the other officers surrounded her.
"Give me your position."

"I'm six miles outside of Erwin on a farm-to-market road called Greenbriar," Bell said, cupping a hand over her eyes to block out the haze.

"Okay, I know where that is."

"There's a forest about one mile up the road and what appears to be a rather large swamp past the tree line.

That's not state land or a park, correct?"

"No, but be careful, Bell. That's not just a good place to hide a body. It's a damn good place to disappear."

"It looks like God's country."

"More like the devil's."

The road met a dead end of cloying green. Not trusting the muddy earth fronting the forest, she brought the Rogue to a stop halfway down the road. The wind carried the pungent smell of standing water as she exited the vehicle. Knotted weeds and moss-covered trees blocked the way forward.

At the dead end, she noticed deep tire tracks in the mud. Careful not to disturb the impression, she stood upon a patch of grass and snapped a photograph. Lason had provided her a picture of the tracks at the park. From her phone's gallery, she retrieved the picture and compared it to the new impression.

Her pulse race as she scanned the pattern. She wasn't an expert, but dammit, the patterns looked identical.

Additionally, two distinct track patterns cut into the mud—tires from a vehicle and trailer.

The tracks veered from the road into the field. A graveyard of broken stalks and matted grass marked the vehicle's path. Had the killer followed the dirt road to the dead end and backed into the field to reverse course?

As Bell took pictures something large splashed into the water inside the dark forest. She touched her gun and stepped back. Thunder rumbled, an angry sound.

Surveying the darkening sky, Bell removed the Glock from her holster and pushed through the trees. The wind died inside the forest, the grounded littered with seasons of fallen leaves. A branch snapped when she stepped down. She swung the Glock over the shadows until her eyes adjusted.

The terrain sloped down to the bog, the soil black and loose. She slipped and grabbed a tree limb before she slid down the embankment. More splashing sounds came from below. She slapped at her neck. The mosquitoes had found her.

The stench hit her halfway down the slope. Death. Carrion festering on a rainy day. She plugged her nose as she edged down the path. The ground gave way, and she slammed hard on her back after her feet flew out from under.

Falling. Gray slashes of light through the trees somersaulting around her.

She came to rest beside the swamp and recoiled when she saw the bloody stump of an arm protruding out of the tall grass like a sleeping anaconda. A cloud of swarming flies lit upon the meaty flesh.

Bell clamped her mouth shut and averted her eyes before she regurgitated.

CHAPTER THIRTEEN

Led by Lason, the police arrived thirty minutes after Bell placed the call. There was no hiding her presence anymore.

Thunder rolled over the distant ocean. The full brunt of the storm had moved out to sea, but a clinging mist sopped Bell, who shivered with a blanket around her shoulders.

A bear of a man, Chief Haggens stroked his auburn beard as he towered over Bell. He kept glancing between Bell and her gory discovery as if she'd murdered the victim and buried the body parts in shallow graves. Each time Officer Lason tried to intervene, Haggens snapped off an expletive-laden tirade about feds interfering in his investigation.

"Give me one goddamn reason why I shouldn't phone your supervisor and asks him why the hell a field agent on administrative leave dug up body parts in my backyard."

"I didn't dig them up, sir."

Haggens slapped his cap against his leg and stomped in a circle.

"Same difference. As if I don't have enough problems to deal with. Now I've got a rogue field agent snooping around murder scenes. How did you say you came upon our vic, Agent Bell? What brought you out to a random swamp in the Georgia countryside?"

"I followed a hunch."

"Based on?"

"Your team already determined the killer is pulling a trailer." Technically, the city crime techs and the FBI had pieced the evidence together, but Bell knew to stroke the police chief's ego. "He can't hide a trailer in plain sight, especially with the entire town looking for him."

"But why the swamp?"

"Water plays an important role, perhaps something symbolic."

"You haven't seen the case evidence, and you're already making assumptions about the murderer."

Lason caught Bell's eye, a warning not to tell Haggens they'd shared details about the case.

"Not assumptions, Chief. More like educated guesses."

Haggens nodded at Bell's cheek.

"You have a piece of…arm…on your cheek."

"What?" Bell thumbed a pulpy chunk of flesh off her face. "Oh, Jesus."

Haggens dug a handkerchief from his pocket and offered it to Bell.

"It's clean."

"Thanks."

Bell brushed the cloth over her face, and the corner came away red. She held it out for Haggens, who shook his head.

"Keep it. I got plenty. Tell me, Agent Bell. How many of these maniacs have you encountered?"

"More than I care to mention. Listen, Chief. You're so close to catching him. With a bolo out on his car and trailer, you've got him hemmed in."

"Perhaps, but what's to say he isn't halfway to Mississippi by now?"

"Because he can't control himself. Two murders and one missing girl in a matter of days. He's acting on a primal level, hunting the same environment until he depletes the game."

And because he knows I'm here, Bell thought. Whatever grisly fate the deceased had met, only his arm remained. Bell, figuring the gators and coyotes took the rest of the body, considered it a leap of faith to tie this victim to the Erwin murders, but the tire tracks matched those found in the park. Then again, the possibility existed the killer dumped the rest of the body elsewhere. Or took it as a trophy.

Haggens paced along the swamp in thought. A harried diver in scuba gear surfaced and drew the chief's attention. A waterfall of swamp water cascaded off the diver as his crime tech partner bagged the dismembered arm. Despite the bugs feasting on the skin, Bell saw the arm belonged to a male. She couldn't determine the age, but it clearly didn't belong to a child.

Had the killer's MO changed?

Haggens chewed a blade of grass.

"Find anything, Paul?"

"I can't see shit along the bottom. I'm doing the best I can. You sure the water is clear of gators?"

"No big boys. They're hiding at the edge of the woods, likely waiting for you to finish."

"As long as they aren't hungry for lunch."

Haggens grunted and set his focus on the other crime tech.

"You there."

"It's Abelson."

"Huh?"

"Abelson. It's my name."

A landscape of wrinkles climbed Abelson's forehead, then gave way to a smooth, hairless scalp. Tall and thin, the tech looked ready to blow away at the first gust of wind.

"Right. Well, Abelson. Estimate when this guy died."

"Seriously? It's just a goddamn arm. I don't have a lot to go on, and anyway, that's a job for the ME."

A low growl came out of Haggens.

"Well, the ME isn't here yet." The chief glanced past the woods where the unmarked dirt road appeared to meander toward nowhere. "Probably got lost. Can't even depend on a friggin' road sign out here. You look like a sharp guy, Abelson. How about an educated guess?"

Abelson gave an exasperated sigh.

"Based on the lack of decomposition, I'd say not long. Could be anywhere from a few hours to several, but time of death isn't my specialty."

Haggens shook his head.

"You guys hedge your bets more than weather forecasters."

The diver plunged beneath the muck-covered water. A line of bubbles followed his progress. Though Haggens appeared confident no alligators swam within the bog, the young officer Bell knew as Schenk kept his gun trained on the water.

Haggens slipped his thumbs through his belt loops and stared a hole through Bell.

"What shall I do about you, Agent Bell? Technically, you haven't done anything illegal, but I gather your supervisor won't take kindly to your being here."

"If I may, Chief, having Agent Bell here could be helpful," Lason said, moving to stand beside Bell.

"Convince me."

"She brings profiling expertise to the table, and she specializes in tracking these psychopaths. I say we bring her on as a consultant." Interpreting the concern on Bell's face, Lason added, "but let's keep the FBI out of it. What they don't know won't hurt them."

"This administrative leave business concerns me."

"The BAU forced Agent Bell out of the field because she made the mistake of bringing murderers to justice. You read about her background, Jack."

That was good, Bell thought. Lason used the chief's first name, made a deeper connection.

"Shot that bastard dead in California," Haggens said, drawing groans of approval from the other officers.

"And you know what Agent Bell did in Florida."

Haggens straightened his back, stood a little taller. Schenk took his eyes off the swamp for a moment and nodded his agreement with Lason.

"Yeah, I remember," Haggens said. He glared at Bell hard, but something dawned in his eyes. An awakening.

A white-haired veteran officer with Donner on his name tag gave Haggens a meaningful look.

"Schuler was a cop killer, Jack."

Haggens spat.

"I'm well aware."

"Agent Bell ended his sorry existence without firing a single shot. I think I speak for everyone here when I say, if the FBI has a problem with Agent Bell taking out cop killers, then the FBI is our problem."

Better than a year's worth of cases working beside Gardy taught Bell to remain cautious around local authority figures. It seemed like an out-of-body experience to Bell, who stoically waited in silence while the officers' arguments shifted in her favor. Now they saw her as some sort of rebel or renegade when all she desired was to capture psychopaths and keep them from hurting anyone again.

"I'll allow Agent Bell to work with us," Haggens said, inciting murmurs of agreement. "On one condition. She answers to the Erwin Police Department, not DC."

"Of course," said Bell. "This is your backyard."

Haggens held her gaze an extra second, enough to ensure Bell understood their agreement included no wiggle room.

"And you'll find the killer and bring the St. Clair girl home to her parents?"

Bell chewed at the inside of her cheek. There was no guarantee Rebecca St. Clair was alive. The killer had kept Dane alive until mere hours before dumping her beside the water. She prayed his ritual hadn't changed, that sufficient time remained to find St. Clair. In the end, she told the officers what they wanted to hear.

"I won't sleep until we find her."

Haggens clapped his hands together.

"So it's decided. Officer Lason."

"Yes, Chief?"

"Get Agent Bell a police radio. From now on, she rides with you, not in her own vehicle. I can't have civilians chasing serial killers." Lason returned to her cruiser as a reinvigorated Haggens barked orders. "Schenk, get on the horn with Savannah. Tell them we're keeping their crime techs a little longer. Find out if they have any missing persons who meet our vic's…uh…description. It's an adult, not a kid this time, thank God. What do you make of that, Agent Bell?"

Discarding the blanket, Bell tossed it beside a kit containing evidence collection supplies.

"Could be he was in the wrong place at the wrong time. Maybe he happened upon the trailer. Our unknown subject murders a certain type."

"Young girls."

"Yes. But he'll kill a potential witness out of necessity."

"I can't think of anyone who'd be out this way except a hunter. Schenk?"

Officer Schenk turned his head and held the phone

over his chest.

"Yeah?"

"Tell Savannah PD I want those missing person reports, particularly missing hunters."

"Somebody in town must have seen the killer's LaCrosse," Bell said, straightening her sweatshirt before it inched up and revealed the Glock-22.

"Two people so far. I've got one eyewitness who spotted a dark colored sedan with a trailer on the south end of Erwin around nine o'clock last night. Another claims a sedan and trailer passed the town park sometime after midnight."

"Are the witnesses credible?"

"The first eyewitness is a member of the town board and a lifelong Erwin resident. The other is an ex-county sheriff's deputy."

Bell pondered the time line. If both reports were to be believed, the killer was tied to Erwin.

Or the killer hadn't captured his ultimate prey—the girl who escaped him twenty-three years ago.

CHAPTER FOURTEEN

Bell, Lason, and Schenk remained with the crime scene techs until the light began its slow afternoon drain from the sky. Bell searched for signs of struggle. No blood splatter or shoe prints led to or from the scene. If additional forensic evidence existed, it was gone now, consumed by animals or insect life and washed away by the rains.

Afterward, Bell followed Lason back to the officer's home in Erwin and parked the Rogue. Then she rode shotgun with the officer through Erwin, Lason quiet during the trip, the radio volume silenced. Lost in somber thought, Lason glared at the empty streets as though seeing them for the first time. Every passing minute decreased the chances of finding Rebecca St. Clair alive, and they still needed to identify the latest victim at the swamp.

"We'll find her," Bell said, instantly regretting her words. It was a meaningless reassurance, but it appeared to have the desired effect on Lason, who perked up.

Before Haggens departed from the murder scene, Bell had suggested the police involve the media. Someone had to know the hunter. A phone call from Haggens to the local radio station got the ball rolling, and several leads had come in. The signal-to-noise ratio was abysmal with media generated phone calls, and false leads wasted time and pulled the police in the wrong direction.

"I've lived in Erwin for the better part of four decades. The only homicide on record dates back to the late nineties, and that involved Bernard Wimble sucking down a bottle of whiskey and getting behind the wheel. Nobody shoots their neighbor in Erwin, and they don't pick up knives and chop up kids. What's happening to our town?"

"He's not from Erwin, Elle. If a tornado touched down on Main Street, you wouldn't blame the town for changing."

"But at least we'd understand a tornado, come to grips with it. Blame it on nature or plain old bad luck. How do you accept child murderers?"

Haggens's voice boomed over the police radio, and Lason reached over to adjust the volume.

"Thirty callers in the last thirty minutes," Haggens growled. "And every one of them a dead end, but I've got another neighbor who claimed a sedan dragging a trailer rolled past the park in the middle of the night."

A chill ran through Bell. No kids would be at the park that late, but the killer might have returned to the scene of the abduction.

Haggens had called every motel in the area, and none of the guests drove vehicles matching the description. Thumbing through her notes, a troubling thought came to Bell, and she grabbed the radio.

"The killer kept Bregan Dane alive for five days before he dumped her body."

"By the creek. You said water held symbolic significance. I don't like that he took Rebecca St. Clair to the swamp. Doesn't that suggest he intended to murder the girl before our hunter walked in on him?"

"The symbolic importance of water is just a theory. Maybe water has a calming effect on our target, or he's religiously motivated. Like baptism and soul purification."

"This guy doesn't sound like any Baptist I know."

"Never forget, Chief, the unknown subject is insane, and any religious belief will be twisted beyond recognition. On any account, it's unlikely he took St. Clair to the water to murder her after less than twenty-four hours. That's not enough time spent with the victim."

"I can't figure out how he keeps slipping through our fingers."

"If I had to guess, he keeps a police band radio with him at all times. That's how he avoids the police. With that in mind, he's aware of the bolo, but it's difficult to hide a sedan pulling a trailer."

She heard Haggens lower the radio and speak to another officer.

"Sorry. Sounds like this guy needs to flee the area or get off the road."

"You and your officers know this area better than I do. Look at your maps and find a similar location, preferably an area with a water feature. Someplace he can take St. Clair without drawing attention."

"Like a vacant house with a pond or river nearby."

Bell hadn't considered that possibility. The killer couldn't drive and hunt twenty-four hours per day. He needed a place to sleep and privacy with St. Clair. Camp grounds were too risky, and the most likely wilderness location was now a crime scene.

"That's not a bad theory. How soon can you produce a list of vacant properties within a ten-mile-radius of Erwin?"

"I hope you're kidding. There must be hundreds. We don't have the time to work up a list that size."

"Not even if you narrowed it down to properties near water?"

Haggens blew out his beard over the speaker.

"That would take longer if we had to cross-reference empty houses with the surrounding terrain. We're not as technologically proficient as the FBI."

Bell considered Harold at the BAU. Between his skill and the database at his fingertips, he could give them an answer in minutes. But there was no way she could contact the BAU without Weber finding out.

Unless she went through Gardy.

"Hold on, Chief. I can get you that information."

Lason swiveled her head toward Bell.

"I thought you wanted to keep a low profile."

Bell dug the phone from her pocket, tapping a nail against the screen in indecision.

CHAPTER FIFTEEN

The man's filthy, chapped hand cupped Rebecca's mouth as he dragged her from the trailer. Her legs flailed, kicked, then she bit down on his palm. He grunted and tightened his grip, a warning he'd snap her neck like a twig if she fought him.

They were on a hill somewhere in the country. The clouds had parted after a stormy day. Angry and fiery, the setting sun appeared as a distant hell's reflection.

Rebecca glanced up but still couldn't see his face, only unshaven, pitted cheeks branded by a jagged scar running from ear to chin. He carried her with one arm cupped around her ribs. Each time his bicep contracted, she feared a rib would snap. Hanging at his side like a beaten suitcase, she watched the log cabin drift closer. Darkness pressed out of the cabin windows.

He turned the knob without producing a key, and the door slid open with a screech. She noted the busted, crooked knob and knew he'd broken in. This wasn't his first time inside the cabin. Did he kill Bregan Dane here?

She squirmed in his grip as he crossed the open design first floor. A fireplace smelling of soot took up one wall, and a small kitchen stood on the far side of the room.

In between lay a dusty throw rug. No couch, television, or table. A staircase led to a shadowed loft.

He hefted her over one shoulder and carried her up the stairs as the sun's dying rays colored the upstairs in crimson. An empty bookcase sat against one wall of the loft. An old carpet lay over the landing, a dusty shag that tickled her sinuses when he set her down. No bed. A sleeping bag lay beside a dirt-speckled window overlooking the wilderness. It was hard to look outside with the sun blaring into her eyes, but she thought she saw a creek gurgling along the hill.

Tears crawling down her cheeks, she pleaded for the man to let her go. He raised a threatening hand to quiet her, and she flinched.

Unexpectedly, anger awoke inside her, fury directed at the child killer, and also toward herself for cowering. Better to fight back and die than willingly accept her fate.

"Why did you bring me here?"

No reply. He didn't even look in her direction, just stared into the setting sun as if he took orders from an unknown force lurking in the sky.

"If you're gonna kill me, do it. Get it over with."

"Kill you? You don't understand. This is God's plan. You'll see Him soon."

Grabbing her by the ropes, he dragged her across the room. She ran her legs along the floor, tried to plant her feet, but he was much too strong. Her arms stretched until she was sure her shoulders would dislocate, the room growing darker as he yanked her to the opposite side of the loft where the light failed to reach.

A wooden support beam ran from floor to ceiling. He tied her to the beam. Breathing heavily, he stood over her. Studying.

Satisfied she'd quit fighting, he bent down and pulled on the ropes, ensuring the knots held fast, and wandered back to the window. The light was almost gone now, gray and mottled through tree branches.

He seemed restless, unable to stay in one location for more than a few minutes. Rebecca had a vague recollection of waking inside the dark crypt of the trailer and hearing the car stop. Then footsteps. He left her for long periods of time, she thought. Her intuition told her he searched for another victim, someone he'd force to watch when he finally murdered her.

Then he turned as though summoned and clomped down the stairs. Full dark seeped into the loft, pooling at her feet and rising like a black flood.

"You can't leave me here alone."

Keys jangled. The doorknob twisted.

"You creep! I hope you die out there!"

The door shut, and the silence became loud. Tinnitus buzzed in her ears as she tested her bindings and glanced around the room. Already she'd worked up a sweat, but the knots were tight. Her fingertips tingled with strangled circulation.

Outside the cabin, the squeal of metal-on-metal made her cringe. The noises continued for several minutes until she realized he'd unhooked the trailer. Because the police knew about the trailer and were on the lookout for him? Rebecca's father knew Chief Haggens. They bowled together on Thursdays. Chief Haggens looked oafish, but the chief's simple mannerisms were a ploy. He was smarter than everybody believed. When someone defaced the war memorial with spray paint last year, Chief Haggens figured out it was the Thomas kid and his girlfriend, Deena. And when teenagers broke into the high school and stole a statue of the school mascot, Haggens caught the kids who did it in less than a week and returned the statue in perfect condition.

Caught them in a week.

Rebecca didn't have a week.

She'd be dead by then, and the creeper would catch

another girl.

She lowered her head and cried. The car's engine fired, and stones pinged the underside as he backed down the driveway.

The quietude returned to the little cabin on the hill. She couldn't hear the car anymore. It was as if she was cut off from the universe.

Rebecca fought with the bindings. It didn't take long before she quit. She bumped her head against the beam and brainstormed a way out of this hell.

She grew drowsy, but every creak and bump inside the cabin brought her head up, eyes wide and heart hammering into her throat.

Then she heard it again. Claws scraping down the outer walls. The beast had found her, and though she was much too old for monster stories, she believed.

She trembled as the monster sounds circled the cabin, the thing looking for a way in. But after the unseen beast pawed at the front door, it barked.

A dog.

Rebecca sat bolt upright. It sniffed at the door and wedged its muzzle into the jamb.

"I'm in here. Help!"

She didn't expect the dog to understand, yet the sound of her voice sent the animal into a yelping frenzy. It leaped and slammed against the door, jumped and rattled the window pane. Rebecca recalled the broken doorknob. Could the dog break through, and how had it followed the trailer the whole time? She pictured the animal knocking the door open and scrambling up the staircase. If it got inside, she wondered if the dog was capable of chewing through the ropes before the maniac returned.

When the door refused to budge, the dog raced around the cabin and smashed against the back door. Then back to the front door where it scraped its paws against the wood.

Rebecca cried for help. The dog began to bark and howl.

CHAPTER SIXTEEN

"I've got to hand it to you Bell. Each time I think you've reached a new level of insanity, you raise the bar."

Bell paced the parking lot, the phone cupped between her ear and shoulder, one eye on the glass frontage to Erwin Adventures. Lason had gone inside five minutes ago to inquire if a hunter stopped by recently before heading out to the swamplands. What was taking so long? The sun broke through the overcast a moment before it perished below the horizon and spread bloody reds across the sleepy town.

"I'm a consultant, Gardy, and they're not paying me. There's nothing illegal about what I'm doing and no conflicts of interest with the FBI." It was quiet for a moment. Bell imagined Gardy's chin lifted toward the ceiling, eyes clamped shut in fury. "It won't take Harold more than a few minutes to generate a map of potential hideouts."

"For God's sake, this is just one of your theories, Bell."

"In all fairness, it's a likely theory. The killer is in trouble. Everyone is looking for a trailer attached to a sedan."

"Then he's halfway to Texas by now."

"No, I don't think so. He would have left after murdering Bregan Dane if it were that simple." Another uncomfortable pause. "Come on, Gardy. Harold will get the information if you tell him it's for me. Where are you now?"

"In my office."

Replete with computer monitors, satellite feeds, and various technological gizmos the field agents didn't understand, Harold's office stood at the end of the hall, a short walk from Gardy's office.

"Then go. I'll stay on the line if you like."

"It's not that easy. Weber is still here. I can't run to the bathroom without Weber poking his head out."

"This late? Paranoid as usual."

"That's your fault. Ever since you ditched Flanagan and disappeared, he's hounded me for information about your whereabouts. I can't play stupid forever. He knows you're up to something, Bell. He hasn't figured it out yet, but he will." Bell heard Gardy fighting with indecision. "That's it. I'm coming down there."

"Like hell you will. We'll both end up unemployed. Besides, I've finally got these guys cooperating with me. If another suit shows up, the police will shut me out of the investigation. I can't risk that."

"Then promise me you'll stick to consulting and not go in guns-blazin'. You can joke all you want about losing your job because you crossed Weber, but if you blow bullet holes through a murderer while you're supposed to be on administrative leave, you'll never work again."

Bell shifted the phone to her other ear and checked the shop. Still no sign of Lason.

"Weber has my badge and weapon."

"Do you expect me to believe you aren't packing? Bell?"

"Yeah, I'm still here."

"You didn't answer the question."

"Are you gonna get me this information or not?"

The door to the shop opened, and Lason gave Bell a thumbs-up. Bell placed the phone against her chest.

"Good news?"

"Owner says a guy came through last evening and said he was heading in the direction we found our vic. The owner is trying to dig up the receipt and thinks the guy's name is on it. Did you make progress on your end?"

"Working on it."

Lason made a circle between her thumb and forefinger. Bell smirked, having not seen the okay sign since her childhood. Lason vanished into the shop again.

"He waited five days before he killed the first girl, Gardy. Rebecca St. Clair is still alive."

"I'll see what I can do. Assuming I get past Weber and Harold agrees to help, where should I tell him to send the information?"

Bell gave Gardy the email address for the Erwin Police Department.

"Hurry, please."

Lason clamored down the steps as Bell ended the call. The officer waved a sheet of paper at Bell. A photocopy of a receipt. Lason handed her the receipt, and Bell examined the signature.

"Lonnie Wagoner," Bell said, reading aloud. "I'd hate to be the one to phone his next of kin and ask them to identify Wagoner's arm. I don't recall a tattoo."

"No, but he wore a wedding ring."

"Shit."

"Uh-huh. What did you get out of your BAU contact?"

"Hopefully he came through. We'll know soon."

Another round through the dark streets of Erwin yielded nothing. Rebecca St. Clair's father had phoned Haggens and read the chief the riot act, and Haggens spoke like a kicked puppy when he radioed Lason and Bell.

"Nothing yet from Quantico," Haggens said.

"Check the email again," Bell said, peering out at the empty suburban streets.

Paralyzed by fear, the townsfolk locked their doors and drew the window shades. The orange glow of lamps provided the only proof of life inside Erwin's homes. Lights flared on every porch.

"Nothing new in the Inbox...wait." The mouse click traveled over the speaker. "We got it. Just came in a few seconds ago."

Bell uttered silent thanks to Gardy and Harold. She owed both surf and turf dinners when she got back to Virginia. Lason stomped the accelerator, and the cruiser pulled into the police department lot five minutes later.

Haggens loaded a map on a high definition monitor hanging over the operations center. Schenk and Donner were there, along with three additional officers working third shift. Schenk's and Donner's shifts should have ended two hours ago, and both had labored long and arduous overtime shifts in the last week. Though the room was full of officers with tired, red eyes, nobody complained, everyone dead set on bringing Rebecca St. Clair home alive.

The chief nodded at Bell when they took their place with the other officers.

"Thanks to Agent Bell and our new friends at Quantico, we have a manageable list of vacant properties outside of Erwin, all situated near a water source."

"That's still two dozen properties," a short, graying officer said.

"We'll begin by calling neighbors. See if anyone saw a light inside or noticed the trailer. In the meantime, Officers Schenk and Donner will collaborate with the county sheriff's office and scope out vacant residences. If Agent Bell is right about our killer holing up outside of Erwin, we'll find him before sunrise."

The potential of closing the case and rescuing the teen lit fires in the officers' eyes. Bell had closed in on the psychopath. She could feel it in her bones.

And yet it all seemed too easy, too convenient to Bell.

As if the killer baited her.

CHAPTER SEVENTEEN

The dashboard clock read ten. Officer Lason glued her eyes to the twisting road, the route treacherous at high speeds at night. Shaped like a sickle, the moon floated over the plain. Outside the windows, Bell saw only trees and impenetrable darkness. Occasionally, a pair of glowing eyes blinked. Coyotes and raccoons, Bell thought, but sometimes the shapes appeared larger.

Bell's hand touched the Glock through her sweatshirt, and she pulled it away before she attracted attention.

"You can stop trying to hide the gun anytime now."

Bell glanced at Lason, who remained fixed on the winding road.

"Huh?"

"The Glock. It's under your sweatshirt."

"How long have you known?"

"Longer than you'd believe. You're good, Agent Bell, but I'm better."

Bell swung her eyes toward the officer. Lason grinned.

"We'll see about that."

"Not tonight, we won't. Haggens isn't the sheriff, and he can't deputize you. Your skills are extraordinary, but you're a consultant tonight, not a cop. If all hell breaks loose, stay in the cruiser and radio for help. Understood?"

Bell leaned her elbow against the door and rested her chin on her fist.

"Bell?"

"Yeah, I got it. Where are we, anyhow?"

Lason stole a glance at the route signs blurring past the car. The officer's anxious expression told Bell they were lost.

"Uh, about two miles west of today's murder scene. I think."

"You think?"

"No, I'm sure of it."

Bell remained unconvinced.

The cruiser whipped past a farm with a huge silo that looked like a cyclone in the dark. As if to accentuate the illusion, lightning crackled in the distance and immediately echoed its blast over the radio.

It had been several minutes since the last promising lead fell through. Officers Schenk and Donner responded to a call two miles west of Erwin after a resident claimed a light shone in an abandoned trailer at the top of Harmony Drive. The officers investigated and found a large pond reflecting the moon into the trailer's window. Teams from the county sheriff's department canvassed vacant residences which met Harold's criteria north and south of town and found nothing. Doubt crept into Bell's thoughts. Her theories were wrong. The killer had left the area with St. Clair, and because of Bell they'd never find her.

"You know, I wanted to be you."

Lost in thought, Bell didn't comprehend Lason's words.

"What did you say?"

"Well, not necessarily a BAU agent, but FBI."

"So why didn't you? You'd make a great field agent.

You have all the right instincts."

Lason shrugged.

"I applied out of college. Maybe the application got lost in the shuffle or they didn't feel I was ready. The Erwin PD had openings, and I knew the guys on the force."

"You could have reapplied to the FBI. Hell, you could apply now and use my name as a reference. Wait. That might not help you."

Lason snorted as she navigated the cruiser down a hill paralleling a drainage creek.

"There's a lot keeping me here. Family, memories. Those are positive reasons for sticking around, don't get me wrong. But together they add up to comfort, and comfort isn't necessarily a good thing. Before you know it, you fear change. Stasis is a powerful force, Agent Bell. It's like the universe's Super Glue."

Bell empathized with Lason's reasoning until that last unfortunate analogy. She forced herself not to laugh, but after Lason giggled, there was no stopping it.

"That was sad," Bell said, wiping a tear from her eye. "Sounds like something I wrote in a creative writing project during—"

Something flashed in front of the cruiser. Then the squeal of rubber on asphalt as Lason jammed hard on the brakes. Whatever animal it was, it darted away from the front bumper a split second before impact and bounded into the brush.

Lason sat still with a white knuckle grip on the steering wheel. The engine purred. Bell's heart hammered through her ears.

The cruiser lay crooked across the road, the front end aimed at the drainage creek, the rear bumper poised above the soft shoulder.

"It looked like a dog," Bell said.

"I couldn't see it until the last second. Please tell me I

didn't hit it."

"You didn't."

After taking a deep breath to gather herself, Lason backed up the cruiser and straightened the front tires. But when she touched the gas, the dog bounded out of the grass and into the road. It barked twice and stared through the windshield. Lason and Bell shared a look.

"What on earth is it doing?"

"Your guess is as good as mine."

A beagle's size, the dog shared a labrador's face and wore a black coat. A mutt of some sort. It sat directly in front of the vehicle, tail wagging as Lason touched the horn. The dog didn't flinch.

Several seconds passed, and the dog finally stood and paced up the road. Except it stayed in front of the police cruiser instead of moving to the shoulder. Lason pressed the gas and swerved into the oncoming lane, and the dog ran to block her, barking.

"You've got to be kidding me," Lason said, drumming her fingers on the wheel. "It moved to block us."

"I'm going to get out and coax it onto the shoulder."

"Stay in the vehicle, Bell. Last thing I need to do is explain why a dog took a bite out of your ass when I'm supposed to keep you out of harm's way."

"Look at it. It's totally docile, not even growling."

"Cujo seemed like a nice dog until it tried to eat that family."

"Come on. He's not rabid. I'll get him to move."

"Bell—"

She stepped out from the cruiser in the middle of Lason's argument. As she circled around the bumper, the dog whined and wagged its tail. Was it hurt?

"Come on, boy. Let's get you off the road."

Snapping her fingers, Bell walked to the shoulder. The dog watched her, stubborn and unmoving. Bell jumped when it woofed at her. The driver side door opened, and Lason stepped into the road with her gun drawn.

"Don't you dare shoot the dog."

"Get back in the cruiser," Lason said.

"Give me a second. I'm starting to get through to him."

Trying a different tactic, Bell carefully approached the dog. The dog watched her until she crept up on him, and when she grabbed the dog's collar, it issued a low growl. Bell backed two steps away, and the dog returned to sitting before the car, tail thumping the blacktop.

"Bad idea, Bell."

"Come on, boy. Let's go for a walk."

Inspired by another idea, Bell padded to the cruiser and opened the back door.

"All right, who wants to go for a ride? Fun times in the police cruiser. Hop in, buddy."

All dogs loved going for rides, but this one refused to budge. Bell threw her hands up.

"I give up. I'm out of ideas."

Lason punched the horn twice and leaned on the open door, shaking her head.

"I'm not running over a dog," Lason said, chewing her thumbnail.

"Wouldn't expect you to. But we can't stay here all night until—"

The dog turned and trotted up the road, leaving the two women with mouths agape. About fifty yards up the road, the dog turned and barked. It started away again, then sprinted back to the front bumper. As they watched in astonishment, the dog barked for several seconds, then ran up the road and waited.

"I'll be damned," Bell said, edging toward the passenger door.

"What?"

"Call me crazy, but I'm convinced this dog wants us to follow him."

"You speak canine, Agent Bell?"

Lason waited for Bell to slide into the cruiser and shifted into drive. Creeping the vehicle forward, she glanced at Bell when the dog picked up the pace.

"What are you looking at me for? Follow that dog."

Keeping up with the dog proved tricky. The dog's black coat blended with the night, and he cut over embankments and leaped ditches as if Lason could follow. Whenever the dog ran too far ahead, it turned and woofed impatiently.

Lason pressed the gas, careful not to accelerate and risk running over the dog. She need not have worried, for the animal flew like the wind when it worked up to full speed. It took both women's full concentration to keep the dog in their sights, Bell worrying the chase was another waste of time distracting them from their mission. She was aware of stories in which dogs led vehicles back to injured owners, and she swung her vision over the shadowed terrain for a sign of someone in distress.

Bell felt certain they'd discover a wrecked vehicle around the next bend, but when they saw the dog racing uphill toward a dark cabin, her breath caught in her throat. A trailer stood in the driveway, and a dark sedan sat near the back of the property. She didn't need to creep up on its bumper to know it was the LaCrosse.

CHAPTER EIGHTEEN

The time was late and the cabin silent when Rebecca's eyes sprang open. The first thing she noticed was the dog had left. Abandoned her.

She got to work on her bindings before the slow roll of tires over rocks came up the driveway. Twisting her body, she craned her neck to gain a view out the upstairs window. A faint bloody glow from the taillights washed over the pane. The man kept the headlights off.

Tugging, Rebecca tried to stand, and the ropes pulled her back down. His footsteps circled to the back door where he jiggled the knob. Then around to the front.

The door groaned open. She pictured him in the doorway, immobile and staring into the shadows.

A subtle change in pressure indicated he'd shut the door, though she didn't hear him downstairs until the steps squealed beneath his weight. And by then it was too late to escape even if Rebecca found a way to slip her arms out of the knots.

A shiver ran down her back when his shadow crossed the threshold. He lumbered past the window, and she sought a view of his face, but it was as if the fates concealed his identity. A slash of moonlight caught his cheek and nothing else, then the dark silhouette stalked across the floor. Towards Rebecca.

Terrified, she didn't perceive the smell until he was almost on top of her. Food. A bag dangled from his hand, something greasy and salty inside. He rounded the beam and unraveled the ropes until one of her hands was free. Her arm tingled with pins-and needles. She didn't understand his intention until he dropped the bag into her lap and groaned at her to eat.

Normally, she might have suspected poison and been wary of any food given to her by a stranger, let alone a kidnapper, but her stomach boiled with pent-up hunger, and she ripped the bag apart as soon as the blood flowed into her hand.

The sandwich was chicken or hamburger. Rebecca ate too fast to notice. She dug into a side of onion rings and left nothing but crumbs. Though one of her arms was free, he left her alone while she ate, confident the knots were tight. He returned a minute later with a glass of water which he set beside the food bag.

As he walked back to the window, the man peered into the night as if expecting someone to arrive. She lifted the water to her lips. Dust and grime marred the glass, and she wiped the worst of it onto her sleeve and drank greedily until her stomach cramped. Nausea splashed into her throat and receded. She felt dirty for craving more food.

"I hope you're strong enough for the journey now."

She looked up. He kept his back to her, the nebulous reflection of a shadowed face in the glass.

"She'll be here soon. Together, you will experience the miracle of baptism." He paused. "Or the fires of hell should she refuse the hand of God."

Heavy footsteps shook the floorboards. He grasped her wrist and bound both arms behind the beam. Leaving the remnants of the food bag beside her, he moved back to the window and studied the property.

With a chill, Rebecca realized the man had vanished. She swiveled her head. The man was a phantom, a devil chameleon who blended with the night.

Then a noise.

Barking. The dog.

And she was fearful for the animal and knew the man would kill the dog.

The barking came closer, more insistent. Another sound buzzed through the empty Georgia countryside.

A motor.

CHAPTER NINETEEN

"Was this property on the list?" Lason stammered as the police cruiser climbed the hill.

"Kill the lights."

Lason turned off the lights and radioed back to headquarters for backup. The darn mutt was smarter than most field agents.

The cabin grew larger, a looming crypt turned tombstone-gray by the moonlight. Light warbled in a thin, snaking shape behind the cabin. A creek.

"Stop here," Bell said, leaning over the dash to spy the cabin.

The officer slowed the cruiser beside a treacherous ditch, the lane too narrow to support a shoulder. She made a clicking sound with her tongue and checked the mirrors.

Making up her mind, Lason removed her gun.

"Wait here."

"I'm coming with you."

"That's an order, Agent Bell."

Bell glanced at the cabin and it's dark, dead windows. No movement inside, but the killer was here. She sensed him like the calm before a twister strikes.

"You can't go in there alone."

“I'm only checking the perimeter.”

“Let me back you up.”

“No way. I can't.”

The door clicked shut before Bell could argue, then Lason leaped the ditch and climbed the incline, staying low in the meadow grass. Bell watched Lason until she vanished over the ridge.

She removed the Glock and checked the ammunition, busy work to prevent her from going crazy. The dog watched her from the meadow, and for a fleeting moment Bell thought about ghosts and angels sent from heaven.

Bell lifted her radio.

“Lason, come in.”

Bell counted to thirty in her head. She called Lason again and received no answer. The officer probably had the volume muted.

Or something bad had happened.

Screw the rules. Bell grabbed the door handle, but Haggens's voice on the radio stopped her.

“How did you end up on the other side of the county? Sit tight until help arrives.”

“Too late.”

“Wait, where's Lason? She didn't wait for backup?”

“Negative.”

“Shit. You got eyes on her, Agent Bell?”

“No. Haven't seen her since…” Bell checked the time on her phone. “Five minutes ago. I called her just now and didn't receive a reply.”

“Christ almighty. This keeps getting better and better. What do you see inside the cabin? Any movement?”

“Nothing. I have eyes on the LaCrosse, but it's dead quiet everywhere. At least allow me to check the trailer. What if the girl is inside?”

“We talked about this, Agent Bell. You're ordered to —”

"Act as a consultant. Yes, I know. I'll take the risk, Haggens. If something happens to me, you gave no authorization for me to move on the cabin. I'll take the heat."

"I don't like the sound of this."

"You know, Chief, you remind me of my partner. He always fears the worst when I'm involved."

"Maybe you have a habit of making people nervous."

"Is that a yes?"

Haggens hesitated, then he blew a flustered sigh into the radio.

"Check the trailer for the girl. If it's empty, proceed to the cabin and scope out the perimeter. If you don't see Officer Lason, you're to return to the vehicle and report your findings immediately. Under no circumstances are you to enter the cabin. Are we clear?"

"Clear."

"You got your radio?"

"Got it."

"Fine, go. And don't make me regret my decision."

Insect songs surrounded Bell when she stepped into the road. The moon shone bright enough to light her way, and she slumped down and followed the road until the grass wasn't tall enough to hide her presence.

The dog trotted over to her and sat. She stroked the dog's fur, and it nuzzled against her leg.

"You did good, boy. Help is coming. Make sure they find the road, but don't get yourself run over. I couldn't live with myself if that happened."

The dog cocked its head curiously.

"Go."

The dog darted down the hill and vanished. For a while, its paws clicked against the road before the night sounds swallowed all. Bell jumped the ditch and landed on her palms and knees, the rocky surface tearing a hole in her jeans.

Blood welled from the abrasion as she crawled along the driveway to the trailer. Gun in hand, she set her back against the side and threw her gaze at the cabin. Dammit. Where was Lason?

Holding her breath, she reached for the handle. Issued a silent prayer the door wouldn't squeal when she yanked it open.

On three.

One…two…

She pulled the door open a crack and beamed the flashlight into the interior with her gun aimed. The light cast shadows which violently thrust off the walls.

As expected, the inside was empty. Using the trailer as a shield, Bell moved up the driveway. The sedan lurked in the grass near the back of the house. She couldn't tell if anyone was inside.

After peeking around the corner, she raced from the trailer to the side of the cabin. Gun flicking back and forth, she followed the wall to the rear of the cabin and approached the sedan.

She spun from the bumper to the driver side window. Empty. Then along the back wall where Bell located a rear entry door framed by wilted flowers in dry planters.

"Lason?"

Her whisper died beneath the whistle of wind snaking around the cabin.

She tested the doorknob. A gentle twist to confirm if it was locked or open. The knob turned in her hand, and the paranoia the killer had lured her to the cabin grew stronger. Checking the police radio, Bell made certain she'd cut the volume.

Now she stood beside the unlocked door, back pressed against the cabin, the Glock a small comfort against evil incarnate.

The devil waited inside.

She grasped the doorknob and slipped into the cabin.

CHAPTER TWENTY

Smothering dark met Bell inside the cabin. The first level was all shadows and indistinct contours, and she needed to wait for the shapes to take form.

Crouching beside the door with the moonlight beaming through grungy panes to either side, Bell steadied her breathing and swung the gun around the downstairs.

Without furnishings, the living room and kitchen were nearly indistinguishable. The front door stood across the room, a tinge of gray light seeping around the broken knob. Gun thrust before her, she edged toward a wooden stairway.

Backup was at least fifteen minutes away. She couldn't wait that long. Not with Lason missing and the St. Clair girl somewhere inside.

Poised beside the foot of the stairs, she listened. Dead quiet followed from the second floor.

Bell swung out of hiding with the Glock aimed up the staircase. A pool of gray light glimmered on the landing, and Bell recalled the huge second-story window affixed to the cabin. She crept along the wall, worried the steps might creak and give her away. Halfway up the stairs, the hairs prickled along her arms. Something was wrong. Too much silence.

At the landing, she aimed the gun into the dappled moonlight and perceived life in the darkness. An imperfection in the shadows. A cylindrical shape grew to the ceiling. A beam with a body slumped against its base.

Throat tight, she edged past the window, careful to avoid the revealing moonlight. But he was here. Jillian's killer.

She was close enough to make out a body tied to the beam. A girl's body. Rebecca St. Clair. Gloom hid the girl's face, but her chest swelled and receded. She was alive.

Feeling someone coming up behind her, Bell swung around to the empty landing. No one. She flicked the gun around the room and advanced toward St. Clair. By the time the light caught the girl's shaking head and gagged mouth, it was too late for the teen to warn her.

The fist hammered down on the back of Bell's neck. Her knees buckled, and the gun dropped to the floor as she fell. The man struck her again. Her legs spasmed and went still, eyes frozen open and staring at Lason's crumpled body at the back of the room.

Then he stomped on the back of her skull. The room turned black.

CHAPTER TWENTY-ONE

When the benzene scent pulled her out of her stupor, Bell struggled up to her elbows and collapsed, too groggy to support her weight.

She spun her head when she recognized the scent of gasoline. It lay thick along the walls and toward the landing.

Pulling her legs into her chest, she felt a doughy weight sag against her shin. Lason's body. Bell crawled to the officer and touched her neck. Warm. Bell discerned a pulse.

Bell sensed eyes on her and twisted to her side. Rebecca St. Clair stared, eyes wide and impossibly bright in the shadows. Still woozy, Bell dragged herself to the girl and checked the bindings. Multiple knots held the girl's wrists behind the beam. It would take a long time to untie all of them, time they didn't have. She loosened the gag until it fell around the girl's neck.

"Where is he?"

"Downstairs. Hurry before he comes back."

The Glock was gone, taken by the killer, who'd also pilfered Lason's holster. She started unraveling the ropes, all the while attuned to the footsteps stomping through the downstairs.

"Are you her? The woman the man said would come?"

The reply caught in Bell's throat. She swallowed and met the girl's eyes.

"Listen to me. I'm an FBI agent. Stay calm, and I'll get you out of here."

"He hurt the other woman bad, the police officer. He beat her until she started shaking. I think she had a seizure."

Bell scrambled over to Lason. The officer's skin looked pallid, diseased in the low light. Bell worried the woman had a brain bleed and required medical attention.

The hollow clunk of the killer setting down the fuel echoed from below. Gasoline vapors ascended the stairs. The maniac intended to burn everyone alive.

She untied one knot, but several more remained. The man climbed the stairs now, a black shadow growing against the moonlight.

A second knot popped loose, but he was almost to the landing.

Bell placed her finger against her lips, and after Rebecca nodded in understanding, she placed her hands together and lowered her cheek to the top of her hand, a signal for the girl to pretend to sleep.

Quickly, Bell slumped to the floor. Checking her surroundings, she inched backward until she lay where the killer had left her. Lason's shallow breathing whispered behind Bell.

He shuffled onto the landing, dragging his feet as a zombie would in a horror movie. Bell squinted one eye, tried to get a look at his face, but the shadows ran too deep.

He stopped before Rebecca and nudged the girl's shoulder. Bell's pulse raced, yet the girl stayed calm and put forth a convincing act.

Grunting like an animal, he stalked to Bell and stood

above her, his breathing deep and monstrous. He fished inside his pocket and produced a matchbook.

When the match flared, Bell's fist shot up and caught the stunned kidnapper in the stomach. He doubled over, and she caught hold of his wrist and twisted. The lit match tumbled from his hand, fell upon gasoline splatter, and kindled a blue flame.

Bell released her grip and dived at the flame, but it spread faster than she could move. Then the fire leaped to the corners where he'd splashed the most fuel, and a blinding blast of flame exploded up the wall.

Two fists crushed her head from behind. She pitched forward with the maniac astride her back, hands squeezing her throat. Bell fought up to her knees, and he crashed his weight onto the small of her back. Flattened against the hardwood, Bell coughed and choked, the fire growing by the second.

"I knew you would come, Scarlett. Accept the hand of God."

She twisted her neck. Fought to look at the face of her nightmares.

Grabbing her hair, he drove her head against the floor. Blood poured from her nose and mouth as Rebecca screamed over the roaring inferno. She threw her head back and cracked the bridge of his nose. When he weakened, she slid up to her knees and drove her elbow into his throat.

He tottered toward the wall, the fire almost catching him as Bell struggled to her feet. Smoke clouded the room. It was impossible to see Rebecca, only the hint of her shadow amid the billowing cloud.

He screamed as the fire spread down one arm. Dropping to the floor, he rolled under the smoke, and she lost sight of him. Eyes stinging, Bell groped blindly for the teenager. She followed the girl's coughs and bumped headfirst into the beam. She bent down and groped at the knots. Somewhere in the smoke, the man bellowed and crashed against the floor, fighting to reach the staircase.

The knots unraveled in Bell's hands, but there was always one more she hadn't discovered trapping the teenager. Bell doubled over, choking while the fire spread toward the landing, cutting off their only escape route. Smoke cloaked the room, crawling over the ceiling like a virulent ghost.

Just when Bell was certain she'd never locate the last of the knots, the ropes sprang apart. The girl slumped forward, unable to support her own weight.

An explosion below rocked the cabin and spit dragon fire up the stairway. Holding Rebecca's hand, Bell remembered Lason. She'd last seen the officer beside the back wall where the fire raged toward the ceiling.

Closing her eyes and holding her breath against the noxious fumes, Bell reached into the smoke and closed her hand over Lason's ankle. She tugged and dragged the prone woman toward her, relieved when Lason moaned. Still alive.

Rebecca grabbed Lason's other ankle and helped pull the officer away from the fire. As Bell placed a comforting hand on Rebecca's shoulder, a chunk of ceiling rained down on the landing and spurred the inferno higher.

"What are we going to do?"

The newfound bravery drained from Rebecca's face as the fire cut them off. Bell eyed Lason, wondering how she could carry the woman to safety if she found a way past the flames. Lason coughed as Bell supported the woman's head in her lap.

"The window," Bell said.

"It's too high to jump."

Risky, yet preferable to burning alive. Then she remembered the ropes.

With the roar of the fire drowning out their voices, Bell motioned at the spool of rope as she attempted to rouse the groggy officer. The girl gathered up the rope and pulled it away from the beam, the fire smoldering where the ceiling and beam met.

"Get up, Lason. I can't carry you."

Glassy-eyed, Lason struggled to focus. She shook her head.

"Get the girl out of here. I'll take care of myself."

"On your feet, Officer."

Bell helped Lason onto her hands and knees. Unable to hold herself up, Lason pitched forward. Bell caught her before Lason slammed her head against the floor, and then Rebecca was by her side, helping the officer up to her knees. Together they edged Lason toward the window.

Another explosion boomed from the first floor. A black cloud twisted up the stairs and curled around the landing as though seeking them.

By the time they reached the window, Lason crawled on her own, but Bell doubted the woman had enough strength to climb down. Bell saw how high they were and contemplated the length of the rope.

The window was double-pane, and Bell tore the sweatshirt over her head and wrapped it around her arm. Smashing her elbow against the glass, she winced. The window shattered. Lason and the teenager chipped at the jagged shards.

Feeding off the new source of oxygen, the fire tore across the walls, burgeoning with terrifying velocity. Bell grabbed the rope and searched the room. There was nothing to tie the rope to except the beam, now burning.

With no alternative, Bell wound the rope around her hip.

Lason grasped Bell's arm.

"What are you doing? Who's going to lower you down?"

Bell shook her head.

"I'll figure it out later. Grab hold of the rope and help me." Noticing the terror on Rebecca's face, she grabbed the girl's hands. "You can do this."

"I can't," the girl said, averting her eyes from the window.

"You have to. There's no time to argue."

The ceiling cracked. Flaming plaster rained around them.

Rebecca wrapped her hands around the rope and climbed over the pane. A thin ledge gave the girl somewhere to place her feet, but as Bell and Lason began to lower the girl out the window, Rebecca's feet slipped off the edge, and she plummeted down the side of the house.

A scream.

Bell and Lason grabbed the rope. The sudden force whipped Bell forward and slammed her against the wall. Bell dared not look out the window, but after her muscles stopped shaking and she was able to brace her body against the window frame, she felt Rebecca dangling below. The girl hadn't let go.

With Lason's aid, Bell wrapped the rope over her shoulders and got control of Rebecca's weight. The teenager scrambled her legs against the outer wall but couldn't gain solid footing. Momentum ricocheted the girl against the cabin. Bell let several inches of rope go, the fibers burning streaks into her palms.

Then another several inches. The girl seemed heavier now, muscle fatigue setting in for Bell. The fire crept out of the corners. Hemmed them in. Bell leaned her head out the window and saw the girl hanging halfway down the cabin. The tremors in Rebecca's arms told Bell she couldn't hold on much longer.

"Jump, Rebecca. You're almost there."

The girl raised her eyes, and Bell saw stark terror. The teenager might get out of this with nothing more than a broken ankle, but plenty could go wrong falling an entire story. And if Rebecca landed on her head…

Lason screeched when a rogue flame caught her shirtsleeve. Bell smothered the fire with her body, somehow able to keep hold of the rope. A scream came from outside the window. The rope went slack, Bell nearly stumbling backward into the advancing fire before Lason caught her.

Bell saw the girl curled on her side. The teenager had the wind knocked out of her. The way Rebecca grabbed her ankle made Bell think it might be sprained, but as a piece of the roof exploded, the girl had the wherewithal to drag herself toward the creek.

"You're next, Agent Bell."

Lason accepted her fate. It was clear on her face as Bell pulled the rope through the shattered window.

"No way, Elle. Wrap the rope around your waist."

"I'm heavier, and you're too exhausted to lower me."

As Bell argued, a portion of the roof collapsed and swung like a guillotine across the room. Before Bell got the warning out of her mouth, the roofing clipped the officer's head.

Bell caught hold of Lason. As she supported the woman's crumpled body, Bell spun the rope around Lason's hips and tied it off. Something bit at her ear, and she yelped and brushed the fiery ember off her hair. She hauled Lason to the window and tied the other end of the rope around her own waist. It was a fight to prop the unconscious woman onto the sill, and she implored Lason to awaken and support herself.

The officer teetered for a moment. Bell caught her before she plummeted out the window and dragged them both to their deaths. Her mouth covered against the smoke, Rebecca limped below the window to catch Lason.

"I'm going to lower her," Bell called down to the girl. "I don't know how long I can hold her though. When she's close to the bottom, grab her so she doesn't land on her head."

Bell didn't wait for acknowledgement. She spooled the rope around her body until it was tight. Jamming herself against the wall, she let Lason topple over the sill. The ropes constricted around Bell's chest and drove the air from her lungs. The woman's bulk threatened to yank Bell up and over the frame. Yet she held on, the small of her back screaming as she twisted her body and released another foot of rope.

The dead weight of the officer dragged against the cabin, twisting in the wind. Bell forced herself not to hurry despite the agony. Sweat bubbled from every pore, her shirt a second skin as the hellfire roared closer. She would die here, and it would be worth it if she saved Rebecca and Lason while Jillian's killer burned to ashes below.

Shouts outside the window told Bell something was wrong. As she lowered Lason another agonizing inch, she peeked over the ledge and realized with horror the rope had risen past Lason's chest to her shoulders and would soon become a noose. Cursing, Bell let another foot of rope go. Lason was halfway to the ground.

A man's shout brought her head up. Officers Schenk and Donovan had joined Rebecca. Red and blue lights flooded the yard and reflected off the creek as the banshee cry of an approaching fire engine echoed off the ridge.

"Another few feet and we'll catch her!" Schenk yelled over the fire.

The presence of the officers invigorated Bell, gave her the will to strain against Lason's weight a little longer. She cried out, back wedged against the sill, and unwound the rope. A tug came from the other end, and Bell collapsed in exhaustion as Schenk and Donovan caught Lason.

And that was when the rope slipped from Bell's hands and snaked out the window. She lunged for the end as it disappeared into the night.

When the rope hit the ground, Schenk looked up at Bell, his mouth frozen open. Recognizing what happened,

Donovan sprinted down the driveway and waved down the fire engine climbing the hill toward the cabin.

The stairs fell away and took the landing with them. Body shaking with fatigue, Bell pulled herself onto the ledge and looked down. Schenk put his arms out, but the officer couldn't catch her. Too far to fall. She'd likely kill them both.

Led by Donovan, a crew of firefighters rounded the cabin with a ladder. It didn‘t matter. The fire was almost upon her now. Better to plunge to her death than burn.

The upstairs detonated. Flames lunged for Bell as the force of the explosion smashed against her back.

A cry. Was it her own voice?

Bell lost consciousness as she tumbled off the ledge.

CHAPTER TWENTY-TWO

Smoke choked the air as sirens converged on the hillside cabin.

Bell's eyelids drifted apart, drooped closed, then popped open with the shock she was alive. An EMT with a walrus mustache and potato chips on his breath crouched beside Bell. An oxygen mask enveloped her mouth and nose, and a female EMT with flowing braids assisted her partner in lifting Bell onto a stretcher.

"You don't have to do that. I'm fine," Bell said, pulling the mask away.

The braided woman cocked a doubtful eyebrow and shushed her.

"We're treating you for smoke inhalation. You're lucky you didn't break your neck."

Everything hurt. Her head, back, legs. Bell shifted and cried out at the pain biting through her ankle.

"I don't think it's broken," the woman said, biting her lip as they hoisted her into the ambulance. "Somebody smiled down on you tonight. Try to remain still."

Bell lay in the ambulance and stared at the ceiling. An open cabinet full of medical supplies stood to one side of her, a wall of monitors on the opposite side. It was noticeably quieter inside, drowning out the shouts of the firefighters as they waged a lost war with the fire.

The vehicle shook when Schenk climbed into the back.

"How you doing, Wonder Woman?"

Bell tried to smile and grimaced at her parched, cracked lips. She ran her tongue over them and tasted blood along the split.

"Where's Elle?"

"She's on her way to the hospital. The EMTs think she has a concussion and a cracked rib, but we'll know more when the doctors get a look at her. How you feeling?"

"Like I got kicked by a horse."

The moments before she lost consciousness at the window were lost in a haze, but now she recalled climbing onto the ledge a heartbeat before the second floor burst.

"Wait a minute. How am I alive? I couldn't have jumped."

"You tried to. Damn foolish. While you clung to the ledge, the fire crew threw a ladder against the cabin and reached you. You were lucky, Bell. One of them pulled you onto the ladder before your fingers slipped."

Bell didn't remember the near fall, only the blast ringing in her head when the roof collapsed.

"Shit."

"What's wrong?"

"The killer took my phone and keys. How the hell am I going to get out of Erwin?"

Schenk smiled and stood, making way for the EMT crew.

"You ever see *Doc Hollywood*, Agent Bell? You might come to like Erwin once you give it a chance."

CHAPTER TWENTY-THREE

Bell spent two nights in the county hospital a few blocks from the swelling Atlantic. The doctors released Officer Lason on the same morning, and Bell drove Lason home. Due to the seizure, the doctors wouldn't allow Lason to drive for a minimum of six months, though they expected a full recovery.

Lason invited Bell to sit on the deck and watch the hummingbirds flutter around the flower garden, but Bell wanted to drive into town for a new phone first. She'd stored her wallet inside the cruiser, or she would have lost her driver's license, too.

Bell's phone hummed to life as soon as the world reconnected. By now, her name was all over the news. She expected Gavin Hayward was already penning a front-page article for *The Informer*.

Trying to get ahead of the story, she sent a text to Lucas and admitted she'd lied. His reply came immediately.

How soon before you get back?

Bell pushed the car seat back and winced. The bruised back seemed to double her age.

I can't think of a better place to heal than home. I'm

leaving first thing tomorrow.

Bell rubbed at her temples and turned the radio off before the news about the case repeated. She figured she'd lost her job with the BAU. She expected Weber's call soon.

When Lucas didn't reply, she sent another text.

Hey, I might be home a lot more from now on. What do you think of dinner on the deck every night? You catch them, I'll cook them. We'll make a game of it.

For Bell, no better medicine existed, and for the first time, she realized she didn't care about her career. There comes a point when one defines victory as walking away from inevitable loss.

I'll be waiting for you, Scarlett.

The little town had emerged from its hibernation now that Rebecca St. Clair was home. The Renaissance Cafe bustled with activity and shoppers crowded the sidewalks. Erwin would mourn Bregan Dane for a long time, but the nightmare was finally over.

Bell reached for the ignition when her phone rang, unsettlingly loud with the windows shut.

She recognized Gardy's number and considered ignoring the call. After several rings, she answered.

"Tell me you're still in Georgia."

"Hey there, Gardy. Yes, I'm feeling much better. Thanks so much for asking."

"Are you alone?"

Something in Gardy's voice worried her. Bell checked the mirrors. The mobile phone shop's parking lot had emptied now that lunch hour was over.

"I'm on way back to Officer Lason's house. If you called to warn me about Weber—"

"This isn't about your job, dammit. Listen to me. They didn't find a body inside the cabin."

Bell reached for the missing Glock and felt naked.

Checked the mirrors again. A man watched her from the park.

"There must be a mistake. The cabin collapsed. Nobody could have survived."

Bell stepped out of the Rogue. The park was empty now.

"Bell?"

"Yeah, I'm here."

"I'm sending an officer to Lason's residence. You aren't to leave the house until I get there."

Sliding back into the SUV, Bell locked the doors.

"You don't need to come to Erwin, Gardy."

"I fly into Savannah at four. It's a one-way ticket. Tomorrow morning, we'll drive the Rogue back to Virginia."

"Come on, Gardy. None of this is necessary. He won't try to kill me on I-95."

"They found photographs of you in his car. Candids. Bell, you couldn't have been more than nine or ten."

Dread crawled down Bell's back. Her hands trembled. She didn't think she could drive.

"There's something else. God, I wanted to tell you face-to-face."

"Just tell me, Gardy."

"Have you received texts from Lucas today?"

"Yeah, why?"

Silence.

"Gardy!"

"They aren't from Lucas, Bell. He's dead."

"No, that's impossible. I talked to him a few minutes ago."

Yet the cold horror clutching her bones told her it was true. A tear crawled down her face, perched on her chin and lingered.

"Someone broke into the beach house this morning

and stabbed him in his sleep. Took his wallet and phone as far as the police can tell. Bell, what if it's the same guy? Bell?"

The words refused to come.

Bell ended the call and clutched the steering wheel.

She didn't want Gardy to hear her scream.

THE DEVIL'S HOUR

CHAPTER TWENTY-FOUR

Fire me. Get it the hell over with.

But he couldn't fire her, Special Agent Scarlett Bell thought as she sat across from Deputy Director Weber's desk, not with the media firestorm and court of public opinion on her side.

It seemed unusually bright inside Weber's office as if one too many floodlights shone. These were just after effects of the fire she escaped in Georgia.

Weber fidgeted in his chair, brow dotted with sweat. The story of how Bell rescued teenager Rebecca St. Clair and police officer Elle Lason from an at-large serial killer and risked her life to save them from a burning cabin had gone national, and now everyone from CNN to the Washington Post wanted to interview Bell.

"You defied FBI orders by involving yourself in the Erwin murder case. In my day as a field agent, insubordination of this magnitude would get you fired, no questions asked."

Weber swiveled in his chair, eyes fixed on the ceiling as if asking a higher power for forgiveness. His grimace thin and tight, he reached for the intercom and pushed the button.

Candice, Weber's new administrative assistant, answered.

"Yes, Deputy Director Weber?"

"Candice, call Neil Gardy to my office."

"Right away, sir."

Weber had the look of a man two moves away from checkmate, so it was wholly unexpected when he reached into his cabinet and slid her Glock and FBI badge across the table. Bell looked down at the items, then up at Weber.

"I don't understand."

"Sure you do, Agent Bell."

"Am I reinstated?"

"Effective immediately." She reached for her badge and gun, and his hand shot out and slapped down on them. "Make no mistake about it, Agent Bell. While I'm willing to put the public image of the BAU above my desire to fire you, there will be repercussions for crossing the deputy director of CIRG. This isn't over."

The door opened, and Neil Gardy, Bell's partner, poked his head into the room. Dark-haired, middle-aged, and fit, Gardy was the BAU's senior agent and respected by his peers.

"You wanted to see me, sir?"

"Yes, Neil. I was just speaking to your newly reinstated partner. Please have a seat."

A wolffish grin crossed Weber's face. He only flashed it for a second, but it was long enough for Bell to discern Weber's true intentions. Weber didn't dare go after Bell, not until the national attention ran its course and died off. Instead, he meant to destroy Gardy's career.

Damn, it made sense. Gardy remained the heir apparent to Weber's position, and there wasn't an agent inside the BAU who didn't think Gardy deserved the title.

The FBI should have selected Gardy over Weber in the first place. Political pressure to force Weber out of CIRG grew every month, but only because a more worthy successor was in place. Get rid of Gardy, and Weber could rest easy.

Gardy sneaked a look at Bell. She pressed her lips together, a signal for him to watch his step.

Weber passed a folder across the desk to Gardy.

"The letter on top arrived on Congresswoman San Giovanni's desk yesterday afternoon."

Gardy scanned the letter and glared at Weber.

"This is from the Erwin killer. Why wasn't I informed of this earlier?"

"As I'm certain you can appreciate, it was important to verify the authenticity."

"Is it the real deal?"

"We believe so. He mentions details about the Bregan Dane murder which we withheld from the media."

Gardy handed the folder to Bell and shifted his seat closer to the desk.

"He signed it God's Hand. This is new."

"It seems our unknown subject desires attention. Perhaps he hired Agent Bell's publicist."

"Why write San Giovanni?" Bell asked, biting her tongue.

"The congresswoman is one of the brightest and most vocal of the new freshmen," said Gardy. "If you want to make a splash, go after the biggest fish in the pond."

"Sure, but he only warns he'll take another girl soon. At no point does he threaten San Giovanni's family. Does the congresswoman have a child?"

"A thirteen-year-old girl, and she has two nieces in their mid-teens, so I can imagine San Giovanni is at her wit's end."

Bell handed the folder back to Gardy and winced when her skin stretched. Pink tinged her flesh from neck to forearm. It was little more than a bad sunburn, and Bell felt lucky she'd escaped a far worse fate inside the burning cabin.

"Am I to understand the God's Hand case takes precedence over capturing Logan Wolf?" Gardy asked Weber as he thumbed through the notes.

"Indeed. All of Washington is watching how we handle this case, Agent Gardy. These are the cases which make or break careers."

After Weber dismissed the agents, Bell followed Gardy back to his office.

"What the hell was that line about? Making or breaking careers."

"Don't read anything into it. If Weber wanted to fire you, he'd have done so already. It's not like you haven't given him a few dozen reasons over the last year."

"Funny," Bell said, except she didn't laugh. She was tempted to tell Gardy her fears about Weber targeting his job and setting them up to fail, but when she opened her mouth, Candice strode into the office and slapped another folder down on his desk.

"More notes on the case, including a psychological profile of the killer from George Mason."

Overweight in heels and a power suit, Candice swung and huffed back to her office before either replied. Bell had underestimated Weber. He wanted to eliminate both of them, and feeding Gardy and Bell a flawed profile would ensure their failure and allow Weber to point the finger of blame at his agents when congress came down on the BAU.

"Still trust Weber? Now he's going outside the BAU for psychological profiles."

"Calm down, Bell. He's covering his ass if the case goes south. Weber needs to demonstrate the BAU utilized every resource to catch this guy."

"Every resource, my ass. He turned a blind eye to the

Erwin murder."

"In all fairness, Weber hadn't reinstated you yet. He couldn't send you into the field until the psychological evaluation—"

"Came back clear. Yes, I remember. Doesn't it seem a little funny how long Weber dragged his feet on the evaluation? Keep in mind nothing happened until the case made the national news."

Gardy threw his jacket over his shoulder.

"I'm heading down for a smoothie. Walk with me."

"I can't," she said, sliding her badge into her lanyard. "I promised my parents I'd stop by after work."

Gardy watched her from the corner of his eye.

"Bealton is a long drive. Sure you're up for it?"

Physically, she wasn't, but driving cleared her head, and Bell needed to exorcise a few demons.

In the parking lot, Bell closed the door and let the silence fall over her. The quiet times were the most painful. If she listened closely, she could hear Lucas whispering in her ear. Though she'd known him only two months, she imagined marrying Lucas someday. Memories from the funeral bit her heart when she least expected. The gathering had been tiny, just a handful of cousins and his parents, who were much older than Bell anticipated. They'd had Lucas in their forties, an unexpected late-life gift, and when Bell offered condolences, they were too stricken to respond.

The mirror revealed red and puffy eyes. She wiped the tears on her sleeve and tried to convince herself Lucas's death wasn't her fault. The killer, the man who now referred to himself as God's Hand, murdered children. He killed adults out of necessity, including a hunter outside of Erwin who'd figured out God's Hand held a kidnapped teenage girl in his trailer. Lucas's murder was personal. God's Hand murdered her neighbor and boyfriend to send a message to Bell.

And that meant God's Hand knew her address, as did fugitive serial killer and former BAU agent Logan Wolf.

For once, she felt thankful an unmarked FBI vehicle watched her apartment at all times.

CHAPTER TWENTY-FIVE

Two decades had passed since the last time Bell visited the creek where the killer abducted her childhood friend, Jillian Rossi, and later dumped her body. In the ensuing years between high school graduation and her adult life, Bell refused to return despite the creek's proximity to her home.

It was as she remembered—the soft gurgle of water hugging the creek's many twists and bends, the dappled sunlight through branches which displayed the season's first buds. And the solitude. When Bell was a child, she'd sit upon the banks and read, and sometimes she'd lay in the soft grass and watch the clouds swim through an ocean of blue.

And yet it was different. The neighborhood had expanded across the meadow, a new upscale development fifty yards from the banks. Bell knew the homes would flood during the spring, but she was certain the wealthy owners could afford the cleanup and elevated insurance premiums.

The creek rippled back toward the woods where the shadows grew thick as blood. Something moved among the trees. A deer, most likely, but one could never be certain what lurked in the darkness. Something loud thudded against the ground, and Bell, having seen enough of the creek for today, backed away and headed for her Nissan Rogue.

Her parents, Sean and Tammy Bell, were outside when Bell pulled into the driveway, a load of excavated weeds in Mom's arms, Dad busy realigning the garage door. The hinges were rusted orange, and one had snapped two years ago.

"Wouldn't it be easier to replace the door?"

Dad grinned and stood, hands rubbing at the small of his back.

"The new ones have too many gadgets built into them. The Sennets had their snowblower stolen over the winter. Seems Alexa decided to raise the garage door in the middle of the night."

Bell fell into her father's arms. Sean Bell stood five inches taller than Bell, yet he seemed to lose an inch after his cancer scare last year. He kissed Bell on top of her head as he'd done all her life. Smiling and trying to figure out what to do with her dirty hands, Tammy leaned in and pecked Bell on the cheek.

"Sorry, baby. I don't want to get your work clothes dirty."

"Don't worry about my clothes, Mom."

Caught in the same time warp as the creek, Bell's childhood home never changed. The soft pile carpet in the living room was new, yet the color looked identical to the beige rug they'd had for two decades. The walls remained white, even though two new coats stood between Bell and the paint that covered the wall when she left for college.

End of day sun burned through the kitchen window when Bell took her customary middle seat at the table. Mom always sat on the left, Dad on the right, and this reassuring stasis brought a grin to Bell's lips. The injury was plain on Mom's face when she set a glass of lemonade in front of Bell. Tammy Bell danced around Lucas's murder the way one gives a shattered glass on the floor a wide berth. Bell's parents had never met Lucas, the relationship too brief.

Mom made small talk and gave Bell all the town gossip. The Clark girl at the end of the block was engaged, and old Mr Slater fell in the tub last week and would need to move to a seniors' home. As she talked, Dad adjusted uncomfortably in his chair, knowing no one would get a word in edge-wise unless his wife went hoarse. When she began to tell Bell about Richard Younker's new Mercedes—a nod to Stephen King, Tammy Bell simply referred to Younker as Mr Mercedes these days—Sean broke in.

"That's enough, Tammy. Scarlett didn't drive all the way to Bealton to hear about Mr Bigshot Mercedes."

Mom waved the thought away and sipped at her lemonade.

"It's not that long a drive," Bell said.

"Long enough," said Mom, wiping a condensation ring with her shirtsleeve. "Otherwise, she'd visit more often."

The kitchen fell quiet, the frightened-mouse silence that ensued at the sound of a distant explosion during wartimes. It never took long before Tammy Bell stirred the pot. Next, she'd revisit the same tired arguments that women weren't fit to be FBI field agents.

Staving off the animosity, Bell pretended not to notice.

"There's something I want to ask you about."

"Sure, honey," Mom said, thankful for the reprieve. "You know we're always here for you."

Bell looked from Mom to Dad.

"I want to warn you before I start. It's about the man who murdered Jillian."

At the mention of Jillian's name, Mom's hiss pulled the air out of the room. She visibly composed herself, distractedly picking at the dirt specks on her gardening shirt.

"Sorry, Scarlett, it's just that we haven't spoken about

it in a long time," Mom said as Dad looked down at his hands.

Bell trembled. She'd broached the subject for the better part of her life and ended up in therapy with Dr Morford, unsure if Jillian's killer chased Bell at the creek or if she'd dreamed the encounter. She breathed deeply and waited for the shakes to abate.

"I'm seeing a doctor about what happened. To Jillian, I mean."

"That's good, Scarlett. It's always good to have someone to talk to when bad things happen. Isn't that right, Dad?"

"Let her finish, Tammy."

Mom returned to fretting over the water droplets on the kitchen table.

"I dream about the man who took Jillian." She glanced over. Mom bit her hand, eyes glassy. "Actually, I've had the dreams since the murder."

"Of course," Mom said, sniffling. "What happened was a horrible, horrible tragedy, and it's completely normal to have nightmares."

"That's not all. You see, I can't recall everything that happened in 1995. It's like I can't tell dream from reality." Bell pushed the glass away. She'd lost her appetite. "Did Jillian's killer come after me, too? Or was it only a dream?"

Nobody spoke. The old clock ticked from the living room. After what felt like an eternity, Dad brushed the gray hair back from his forehead.

"Don't you remember, Scarlett? You were the reason the police almost caught him."

CHAPTER TWENTY-SIX

Five miles outside of Bealton, Bell pulled the Rogue onto a quarry road where she and her friends partied during their high school days. The sky was black and lit with stars as Bell unbuckled the seatbelt and buried her face in her hands. She killed the engine and slid the seat back. The sobs came loud and harsh, little duck calls she choked on.

Upon her father recounting the events of 1995, the pent-up memories flooded back to Bell. She'd gone to the creek on a foggy morning before her parents awoke, and the killer, revisiting the abduction scene, had come out of the woods. After chasing the screaming Bell back to the neighborhood, he caught her two blocks from her house. Ripped her from the bike and dragged her toward his car. When he threw her over his shoulder, Bell saved herself by gouging at the man's eyes and biting down on his cheek, not letting go until his blood poured.

The police came, and Bell remembered the make of the vehicle, a stolen Dodge Shadow, and the license plate. Her information led to a bolo, but despite roadblocks, police checks, and continuous news coverage, the man evaded the police. A month later, they found the car at the bottom of a ravine in Northern Virginia, the interior burned out and the body crumpled beyond recognition. No sign of a body.

God's Hand had remained a ghost until the Erwin murders, though Bell wondered how many cold cases involving murdered and kidnapped children could be tied to him. Logan Wolf had told Bell the killer was active again, warned her in his own sick and nebulous way of what was to come in Erwin.

Bell dabbed her eyes dry and adjusted the mirror. The ride home was a long one, and she wouldn't arrive at the apartment until late.

She jumped at the unexpected sound inside the car and snatched up her phone, forgetting she'd set the ringer to vibrate.

Gardy's number. She answered.

"You still in Bealton?"

"Uh..." Bell swallowed the tremors rolling through her throat. "I'm heading out now."

"You don't sound good, Bell. Everything all right?"

She cleared her throat and wiped her nose.

"Just thinking about things."

A quiet moment, then he spoke.

"Sorry."

"It's fine. Just gonna take a while before I process everything."

"Hey, why don't you grab a hotel for the night. Drive back in the morning after you've had a good night's sleep and too much to eat at the breakfast bar."

Bell snorted.

"Oh, man. You remember California when I hadn't eaten for twenty-four hours?"

"Many a Belgian waffle paid the ultimate price."

She realized she was laughing and regretted it. Lucas dead, Jillian's killer back, and old graves unearthed inside her parents' house.

"Anyhow, I talked to my parents."

"Wait, about the dreams?" She told him her father's

story. “Damn, Bell. I don't know what to say.”

“You don't need to say anything. That’s why God's Hand targeted me. I'm the one who got away. Shit.”

“We can use that against him, Bell. Don't forget he texted you with Lucas’s phone. The minute that phone turns on, the entire bureau will be all over him.”

“That was over a week ago. He won't use it again.”

“Take my advice. Stay the night.”

“I wouldn't sleep a wink, Gardy. It’s like twenty-three years of secrets are flooding back at me. If I stay, I’ll end up pawing through the dark along the creek, searching for some ancient piece of evidence that went unnoticed over the decades. No, I'll drive back and deal with the exhaustion tomorrow.”

“At least write me when you get home.”

She drummed her fingers on the seat.

“Thanks for letting me know you care.”

“Come on, Bell. You don't need to joke about it.”

“Who's joking? I mean it. Thanks.”

“Oh…well, you're welcome.”

“Hey, I've got two bluefish filets in the fridge I need to cook before the apartment starts to smell like the Atlantic. If you're free, I'm eating at four.”

Gardy didn't answer for a while. Bell started to think the call dropped.

“As it so happens my schedule is free tomorrow afternoon.”

“Then it's settled.”

“I'll stop by at three and sit on your deck. Overstay my welcome and such.”

“Nobody does it better. And, Gardy?”

“What?”

“Thanks for making me laugh.”

The cars on the highway buzzed along the ridge. Down on the quarry road, the insect songs rang, and darkness swam over the crumbling blacktop. She couldn't see the water pit where they swam, but now and then a rock plunked into the water. Insanely risky they used to swim after dark at a gravel pit. A kid drowned when Bell was in middle school. The police occasionally cracked down on kids sneaking out to swim, but they still came to this day.

She wondered if several teens were out there right now, looking back at her vehicle. How many of them did God's Hand stalk without them knowing?

CHAPTER TWENTY-SEVEN

The doorbell rang while Bell hustled between the cupboards, confused how she could lose spice bottles on a weekly basis. Gardy stood in the doorway in flip-flops, Bermuda shorts, and a sage v-neck.

And held a bottle of wine.

"You look like you fell off a cruise ship."

"And you're a bundle of laughs as always."

Bell invited him inside, and Gardy fidgeted beside the counter as Bell rummaged for the correct pan. Pans vanished as often as spices.

"Here, let me take that," she said, and Gardy handed over the bottle. She examined the label. "Ooh, a Finger Lakes Riesling."

Gardy glanced about the room as if worried their parents might walk in on them.

"Full disclosure. I have no idea if the Riesling goes well with bluefish."

"Pour us two glasses and we'll figure it out."

"Oh, yeah…sure. Didn't figure you'd want to drink a lot given the last several…uh…I'm going to shut up now."

Bell snickered and reached into the upper cabinet for glasses. She could give a hundred reasons for hitting the wine hard this evening, but what were his?

"You don't need to treat me with kid gloves, Gardy. And to answer your question, I plan to get utterly blotto tonight, so start pouring."

Gardy filled the glasses a quarter, and when Bell tutted, he poured her glass halfway full. He handed her one glass and raised his own.

"What shall we drink to?"

Bell squinted at the ceiling.

"Taking out God's Hand once and for all."

"And Logan Wolf."

Already into her first gulp, Bell lowered the glass and nodded uncomfortably.

Gardy took his glass and a bag of pretzels to the deck and sat with his feet on the rail. More people than Bell had seen in weeks combed the beach while enjoying the pleasant March temperatures.

Gulls circled above Gardy, and before the warning was out of Bell's mouth, one of the winged thieves pilfered a pretzel and flew off with the prize. Bell tried not to laugh too loud. The deck was open to the screen, and he could hear her.

Dinner went off without a hitch. The bluefish was a tad dry to Bell's palate, but she was used to fresh-caught fish and Lucas's experienced preparation. If she lived another eighty years, she'd never cook as well. She swallowed the thought before depression sank its claws in.

Gardy washed the dishes and Bell dried. Together they finished the task in five minutes and caught the elusive green flash over the ocean after sunset.

"You up for a walk on the beach?" Gardy asked, leaning his forearms on the deck rail while the sea breeze rushed at them. "But if it's too soon..."

The wind mellowed Bell, made her arms and legs tingle.

"No, I could use the walk. I should get out of the apartment more often."

They followed the ocean toward a distant pier they'd never reach before full dark, Gardy careful to lead her away from Lucas's beach house. Lucas's parents had told Bell to take anything she wanted before they cleaned, but she hadn't stopped by. The little beach house, the home by the water which brought her so many fond memories, felt haunted to her now. She couldn't venture inside without sensing the killer's presence, fear him lurking in dark places.

"Sorry," he said, looking pensively over the water as the tide smashed against the beach.

"What are you sorry about?"

"Everything, I guess. I didn't know what to say after we found out about Lucas, and I should have been there for you in Georgia."

"Stop, Gardy. What would I say if this happened to you? There are no right words. And I drove to Georgia without telling you."

"Yeah, about that. Don't do it again. Please."

"But I was right about Jillian's killer. Which leads to my next question. What are we going to do about Weber meddling in the investigation?"

"I read the George Mason profile after you left."

"And?"

"You were right. We'll need to work up our own if we want to catch this guy."

"I'll take a look at the report. I remember the professor who worked up the profile. He's a genius, but profiling was never his strong point. It's like they brought their best pitcher off the bench to bat in the bottom of the ninth."

"Rebecca St. Clair told police during her interview the killer claimed God sent him to save her. That fits the visionary profile. I'm guessing a psychotic break with reality."

"Like Berkowitz. The fact that he's calling himself God's Hand suggests his psychotic break is worsening."

"And what do we know about visionary serial killers?"

"They're highly disorganized, too impulsive to avoid eventually being caught."

"And yet God's Hand evaded the police for over twenty years. How's that possible?"

The cold ocean surged up the shore and rolled around Bell's ankles. She pulled her sweatshirt hood over her head, staring down at wet sand as she walked beside Gardy.

"What if he wasn't active all those years?"

"Are you suggesting he quit? That isn't likely."

"No, he wouldn't have quit on his own."

"What are you suggesting?"

"That our killer spent time in prison, possibly institutionalized."

Gardy looked at her sidelong.

"How long have you had this theory?"

Bell shrugged.

"It makes sense, doesn't it?"

"That's not an answer."

Logan Wolf had told Bell Jillian's killer was back. She never pressed Wolf on the issue, but she felt the fugitive had given Bell a subtle clue. Wolf, the best profiler to come through the BAU, understood as well as Bell a madman like God's Hand never stopped killing.

Gardy sensed Wolf's involvement. Somehow he knew.

"I want to rework the profile and have Harold search for violent felons incarcerated between 1995 and this year," said Bell, bending to retrieve a shell.

"He'd need to be a felon, or he wouldn't have spent so long in prison. But maybe we're off base on this. What if the guy was out of the country?"

"No, he's too disorganized to be that strategic. He spent time in prison. I'll put my thoughts on paper tonight and email you a copy. Keep it between us and Harold until I'm sure we can trust Weber's intentions."

"I hope you aren't serious. I can't stand the guy either, but he wouldn't undermine our efforts to capture God's Hand."

Night turned the water black and made the beach difficult to see. When they reached Bell's apartment, clouds swallowed the moon. The walkway to the stairs was nearly invisible in the dark. Bell almost walked into a woman headed in the opposite direction.

They were halfway up the stairs when Bell looked over her shoulder. Lucas's beach house was a black, rectangular husk against the night.

CHAPTER TWENTY-EIGHT

Outside of DC in Fairfax, Virginia, Joelle San Giovanni locked the bathroom door to hide from her mother and brushed mascara through her eyelashes. Lana San Giovanni, star congresswoman leading the charge for the new wave of Washington democrats, sipped champagne downstairs with her date, a cookie cutter beau who appeared plucked from GQ. Liberal with her politics, Lana San Giovanni instituted Reagan-era conservatism when it came to her daughter's social life and didn't approve of her young daughter wearing makeup.

But Joelle's mother had consented to the girl's request to attend Jackie's birthday party, provided the secret service escorted the town car carrying Joelle to-and-from the party. That put a major crimp in Joelle's plans to kiss George tonight, but she thanked the benevolent power writing the story of her life that her mother allowed Joelle to leave the house at all after the God's Hand letter.

"Ready to go, Mother," Joelle said, clicking down the stairs.

Lana San Giovanni, a diminutive, young woman with dark curls past her shoulders, tsk'd when her daughter descended the steps.

"Oh, no. You aren't wearing heels."

Joelle looked down at her shoes.

"What's wrong with my shoes?"

"Eighteen-year-old girls in heels are fashionable, and thirteen-year-olds merely strumpets. Besides, you know the photographers will be there. I don't want to read tomorrow's headline about the congresswoman's middle school daughter in hooker heels."

"So I'll be the only one at the party looking like a nerd."

"Nobody will think you're a nerd because of your shoes, Joelle. Run upstairs and change before the town car arrives. Flats or sandals. Your choice."

Joelle huffed. At the doorway, a young man in a dark suit touched his ear piece and talked into his shoulder. Joelle spun, tripped on the wobbly heels and caught the rail before she twisted an ankle.

"See what I mean?" Her mother called from the bottom of the staircase. "You can hardly walk in heels. I won't have you tripping drunkenly in public."

Joelle smirked when she got back to the room. She knew Lana San Giovanni would never allow her daughter out of the house in heels. The black, lace-up sandals were the true goal, only her mother would have balked at those had Joelle not donned the heels. The art of negotiation.

Take that, Congresswoman.

Lana hardly gave Joelle's feet a second look after determining she'd ditched the heels. Hands clasped at her waist, Joelle patiently waited while her mother instructed the secret service agent.

"She's not to drink, smoke, or kiss boys." Lana shot Joelle a don't-say-anything-sarcastic glare. "Or girls, for that matter."

"What about gender neutrals?"

"Don't get smart, Joelle." Lana swiveled to the man in

the dark suit. "Are we clear, Agent Kerr?"

"Yes, Congresswoman."

But the look he gave the woman said he wasn't a goddamn babysitter, and Joelle rolled her eyes in sympathy with the agent when her mother turned.

The long, black town car idled curbside in front of the San Giovanni estate, or compound as Joelle liked to think of it. A tall man wearing a suit and top hat awaited their approach before opening the back door. As Joelle slid inside, she heard the secret service agent.

"Keep me in your mirrors at all time. Are we clear?"

"Yes, sir.

The door closed. Inside the town car, a stuffy stench weighted the air. Cigarette smoke and alcohol, Joelle thought. Last year, her mother dated a smoker. Though he'd only been to the house twice, Joelle could still smell the stale death of cigarette smoke in the couch.

"Any requests?"

Joelle looked up. She couldn't see the man's face in the mirror, only his eyes greeting hers. Something old from the Backstreet Boys, music from her mother's middle school years, played over the speakers.

She shook her head.

"I'll change it for you."

The man scanned the satellite radio and settled on an aggressive, thumping beat. Good. Mother hated hip-hop.

He flipped on the air conditioning. While the chill circulated through the car, the stale smell strengthened. It came from behind her.

Joelle twisted on the leather backseat. Her jeans made squeaky noises as she searched for the origin of the smoky stench. Several car lengths behind them, the black Ford Escalade followed the town car through a red light. She wondered if the police could pull over secret service agents and write them tickets.

"That too cold? I'll turn on the heat."

His eyes watched her through the mirrors again. She rubbed the chill off her arms.

"Yes, please."

"Okay. I'll make it warm again."

A strange and cringe worthy reply.

As his fingers curled over the temperature controls, she noted the blisters on the back of his hand. Though the injuries repulsed her, she wanted to ask the driver if he'd burned himself.

The heat blew down from the vents, warmer than she preferred. It didn't take long before the chill was a forgotten memory. Sweat broke along her neck and her eyes itched.

"Thank you. It's warm enough now."

She sought him in the mirror. His eyes flicked to hers and returned to the road. Maybe he hadn't heard.

"Please, mister. It's getting really warm back here."

She felt relieved when he reached for the temperature controls. He raised it from 78 to 81.

Now the heat barreled out of the vents in a jet engine roar. The shirt stuck to her back, itched. She checked the window and noticed the pink welt under her eye, flare-ups which returned when Joelle was too hot or nervous, and she was both in spades.

Joelle turned and looked for the Escalade. Her heart stopped when she didn't see it, but then it emerged around the bend and took its place behind the town car. She waved to the man, wanted to tell him something was wrong with the heat. The man drove at a non-threatening pace up the thoroughfare, one hand on the wheel. If the secret service agent saw Joelle, he didn't react.

The cigarette stench was at its strongest behind her. She glanced down. A leg stuck out from under a black blanket in the rear of the vehicle. She pulled the phone out of her pocket when the fist smashed her jaw. The force rolled her eyes around in her head, turned the world into a blurry haze like dew-glazed windows on a humid evening.

Joelle's brain tried to piece the puzzle together as he grasped her by the hair and rammed her head against the passenger window.

She slumped down on the seat, her indistinct mumbles slurred as she grasped for his seat back. The town car swerved, and her head swung against the side panel.

As Joelle lost consciousness, the driver waited until the town car rounded a curve and took a sharp right down an alley before the Escalade cleared the corner. He killed the lights and dodged a dumpster. In the rear-view mirror, the Escalade shot past at 50 mph.

The agent would double back in a moment when he didn't find the town car.

God's Hand had anticipated this, planned every minute detail. After slicing the real driver's throat and tossing his body in the back, he awaited the blind curve and knew the alleyway lay ahead. What's more, the alley ended at a T, a one-way street that emptied onto the interstate.

He checked the girl. She hadn't moved. Good. While the engine grumbled, he stepped out of the town car and shoved a row of garbage cans across the alley. Not that the Escalade couldn't plow through the obstruction. He wanted to give the illusion the alley was closed to traffic.

He edged the car out of the alley and fell in behind a tour bus headed for the coast. Then onto the interstate where he broke free before the authorities cast their nets.

CHAPTER TWENTY-NINE

The ringing of the phone brought Bell awake. She'd fallen asleep on the couch with the television on, Gardy curled in a chair with a blanket pulled to his chin. After they'd finished half the wine bottle, Bell pocketed his keys with the understanding she'd revisit his ability to drive in the morning.

Lifting the phone to her ear, she squinted at the clock. Ten. Christ, it felt like four in the morning.

"Agent Bell?"

"Yeah." It took a moment for the synapses to fire. It was Weber. "Yes, sir."

"You don't sound good, Agent Bell. Whatever ails you, get it out of your system now. I want you at headquarters at 0000 hours."

Bell scrubbed at her eyes. The insides of her face felt like rubber, stretched and deformed as she willed herself awake.

"0000 hours. I'll be there. Is this about God's Hand?"

"I'll brief you when you arrive. Agent Gardy isn't answering his phone. Do you have any idea where he is?"

Yeah, he's sound asleep in the next chair. Bell glanced at Gardy's phone on the coffee table, the screen lit with missed calls. He must have muted the ringer.

"Gardy had trouble with his phone earlier."

"I see." The doubt was evident in Weber's voice. He knew Gardy was there. "I'll continue to attempt reaching Agent Gardy, but if you happen to bump into him in the next few minutes, I trust you'll relay the message."

Bell shook Gardy's shoulder. The blanket drooped down to Gardy's stomach, and his shirt slid off his shoulder and revealed a scar. The Milanville sniper. He'd almost died while saving Bell in the process.

"Gardy, wake up." He muttered incomprehensibly and reached for the blanket. "It's Weber."

His eyes shot open. Blinked as he took in the unfamiliar surroundings.

"Shit. I must have fallen asleep. Wait, did you say Weber is here?"

She swatted his uninjured shoulder.

"Clean yourself up. He was on the phone. Sounds like God's Hand struck again."

Gardy leaned over and shook his head the way a dog does after swimming.

"How soon does he want us?"

"0000 hours."

Gardy checked his watch.

"How are we going to pull this off? I can't walk into Weber's office looking like...you know."

"What? Like you woke up beside me?"

Gardy's face contorted as though she jabbed a dagger through his ribs.

"I wish you wouldn't say things like that. Goddamn, I drank way too much wine."

"Sober up, Buttercup. I'll grab you a change of clothes. I have a sweatshirt that will fit you."

Gardy sprang from the chair and rushed to the bathroom mirror where he stared at the monstrosity reflecting back at him.

"No way I'm meeting Weber in one of your sweatshirts," he said, squeezing toothpaste onto his finger and rubbing it over his teeth.

"Relax. It's not like he expects you to roll out of bed in a suit and tie. Besides, it's a guy's sweatshirt. Hope you like the Virginia Cavaliers."

He spat the toothpaste and gargled water.

"Not particularly. I'm more of a Florida State guy. Can't we stop by my place? It's on the way."

"No time. Not unless you want to incur Weber's ire."

When they arrived at headquarters five minutes before midnight, Weber was in the briefing room. A mix of junior and senior agents filled the front row, many looking like they'd rushed home for a change of clothes after a long evening in the clubs. Peterson and Glick sipped coffee from Styrofoam cups with an air of desperation. Harold rushed between the podium and the monitors, troubleshooting a computer glitch as Weber glowered.

"Agents Bell and Gardy, thank you for finally joining us."

Bell glanced at the clock and opened her mouth. Gardy shook his head.

They took two open chairs in the second row. With the briefing room only a quarter full, voices echoed off the walls. It seemed colder at night, the walls too white, the vaulted ceilings impossibly high.

Weber barked at Harold until the overhead monitor lit with the face of a preteen girl with long, black hair. Bell's heart skipped. The facial resemblance to Congresswoman San Giovanni was unmistakable.

"Shortly after 2130 hours, a Fairfax town car carrying Joelle San Giovanni, the thirteen-year-old daughter of Congresswoman Lana San Giovanni, vanished on Inglewood Drive two miles south of I-66. A secret service escort lost sight of the town car after coming out of a wooded section on the edge of town. We put a bolo out for the town car, but if someone abducted San Giovanni, we expect the kidnapper changed vehicles. There is also a bolo out for a sedan, possibly a LaCrosse, dragging a trailer, per the abduction and murder case in Erwin, Georgia."

Weber clicked the laser pen, and a photograph of a ruddy-faced bearded man appeared on the monitor.

"Gordon Thies, age forty-seven of Fairfax, Virginia, sixteen years with Exceptional Town Car. Before taking his current job, he drove taxis for several outfits in the Baltimore and DC areas. Except for a multitude of speeding violations, Thies has a clean record. He was seen leaving the Exceptional Town Car garage at approximately 2100 hours. At 2120 hours, Secret Service Agent Jonathan Kerr briefed the town car driver outside the San Giovanni residence. Agent Kerr confirms the man in this picture and the man he met are two different people."

Agent Glick sat forward.

"You suspect the God's Hand killer abducted the San Giovanni girl?"

Weber pointed the pen at the monitor, and the image switched to God's Hand's letter.

"Given the recency of this letter arriving on Congresswoman San Giovanni's desk, we suspect God's Hand is responsible for Joelle San Giovanni's disappearance. Now, whether that means Gordon Thies is a willing accomplice, or God's Hand attacked Thies and took control of the vehicle, we're still piecing the puzzle together. Mrs Thies claims her husband should have gotten home a little after eleven. She hasn't heard from him tonight."

"Does the Secret Service have an idea what route the town car took to evade the escort?"

"Agent Kerr believes the car turned down an alley between the Ulster Inn and Kensington's Restaurant. The light was red at the Main Street intersection with two vehicles stopped at the crosswalk. No way the town car could have blown around them without drawing attention. He found garbage cans lined across the alleyway. I'd expect the cans would be against the wall, which makes me think someone placed the cans with the intent of blocking passage. The local PD is dusting the cans for prints right now, and I'm waiting to hear back from their lead detective. In the meantime," Weber snatched a folder off the podium and waved it over his head. "I'm passing around copies of the George Mason profile of God's Hand. The professor who constructed the profile is one of the world's foremost experts on child kidnappers and murderers. This is your template for God's Hand, the skeleton upon which you will build all future knowledge regarding our unknown subject."

Bell mumbled under her breath. Gardy raised his eyebrows as if to say, "what do you want me to do about it?"

"If I may speak frankly for a moment," Weber said, folding his glasses and slipping them into his jacket. "We're all under a lot of pressure on this one. Don't think I'm unaware. All of Washington has eyes on us. We know from experience God's Hand keeps the children alive for four to five days before he kills. That gives us seventy-two to ninety-six hours to identify God's Hand and save the girl's life. And we will save her life, even if we go four days without sleep."

Weber wrapped up the briefing by giving the agents their orders. He assigned Bell and Gardy to follow up with Gordon Thies's wife and Agent Kerr. The police had constructed road blocks at all the major interchanges surrounding DC.

"They're too late," Bell said, sliding the FBI jacket over her head. "He was outside their radius by the time Weber called me two hours ago."

CHAPTER THIRTY

The Thies and Kerr interviews yielded no new information, and Bell felt the case racing away from her.

Joining Peterson and Glick, Bell and Gardy arrived at the San Giovanni estate at four in the morning. Voices shouted and camera flashbulbs sparked from the sidewalk as they made their way past the topiary and up the landscaped walkway. Someone had tipped the media off.

A late-middle aged woman Bell took to be San Giovanni's mother sat in the living room. She possessed the same jet black hair, though Bell suspected the woman colored hers.

Joelle's room seemed a typical teen's, except there was a lot more of everything: posters on the wall of alternative bands, a small jewelry box atop an overstuffed dresser, a cardboard box filled with love notes hidden under the bed. The closet pulled the biggest reaction out of Bell. It was three times the size of her own and filled with designer clothing and expensive shoes.

But nothing indicated the identity of the man who took Joelle. God's Hand had taken another child, but like Lucas, this was a personal attack on Bell. Bait to draw her out of hiding.

After the investigation, Peterson issued the usual platitudes to San Giovanni. The BAU wouldn't rest until Joelle came home alive, and above all, the congresswoman should stay calm and alert them if the killer contacted her. As the team departed the estate, San Giovanni, mascara dripping beneath her eyes like black tears, pulled Bell aside.

"Your celebrity status doesn't impress me, Agent Bell. Bring my daughter home alive, or I'll see to it you never work in my city again."

Bell promised to do her best, an answer the congresswoman didn't find sufficient. On the sidewalk, Gardy whispered into her ear as Peterson and Glick walked ahead.

"What was that about?"

"Oh, nothing. Just another threat of career destruction should the case go south."

When Bell and Gardy climbed into their car, Gardy's phone rang. Gunning the engine, he pulled off the curb. He said little more than "yeah" and "okay" as he followed the signs to the interstate.

"That was Weber," he said, pocketing the phone. "The only prints on the garbage cans belonged to the restaurant help. For a disorganized killer, this guy is pretty careful. Or damn lucky."

Predawn seeped up from the ocean when Gardy took the on-ramp. Bell paged through the George Mason report, eyes flicking to-and-from the road as a pair of weaving tractor trailers cut in front of the car.

"This is all wrong." Bell snapped the folder shut. "The report pegs him as a power and control killer and barely touches upon the visionary aspects. I was there, Gardy. This guy believes he's serving God."

"I noticed they estimate his age around thirty-five."

"This is the sort of dumbed-down, by-the-numbers analysis you'd expect in a tabloid article. They're ignoring that he murdered Jillian in 1995 like it's an inconvenient truth. What are we doing, Gardy? Combing a teenage girl's bedroom as if we'd find evidence linking her to the killer? He all but boasted he'd kidnap Joelle, and then he took her under the nose of her Secret Service detail."

"What would you prefer we do?"

"Something. Nothing. Hell, I don't know. All we're doing is waiting for his next move and letting him call the shots. We're not closer to catching him."

The highway congestion cleared, and Gardy pushed the speedometer past seventy. The phone buzzed in Bell's pocket. She didn't recognize the number.

"Good morning, Scarlett."

The blood drained from Bell's face upon hearing Logan Wolf's voice.

"Is everything all right, Dad?"

Gardy glanced over. Bell waved him away.

"I sense you're not alone, Scarlett. I trust the knightly Neil Gardy is by your side as you hunt the monster who calls himself God's Hand."

"Yes, that's correct," Bell said, torn between alerting Gardy and concealing Wolf.

"Our last conversation ended on an unfortunate note, and I fear I am to blame. Let me first offer my condolences. I should have called sooner after I heard what our man did to young Lucas. You see it's personal now, don't you?"

"It's obvious."

"Good. Knowledge will keep you from getting killed, Scarlett, and I rather believe the world would be worse without you. But you'll never catch him. Not before he dismembers the star congresswoman's progeny beside the Potomac. Or will it be the Atlantic this time? Imagine the shock when the Virginia Beach spring breakers find little San Giovanni in pieces, the seagulls picking at her insides."

"I assume there's a point to this."

Gardy looked over again, eyebrows raised when Bell snapped.

"I won't waste your time, Scarlett. If a better profiler exists, I'm unaware, and I have full faith you'll capture God's Hand and avenge poor Jillian. But you won't do it in time to save the princess. If you want to catch him today, I'll tell you who he is."

Noticing Gardy staring at her, Bell pointed an angry finger at the road. He pursed his lips and turned away.

"Then do so. Mom's waiting."

"And the congresswoman will wait a lot longer unless you meet my demand. Promise me you'll build a profile of my wife's killer, and I'll give you God's Hand."

"You know I can't do that."

"Can't or won't? I see no downside for you, dear Scarlett. You'll catch two serial killers. The news will worship you, including Gavin Hayward and *The Informer.*"

"Even if I wanted to help you, I'm in no position to do so at this time."

"Yes, with Agent Gardy sitting beside you. Shame I didn't call on you last evening after the wine kicked in."

Bell's heart kicked into second gear. Twisting to face the door, she cupped her hand over the phone and whispered to Wolf.

"You stalked me."

"I prefer you think of me as a benefactor. From time-to-time, I check my investments."

"Is that what I am to you? An investment?"

"Calm yourself, Scarlett. I see you as much more than an investment. You needn't provide the profile over the phone. I'll come to you."

"Wait, what?"

Scarlett swiped at her phone, but the call had ended.

"Everything all right with your folks?"

His voice pulled her out of the waking nightmare.

Gardy navigated, one hand on the wheel as Bell tapped the phone against her knee.

"My folks? Oh, yeah. They're fine."

"Because you sounded upset."

"You always listen in on other people's conversations?"

"No, of course not. I mean...well, we're in the same car and the windows are closed."

"Yeah, I know. I didn't mean to snap at you."

"I didn't think you had. You're scaring me, Bell. You haven't been yourself since you came back from Georgia."

"I wonder why."

Bell leaned her head against the window.

CHAPTER THIRTY-ONE

A gentle susurrus flowed at the edge of her consciousness. Like wind through meadow grass.

The air seemed weighted down and stuffy, and Joelle coughed into her hand.

Blinked.

Opened her eyes to black.

"Hello?"

Her voice rolled around the trailer and returned. Trapped like her. She heard birdsong and the whisper of leaves. Some time ago, the vehicle stopped after the trailer jounced over an unpaved surface. She'd heard the brittle lock snap. His first mistake. If only she could break free of the ropes.

Footsteps followed around the trailer and stopped at the door, then the man walked off, pushing through trees and cracking branches underfoot. Always near.

After they stopped, Joelle dozed periodically. Some unidentified noise always pulled her awake. Which was fine, because she didn't want to sleep, not with her kidnapper outside the trailer.

She concocted a fantasy in her head and turned the kidnapper into a political foe or a criminal bent on monetary gain. Then why hadn't he issued ransom demands?

Because he was the God's Hand killer, the monster who threatened her mother and forced Joelle to have a Secret Service escort. So much for the agent's ability to protect her.

The trailer door jetted open. She jumped and twisted her neck. He stood among the blinding light, a serrated hunting blade in his hand. The trailer shook as he climbed inside. She was certain he'd plunge the knife into her back, but he jammed the hilt between his teeth and worked the ropes off her wrists.

Joelle begged him to stop as he yanked her out of the trailer and into the unknown. One powerful hand clutched her shoulder. Squeezed.

"Do you see?"

Except for a dirt access road that descended into darkness, forest surrounded her in all directions.

"Do you see?"

Wobbling on her feet, dizzy after the long confinement, she stumbled into him. He grabbed her chin and twisted. Angled her vision toward a stream. Water chuckled over rocks and slithered around bends, flashes of sun reflecting off the surface.

"Do you know who I am?"

Joelle swallowed, shook her head, then thought better of it and nodded.

"Tell me. Speak my name."

She glanced up. The sun burned behind him, turning his face into shadow and unspeakable horror.

"Speak my name."

"You're…you're God's Hand."

His grip relaxed. She massaged her neck and chin.

"Do you know why I brought you here?"

A hawk shrilled among the treetops. The wind set the leaves in motion, brought the forest to life.

Joelle whispered, "No," choking on the word.

Now he pushed her shoulders from behind. Prodded her forward. She shuffled uncertainly, his shadow swallowing hers as if they were one expanding ink blotch staining the forest floor, until they came to the edge of the stream. Clutching her hair, he forced Joelle to her hands and knees, head over the banks.

He'll drown me, she thought. Her frightened-eye reflection looked back at her, deformed by the water.

"Now do you understand? Let us draw near to God with a sincere heart and with the full assurance that faith brings, having our hearts sprinkled to cleanse us from a guilty conscience and having our bodies washed with pure water. Do you understand?"

She vomited spittle into the stream and watched it swirl and expand before the water rushed it downstream. Coughing, she felt a second surge leap into her throat. He yanked her hair back, dragged her from the water.

"You are not ready! When will you be ready?"

Joelle fell limp against his body as he threw her over his shoulder and carried her to the trailer. The trees seemed to drift away from her, little spotlights of sun beaming around the branches.

Drooped in the chair, Joelle struggled to hold her eyes open. He spun the ropes around her chest, pulled her arms behind the chair, and tied the ropes off around her wrists.

Then the trailer door thundered down. And it was very dark again.

CHAPTER THIRTY-TWO

Bell and Gardy purchased a late lunch from a food truck two blocks from headquarters. Two senior FBI managers she rarely crossed paths with sat two tables away, the short, barrel-chested manager named Zale sneaking looks in her direction. Like watching a dead woman walking, she thought. By now, Bell's fate was common knowledge. Should they fail to rescue San Giovanni's daughter, her career would be over, and she didn't put it past the congresswoman to make her future civilian life as difficult as possible.

"Eat your fish sandwich," Gardy said, putting the finishing touches on a basket of shrimp and fries.

Bell peeled the bun apart and eyed the suspicious fillet. Might have been cod. Might have come from a box with a gruff, bearded fisherman on the front.

"It's yours if you want it."

"You gotta eat, Bell," he said between bites. "I don't want another fasting situation like we had in California."

"Fine, Dad."

Bell bit a chunk off the sandwich, chewing it as if in an eating contest, a trick she'd learned during her childhood whenever Mom plated a meal she didn't care for. Especially meatloaf and quiche. Get it over with before her taste buds caught on to the scam.

After Gardy refocused on his meal, Bell scanned the faces in the shopping center parking lot. A woman in blue jeans and a sweater pushed a young boy in a stroller. Two men in baseball caps debated the pitching rotation for the Nationals. Across the street, a dirt path led into a maze of hiking trails. When Bell saw a man wearing a black coat among the trees, she stood up from her chair.

"Something wrong?"

Gardy stood. A woman appeared on the trail, and the man put his arm around her shoulder. Laughing, they strolled out of view.

Bell sighed.

"It's nothing. This case has me spooked."

But as Gardy tossed his basket into the trash and scanned his phone, Bell sneaked glances over her shoulder. Logan Wolf didn't make idle threats.

Back in her office, Bell went over the Thies and Kerr interview notes. Overlooking the parking lot, her desk caught the sun. Every time she looked at her Rogue, she swore she saw a shadow move across the backseat.

The quiet overloaded her mind, forced the wheels to spin too fast. It was enough to make her drop her pen and rub her eyes. When she opened them, she half-expected to see Logan Wolf staring up at her from the parking lot. He'd disappear after she blinked again, an old horror movie trick. But this wasn't a John Carpenter flick, and the parking lot lay empty of people. Just the harsh glare of sun against aluminum.

Having slipped her shoes off under the desk, she padded in stocking feet down the hallway and past Weber's office. Candice leaned over his desk, going over Weber's schedule. Bell quickened her pace before either noticed her.

The coffee maker was on the fritz in the break room.

It made a whining noise that hurt her ears as she lifted the pot and sniffed inside. Burned, but salvageable. Pouring the black gold into her mug, she leaned against the counter and smiled at a female intern munching on a pastry.

Bell was three sips into the coffee when her stomach somersaulted. Quickly, she dragged the garbage can over and threw the top open. The queasiness subsided, but she already felt it gearing up for a second run.

The intern gave her an uneasy glance as Bell rushed from the break room. It was a long run to the bathroom, the door at the end of the hall. She kicked herself for not wearing shoes and prayed the cleaning staff had mopped the bathroom. A yellow closed for maintenance sign stopped her at the door. Cursing to herself, she glanced around the hallway and grabbed her stomach when the nausea started again.

The floor below had a men's room. It would have to do.

She threw the stairwell door open and moved as fast as her stomach allowed. Descending one flight almost made her faint. Nobody milled in the hallway when she pulled the door open. Voices carried from the multitude of offices, none she recognized. In front of the men's room, she pounded on the door. When nobody answered, she pushed inside and hurried to the first stall.

She locked the door and bent over the toilet, convinced she'd see the ill-fated fish sandwich again. Sweat beaded her forehead, skin slick and clammy. Several heartbeats later, the sickness abated.

Bell exhaled and sat down, unconvinced her stomach didn't hold another nasty trick up its sleeve. The men's room floor was gritty and disgusting beneath her feet. A chill rippled through her body, and she raised her feet up on tiptoes to minimize contact with the grimy real estate.

She closed her eyes and willed her body to relax. Then the door opened. A breeze preceded an intruder who moved on cat's paws into the lavatory, so quiet she wondered if he'd left without her realizing.

"Hey, just wanted to let you know I'm in the first stall." She paused, expecting a surprised reaction. No reply came. "The women's room is out of service. Sorry, I had no choice."

Her disarming giggle made a hollow echo.

"Listen, I don't mind if you don't mind," she said, craning her neck for an answer. "I'll be out of here in a second."

When the man didn't answer, she edged down from the seat. As she bent to peek beneath the stall, her hair flopped down. She sat up and wrapped her hair into a makeshift ponytail. Holding it with one hand, she bent down once more. At first, she didn't spy anyone inside the restroom, and she felt stupid for holding an awkward discussion with a ghost. Then she spied a man in black shoes and pants beside the sink.

Breaths flying through her chest, she sat up before he noticed.

Logan Wolf.

No. That was impossible.

Confused thoughts spun through her head. A civilian lacking official credentials couldn't walk past security and wander upstairs.

Yet Logan Wolf seemed capable of anything.

She raised her legs and rested her bare feet on the seat, her back thrust against the piping.

No phone, no gun. Nobody knew she was here.

"Wolf? Is that you?"

Still no reply. The water didn't run, and the only sound inside the lavatory was her breathing.

Her body shivered, the cool interior of the bathroom milking her anxiety. She didn't know how long she sat in silence. Seconds, minutes.

When she ducked her head under the stall door, the room was empty.

CHAPTER THIRTY-THREE

Though Gardy busied himself with case notes when Bell breezed past his office, he noticed her and called out. She halted beside the door and contemplated if she should let him see her like this.

"I wondered where you disappeared to. Pull up a chair. I want to ask you something."

She patted forehead perspiration on her shirtsleeve and took a composing breath. Gritting her teeth, she entered the room.

"Close the door."

He hadn't looked up from the papers as she edged the door shut. A wilting bamboo palm drooped in the corner. Most agents had pictures of spouses and family members on their desks. Gardy had one photograph—a red and orange sunset over the Atlantic, something he'd taken with his phone and printed at Target or Staples.

Bell sat across from the desk, crossed her legs, and tried to appear casual. She didn't know whether to feel safe or stupid. Black shoes and pants were standard fare for some agents. The unknown man probably left the restroom embarrassed to discover a woman behind the stall.

Gardy shuffled the papers, sighed, and glanced up

with a smile. His eyes returned to the notes for a millisecond, then shot up when his brain caught up with his vision.

"What the hell happened to you?"

"It's nothing. I got a little sick."

"Gee, Bell. Head home for the day. You're no good to the BAU if you aren't getting enough rest."

"Seriously, Gardy. I'm fine. The fish sandwich didn't agree with me."

"Hmm. My stomach has been off since the shrimp. I suppose we should scratch the food truck off the list." He burped into his hand and tapped his pen on the desk. "Wait, are you barefoot?"

She uncrossed her legs, but he'd already seen. Gardy snickered.

"Going extra casual today?"

"Stop. My feet are killing me. I only removed my shoes before I wandered to the break room. The sickness hit me before I could go back to my office."

"But the women's room is closed. Something about a leaking pipe. Candice complained to Weber."

Bell pinched the bridge of her nose and squinted her eyes shut.

"I handled it."

Gardy raised his eyebrows.

"At least you didn't commandeer the men's room." Realization dawned on his face. "Oh, man. You did, didn't you?"

"Focus, Gardy. You wanted to talk to me about something?"

"Right, sorry." He glanced over her shoulder and confirmed the door was shut. Leaning back in his chair, he rubbed at his eyes and sighed. "I've been giving God's Hand more thought. We've established it's the same man who abducted Jillian Rossi, and your parents confirmed he tried to capture you."

"Yeah, I'm the one who got away. It's personal."

"Right. I did some digging and called the Bealton PD. It took some doing, but they figured out the exact date of the attempted abduction. August 5, 1995. Jillian's abduction occurred on July 7, the murder five days later."

Bell shifted uncomfortably.

"So he would have murdered me sometime around the tenth if I hadn't escaped. How does this help?"

"I had Harold run searches, and we couldn't find a similar case—young girl murdered and left beside the water—during 1994 or 1995. But he found three more over the following eighteen months."

Gardy lifted three manila folders and tossed them to her side of the desk. She paged through the cases, the forgotten nausea gurgling inside her stomach. The girls were young, white, pretty for their ages. Bell wanted to look away, but she forced herself to study the names and case notes, wondering how a child serial murderer stalked the eastern seaboard for two years without her knowing. Surely it had been national news and Bell's parents insulated her from it.

"He was active from the Maryland coast down to Georgia for two solid years," Gardy said. "Then he fell off the map. Last night, you theorized he did prison time."

"It's the only explanation for the murders stopping. Did Harold find anything?"

"The list of violent offenders incarcerated from 1996 until this year is too long."

"But Harold employed his arcane magic."

Gardy winked.

"You know it. We added search variables. Why did he start killing in 1995?"

"Because of a stressor. Something tragic set him off."

"Exactly. We looked for deaths of abusive parents,

family sickness, loss of employment. The usual."

"And?"

"We got the list down to eighty-seven names."

Gardy slid the list across the table, and Bell picked it up.

"That's a lot of names, Gardy, and we can't guarantee he's on this list."

"No, but we're getting somewhere. I'm running the list by Weber in a minute if you wish to join us."

Beyond the desk, Gardy's window lent a view of the parking lot.

"You know what? I think you're right about the rest thing."

"Good, you're finally listening to reason. I'll fill you in on the details tomorrow morning."

As Bell rose from her chair, Gardy said, "Are you sure there isn't anything else you need to tell me?"

Bell's eyes swiveled between Gardy and the door. After a moment of consideration, she told Gardy Wolf had phoned her. Bell swallowed her humiliation over the bathroom scare and recounted the strange man who didn't answer her.

"Could be you caught the agent off guard, and he departed to save both of you a lot of embarrassment. You're right to be concerned about Wolf, but no way I see him getting past security. Regardless, you should have come to me about the phone call."

"To what purpose? My apartment has constant surveillance when I'm home."

"This isn't only about you. He's a wanted man, the most dangerous fugitive in the country. When he contacts you, the FBI needs to know." Gardy steepled his fingers and bounced his chin off the tips. "So he's willing to tell you God's Hand's identity if you meet with him."

"Only if I work up a profile of his wife's killer."

Gardy laughed.

"He's still trying to convince you he didn't do it." Gardy closed his eyes in thought. "What if we set up a meeting? Someplace safe with plenty of eyes on you. Wait until Wolf gives up God's Hand, then we take him down."

"You have to be kidding. Wolf is too smart."

"Smart, yes. But is he desperate? He's contacted you multiple times, probably including a few times you neglected to tell me about."

Bell turned for the door.

"That's my cue to exit stage right."

"Not answering can be construed as an admission of guilt."

"Uh-huh."

"Okay, Bell. Feel better. I'll contact you if we get a break on God's Hand."

CHAPTER THIRTY-FOUR

Eighty-seven names.

By the time the BAU sifted through the morass and identified God's Hand, Joelle San Giovanni would already be dead. As Bell turned down the coast road, the radio silenced to facilitate clear thinking, she considered Gardy's plan. Wolf knew the killer's name, she was certain. Checking the clock, she noted nearly twenty-four hours had passed since the madman abducted the congresswoman's daughter. At best, she had three or four days to save the girl.

Dusk reflected darkly in the waves as Bell pulled the Rogue to a stop in her parking lot beside the FBI SUV.

She tapped on the tinted glass, and the window lowered. Agent Flanagan glowered at her.

"We had an understanding, Agent Bell. You're breaking my cover."

Dark-haired and thin, the junior agent possessed green eyes that looked like crystal balls set over a hawk's beak. In Bell's experience, there were three types of agents: duty, career, and power motivated. Weber was the latter, and in Bell's estimation, so too was Flanagan.

"Relax. I want to apologize for giving you the slip and

driving to Georgia."

Flanagan's face reddened with anger or embarrassment. Probably both.

"If you stopped by to humiliate me—"

"Give me a little credit, Agent Flanagan. I really am sorry, and I appreciate you keeping an eye on my place."

He glanced at Bell from the corner of his eye.

"I'm waiting for the punchline."

"No joke this time. And to show you how thankful I am, I'd like to make you something good to eat this evening."

"I brought food with me."

Bell eyed the greasy bag on the front seat.

"That stuff will kill you before you're fifty. You're from Philly, right?"

"Yeah."

"How about a homemade hoagie? I've got organic roast beef and turkey breast, and I'll bring you down a kombucha. That'll settle your stomach better than all that cola you consume."

Two empty Pepsi cans littered the backseat. She'd left him speechless.

"Let me change out of this damn suit and clean up," she said. "I'll bring it down to you."

"You don't need to do this."

"I want to." She reached over him and plucked the greasy bag, holding it between her thumb and forefinger as though the cholesterol might seep through her skin. "And I'll deposit this in the nearest hazardous waste container. Hope you're hungry, Agent Flanagan."

"Well, I will be now."

Bell tossed the bag in the dumpster and climbed the stairs, smiling to herself. The key fit into the lock, but the knob refused to turn until she jimmied it. Inside, the apartment was dark as night, a shimmer of gloaming reflecting on the deck. She set down her belongings and opened the refrigerator. After she ensured the promised sandwich fixings waited inside, she angled toward the bedroom, humming to herself as she imagined how nice a hot shower would feel.

She shut the door and flicked on the bedside lamp. It didn't turn on.

Her fight-or-flight instinct kicked in too late. The shadow slipped out of the darkness and stole the Glock from her holster, fixing it on her. He was a sharp outline against the dark, invisible otherwise.

"I'm warning you, Wolf. There's another agent downstairs."

"In the parking lot, yes. Black SUV. How original. Do you know how many times I've visited your apartment without the FBI knowing?"

He twisted the door lock.

"Agent Flanagan won't check on you, Scarlett. Not until you fail to produce his dinner. Very kind of you."

"How did you—"

"I suggest we skip the small talk. Time is of the essence for young Joelle, yes? Tick-tock, tick-tock. Are you prepared to produce the profile I requested?"

"Give me God's Hand, and we'll discuss the profile."

"No deal, dear Scarlett."

The longer she stood within the darkness, the more her vision acclimated. Though his facial features remained cloaked in shadow, the waning dusk slipped past the curtains and curled around his legs. He wore black pants, black shoes.

"I don't have enough information to profile your wife's killer. Where do I start?"

"Begin as you always do, Scarlett. With a walk-through."

He lifted an object and pointed it at her face. She

thought it was a gun before the spray wet her nose and lips, and then her legs wobbled and the room went dark.

Logan Wolf caught her as she fell.

CHAPTER THIRTY-FIVE

A blur of shooting stars dazzled through the window. Bell's eyelids fluttered and drooped, lethargy weighting her down, her arms rubber bands attached to her body by thumbtacks. She sat scrunched between the passenger seat and the dash with her head leaned against the cushion. Vivaldi's Four Seasons was the soprano to the rolling bass of tires humming along a paved road, and as Bell forced her eyes open, she saw the stars were streetlights.

"Where the hell…"

Her words blended with the strings, drifted away with the instruments like a leaf caught in a whirlpool. Bell fought to stay awake as her mind connected the dots. She was inside a car with fugitive serial killer, Logan Wolf. He'd sprayed her with Chloroform. His last words…something about a walk-through.

"Almost there, Scarlett. My humble apologies, but you'll understand my crude methods are necessary given your lack of cooperation."

As she grabbed the seat and attempted to pull herself up, her arms gave out.

"Don't worry. The effects of the Chloroform will soon

wear off. You might have a headache or feel unsteady in the stomach, but your strength will return."

She rested her head on the cushion and watched him. He drove with one hand on the wheel, the other conducting to Vivaldi. The streetlights caught his face at regular intervals and revealed his deep-set, black eyes and the unsettling tranquility of his expression.

"They'll arrest you," Bell said as the feeling returned to her arms and legs. "Kidnapping a federal agent will get you hard time."

Wolf laughed.

"A kidnapping charge is the least of my concerns."

A glowering moon lit the sky. Otherwise, Bell didn't know how late it was or where Wolf had taken her. Her stomach dropped when the car took a sharp turn, then they climbed a hill. She summoned enough energy to drag herself onto the seat and looked out the window. Wolf aimed the Glock at her, conducting with the weapon.

"You plan to shoot me with my own gun?"

"A simple deterrent. As I've made abundantly clear, I have no intention of harming you. As I did in the warehouse, I will hand over the gun once I'm certain your trust for me equals mine for you. Besides, it would be an abomination to interrupt the music."

She laughed without mirth and shook her head.

As the car climbed, the real estate value grew commensurate with the size and privacy of the yards. Looking in the mirror, she expected distant city lights. Ancient, hulking trees blocked the view and walled away civilization.

They passed a Victorian mansion fronted by a topiary maze and a wraparound driveway. To this point, the mansions had appeared at regular intervals. Wolf drove another half-mile and swung the wheel to the right.

The car passed through an open wrought-iron gate and descended a winding drive that ended before a brick

Georgian mansion. Twin porches, one ground level and the other along the second floor, stretched the length of the home. At one time, intricate landscaping had provided a focal point for the front yard, but now the bushes grew in jungle tangles, and dead husks marked where flowers once bloomed.

Without a word, Wolf exited the car and followed the front bumper back to the passenger side. He kept the gun trained on Bell while he opened the door and offered his hand. She waved it away and wrestled herself off the seat. He grabbed her when she pitched forward.

"Take it slow, Scarlett. Move too fast, and the Chloroform will make you sick."

Spittle dangled off her lip, her legs buckled like a newborn calf's. Biting back a curse, she clutched his offered arm and pulled herself to a standing position. Wolf was right about the aftereffects. Her head cleared as she stood upright, and after several deep breaths, she found her sea legs and walked with assistance up the sidewalk.

Dead leaves littered the walkway. A juniper tree leaned against the house, the top snapped by a long ago storm.

"Now do you know where we are, Scarlett?"

"Your old home on Nichols Mountain. That's where the FBI found your wife."

"Very good."

At the front stoop, Wolf produced a key and slid it into the lock. The mechanism opened with a screech, and the door swung into the room.

"My apologies for the lack of upkeep. You'll appreciate it is unwise for me to visit Nichols Mountain." The downstairs was desolate except for a few moldering rugs and a lone chair thrust beside a brick fireplace. Stirred by their intrusion, dust motes levitated and glistened in a moonbeam. "The authorities sold our belongings, or I'd offer you a place to sit."

Bell's nose crinkled at the massing allergens.

"No thanks, I'll stand." The Chloroform worn off, she no longer needed his assistance to stay on her feet. She swung her eyes over the spacious interior to a wooden stairway leading to the upper floors. "Can't believe no one bought this place."

"There is the little problem of a murder on July 21, 2013 softening the market for this fine piece of real estate."

"It's beyond *fine*, Wolf. The FBI pays well, particularly if you're a senior BAU agent with your expertise, but no way you could afford this mansion. Minus the little murder problem, a house like this lists for at least two million."

"That would be an underestimation, but as the old game show professed, the winner makes the closest guess without going over."

Their footsteps rung off the high ceilings and repeated through the mansion. It gave the unsettling effect of other people shuffling through the dark corners of the abandoned home.

"So how?"

"How?"

"How did you afford this place? You don't strike me as the house-poor sort."

He shrugged.

"My father died when I was young and left a considerable sum of money. I've always invested, and while the rest of the world panicked, I made a few prudent purchases during the 2001 stock market crash."

Wolf lowered the Glock to his side and let it hang from his fingers. The temptation was there for Bell to snatch the weapon, as though she was quick enough given her cloudy head. She held a modicum of trust for Wolf. He'd passed up multiple opportunities to murder her. The dark thought led her back to Flanagan guarding her apartment.

"About the FBI agent outside my residence."

"Ah, yes. Flanagan."

"How do you know his name?"

"I make it my business to study my enemies, dear Scarlett."

"You didn't…"

"Slice his throat and cover his head with a sack?" Bell quivered at Wolf's trademark. The FBI had discovered too many grisly scenes in the serial killer's wake, the first being Wolf's spouse. "No, there was no need."

"How did you get by him?"

"The same way I did last evening when you entertained my old friend, Neil Gardy. An agent of Flanagan's skill level doesn't see me unless I require him to. By the way, a less than optimum choice with the Riesling."

Bell coughed into her hand, the aftertaste of the Chloroform mingling with the dust.

"Then you made a fatal error this time, Wolf."

"Explain."

"Agent Flanagan expected me to return. When I didn't show, he alerted the FBI."

"I assumed as much, Scarlett. Our time together on this fair night is precious. Don Weber must suspect my involvement, and soon he will send his goons to save you from my evil clutches. Nichols Mountain is a good first guess, even for a cretin like Weber, so I suggest you get to work."

Shoulders slumped, she followed his lead into the kitchen. A long island divided the kitchen, and a shadowed walk-in food pantry waited in the corner. State-of-the-art appliances rotted from disuse. This is where they'd discovered Renee Wolf's body on a suffocating night in the middle of July.

"I don't know what you expect me to do. This is a six-year-old crime scene, no body, a layer of dust suffocating any hint of evidence. Besides, I'm working against an inherent bias."

"Which is?"

"My belief that you're the killer."

A dark discoloration marred the hardwood flooring and formed the vague outline of a body. Something skittered down the wall and disappeared beneath the refrigerator. Left to its own devices, even stately mansions invited roaches inside.

His posture slouched, and she swore she caught a tear crawling out of his eye before he turned his head away.

"Is there nothing I can do to convince you I didn't murder my wife?"

Beyond the mansion's walls, the night waited in silent anticipation. The kitchen gave off a preternatural chill. She cupped her elbows as her teeth chattered.

"Let's assume I murdered my wife," Wolf said, lifting his chin as he holstered Bell's gun. "What was my motivation?"

"God's Hand's motivation for killing children is the voice in his head. He's insane. What more does a visionary serial killer need?"

"Is that what you think I am, Scarlett? A visionary serial killer? I've never professed to a higher power bidding me to murder."

"No."

Wolf twisted around to stare at her. Bell struggled not to look away.

"And if you suspect a psychotic break, there must be a stressor. Think, Scarlett. Analyze me first, if you must."

Bell placed her hands on her hips and walked around the island, nodding to herself.

"Perhaps you discovered your wife cheated on you. Spouses have murdered over less."

"A logical conclusion except I harbor no ill will for my

wife. My spite would only grow had I killed her, for I'd need to justify my actions." Indeed, Wolf had appeared distraught at the mention of his wife's death in Kansas and tonight. "Continue, please."

She glared at the dead light fixtures as if the answer floated across the ceiling. She stopped at the far edge of the island and shook her head.

"So you murder Renee Wolf in cold blood. Open her throat with a knife and place a sack over her head. A ritualistic murder."

"Go on," he said with a tremble in his voice.

"Then you conceal the weapon, and lord knows this hill holds countless options for hiding a bloody knife."

"Very good, I agree."

"Next you return to the mansion and phone the FBI, foregoing the local police."

"A poor choice for a budding serial killer," Wolf said, his grin displaying too many teeth. "The logical step is to call the small-town police department. Their detectives don't possess the FBI's skill and are likely to bungle the evidence before the experts have their say."

"True. But bringing in the FBI is a smart tactic if one wishes to give the false impression of cooperation and innocence."

"You're over thinking."

From the dead of night, an approaching siren screamed and was soon joined by another.

"Looks like they're on to us, Agent Bell." Wolf waved the Glock at her. "We're leaving now."

CHAPTER THIRTY-SIX

Nearly two decades after a pair of hijacked airliners flew into New York's Twin Towers, Washington remained hyperaware of terrorism and threats against public officials and their families. At midnight, a white van with Ted's Cleaning Services written in flowing cursive across the side, parked three houses from Lana San Giovanni's estate. Two FBI field agents sat inside the vehicle, a young female sweeping binoculars across the estate's grounds while a grizzled male huffed and dealt the cards in an old school game of Solitaire. A tap existed on San Giovanni's landline, and a secret service agent named Revert patrolled the downstairs. She'd refused the tap on the mobile phone, stating the number was private and only family used it. Agents vetted mail which arrived at the congresswoman's office and home, and the agents inside the van recorded the license plate numbers of every vehicle passing the estate.

So it came as a shock when Lana San Giovanni uncovered an unmarked envelope among a stack of junk mail and correspondences. She threw the other letters aside on the bed and held the blank envelope in her trembling hand. Without opening the letter, she couldn't know it came from God's Hand, yet her instinct insisted he'd sent it. Her hand reached for the phone and stopped short. Until she read the note, she didn't wish to alert Agent Revert, who'd done nothing to bring her daughter home. Better than a day had passed, and the so-called experts were no closer to rescuing Joelle.

She tore the top open and stared at the folded paper inside the envelope. The ghosts of typed words bled through, though it was impossible to discern their meaning without unfolding the paper. San Giovanni gripped the note as her eyes moved to the closed bedroom door, then to the curtained windows. Closing her eyes, the congresswoman pulled the letter from the envelope and unfolded the paper.

I have no intention of harming Joelle.
Bring me Agent Scarlett Bell, and I will release Joelle into your custody.
Instructions to follow. Share this note with no one if you value Joelle's life.

San Giovanni dropped the note and bit her hand to suppress a sob. An unexplainable air of paranoia blanketed her, and she stuffed the letter beneath the mattress.

Bolting off the bed, wide awake despite only a brief nap since her daughter went missing, she paced the room. As a political figure, she made difficult policy decisions. The world was not black and white, but stippled in shades of gray. Yet she'd never again face a decision this critical.

Torn between the killer's warning and the temptation to bring the letter to the FBI, she parted the curtains and studied the night. How did the letter get past the agents and reach her hands? Was it conceivable someone in the government, a political foe perhaps, aided God's Hand?

She slumped into a chair and ran her hands through her hair. A government official or politician aiding a serial killer? Unrealistic.

But what did they know about God's Hand? The

serial killer hadn't identified himself until last week. The possibility God's Hand wasn't a serial killer at all but a political foe played around in her head, dominated her thoughts.

It made sense. San Giovanni had made more enemies in her first term than any congressional leader in modern times. What's more, a psychopathic killer wouldn't breach security and hand deliver a note. That took power, forethought.

And wasn't the new letter worded differently? Organized. Strategic in its threats. The original letter displayed the ramblings of a madman.

Yes, Joelle's kidnapping was an inside job. She'd thought Agent Kerr incompetent for losing sight of the town car. Now she felt sure someone of immense power, not a deranged lunatic, pulled the strings, with Kerr an accomplice.

Who could she trust?

If the kidnapper wanted Scarlett Bell, she'd deliver the agent's head on a platter.

CHAPTER THIRTY-SEVEN

Logan Wolf drove Bell down a chaotic maze of turns which dumped them on a lonely access road paralleling the interstate. The sirens were a distant memory, and Bell pictured Gardy or Weber and the local police detectives combing the Wolf estate for evidence she'd been there. She prayed for a way to signal the authorities, to alert them to her position, but she gathered they were thirty minutes or more ahead of the police without a trail of breadcrumbs to help them follow.

A fine mist wet the windshield, the beginnings of a dense fog. Wolf ran the wipers on intermittent and peered out at the desolate two-lane roadway while Bell's eyes followed a tractor trailer screaming away on the interstate. Her heart sank when Wolf swung onto a country route and pulled them away from civilization.

A half-hour later with the dashboard clock reading one in the morning, he slowed the car to a stop on a tree-lined pull-off. The cricket songs became loud when he killed the engine, and for a long time they sat in the silence of the vehicle listening to the engine tick and ping. Wolf regarded her, then nodded to himself and popped the cartridge out of the Glock and handed her the gun.

"What's this for?"

"After we learn to trust each other, I'll hand you the cartridge as well. Until then, you'll accept my need to be cautious."

She stared at Wolf as she might a multi-headed exotic animal grazing off the soft shoulder.

"Tell me why you stopped."

Slipping the cartridge into his jacket, Wolf shifted the seat back.

"Because we're safe here. By now, the entire eastern seaboard expects to find us on the road. Best we disappear for a while."

"You mean best *you* disappear."

"Careful who you put your faith in, dear Scarlett. Before the FBI rudely interrupted, you tripped your way into a haphazard profile of the elusive Logan Wolf. Please continue."

Bell studied their surroundings. With dense thickets to either side of the pull-off, the road lay hidden. They might be in Virginia or a neighboring state by now.

"You can't be serious."

"The killer's profile begins with a full understanding of his victims. That's Profiling 101."

Bell blew the hair out of her eyes. Fatigue turned her limp and jumbled her thoughts, and she hadn't eaten since lunch yesterday.

"Where were we?"

"Fledgling killer Logan Wolf alerted the FBI to his wife's murder. What happens next?"

Bell chewed a nail and studied the ghost of her reflection in the glass.

"The FBI calls the police who bring you in for questioning, but they can't hold you without sufficient evidence."

"Yes."

"Yet as the days pass, the case against Logan Wolf

grows, and you flee before they issue an arrest warrant."

Though she looked away from him, Wolf's glare made her flinch.

"What would a legendary serial killer do next?"

Bell stopped in front of Wolf, stuck in the same rut she'd found herself in whenever she constructed his profile.

"I don't know."

"Don't know or don't want to say?"

"This is the point where your actions no longer make sense."

"Do tell. Perhaps I can shed light on your points of confusion. But step carefully, agent. You're so close now."

The moon tracked through the sky, blinding amid so much dark. She felt infinitesimal, helpless.

"The psychotic break which led you to kill your wife careens you out of control, and you repeat the murders over the next several years, leaving the same calling card."

She sensed his glare but dared not turn her eyes in his direction. Bell fixed on a flowering cherry tree turned pallid and frozen by the moonlight. When she opened her mouth to break the deafening quiet, she found her mouth dry.

"In your professional opinion, is that a logical conclusion?"

She shook her head slowly.

"The break in the profile is too extreme," she said, swallowing. "The calling card is the same: throat slit, a sack over the head. Yet reliving Renee's murder requires you seek women, not men, particularly women who remind you of Renee."

"A great many murderers killed across racial, ethnic, and gender lines."

"But switching from one particular type to the polar opposite is extremely rare. No, it doesn't add up. There's no reason to murder men..."

Bell didn't so much pause as seize up. Her lips moved silently, eyes unblinking as her hands curled into fists. Why hadn't she seen the truth until now?

"Go on, Scarlett."

"Christ, you're calling out Renee's killer."

She turned to him. He shook, a split-second from lunging across the seat and ripping her throat out with his teeth.

"That's it, isn't it? You never stopped hunting serial killers when you became a fugitive, only altered your methods for bringing them to justice. Those men you slaughtered…they were murderers, and somehow you found out. Which explains why you were in Pronti and killed The Skinner and how you knew Jillian's murderer had returned. Except one killer forever eluded you, the only serial killer you truly desire to find, so you mimicked his methods to draw him out of hiding. Jesus. I should have seen it."

She slumped against the seat, head spinning, pins-and-needles coursing into her fingers. Her heart hammered to a dangerous beat, and she focused on breathing, unsure if Wolf's blade might sweep across her throat.

When she dared open her eyes, his seat lay back, Wolf prone and focused on the sky through the sunroof. Had he not blinked, she would have thought him dead.

"Vincent Hooper."

The unexpected words made her jump.

"Vincent Hooper. Is that God's Hand's name?"

Wolf handed her the cartridge.

CHAPTER THIRTY-EIGHT

Joelle in the pitch black of the trailer…virulent oil and gasoline scents burning her lungs…

She listened for the man who called himself God's Hand.

Moments before, the car door opened, followed by footsteps leading away from the vehicle. After he relieved himself in the bushes, he stomped back to the car and closed the door. Now it was quiet. He was asleep.

After he last checked on Joelle at sunset, she'd worked on the ropes tying her arms behind the chair. In his demented anger after the incident at the creek, he'd haphazardly tied her wrists. As he dragged the trailer to a new and unknown location, she slipped one arm free. Now she stood up from the chair and fought to free her other arm, careful not to wake him as she stepped upon the wooden floor.

The final knot trapping her arm proved the most daunting. She couldn't see it in the dark, but her fingers grappled with the fibers and loosened the binding. When the loop relaxed by a fraction of an inch, she bent over and clamped her teeth on the knot. Pulled until her jaw threatened to dislodge.

The rope unraveled. Joelle yanked her arm free and tumbled into the door, rocking the trailer. Holding her breath, she worried he'd heard. When the man didn't come, she wiped the sweat onto her shirt and knelt beside the trailer door.

During the day, sunlight oozed inside the trailer through the warped door. Now she placed her ear to the opening and listened to the night sounds. All she needed to do was pull the door open past the busted lock, but opening the trailer caused a screech that drove wraiths from a graveyard.

Rust crusted the track. She doubted she had enough strength to lift the door.

Slipping her fingers beneath the door, she pulled. It held held fast. She tried again, and the door lifted half an inch and descended like a guillotine. Gasping, she pulled her fingers from under the door before it crushed her knuckles.

Her heart raced as she leaned against the wall. The wilderness sounds buoyed Joelle. The promise of freedom. She bent her knees and yanked. When the door raised a few inches, her arms trembling from exertion, she slipped the toe of her sneaker into the opening. It hurt when the door came down on her foot, but she'd won the leverage necessary to muscle the door open.

She bent and lifted. Strained. Neck muscles popping beneath her skin like garter snakes on the hunt.

The jam released at once. The door shrieked open, and she stood on the precipice of freedom, lips quivering.

She leaped out of the trailer as the car door swung open. He roared. A guttural scream that prickled the hairs on the back of her neck.

Joelle hit the ground running, God's Hand steps behind and crashing through the brush. She felt him gaining on her, imagined his claw-hands reaching out.

It was too dark to find the dirt road leading into the

woods, and even if she had, she'd lost her sense of direction.

His breaths puffed from behind. Touched her neck. The trees flew at her. Branches lashing at her flesh, gouging her eyes. Then a hillock above a stream, too dark to gauge the drop.

She leaped. And fell, and fell.

Slammed against the bank, elbows and knees taking the brunt of the collision. But she was up and limping when he splashed into the stream. Cutting between trees, sandals crunching twigs and a carpet of leaves.

He fell further behind, yet she made too much noise as she fled and gave him a beacon to her position.

Between two oaks, she stopped and stood upon a bed of moss. Silent. Out of breath.

For a long while, she thought she'd lost him, then his footfalls clambered through the overgrowth. He came closer. She was trapped. The moment she sprinted from the soft moss onto the fallen branches, he'd locate her.

Slumped against the larger of the two trunks, she rubbed her heels and cursed herself for refusing to wear sneakers to the party. Her feet were a war zone of scratches and bloody streaks. The prickers had gnashed chunks off her flesh as she ran, and her twisted ankle begged her to rest.

When the killer was almost upon her, he veered off and stalked deeper into the forest. Still Joelle waited, convinced it was a trick and God's Hand waited in the shadows.

As the humid night slicked her skin, and the mosquitoes buzzed at her ear, she backtracked and searched for a way out of the woods.

All paths led to dead ends.

CHAPTER THIRTY-NINE

Drained after she learned the truth about Logan Wolf, Bell sat in the driver's seat of his car, head hanging against the steering wheel.

She'd promised Wolf a profile of his wife's killer, and that had been enough for the ex-BAU agent turned serial killer, who handed her the keys and crawled into the backseat with nothing more than a nebulous agreement to accompany her until she reconvened with Gardy. At that point, Wolf would become a ghost.

"You're giving me your car?"

"Oh, Scarlett. I haven't owned a car or home in six years. Now if you don't mind, I haven't slept in two days."

"You and me, both," she muttered to herself so he wouldn't hear.

Perfect. A stolen car. How would she explain this one?

She warred with indecision, uncertain if she should trust Wolf. In truth, she didn't. Couldn't. Taking his story at face value, the man was still a serial killer though he hunted other killers.

Vincent Hooper. Bell had notified Gardy she was safe and knew God's Hand's name. He crosschecked Vincent

Hooper with Harold's list and found Hooper's name near the top. The FBI was already procuring a search warrant for his address outside Fredericksburg. She danced around why she'd disappeared from her apartment and how she unearthed Hooper's name, saying only he fit the profile and she'd tell him more when she met Gardy at the address.

Reflected in the mirror, Wolf curled on the backseat, lethal as a viper as Bell pulled out from the concealed pull-off and backtracked toward the interstate.

On I-95 an hour out of Fredericksburg, her phone rang. She didn't recognize the number, and answering, she was shocked to hear Congresswoman San Giovanni's voice.

"Yes, Agent Bell, I'm aware of the raid on Hooper's residence and helped expedite the warrant. Listen, I'm contacting you because you are the only one who can bring Joelle home alive."

"Me? I don't follow."

"He called me moments ago."

Bell clamped the phone between her shoulder and ear and weaved through slow traffic.

"God's Hand? How did he get your phone number?"

"It doesn't matter. What's important is he won't hand Joelle over to anyone but you. I don't know why it has to be you, but he insists you come alone. Otherwise, Joelle dies."

An angry horn honked as she swerved around a truck. The driver's high beams stroked her mirrors.

"Congresswoman, I'm not far from Fredericksburg. Give me the details, and I'll discuss the matter with my partner."

"No!" A moment of quiet, then San Giovanni sniffled. "I'm sorry…I'm under pressure and losing control. Please, Agent Bell. My daughter is my life. If you involve the FBI, he'll know. He managed to push a letter past security and figured out my phone number. At least let me give you the address."

Tearing open her notepad, Bell copied the information as she drove. It wasn't lost on her the address was a stone's throw from her hometown, Bealton. Five miles, at most.

"Give me five minutes to compose my thoughts. May I call you back at this number?"

"Of course. But please hurry. He'll kill her at dawn if you don't agree."

San Giovanni's words repeated in Bell's head as she looked for a rest area, somewhere to clear her thoughts. Her brain raced on overdrive.

"San Giovanni called you?"

She screamed at Wolf's voice and saw him glaring at her in the mirror. Bell nodded.

"The crocodile conceals its jaws below the waterline," he said, grinning. "I hope you don't trust her."

Three in the morning, and she drove a stolen car with a murderer in the backseat, while a power-hungry politician begged her to go rogue and apprehend God's Hand without backup.

"God's Hand called San Giovanni."

Wolf's eyes glimmered.

"Go on."

Bell recounted her conversation.

"Tell me something, Scarlett. Is God's Hand an organized killer?"

"No, just the opposite. He's disorganized, visionary, and deep in the throes of a psychotic break."

Wolf leaned forward, arms folded over the front seat.

"Let's say you wished to sneak a threatening letter into San Giovanni's estate. Could you do it?"

Bell chewed her lip.

"Maybe. I'd need to study the grounds, figure out the security workers' schedules and determine the most vulnerable times of day."

"Under normal conditions, yes. But with young Joelle in the clutches of God's Hand, you'd need to dodge secret service and FBI surveilling the estate."

"You're right. I couldn't breach the mansion without divine intervention."

Wolf's grin reflected off the windshield as the head beams from a passing van touched the glass.

"If the resourceful Scarlett Bell can't break San Giovanni's security, how can a psychopathic killer who believes he has a direct line to God?"

Wolf hadn't told Bell anything she wasn't already thinking, but hearing him echo her thoughts amped up her suspicion.

"He couldn't."

"And she claims God's Hand called her?"

"Yes, and for what it's worth, I believe her. She's terrified for her daughter."

"We make critical errors when we don't keep our wits about us, Scarlett. She spoke to someone who claimed to be God's Hand, yes. But do you believe it was him?"

Bell considered her answer.

"The odds are against it. In an emergency, I could obtain San Giovanni's number, but I'd jump through hoops unless I went straight to Harold."

"Ah, yes. I miss few things about the BAU, but Harold was a delight. Scarlett, to breach the enhanced security surrounding the esteemed congresswoman takes connections."

Bell tapped her fingernail against the phone case.

"You're suggesting this was an inside job."

"Perhaps."

"But why? I see no reason to fool San Giovanni into sending a field agent to the wrong location."

"Have you considered San Giovanni isn't the target for this misdirection?"

The interstate hummed beneath the tires, the white dividing lines shooting toward the car like a snow squall. A road sign popped out of the dark.

Fredericksburg 28 miles.

"Where is the faux God's Hand supposedly holding young Joelle?"

Bell recited the address—just outside of Bealton and thirty miles south of Hooper's residence. It made sense for God's Hand to hold Joelle close to his home. In a place he'd scoped out. Yet the facts didn't add up.

Despite misgivings over the authenticity of the letter and phone call, her sense of duty pushed her to save the politician's daughter. Or was it the memory of Jillian driving Bell to avenge her friend's death?

"I have to call the congresswoman and give her my answer."

In a blur, Wolf's hand ripped the phone from her grip.

"If you are fool enough to gamble with your life, don't show your cards. Whoever awaits your arrival mustn't expect you."

He dropped the phone on the passenger seat. The screen turned black from disuse.

Bell set the GPS and ensured the Glock was ready.

CHAPTER FORTY

Hours before sunrise, night shadowed a field and old barn overlooking a rural valley of wild grasses and weed reincarnated by spring's return. The early morning carried a heavy fecund scent, the air thick as a sodden washrag. Bell parked the car on a sloped tractor turnaround above a drainage creek.

"There's nothing here," she said, eyeing the dilapidated barn with suspicion.

"I advise you leave. You won't find the congresswoman's daughter here."

Behind the barn, a heap of strewn and charred timbers slumbered upon the ridge. Fire had consumed the home, and the barn stood abandoned fifty yards from the destroyed residence. A good place to hide a kidnapped girl.

Bell was first to step out of the car. The back door clicked open as Wolf followed.

When they were less than a mile from their destination, Bell had killed the headlights to hide their arrival from God's Hand, or whoever contacted San Giovanni. Yet as they stood in the shielded dark, invisible to anyone inside the barn, she sensed eyes on them.

"Stay in the car, Wolf. This isn't your fight."

"On the contrary, I've taken a strong interest in your wellbeing, Scarlett. After we finish this childish scavenger hunt, you will deliver on your promise."

Before they edged out of the field, a swishing sound up the hill brought Bell to a stop. It might have been an animal crawling down the ridge. It might have been anything.

She turned toward Wolf. Couldn't see his face, only his head shaking. A final warning.

Gun in hand, Bell bent beneath the overgrowth and angled toward the country road. Once she broke out of hiding, she'd be vulnerable until she crossed the blacktop to the opposite ditch. A click brought her head around. Wolf held a gun, something smaller than the Glock and equally deadly. Though she'd never worked with a partner other than Gardy, the unspoken language between them came naturally as Wolf motioned her forward and indicated he would cover her.

She slipped into the blue-gray moonlight. It felt cold and forsaken. Knife-edged.

Wolf passed her and took his place beneath a willow tree. All she saw was a shadow as he breezed past.

From the ditch, the barn hid from her sight. Eventually she'd need to cross the meadow. Her instinct told her they weren't alone. The man awaiting her arrival wasn't God's Hand, nor did he hold the congresswoman's daughter.

Wolf slipped out from under the willow and took the forward flank, moving up a gravel road. By now, she should have heard his shoes scuff the rocks, yet he was barely a whisper as he tracked along the hillside, weapon raised to cover her.

Bell climbed from the ditch a second before the gunshot exploded off the hillside.

A hissing sound.

Then Wolf hit the ground, curled and twitching.

CHAPTER FORTY-ONE

After the call went to Bell's voice-mail again, Gardy killed the connection and put his phone away.

"Problem?"

Gardy looked at Agent Peterson who rode shotgun to Glick in the SUV. The vehicle's headlights sliced the country route and colored the blacktop.

"No problem. Service out here is less than optimal."

Gardy withheld his inability to reach Bell and preferred the other agents work under the assumption she was traveling a long way to join the raid on Hooper's residence, and maybe that was true. But an undefinable need to protect Bell glued his lips. He'd missed something important.

Peterson nodded and focused on the road as they followed a local PD cruiser. Its flashers were off. Why bother? Keeping a low profile seemed impossible with a four-vehicle motorcade of FBI and police driving through rural Virginia at four in the morning.

Gardy glanced out at the dark fields.

"How much farther?"

As if the officer in the lead car heard, he answered over the radio, "Two more miles after we crest the next ridge." Gardy checked his gun. A nervous habit, but a necessary distraction from his worries.

A minute later, the vehicles killed their lights and slowed. The cruiser's brake lights stained the macadam red, and Gardy pictured the gates of hell opening to admit the unsuspecting officers.

Vincent Hooper's house stood a quarter-mile down Yancy Road, ten miles from the city lights. A single-story residence with chipping gray paint and a car port, no lights burned inside. And no vehicles rested in the driveway.

Two of the police cruisers fanned out to block both ends of Yancy Road. On the shoulder outside Hooper's residence, a third cruiser pulled behind the FBI SUV.

With only the starlight to guide them as they approached the front door, it was difficult to follow another team of officers circling around the back of the house. Gardy gave them time to get into position, then he nodded at a burly local cop named Ewing who held a battering ram as though it was a softball bat.

On Gardy's signal, Ewing swung the ram against the door. The flimsy construction proved no match, and the door crashed open, a chunk of splintered wood jutting into the room. Simultaneously, the back door imploded, and the second team forced their way inside.

"FBI!"

Leading the charge, Gardy swept his gun across a dingy living room as Glick and Peterson checked the corners. When the living room was clear, they moved through a small kitchen with a sink full of dirty dishes and pans, the stink of rot rising out of the garbage disposal. The police stormed the hallway. Flashlight beams uncovered the dark corners.

The teams convened inside Hooper's bedroom. When Gardy led Glick and Peterson into the room, the closet door stood open with a mess of unlaundered clothes spilled onto a throw rug. The bed was unmade, white sheets tinged gray and yellow and smelling of filth.

"He isn't here," Ewing said, lowering his weapon.

"Still need to check the storm cellar," said Gardy as he scanned the room for some sign of where God's Hand had taken the congresswoman's daughter.

Satellite imagery of the residence had confirmed the backyard storm cellar. Now outside in the starlight, Gardy's adrenaline raced as they surrounded the strange concrete structure poking out of the earth. To Gardy, the storm cellar looked like a crash-landed spaceship. A rotating vent fan spun with the wind. Secured by a padlock, a reinforced door offered entry.

Gardy made way for Ewing, who produced a pair of industrial-quality bolt cutters. The officer's veins stood out on muscular forearms as he strained. With a loud crack that echoed through the countryside, the padlock snapped and fell away. Ewing pulled the door open as the officers plowed down the stairs.

The cellar wasn't as musty as Gardy predicted. As if God's Hand used the structure recently. Instead, a metallic smell wafted out of the shelter, little more than a bunker fit for a small family,

Pulse thrumming, he prepared himself for the worst as the officers checked inside. He let out his breath when they didn't discover a corpse.

"What do you see?"

"Pictures," Ewing said, shining his light into Gardy's eyes when he looked up.

"Photographs?"

"No, like paintings."

"Let me down there."

Ewing remained in the shelter with his flashlight aimed at the wall while the other officers cleared out. Enough room existed for Gardy and Peterson to descend the steps and squeeze beside the lumbering officer.

A practiced hand had painted the pictures, four of which wallpapered the shelter. In one painting, heavenly light burst through dark clouds to spotlight a man dipping a child into water. In the others, fire engulfed a cabin which surely represented Erwin, Georgia, and a tranquil creek ran between a deep green forest and a suburban neighborhood.

But it was the final painting which took Gardy's breath away.

"My God."

A monstrous, clawed hand reached for a woman with straight blonde hair and green eyes.

Bell.

CHAPTER FORTY-TWO

A sound in the forest snapped Joelle awake. She panicked upon realizing she'd drifted asleep. Leaned against a tree and surrounded by the talons of pricker bushes, Joelle rubbed the chill off her arms, teeth chattering as she climbed to her feet.

Everything hurt. As if she'd run all night.

A cool mist curled through the woods. She sneaked a look over the prickers. Where was God's Hand? She'd last heard him hunting through the forest, yet she could never be certain of his position or if he was close. Noises echoed off the trees and ridges and fooled her.

With no idea how late it was, frightened the sun would never rise again, she struggled out of the brush and weaved through the woods. Her ankle screamed, then it loosened while she walked, and she concentrated on putting one foot in front of the other, praying the real God would lead her back to her mother.

She walked for too long and began to believe she'd never make it out of the woods alive. Then she saw a light bobbing in the distance and threw herself behind a tree, believing it was the killer's flashlight. But as she sneaked a glance around the tree, she noticed the light only moved when she did. Not a flashlight, but a streetlight. Or a lamp shining through a window.

Soon a second light joined the first, and Joelle realized a neighborhood lay in the distance. A sob choked her, and she hobbled with greater urgency toward the lights. Toward safety.

In between the boughs, moonlight spotlighted her before she vanished beneath stands of trees. A creek glistened in the distance, and she stopped, reminded of the insane killer's biblical ramblings as he threatened to drown her.

She started for the lights again, keeping an eye out for the sedan and trailer and listening for the madman's footsteps. The pursuit seemed to follow her from all directions, but it was her own footfalls reverberating through the woods.

Joelle entered a clearing and found him waiting for her. A black shadow against the alien blue light. Before she could scream, his filthy hand clamped over her mouth. He dragged the flailing girl into the dark.

CHAPTER FORTY-THREE

Bell swung the gun across the meadow and toward the barn.

Nobody.

Where was the gunman?

Another blast echoed over her head, and she dropped flat and crawled toward the shoulder where Wolf lay. Pushing herself up to her elbows, she dragged her body across the meadow. The next shot ripped through her arm. She dropped and clutched the wound. Winced at the hot agony. Her trembling hand came away covered with blood. The bullet had clipped the outside of her arm and excavated a finger's length of flesh. She felt lucky the bullet hadn't lodged in her triceps.

Running footsteps brought her head up, and she saw the silhouette of a man crouched beside the rusted bulk of an old tractor.

Don't panic. Breathe.

In the dead gloom of early morning, Bell bit her tongue and crawled along the ridge base, careful to remain quiet. Almost to the road, she maneuvered behind a chestnut tree and peeked her head around the trunk. The man's gun aimed where the bullet had grazed her. Unaware she'd crept up on him.

She placed both hands on the gun. Aimed, using the trunk for support.

But a clear shot didn't exist.

From the corner of her eye, she spied Wolf. He lay still now. She didn't discern breathing.

A fallen branch leaned against the tree. Carefully, she lifted the branch, one eye fixed on the gun poking out around the tractor. She whipped the branch toward her previous position in the field. It whistled as it spun, and as a night wind snaked through the tall grass, the shooter jumped out of hiding and fired into the meadow.

Bell was too quick for him. Before he caught on to the con, she fired three shots in succession. One missed. One exploded through the shooter's cheek and stole a quarter of his face. The last hammered the shooter's forehead and whipped his head back.

The man crumbled and hit the ground. Bell spun off the tree and hurried up the hillside, staying beneath the meadow grass in case the gunman was still alive. His legs splayed beside the tractor when she broke out of the field, arms outstretched as though welcoming a benevolent power in the sky. Cautiously, she approached the man. The gun lay beyond his reach, hurled backward when his body convulsed at the bullets' impacts.

He was bald and blue-eyed, the left side of his face a horror show of gore as he gazed at the unforgiving stars. She touched his neck, checked for a pulse and found none. His dark coat held no wallet, no identification, but a silver chain and pendant hung off his neck. She turned the pendant to the moonlight and recognized the symbol as special ops. Checking his hands for a hidden weapon, his smooth fingertips brushed her palm. She held his hands up to the light. No matter what he touched, this man left behind no fingerprints.

Shit.

A scan of the property verified no additional enemies waited. If one had, she'd already be dead. As the arm wound throbbed and trickled lifeblood, she crossed the yard and checked the barn. Joelle San Giovanni wasn't here and never had been.

The phone buzzed inside her pocket. The congresswoman. She touched *Ignore* and hurried down the road, no longer worried over stealth.

She knelt beside Wolf and found him breathing, eyes closed. A dark, wet blemish between his chest and shoulder marred his jacket.

She reached for the wound. His hand shot out and snagged her wrist.

"I trust you took the shooter down," Wolf said, blood speckled against his gritted teeth. "Were you injured?"

"Don't worry about me. Save your strength."

"Did you recognize the man?"

"No, but he's not FBI."

"How do you know?"

"Well, first of all, he smoothed the prints off his fingertips."

His laughter morphed into a wet cough that made her cringe.

"What else?"

"He wore a pendant. Special ops."

"You've entered a maelstrom, Scarlett. Someone very powerful wants you dead."

"I'm popular like that," she said, locating the hole in his shirt and tearing it open.

He flinched and found her eyes.

"It's inside me, Scarlett. The bullet. You'll need to cut it out."

"Forget it, Wolf."

"Reach into my jacket. You'll find a knife in the inside pocket."

She sighed and searched for a pocket, then she touched the sheathed weapon through the fabric. When she removed the knife, ice water trickled down her spine. How many lives had this blade claimed? He recognized her reaction and smiled.

"Run back to the car. I keep a kit in the trunk. Needle and thread. Gauze. A lighter to sterilize the blade."

"I thought you stole the car."

"I did, but it pays to stay prepared."

The awful cough came again, and this time Wolf lowered his hand to his stomach. A memory surfaced. Logan Wolf caught on the convenience store security camera in Pronti, Kansas, purchasing stomach medication.

"Are you sick?"

"I'll be dead soon if you don't get this bullet out of me."

"What you need is a doctor."

"You know what will become of me if I check into an emergency room." He hissed as if the bullet had teeth and was chewing deeper into his flesh. "I know a man who will treat the wound properly."

"Then tell me where he is. I'll take you to him."

"No time. Hurry, Scarlett."

She met his eyes for a second. His dark, piercing stare glazed over, lost a flicker of life.

Bell rushed down the hill, stumbling twice over holes in the pavement. The FBI would be storming Hooper's house by now, Gardy wondering where she was. Ultimately, she'd owe the FBI answers.

In the trunk, Bell rummaged for a first aid kit. She expected a store-bought kit with the first aid symbol on the box. Instead, she located a nondescript toolbox containing the promised supplies.

She walked a brisk pace back to the fallen murderer, concerned she'd trip on the rutted road. His eyes lay closed when she found him. Chest steady.

She thought herself too late until those deadly eyes popped open and fixed on her. Smiling through the pain, he watched her remove the knife from its sheathe. She glared at him.

"I can't do this."

"You can and you will."

Bell bit her lip and ran the lighter's flame along the blade.

CHAPTER FORTY-FOUR

Bell sniffled and fought to keep her hands steady as she threaded the needle through Wolf's flesh.

Blood slicked her fingers and stained her through the cuffs of her jacket. She yanked her jacket off and tossed it into the road. In short sleeves, her arms rippled in goosebumps as the morning air touched her sweat-beaded skin.

She tied off the last stitch and sat back on her hands, exhausted. The legendary serial killer and former BAU agent had fallen unconscious from the pain, yet his chest continued to rise and fall, his eyes closed to the constellations looking down on him.

Bell wiped her nose on her forearm, surprised to see her own blood. She recalled diving beneath the gunman's bullets. Though the event was a blur, her face must have struck the earth. She checked her phone. Gardy should have called or written. That he hadn't confirmed she was far from the nearest cell tower. No doubt the gunman chose this place knowing she couldn't contact her partner.

Bealton lay over the next hill, and when she started driving in the direction of her home, she'd reconnect with the world and get an update on the raid. She exhaled and fretted over Wolf. She couldn't leave him to die. Regardless of his murderous past, she refused to abandon the man who risked his life to protect hers.

No time to worry about complicating his injuries, she lifted him by the shoulders and into a sitting position.

"Time to wake up, Wolf. Let's go."

He slumped forward, and she locked her arms around his chest to support him. After several breaths, he came around. He coughed again and splattered blood on her arms.

"I can walk."

She pulled him to his feet, but when he tried to walk, he stumbled into her. Throwing his arm over her shoulders, she helped him totter down the road, loose gravel vying to trip them up.

By the time they made it back to the stolen car, fatigue gripped Bell. Wolf regained enough strength to limp to the vehicle and slide across the backseat.

"Where to, dear Scarlett?"

"East to Bealton."

"Ah, your old home. It would be a great honor to meet the parents who produced the finest profiler the BAU has ever seen."

She slammed the door and glared over her shoulder.

"Get one thing straight. My family is off limits."

"As you wish."

"I mean it, Wolf. Take one step onto their property, and I'll skewer you myself. Until then, I'm driving until my damn phone finds a bar, then we'll discuss this doctor friend of yours and how we'll get you to him."

The engine stuttered upon starting. She found him in the mirror.

"Next time, steal something with a heartbeat."

She pulled the car out of hiding and crawled back to the road. Then she accelerated toward the hills with a bubble of gray visible on the eastern horizon. It took a few turns before she remembered the quarry outside of Bealton sat on the other side of the ridge.

Halfway to Bealton, her phone connected and chimed with dozens of missed calls and messages. She saw Gardy's name on most of them.

"This jalopy have Bluetooth, Wolf?"

He didn't answer. When she checked the mirror, he was too low on the seat to see.

She clicked redial on Gardy's last message, received ten minutes ago. Phone pressed to her ear as she navigated the twisting road around a blind curve, she waited. He answered on the second ring.

"You're alive," he said, irritated. "That's one less thing I have to worry about."

The ditch flew at her, and Bell cranked the wheel and screeched the tires to right the car.

"Hold on, Gardy. I'm putting you on speaker phone."

Aware Wolf could eavesdrop on the conversation, she placed the phone in the cup holder. Bealton and access to the interstate waited three miles down the road.

Gardy spoke in a hushed voice, a clue agents stood nearby.

"Dammit, Bell. That's twice tonight you've fallen off the face of the earth. Harold ran a locater on your phone, but it must have been off."

"Or out of cell range."

"And I don't suppose you'll tell me what you were doing out of cell range. It's been a shitty night, Bell."

"Really? How many people tried to kill you so far?"

"Wait, what? Did you just say someone tried to kill you?"

She checked the mirror for Wolf. He coughed, and Bell snatched the phone and buried it against her body. The serial killer spiraled toward an open grave. After the hacking ceased, she placed the phone back in the cup holder.

"Bell, you sound horrible."

"Swallowed down the wrong pipe. Listen, Gardy. There's a dead man a few miles in my rear-view mirror near a burned out farmhouse. I'll feed you the coordinates."

She told him of San Giovanni's call and how the shooter ambushed her upon arrival.

"You entered a hostile situation without contacting the FBI? What the hell has gotten into you?"

"The congresswoman swore me to secrecy. Claimed God's Hand would murder Joelle if I brought backup."

A pause. She pictured Gardy ripping out chunks of hair.

"You can't think the congresswoman had anything to do with this."

"Why not? She told me God's Hand held Joelle at the barn. She set me up."

"Bell, God's Hand is in Bealton."

Bell lost control of the wheel and skidded to a stop.

"Bealton? How do you know?"

"The evidence points in that direction. Look, we found paintings, one of you, others which appear to recreate the scene at the creek when he killed Jillian."

"Where he almost killed me."

"We think he took Joelle San Giovanni to the creek with the intent of reliving his first kill and attracting you. He wants to finish what he started in 1995, but we're taking him down first."

"The son-of-a-bitch."

"Bell, I need the coordinates now. We have enough team members to divert—"

"No one is to know about the gunman."

"That's not an option. I'm not brushing an attempt on an agent's life under the rug."

"I'll give you a reason."

"Like?"

"Suppose someone in the government is behind the shooting."

"Drop the conspiracy theories. Next you'll claim Weber ordered the hit."

She didn't answer. Gardy put the phone against his jacket and spoke to another agent, the conversation too muffled to make out.

"When I get an ID on the shooter, you'll be the first to know. Listen, I'm en route to Bealton. We should get there in a half-hour, forty-five minutes max. Where are you now?"

"Just outside Bealton. Gardy, I can get there faster."

"Under no circumstances are you to pursue God's Hand alone."

"I can't depend on the killer keeping the girl alive until —"

"Dammit, Bell. Stand down until we arrive. That's an order."

Bell killed the call. The demonic laughter of the world's most dangerous serial killer rose up behind her.

CHAPTER FORTY-FIVE

Bell deposited the car behind the neighborhood where the road ended and the path to the creek began. She pocketed her phone and left the keys in the ignition for Wolf who slumped against the back door.

"If you're smart, you'll drive the hell out of here before the FBI arrives."

Wolf grinned.

"And miss the great Scarlett Bell in action? Not for the world."

She stepped onto the road and leaned her head through the open window.

"They won't ask questions before they arrest you."

Wolf struggled into a sitting position, one blood-crusted hand covering the stitched wound.

"If the FBI could bring me to justice, they would have caught me six years ago. Now go. I'll be right behind you."

That's what I'm afraid of, she thought. She didn't wish to be alone in the dark woods with two bloodthirsty serial killers.

The telltale signs of the coming dawn grew to the east, but the looming forest was pitch black as she approached the creek. With no way to cross, she waded through the frigid shin-deep waters, thoroughly soaked through by the time she ascended the far bank.

And then it hit her. In all her years living in proximity to the creek, she'd never set foot inside the forest. During her childhood, the woods were a place of monsters, cackling witches, and untold horrors. Now she knew the horror was real.

The forest floor was soft underfoot. Quiet. The bushes rattled, and she swung the gun at the shadow of a small fleeing animal.

She stepped deeper into the woods, a place where the forest entry vanished. The creek didn't run in a straight line. Instead, it meandered and curved through the darkest regions of the woods. Though she'd never ventured inside, she was aware country roads paralleled the forest and offered access to fishers and hunters. Good places to conceal a trailer near the water.

She followed the water beyond rises, over which the creek tumbled in waterfalls and produced fine mists, and down into lowlands where the water spread and formed bogs of peepers and buzzing mosquitoes. Still no sign of the killer.

But as she rounded a bend in the creek, she spotted the trailer parked amid dense vegetation and cloaked by the forest canopy. With the moon and starlight blotted out, the water appeared black and bloody.

Bell threw her back against a tree. Breathed. Felt the bark scrape.

Both hands on the gun, Bell winced at her throbbing arm. Wetness soaked her shirt down to her elbow. The wound needed stitching, but no way she'd allow Wolf near with needle and thread.

A whimper came from inside the trailer. Bell's heart accelerated with the knowledge Joelle was still alive. Bending low, she scrambled toward a wall of bramble and peeked over the top. The car and trailer stood twenty paces away. She flashed the gun toward the water. God's Hand was close. She'd sensed his presence since she was nine, always watching her from the shadows, stalking her dreams.

In that moment, she pictured Jillian's face and flashed back to quiet times together along the creek. Mischief, bike rides with streamers hanging off handlebars during endless summers. All stolen by one man. One monster.

Under the cover of darkness, the night sky conspiring with the woods to cloak her movements, she followed the overgrowth and set her back against the trailer. Slid along the side until she found the door, warped and askew compared to when she'd last encountered the trailer at a cabin in rural Georgia.

She checked her surroundings again and squeezed her fingers beneath the door.

Lifted.

The door squealed open. Bell aimed the gun and saw the girl bound to a chair. Bolts pinned the chair to the floor, and a kerchief pulled the girl's lips into a painful rictus.

She leaped inside and unraveled the ropes. Joelle San Giovanni's eyes widened. The girl shook her head, a warning Bell received too late.

God's Hand struck her from behind. Bell's face slammed against the wall. Blood poured from her nose as he snatched her by the hair and dragged her away from the trailer.

She shook the cobwebs from her head and reached for the Glock. He snatched her wrist and twisted. Hurt her. She cried in anger when the gun fell from her hand.

Unconcerned over the fallen weapon, he dragged her by the hair with both hands digging into her scalp. She twisted and flailed, groggy and dizzy, but he was too strong.

"I knew you'd come, Scarlett. You came home."

She heard the creek before she saw it. The waters trickled silver and gray. Above the canopy, the sky lightened.

He yanked her down the bank and plunged her head into the icy water. She spat and choked, legs slamming the bank behind him as he forced her cheek onto the grime and stone below. He ripped her head back. Water poured from her mouth and off her drenched hair.

"Accept your God," he said, and dunked her under.

Ripped her head up.

"And you will be cleansed."

Bell rolled onto her back and snaked her arms around his neck. She pulled him into her and twisted like an alligator rolling prey. Now she reversed their positions, he submerged and coughing creek water as she drove her forearm against his windpipe. Their eyes met, and Bell couldn't discern a rudimentary understanding of good and evil, only a monster taking orders from his dark god.

Stronger than Bell, he threw her backward. She toppled into the creek, her outstretched hands stopping her from concussing herself on the rocks. He lumbered to his feet, stalked toward her. A horror movie beast come to life.

He drove a boot into her ribs. She cried out, and his backhanded slap whipped her neck.

When he dived at her, she turned and used his momentum against him. She shoved his head into the water's depths. Closed her hand over a rock and hammered it down on the back of his neck.

She dug out a heavier rock, a sediment-crusted stone with jagged edges that would tear flesh and crush a skull. Hoisted the rock from the creek bed as generations of mud and slime drizzled off the weapon. As she raised the rock over her head, he burst out of the water and swung a fallen branch. The waterlogged limb struck her head and dimmed her vision. Bell's knees buckled, arms useless at her sides. She sensed her body falling as though in a dream. Tumbling impossibly slow. Plummeting. Until her cheek struck water and stone.

As though it smelled blood, the creek rushed at her mouth and filled it with unrelenting glee. Choked and suffocated. She hacked on the water and spat, arms locked while she fought to press herself up. He stomped through the water. Closed in on his wounded quarry. Though she heard him coming, she couldn't move. Her body refused to obey.

A girl screamed. Bell turned to see Joelle leap upon God's Hand's back, fingernails gouging his eyes. He squealed, yet the girl held on while he thrashed at the water's edge.

"Joelle, run!"

Joelle looked up, and in the strange, mottled light of the coming dawn, Bell saw Jillian as she would have appeared as a young teen. The illusion vanished, and God's Hand grabbed Joelle's hair and tossed her over his shoulder. The earth flew up and bludgeoned the girl. She lay curled in a ball, hacking for air.

Bell exploded out of the water, but the monster was ready for her. A clawed hand gripped her throat and hoisted Bell so they stood face-to-face, and she saw him as a vengeful god, a demon risen.

The madness of his eyes jolted Bell out of her stupor. She struck out, palm rising up against his nose to break his grip.

His head whipped back with a spurt of blood. He stumbled on his feet, righted himself, and lunged at her.

But she was faster, fueled by rage and hate.

God's Hand seemed to notice this change in her, for a wary confusion contorted his face as he attacked.

Bell spun on the slick creek bed and crumpled him with a roundhouse kick. When he dropped to his knees, she swung her leg against his jaw and drew more blood. He gasped and sucked air into his lungs as she peppered his ribs with kicks, then she drove her knee against his face and shattered his nose.

"Get out of here!"

Joelle's head lifted, and she nodded at Bell, scrambled through the creek, and ran for the neighborhood.

Now the hunted, the killer crawled toward the banks. Forsaken. Bleeding.

Bell followed, and as she watched the water pull his blood downstream, she knew it would pass the flowered banks where she spent summers with Jillian, where he stole the young girl and brought endless pain and suffering to her family. And to Bell.

He lay injured against the bank, one leg in the water, the other drawn to his chest. The broken nose muffled his insane rhetoric, but she discerned Jillian's name as his lips curled into a smile.

She leaped atop God's Hand and pummeled his face with closed fists. For Jillian. For Lucas. For Bregan Dane and every child the maniac slaughtered. Each punch split lips and blackened eyes, his face a bloody pulp as she rained justice down upon him. He snatched her neck and squeezed, and his resilience and strength stunned her. She drove her elbow against his cheek to break his grip. His neck lolled, tongue rolling over his lips, a dying animal.

The dark seeped out of the sky as Bell grabbed his shirt collar and hauled him to his feet. Bloodlust blinded her. God's Hand was a death bringer and deserved nothing less than to die by the sword. She pulled her fist back, loaded it.

"End him, Scarlett."

She turned toward the shadowed figure on the banks. Wolf removed the knife from its sheath and held out his hand.

"Take it."

Bell glanced down at the man who called himself God's Hand. The killer's eyes fluttered open and fell shut.

"No. I'm not like you."

"You're exactly like me, Scarlett. Take the knife and

do what must be done." Wolf edged down the bank, the chest wound sapping his strength and turning his gait drunken. The gray light found his burning eyes. "The system will institutionalize him. Rehabilitate. Some attorney will claim his mother abused him as a child and sway the courts to show mercy. Don't let it get that far."

Bell reached behind her for the handcuffs. Wolf closed the space between them.

"Dear Scarlett, do you wish to spend the rest of your life counting down the days until the system releases him or he escapes? You'll never be free. He'll always be under your bed, hiding in the closet at midnight. Take the knife."

The look of disdain on Bell's face stopped Wolf in his tracks.

"You can go to hell."

She cuffed one wrist. God's Hand, playing possum, stole the knife from Wolf and sliced the blade at Bell's neck.

Then she became a blur of motion, a part of the flowing creek and the whistling wind.

While the knife arced toward her neck, she ducked beneath certain death and swept his legs.

He toppled to his knees, and she twirled behind him and grabbed his head and chin.

One violent twist of opposing motion.

She broke his neck.

God's Hand pitched forward into the creek. Bell screamed until her strength abandoned her.

As perpetual dark lifted from the haunted neighborhood, Bell slumped against the bank. Across the creek, a porch light flicked on, followed by another as people ventured outside to find the source of the commotion.

The first sirens approached.

CHAPTER FORTY-SIX

A blanket lay over Bell's shoulders. Sunlight scorched the once-dark woods, and a pair of ambulances joined the FBI and police cruisers.

Wet hair matted her cheeks. Gauze covered her throbbing arm. Stitches and shots awaited her at the hospital.

The boots were the last she'd seen of God's Hand moments before the medical examiner zipped the body bag. Then two officers lifted the killer onto a gurney and whisked him away. Forever this time. The killer's death lifted a shroud off her, yet it left her empty. Drained.

The graying male paramedic with the naval tattoos stressed the urgent need to get Bell to the hospital, but Gardy requested two minutes alone with his partner, and the paramedic conceded with a scowl.

"I don't know where to begin," Gardy said, body slumped forward as he sat beside her, face buried in his hands. "Have a death wish on your own time. Too many people depend on you."

She refused to look at him.

"To heck with you if you don't want to listen," Gardy said, zipping his jacket and standing. "But you'll have plenty to answer to for your actions. I can't protect you this time."

"I have nothing to hide."

"Then you should begin with your whereabouts last night and how you arrived in Bealton. Where's your Rogue?"

"Am I under suspicion, Gardy?"

"It's a little suspicious that you deflect all of my questions."

Bell looked up from her hands. Through the trees, she viewed an awakening neighborhood of backyards where children would soon play. Had she laughed or run with her friends after the age of nine? She wondered if her parents heard the sirens and had any idea she was here, or if the ambulance would pass her old house on the way to the hospital.

No sign remained of Wolf's stolen car, the serial killer having vanished minutes before the authorities stormed into Bealton.

"You know what pisses me off, Gardy?" She swung her eyes to his. "Someone tried to murder me this morning, and an hour later I stopped a child serial murderer and rescued a congresswoman's daughter, and all you can do is question my whereabouts. Maybe I was here visiting my parents and parked in their garage."

"Shall I check?"

She picked the head off a dandelion and flung it.

"Do as you must. I don't give a shit anymore."

He sighed and set a hand on her shoulder.

"Let's not do this. I'm on your side."

"Then ID the shooter."

"There's a little problem."

"Of course."

"Peterson and Glick found the barn. But they didn't find a body. They have a team scouring the area for shells, anything to prove a gunfight took place in the field."

"Let me guess. They haven't found anything."

"Nothing yet."

"I'll save you the suspense. The evidence is gone. Whoever wants me dead is thorough."

"You still think the guy was special ops?"

"I saw the pendant."

He nodded, itched his head, and glanced around at the agents and crime techs combing the woods. He regarded the agents differently. Perhaps not suspicious, but wary.

"That doesn't prove anything. These days, you can probably buy replicas on eBay."

But the wrinkle to his brow revealed troubled thoughts.

Gardy tapped the ambulance twice.

"She's all yours."

Bell huffed as the paramedic returned to escort her into the vehicle.

"I keep leaving in these things," Bell said from the back of the ambulance. "Street cred, remember?"

"You should rethink your life goals."

The paramedic shot him a meaningful glance, and Gardy backed away from the vehicle.

"I'll meet you at the hospital. We'll discuss all of this and figure out what to do."

She gave him a thumbs up, and the door closed.

Then the motor rumbled, and the ambulance backed onto the access road and took Bell from this place of nightmares.

She closed her eyes, and the rumble of the tires brought back long trips in the car with Mom and Dad.

Before sleep took her, a young girl appeared to Bell, bright and hopeful as she'd been when they ran these fields together, inseparable and forever bonded. A tear curled from Bell's eye. She reached her hand out to Jillian as the jubilant colors of sunlight intermingled with meadow grass and consumed her friend. Before the girl vanished, Bell read her lips.

Thank you.

Bell fell asleep smiling.

CROWN OF THORNS

CHAPTER FORTY-SEVEN

Scarecrows don't move. Of that, Shelly LaFleur was certain.

LaFleur shaded her eyes and stared over the corn, a field of verdant green that stretched a football field's length into the westering sun. Leaves flapped like skittish birds. Insurgent weeds sprouted among the paths and hunched over where she'd shoved them aside during the morning rounds.

The scarecrow hung above the center of the field. Two black crows perched on either arm and squawked, not phased by LaFleur's faux watchman. So it hadn't been the scarecrow she saw moving through the field. So what was it? A shadow, perhaps. Or maybe she was overdue for new prescription glasses. Whatever it had been, it was gone now. She shrugged away momentary uneasiness and set off for the barn.

A wind borne of the Gulf, gummy and suffocating, slithered through the field and stuck to her face. It was too hot, too sultry for early June in Northern New York. If this was a sign of things to come, she wouldn't be able to breathe come August.

Though slashes of shadows cloaked the inside of the barn, the heat felt worse inside, the hay and baked wood scents overwhelming. No wind, the air pent up and stagnant, a dead thing.

She snatched up an old bucket of hay and alfalfa and walked it over to the horse stall, where Winnie paced and pawed at the door latch.

"Hungry, girl?"

LaFleur offered a handful to the horse. The old mare dipped its face into her hand, the horse's teeth and tongue tickling her palm as it fed.

The mare neighed as she set the bucket down.

"Easy now. I'll let you into the pasture as soon as I'm sure a storm ain't brewin'. "

To LaFleur, it seemed a storm hid on the horizon, somewhere over Lake Ontario. She sensed it the way one does eyes on her back, a distant energy that wanted to unleash its fury on the lake plain. But as she stepped out of the barn and surveyed the hills, she saw only hazy blue and the shredded contrail from a long departed airliner.

The sensation of being watched grew when she returned to the corn. Though the rows needed clearing before the field became an impassable jungle, she found it difficult to put one foot in front of the other. An unidentifiable fear.

Shadows in the corn. An unseen storm over the lake.

These were the paranoid worries of a woman who spent too much time by herself. No husband, no child. The concept of a nuclear family never appealed to her. The farm was all the family she needed, just the earth and the seasons to keep her company.

She liked it this way, though the men outside the general store whispered about her, and the locals held pity in their eyes when they visited her booth at the farmers market as though she were a charity case. No matter as long as they kept buying.

She was halfway up the tractor when the scarecrow leaped off the cross and plunged into the corn. LaFleur caught her breath, uncertain what she'd seen. The crows winged off in opposite directions while the perch wobbled with unspent momentum.

The scarecrow had fallen before, but she was sure she'd secured it well. Damn crows probably pecked at the ropes. The irony might have provoked laughter were she not a bundle of nerves.

Not chancing the possibility of some animal prowling through the field, she grabbed her rifle off the back of the tractor. After retrieving rope from the barn wall, Winnie fretful and strutting around her stall, LaFleur started toward the field, looking at the empty perch with annoyance and a terror she couldn't place.

Inside the rows, the growing stalks emitted rich scents which always brought her back to childhood days spent on her parents' farm. An only child, she'd busied herself with chores, the fantasy adventures she concocted in her head a substitute for friends. Sometimes she explored rainforest jungles or explored the darkest reaches of Mordor. Mom and Dad found her a tad odd, but no one worried over her imagination provided she finished her work and kept her grades up in school.

Solitude was a gift, not a disease or a reason for the townsfolk to take pity on her.

Fighting through the overgrown weeds, LaFleur made it to the middle of the field. The scarecrow lay face down, arms splayed as if it had belly-flopped off a diving board to nowhere. The crows circled and cawed in the sky.

Unraveled rope lay to either side of the scarecrow. Frays in the fibers suggested someone cut the scarecrow down. But why? She gripped the rifle, sweat trickling into her eyes. Kids might play a practical joke, but the scarecrow stood too tall for a child to reach.

The stalks shifted behind her. She spun and pointed the rifle into the corn.

"Who's in there?"

Even with the sun strong on the horizon, darkness curled among the rows.

"Come out now. That was a fine trick you played, but the joke's over."

Her voice wavered, belying the courage of her words. And the noise came again. A parting of the stalks as though someone circled her.

"That's enough. Show yourselves, or I'm calling the sheriff."

LaFleur hauled the scarecrow into her arms. It slumped over her shoulder, lifeless, black eyes glaring into the rows. She spat and hoisted the scarecrow onto its perch and tied the rope around one of its arms. Then she started to secure the next, one eye sweeping through the sea of green as the stalks danced and swayed with the growing wind.

Irritated over the scarecrow, she forgot her fears and let down her guard. The rifle stood on end, propped up against the post, when the thing crashed out of the corn. At first, she saw a goat's head and thought someone's pen had busted, but the head stood too tall above the rows.

LaFleur grasped for the rifle as the monster tore out of the corn. The sight of the goat-headed man stunned her. She pulled the trigger as he pummeled her head with a knife hilt. The rifle thundered and kicked back against her shoulder.

The hilt battered her skull while she kicked and thrashed beneath the man's weight. He leered down at her. Eyes wild, crazed.

Behind him, the scarecrow dangled by one arm. The last thing LaFleur saw was the dead goat eyes glaring down at her. Then the hilt smashed her between the eyes, and the sky went black.

When LaFleur ceased moving, the man removed the goat's head and placed it beside her. He removed a video camera from his shoulder and focused the lens on the farmer's sleeping face.

And he began to film.

CHAPTER FORTY-EIGHT

Special Agent Scarlett Bell grabbed the door handle when Neil Gardy took the curve too fast. His brown hair speckled by gray, Gardy eased off the gas and avoided turning the rental into a ditch.

"Trying to lap the field, Dale Earnhardt?"

Gardy eased off the gas and clicked off the satellite radio.

"I forgot how much these back roads twisted. Hey, aren't you the one with the lead foot?"

"For the record, I've never put us in a ditch. Or hit a tree for that matter."

Gardy snickered his Muttley the cartoon dog laugh.

"That tree was completely out of place."

"In a forest, yes."

An hour ago, they'd landed at Syracuse airport with a strong sense of deja vu. A year earlier, the two FBI Behavioral Analysis Unit agents captured serial killer Alan Hodge at nearby Coral Lake. Now they raced against the setting sun to reach the rural village of Golden, situated a stone's throw from the glistening blue waters of Lake Ontario.

Gardy tapped the case file on Bell's lap.

"Our contact is Sheriff Kemp Marcel."

She screwed up her face as if she'd bit down on a lemon.

"Why do I sense another border war with local law enforcement brewing?"

"Stay positive. Coral Lake is the next county southward. Different sheriff."

"He find the victim?"

"She didn't show for the farmer's market last Saturday and stopped answering her phone. Sheriff went out to have a look and found...well, you'll just have to see how he found her. It's not pretty."

Bell paged through the case notes.

"Shelly LaFleur, farmer on the outskirts of Golden, New York."

"Sheriff says she's a bit of a recluse. Except for market, nobody saw her. Thing is, the farmer's market was her livelihood. She never missed a day."

"Until last Saturday."

Green hills accented by wildflowers rolled past in colorful streaks. With the windows open, the scents traveled into the rental SUV and brought to mind childhood days in Bealton, Virginia when school let out for the summer. The undulating terrain looked similar to Coral Lake, but without the population. This was God's country, a place industry wouldn't discover for another few centuries, if ever.

Gardy turned down a dirt and gravel road, the stones loud beneath the SUV. Tree-covered hills grew as far as the eye could see. Atop one ridge, a trio of windmills twirled over the countryside like benevolent giants. She could hear them with the windows rolled down, the sound pleasing compared to the static from the AM radio.

The occasional farm sprang out of the wilderness. A road sign proclaimed Golden lay only two miles ahead as they came upon a tractor heading in the opposite direction. The face of the tractor driver was shriveled and parched from decades in the sun. He eyed the agents and gave an almost imperceptible tilt of his hat as the two vehicles passed.

"This is it," said Gardy, stomping on the brakes when an unmarked road popped up on their left.

In a swirl of dust, the rental plodded down another dirt road. Bell couldn't see more than ten yards in front of the vehicle until the dust settled. A cornfield and old barn appeared down the road as though a London fog parted. Something hung suspended above the crop. A scarecrow, Bell thought, but too bulky to be a dummy. Crows set down upon the arms and pecked.

The victim. Bell's stomach flipped.

She leaned forward for a better view and pointed at a truck parked between the barn and field.

"There's the sheriff's vehicle."

Gardy, also staring at the macabre scarecrow, rubbed at his eyes and turned into the driveway. Two more sheriff department trucks stood beside a white farmhouse, and the county coroner's wagon, ebony and hearse-like, sat parallel to the field. The elderly female standing with her arms folded looked out of place beside the sheriff and his three male deputies. Bell wondered if the woman was the county medical examiner. They all turned their eyes toward the agents.

After Gardy killed the engine, the only sounds were the dying breeze and the murmured voices of the deputies. They fell silent when Gardy and Bell stepped out of the SUV.

Bell's eyes traveled between the officers and LaFleur's house. The home was recently painted, quaint and homey on the outside. A long porch welcomed visitors, though Bell figured she could count on one hand the number of people who called on LaFleur. One lonely rocking chair seemed to move on its own when the wind set the corn in motion.

The oldest of the officers, an imposing figure with a wavy spill of gray below his hat, stepped forward.

"Agents Gardy and Bell, I presume. I'm Sheriff Marcel. Thank you for coming so quickly."

Gardy shook his hand.

"Neil Gardy."

Marcel nodded and offered his hand to Bell. His skin felt calloused, grip firm.

"Scarlett Bell."

The twinkle in Marcel's eye told Bell he knew of her.

"A pleasure. These are my deputies: Monteville, Rasovich, and Greene. And our county medical examiner, Dr Nadia Collings."

The three deputies stood back and eyed the agents. Collings approached Bell and greeted her as if anxious to free herself of the old boy network.

"Not to cut the formalities short," said Gardy, peering over the stalks to where the sun plunged toward the horizon. "But we'd better get moving before we lose daylight."

Kemp removed his hat and fidgeted, wiping his forehead with his sleeve.

"Maybe it would be better if you came with us, Agent Gardy, and Agent Bell accompanied Deputy Greene to the farmhouse."

Bell fought the urge to chew her lip. Gardy shook his head.

"If anyone should view the body, it's Agent Bell. Nobody profiles serial killers better."

Marcel raised his hands.

"I'm certain what you say is true, but once you see the body—"

Bell threw her evidence bag over her shoulder.

"Thanks for the concern, Sheriff, but like Agent Gardy said, we're losing the sun."

Marcel paused, searching for a reason to exclude Bell. Then he shrugged and stepped onto the pathway.

"Follow me."

Weeds choked the path and tripped them up. Beneath the stalks, animals skittered away at their approach. Monteville and Rasovich yammered about last night's baseball scores and whether the Yankees had enough pitching to win the series this year. Greene, the youngest of the deputies, followed at their heels, a puppy dog seeking approval.

It took several minutes to fight their way through the rows, the post holding the scarecrow tauntingly poking up from the field. The anticipation magnified the tension, forced Bell to steel herself from the inevitable horror. If she quaked before Marcel, she'd vindicate his belief that she should have remained back at the farmhouse. A woman's place is in the kitchen, she pictured him saying.

Collings gasped before Bell realized they'd broken into the clearing. The pale, naked body of Shelly LaFleur hung in place of the scarecrow. Distended. Face purple, tongue lolling outward like a curious worm. Finally at a loss for words, Monteville and Rasovich studied their shoelaces. Greene placed his hands on his hips and turned back to the stalks as if searching for a lost piece of evidence. For Marcel's part, he removed his hat and performed the sign of the cross.

Bell caught her breath. Something wrapped around LaFleur's forehead. Dried blood streaked the woman's face down her nose and cheeks.

"What the hell is on her head?"

She edged closer.

"It's a crown of thorns," Marcel said, cupping his hand over his mouth.

Gardy met the sheriff's gaze.

"You a religious man, Sheriff?"

The sheriff made a gruff sound in his chest and wandered to the corpse. Bell followed, and Marcel looked despairingly at her.

"I warned you," said Marcel as Bell clicked photographs.

After Bell finished, she removed her phone and dictated notes. Later she'd transcribe the audio to paper and begin the profile of the murderer.

"The unknown subject tied the victim's forearms to the crossbar. The bar must be…six or more feet off the ground. Wouldn't you say, Sheriff?"

The sheriff broke out of his daze.

"Sounds about right." Marcel stood beside the crossbar, careful not to touch the corpse. "Yes, I'd say six feet."

Marcel stammered through his reply, his face peaked. Bell kept the sheriff talking and nudged him back into the investigation.

"So our killer must have been a good sized man."

Marcel nodded and swiped the sweat off his brow.

Gardy craned his head up at LaFleur. Thorns cut into the woman's flesh, her skin punctured and torn.

"What do you think, Bell? Do we have another visionary killer on our hands?"

Marcel scrunched his face.

"Visionary killer?"

"It's possible. Visionary killers," Bell explained for Marcel, "often experience breaks with reality. Some claim to take orders from God or Satan."

"Like the God's Hand killer?"

Bell muttered an affirmative, wishing Marcel hadn't brought up the serial killer who murdered her childhood friend.

"Yes, you could say that."

"Heaven help us if a serial killer like that is running loose in Golden."

The original scarecrow lay beneath the stalks, legs extended into the clearing. The three deputies converged on the scarecrow to search for evidence. Likely to put distance between them and the corpse.

"Don't touch the scarecrow," she said as she circled behind LaFleur.

Rasovich, the oldest of the officers turned his pockmarked face toward Bell.

"How's that?"

"Not without gloves. If you don't have your own, Agent Gardy can provide you with a pair."

Rasovich grumbled under his breath, poking at the scarecrow with his shoe as if it might come to life.

"You gonna cut her down?" Marcel asked, swinging his hat at a pair of crows. "Don't seem right."

Bell clicked another set of pictures before she allowed the deputies to untie the ropes. They all wore gloves now, Rasovich's face twisted in revulsion as he and Monteville lowered the woman.

"How long will it take you to determine cause of death?" Marcel asked Collings.

The doctor knelt beside LaFleur's corpse and studied bruises around the mouth and nose.

"The sooner I get her onto my table, the better," Collings said, waving away a swarm of gnats.

Bell ran her eyes over the field. So many places to hide. She wondered how long the killer watched LaFleur before he struck. No obvious trails existed through the corn, and the loss of daylight didn't help matters.

The first stars flickered as night swooped down on the farm. They were almost back to the farmhouse when Gardy's phone rang.

"Yeah, Harold."

Bell glanced at her partner as he spoke. A phone call from Harold was unusual. Gardy or Bell phoned the BAU technician when they required deep background checks traditional law enforcement databases couldn't provide.

Gardy stopped and held up his hand. The deputies shared worried glances.

"Okay, send it to me now."

Gardy needn't have asked the others to gather around. They'd already formed a circle around the agent. He clicked on the link Harold sent him. While they peered over his shoulder, a photograph of LaFleur appeared on the screen as they'd discovered her. The lighting looked different, harsh and bright with the afternoon sun, but the similarity was enough for Gardy to wheel around and stare into the field.

"Can't you trace the picture?" Marcel asked. "Find who uploaded it, and we'll have our killer."

Harold's voice came over the speaker.

"No go, Gardy. Whoever set this up is good. Damn good. He's bouncing the hosting site through multiple servers. I haven't been able to locate the source."

"Keep working at it, Harold. Call me as soon as you know something."

Bell studied the picture, then shook her head.

"Brazen. He wants the world to see what he did."

"How'd your people find the website in the first place?" Marcel asked, averting his eyes from the picture.

Gardy glanced pensively at the screen.

"He emailed the FBI."

CHAPTER FORTY-NINE

The County Coroner's Office was situated in a long, gray brick building with blue shingles. The office lay twenty-seven miles south of Golden, and the drive took nearly an hour in the dark along rural roads.

Bell's phone rang as they pulled into a parking space near the entryway.

"It's my mother," Bell said.

Gardy cut off the engine.

"You better take it."

"You sure?"

"It's your mother. Of course, you should take it. I'll be inside."

"Thanks a million. I'll be right behind you. This won't take more than a minute."

Bell eyed the phone skeptically. Usually when Tammy Bell called, she made it a point to critique her daughter's career choice. Sighing, Bell answered.

"Everything okay, Mom?"

"Yes, everyone's fine. You aren't on another case, are you?"

"As a matter of fact, I am," Bell said, climbing out of the SUV. She leaned against the door and let the night air

—fresh and cool unlike Virginia in June—tickle her awake. "We flew into New York this afternoon."

Tammy Bell harrumphed.

"It seems the FBI should give you a little vacation time, especially after you caught Jillian's killer and saved the congresswoman's daughter. It's like they don't care about your wellbeing. If you don't stand up for yourself, Scarlett, they'll take advantage of you."

"Was there a reason you called, Mom?" Bell asked, shifting the phone to her other ear.

"Oh, right. Listen, honey, I don't want you to take this the wrong way, but your dad and I have been talking, and it's time we had a change a scenery."

"A change in scenery? What are you talking about?"

Tammy Bell cleared her throat.

"Bealton isn't what it used to be, and we found a beautiful little retirement community outside of Phoenix."

Bell paced the parking lot, the lamplight harsh in her confused state.

"Phoenix. As in Arizona?"

"Well, yes."

"All of this seems rather sudden. What will you do with the house?"

"Sell it, of course. I realize this is a bit of a shock to you, but Dad and I talked about this for years. He's retired. All of our friends have moved on. There's nothing keeping us in Virginia."

Nothing keeping you here except your daughter, Bell said to herself. She regretted the thought. It was selfish, and her parents didn't require her blessing. Bell blew the hair out of her eyes.

"What about Dad's adenoma?"

"Your father is healthy, dear. And they have doctors in Arizona."

"But he'll be starting over with a doctor who doesn't

know his health history. Shouldn't he stick with his current doctor until they're sure the coast is clear?"

"Scarlett, we're approaching sixty. I'm sure you don't want to hear this, but the coast will never be clear in the coming years. Which is exactly why we want to do this. While we still can."

Her back against the lamppost, Bell kicked at a pebble. It made a hollow, lonely sound as it bounced across the parking lot.

"I wish you'd think about this a little longer."

"We didn't make this decision overnight, Scarlett."

Gardy paced inside the entryway. Bell tapped her foot.

"I've gotta go, Mom. Let's talk about this when I get back."

She hated ending the call like this. Her mother's timing couldn't have been worse, and once Tammy Bell made up her mind, there was no changing it. Bell clicked the key fob and locked the rental.

The inside of the County Corner's office was well-lit and vacant. Potted plants did little to break up the monotony of the white, antiseptic hallways. The examining room waited at the end of the corridor. Gardy checked his phone outside the door when Bell approached. He glanced up when she drew near.

"Everything okay?"

Bell shook her head.

"Yes. No. I'm not sure."

"That covers the bases."

Bell stuffed her hands into her pockets.

"Lead the way, Kemosabe."

Dr Collings slipped on a pair of gloves as Bell followed Gardy into the examining room. The medical examiner regarded them over her glasses. The body of Shelly Lafleur lay face down upon a stainless steel table which reflected the spotlight like a noonday sun.

Bell put on a pair of gloves, too, and walked to the table opposite Collings.

"What have you determined, doctor?"

"I estimate the time of death at twenty-four hours ago. Suffocation. Notice the bruise marks around the mouth." Collings lifted LaFleur's chin and opened an eyelid. "The eyes are bloodshot, another indication the killer suffocated the victim. Furthermore, I found carpet fibers under her nails."

Collings reached up and redirected the light as Bell leaned closer. The fibers could have come from LaFleur's own carpet, but Bell doubted it. To be certain, they'd test the fibers against those found inside the farmhouse.

"Anything else?"

"Yes. Look at the victim's back."

Bruising stretched across the width of the victim's back.

"Lividity suggests her back lay against a rough surface when the killer suffocated her," Bell said.

Collings nodded.

"I pulled two splinters off her back."

"What about the pole?" Gardy asked. Bell knew he agreed with her assessment but felt a need to test her. "Couldn't her body banging against the pole when the wind blew cause the lividity?"

"No, the markings suggest a wider surface. Something wooden. The pole was no bigger than my fist, and if you look closely, you can see the faint outline from where the body met the metal. On the other hand, lividity is at least twice as large." Bell bent low and examined the skin for additional trace evidence. "But you bring up an important point. The fact that the pole outline is so faint tells me she was dead for nearly twenty-four hours before he hung her."

"He keeps the bodies before he displays them to the world."

The doctor's attention swung between their volleys. She cocked an eyebrow.

"Bodies. Are you saying he's done this before?"

"Or he will again," said Bell, studying LaFleur's neck for indications the killer choked her. There were none.

"So he's a serial killer."

"Yes, though he recently began killing."

"First that crazy man in Coral Lake last year, now this. It doesn't seem possible."

"Doctor," said Gardy, snapping a photo of the lividity markings. "Have you witnessed any suspicious deaths over the last year near Golden?"

"No, nothing like this."

"It wouldn't necessarily be this extreme. It's possible the killer's violence escalated after he gained a taste for killing."

"No suffocations, no suspicious deaths. And I certainly would have remembered a crown of thorns." Dr Collings twisted her mouth. "There is one thing. This wouldn't come across my desk, but my sister-in-law lives in Golden, and she mentioned several dogs went missing during the last year. For a while, the sheriff's department figured someone stole them for dogfighting." Collings noted the meaningful glance Bell gave Gardy. "What? Do you think the crimes are related?"

"It's worth looking into," said Bell. "Sometimes serial killers start with animals, pets, then work their way to humans."

Collings, a woman who didn't appear easily rattled, shuddered.

"Talk to Sheriff Marcel. He'd know about the missing dogs."

CHAPTER FIFTY

Eyes burning from lack of sleep, feet dragging, Bell dropped her bag on the motel room bed and fell into a chair. So much for five-star accommodations. The Golden Lion Motel stashed itself on a country route outside of Golden. Eight rooms and a vending machine. A blinking vacancy sign with two letters out. Nothing but darkness in all directions. Bell hadn't heard a car engine since they arrived.

They'd awakened the manager from a deep sleep upon arrival, his feet on the desk, some grainy slasher movie streaming on the computer screen. The FBI badges jostled the manager. He twice dropped the keys—no modern cards at this motel—and botched the forms. Bell wondered if he had anything to hide or if two feds bursting into his office an hour before midnight provided ample intimidation.

For once, she'd won the argument. Gardy grudgingly allowed Bell to have her own room despite the threat of serial killer Logan Wolf stalking her across the country.

Gardy's room neighbored hers, and a locked adjoining door provided access between the two rooms. Bell didn't plan to open that door unless Godzilla came stomping through the L-shaped motel. She brushed the hair out of her eyes, slid off her pants and shoes, and pulled on a pair of gray sweatpants and sneakers, heaven after the pant suit and heels. A moment after she pointed the remote at the television, her phone buzzed. Gardy had returned with dinner, if you could call fast food burgers and fries dinner. She was hungry enough to eat anything, and out in the middle of nowhere, beggars couldn't be choosers.

Gardy spread the food out on a corner table. Bell entered the room, yawned, and put her hand over her mouth.

"Sorry."

"I'm right there with you, Bell. I'll be unconscious a minute after I hit the pillow."

The restaurant had dusted the burgers and fries with an extra heap of salt. Bell wished for a jug of water to wash the food down.

"So," Gardy said as he crumpled the food containers and stuffed them into the bag. "You feel okay being back in the field so soon after God's Hand?"

The line of discussion would lead elsewhere, Bell guessed.

"Better than locking myself in my apartment. I've done enough of that."

Indeed, she'd undergone a prolonged psychological evaluation and spent the better part of a year looking over her shoulder for Logan Wolf. After Wolf abducted her during the God's Hand case, she became convinced he was innocent of his wife's murder. Her suspicion someone set up Wolf only grew after a sniper tried to kill them both on a Virginia hillside.

"Talked to Marcel about the missing dogs."

"And?"

Gardy gave a noncommittal nod.

"He's going back through the reports and checking to see if they cluster."

"He should have one of the deputies phone the families. Try to find a common link."

Gardy palmed a handful of fries and chased it down with soda. He stared at Bell as he chewed. Bell set down her burger.

"What?"

Gardy took another sip of soda. The casual way Gardy leaned back in his chair belied the interrogation in his eyes.

"Weber's ready to close the book on the sniper shooting."

This didn't surprise her. Deputy Director Weber rarely saw eye-to-eye with Bell and went out of his way to make her job difficult. But burying his head in the sand after someone attempted to shoot her rattled Bell.

"Tell me something I don't know. Shocking he failed to identify the shooter."

"Let's not twist this into a conspiracy. See things from his perspective."

"Which is?"

Gardy sighed.

"No shells recovered on the hill, no blood. Without a dead body, what does Weber have to go on?"

"I killed him, Gardy. He wore a pendant."

"Marking him as special ops. Yes, I remember."

"You think I concocted the story?"

"No, but I fail to see why you drove there alone in the first place."

"I told you. Congresswoman San Giovanni received a phone call from a man claiming to be God's Hand. The man said he held her daughter at those coordinates, and if anyone besides me showed up, he'd murder the girl."

Gardy bit the inside of his cheek. Bell's decision broke protocol. Before he could launch into another long-winded critique, she steered the conversation back to

Shelly LaFleur's murder.

"Let's talk about our unknown subject. We know he's a large man because he perched her up as a scarecrow. Impossible to link the missing dogs yet, but he likely started killing animals. Either way—"

"How about we talk about Logan Wolf?"

Caught off guard, Bell sat back in her chair.

"Okay. Anything in particular?"

"Don't play games, Bell. I can't prove anything, but I'm certain you had contact with Wolf on the night you killed God's Hand."

"You're right, you don't have proof."

"There's a three-hour window when no one can vouch for your location, and somehow you left your apartment without Agent Flanagan's knowledge. It's like you fell off the map. Bell, if Wolf attempted to kidnap you again, there's no reason to hide it from me."

"If Wolf kidnapped me, how did I take down God's Hand?"

Gardy picked at a pile of onion rings, the last of the food.

"In the past, he let you go. Like when he abducted you in Kansas with that insane request."

"He wanted me to profile his wife's killer."

"That's a laugh. You could have held up a mirror."

Gardy turned the box of onion rings toward Bell. She shook her head. As she absently tore at her napkin, he leaned forward.

"You actually believe Wolf, don't you?" She lifted her tired eyes to his. He slapped his palm against his forehead. "No, Bell. I've let you go down a hundred dangerous roads in the past because I trusted your judgment, but not this time."

Here we go again. First Marcel wanted to hide the murder scene from Bell as if she were too brittle to handle the gore. Now Gardy discredited her judgment.

"Don't play parent with me, Gardy."

"I'm the senior agent on this investigation."

"There's no reason to pull rank, and Wolf has nothing to do with this case."

"Strange how you defend him. I'd almost believe you've come to trust the man. Logan Wolf is a master of manipulation and a liar. And a serial killer, in case you've forgotten."

"Wolf doesn't fit the killer's profile."

Gardy laughed and tossed a crumpled napkin into the trash.

"Oh, this should be good."

"You can't explain why he murdered his wife and switched to killing men. Can you?"

"Gee, I don't know. Because he's a psycho, and that's what psychos do?"

"Stop oversimplifying. If this was anyone except Wolf, you'd question the profile."

"But I *know* Wolf. If there's anyone capable of pulling the wool over your eyes, it's him. He concealed his darkness for years. None of us had a clue. You think it doesn't tear me apart that I worked beside the man and never recognized how dangerous he is? Stop the bullshit. Why are you protecting him?"

"I'm not protecting anyone, but I'm open-minded enough to consider the possibility someone set Wolf up."

"Why would someone set up Logan Wolf?"

"Wolf was in line to become Deputy Director. Maybe somebody wanted him out of the way."

Gardy leaned his head back and laughed.

"You can't be serious. Are you suggesting Don Weber murdered Renee Wolf, planted evidence, and masterminded an agency-wide conspiracy because he wanted the promotion?"

Bell took a deep breath to keep from screaming. Gardy wiped his hands and tossed the last of the food into the trash.

"Listen to what you're saying, Bell. Don Weber doesn't get his nails dirty unless he's picking a golf ball out of the sand at Eastwood Pines. I might despise the guy, but this is the last man on the planet who'd slit a woman's throat and place a sack over her head. He doesn't do the dirty work."

"What if he outsourced?"

Gardy pounded the table. Bell jumped.

"This isn't an X-Files conspiracy. Go around claiming one of the most powerful men in the FBI is a murderer, and you'll end up with a lot worse than a pink slip. Logan Wolf isn't some reclamation project. He's a cold-blooded killer. The next time he comes for you, you won't be so lucky. Don't trust him, Bell."

"That's it," Bell said, standing up and shoving her chair back. "This isn't you, Gardy. You're tired, I'm tired. I'm taking a walk, then I'm heading to bed."

"A walk? You think that's safe?"

"I'm an FBI agent, and I'm packing a Glock."

"This discussion isn't over."

"It is for tonight."

Gardy leaped from his chair when she grabbed the doorknob.

"Come on, Bell." She halted as he ran his hand through his hair. "Look, I'm sorry. Don't leave angry. You need to understand I'm responsible for your safety."

"Don't worry about me, Gardy. I can handle myself. I'd hate for you to get in trouble with the boss if I broke a nail or caught a chill." She glanced around the room and sniffed. "And in here, that wouldn't be difficult."

Bell slammed the door on her way out. Another sleepless night awaited her.

CHAPTER FIFTY-ONE

Running at the break of dawn often left Clarissa Scott exhausted during the school day, but she had to run now or she'd find an excuse not to exercise after work. Her sandy brown hair tied in a ponytail, Scott jogged out of her house a little after five o'clock, the sun little more than a promise below the hills as stars melted into cobalt blues. From the center of the village, she could see the brick facade of the Golden central school looming over the homes. A little after eight, she'd have a homeroom of fourteen third-graders chattering about video games. The seven-hour day of teaching concluded with bus duty at three. By the time she walked home, her feet would be sore, voice hoarse, and her head achy. Running would be the last thing on her mind.

Clarissa's Nikes slapped the sidewalk as she passed the general store and turned the corner toward Monument Park. Fog concealed the park, the skeletal tops of the slide and swing set poking out of the mist. In any other town, she'd have passed a neighbor or waved to someone driving for an early morning coffee. Not in Golden. With barely enough residents to justify the outdated school and the dozen or so Ma and Pa stores, half of which closed years ago, Clarissa was more likely to run past a deer or raccoon than another human.

Yet there was another person in the fog. Idling in a van outside the park. In another minute, she'd jog past the vehicle, a long, white van with black lettering etched in cursive across the doors. A landscaping van, she thought, though it was impossible to read from this distance. For now, the van rumbled curbside in a low growl, agitating the mist.

Uneasy, Clarissa crossed the street to run down the opposite sidewalk. News around town claimed someone murdered a farmer on the outskirts of Golden. The sheriff's department provided sketchy details, doing their best to keep the Syracuse and Watertown media at bay, yet rumors swirled around a ritualistic killing and a potential serial killer loose in the countryside. Clarissa believed neither rumor and chalked them up to inebriated banter over beers at Steven's Pub. But logic didn't prevent her heart from quickening when the van's brake lights flared like angry eyes in the fog. Like demon eyes.

A line of old two-story homes bordered the sidewalk, windows dark, no evidence of life inside. She tripped on a rolled newspaper haphazardly tossed across the sidewalk and fell down on all fours, certain she'd injured her ankle. Wincing, she slid her hand across her knees and felt blood. Great. This is what she got for running blind. But it was the shearing pain in her ankle that shocked her, and as she lay clutching her leg, moaning with the crumbling sidewalk digging into her side, the fear she'd injured herself and couldn't struggle back to the center of town sent her into a panic.

She wasn't aware the van sat across the road until a door clicked open. Then the metallic whirl of a sliding door.

Footsteps clonked the pavement. Coming closer.

Clarissa pushed herself up, legs trembling while she braced her arm against a tree.

Then a loud slap against the macadam as the driver

unloaded a heavy bag and tossed it down. Then another. At least she thought they were bags and not dead bodies. Next, he dragged the bags…or bodies…over the curb and toward the shadows of the baseball dugout. She pictured a bloody corpse, the man gripping his prey by the hair. Dragging his quarry into the gloom.

She edged back from the curb and threw a glance over her shoulder at the porch steps. If the man came after her, she'd clamber up the stairs and pound on the door.

It was quiet now, no indication of where the man hid in the fog.

"Hello? Someone there?"

His voice came from the park near the dugout. He couldn't see her, but maybe he discerned her sneakers scraping the pavement when she crept toward the steps.

He lumbered in heavy work boots out of the park, swished through the grass. Heading right for her.

The warped stairs squealed and gave her away when she stepped down. He came faster now, footfalls thumping against the street and zeroing in on her.

But as his silhouette materialized in the fog, a hand clutched her mouth from behind. She screamed into the palm, smelling sweat and an earthy scent. A forearm snaked around her neck and squeezed, her sneakers sliding uselessly against the wood slats as the figure pulled her back from the stairs and behind a shrub.

The last thing she heard was a door slam before the van pulled off the curb. She lost consciousness as the first ray from the sun sliced a hole in the mist.

CHAPTER FIFTY-TWO

The sheriff phoned Gardy a few minutes before noon. Paging through the case notes in the rental parked outside LaFleur's farmhouse, Bell looked up when Gardy's voice altered from casual to concerned.

"How long has she been missing?"

A pause.

Bell mouthed, "What's happening?"

Gardy waved her question away and swung the phone to his opposite ear as he engaged the engine. He activated the GPS and pulled up a map of Golden, just a few lines converging on a small grid of streets in the center of town.

"Four hours isn't a long time, Sheriff…uh-huh…right. Okay, we'll meet you outside the house in ten minutes."

Gardy jammed the phone into his pocket and reversed the vehicle. The tires kicked up a storm of dust as he executed a hurried three-point turn, then they hurtled down the dirt road toward Golden.

"You plan to tell me what's up, or am I still persona non grata?"

Hands clasped to the wheel, Gardy glanced across the seat.

"That was Marcel. A third-grade teacher, Clarissa Scott, didn't show up for school today, and she isn't answering her door."

Bell did the math in her head.

"They declared her missing after four hours?"

"That was my reaction, but the school insists she's the last person to skip out on her kids. And with a killer roaming the area..."

"They're not taking any chances. Okay, got it."

The brief exchange represented the breadth of their conversation since meeting outside the motel at eight. Gardy offered a curt nod before refocusing on the road, a not-so-subtle hint the small talk had run its course. The remainder of the trip, Gardy remained aloof, his jaw set in an irritated clench.

"Here we are," he said before slamming the shifter into park. He exited the vehicle without another word.

Bell sighed and gathered her bag. The rental stood outside a red ranch house with a brick walkway to the door and a pot of flowers beneath the mailbox. A wooden sign hanging above the door offered welcome, though Bell wondered how many visitors Scott received in such a small village.

Sheriff Marcel touched the brim of his hat as Bell approached. She didn't know how to take the gesture. Normally it would have seemed polite, a measure of respect for another law enforcement officer, but coming from Marcel the gesture felt hackneyed and trite, a nod a man reserved for his mother.

After Marcel briefed the agents, Gardy decided they should split, Bell canvassing the neighborhood with one of the deputies, Gardy heading back to the sheriff's office to coordinate with Harold at the BAU. Craving a break from Gardy, Bell agreed. Until Marcel, himself, opted to partner with her.

The sheriff wore a grave expression as they knocked

on doors, barely glancing in Bell's direction as he led the way. An elderly man two doors from Scott's home mentioned the teacher liked to run before school.

"Did you see Ms Scott this morning?" Marcel asked.

The man brushed at his white mustache.

"Yes, but it's not like I spy on my neighbors. She's a jogger, that one. Likes to run through the village and circle back. She's usually dressed and headed out the door by seven, but not today. Made me wonder what happened to her."

For a man who didn't spy on his neighbors, he seemed to know Scott's schedule down to the minute.

"Did you call anyone when she didn't return?"

"I don't poke my nose into people's business."

"Okay. Any idea where she likes to run?"

"Down to Monument Park. Seems dangerous for a woman to be out on her own like that before the sun rises, but I don't pry."

The other neighbors told similar stories. Clarissa Scott seemed like a nice enough lady, someone to exchange pleasantries with now-and-then, but nobody knew her. The Golden townsfolk were old-timers, born and raised in this little village. Scott was an outsider, and that's all she'd ever be to them.

Marcel's truck puffed sunbaked heat when they climbed inside. Bell wished the sheriff would roll the windows down. Instead, he set the temperature control at 72. Predictably, it took ages for the air conditioner to kick in. He pointed the truck toward the village center while Bell gazed out the window, picturing the most likely route Scott took each morning. The misshapen sidewalk flexed and ramped, repaving long overdue, but it wasn't a problem for an experienced runner. Behind them, a county route meandered into the wilderness. Bell, who liked to run along the beach outside her Chesapeake Bay apartment, figured she'd jog the county route as a change of pace on the weekend, but Scott would want to stay close to home weekdays so she wasn't late for school.

"Turn here," Bell said when they reached the corner.

"But the stores are in the other direction."

"And they wouldn't be open at the break of dawn. Besides, she wants scenery when she runs, and abandoned storefronts don't fit the bill."

Marcel thought for a second, nodded, and wheeled the truck to the right.

"Now where?"

Leaning forward, sensing Scott's trail, Bell scanned the possible routes. The way ahead cut between a scattering of ramshackle homes. A baseball field lay to the left—Monument Park, she guessed—and a few well-constructed old homes stood across the street.

"Toward the park."

She opted against explaining her sixth sense for tracking victims and murderers, figuring Marcel would respect her methods as much as he would an astrologist's or clairvoyant's. He tapped the steering wheel to a country song and watched her from the corner of his eye.

"So you're rather famous, I gather."

Wonderful. Another reader of *The Informer*, the tabloid obsessed with serial killers and the sexy FBI agent who hunts them. Their words, not hers. Lacking an appropriate response, she let the comment hang until he spoke again.

"Caught that monster down in Coral Lake last year. Not sure why Sheriff Lerner went straight to the FBI when he could have called us in to help." Bell clamped her tongue against the roof of her mouth and let him continue. "Then again, Lerner's a politician, not a cop. Guy couldn't catch a raccoon pillaging his garbage."

Bell snorted. She wasn't about to badmouth Lerner in front of the neighboring county's sheriff, but Marcel hit the nail on the head. After she captured and killed Alan Hodge, Lerner stabbed the agents in the back and vied for the spotlight, claiming Gardy and Bell intruded on his investigation.

"Yeah, you're quite the celebrity."

Celebrity rolled off his tongue with distaste.

"Not by my own choice."

"No?" He glanced at her, then back at the road, the baseball field rolling out in summery greens fifty feet ahead. "So all that stuff they wrote about you taking down the God's Hand killer single-handedly were lies?"

Bell clenched her hands.

"I was alone. I took a dangerous man out of the world and made certain an abducted girl made it back to her mother. Not once did I consider my popularity. What would you have done?"

Marcel, an imposing figure were it not for the uniform and kindly face, glared down at her from beneath his hat. Bell recognized the look. It was the same one her father afforded a younger Bell when she'd done wrong.

"I would have waited for backup, not rushed in like Stallone in a bad Rambo sequel. You keep driving with the pedal mashed to the floor, and sooner or later you'll take the car over a cliff."

Bell opened her mouth and shut it. The argument wasn't winnable, not worth the aggravation. Steam blew from her ears as the truck passed the park.

"Stop the truck."

"Here?"

"Pull over."

She'd already forgotten Marcel reading her the riot act when she hopped out of the cab.

"Hold up, Agent Bell," he said, but she jumped the curb and pressed herself against the chain-link fence.

Despite the noon sun, darkness billowed out from the

dugout, the ceiling and walls a shield against the daylight. Her heart raced as she considered the possibilities. Scott jogging past the park and hearing something in the dugout. A cry for help, perhaps. No, the scenario didn't feel right. But she was close. The killer took Scott nearby.

She wheeled around and assessed the surroundings. Marcel waddled up to her, a slight limp she hadn't noticed before.

"Leg cramps up on me when I don't stretch it enough. Don't grow old, Agent Bell." He winced and followed her vision. "Why did we stop?"

"There." She focused on a white streak near the curb. Bending down, she scooped the powder into her hand and sniffed it. "Chalk?"

"Sure. The youth league teams start practice this week, so it's time to reline the fields. Not sure how they do it in Golden, but in my hometown, a crew member drops the bags off first thing in the morning, and they line the fields after the dew dries up."

Bell stood and surveyed the sky.

"Sheriff, did it rain last night?"

"No, ma'am. Rained yesterday morning."

"So it stands to reason someone dropped the bags off this morning, otherwise, the rain would have washed it away yesterday."

"I guess."

"Who makes the deliveries?"

Marcel shrugged.

"Local parks personnel? I can check around."

As though she hadn't heard, Bell followed the curb. A muddy tire track curled into the road and vanished before the corner. She photographed the tracks as Marcel came to her side, itching his head.

"Seems like a wild goose chase, Agent Bell."

"How do you mean?"

"Those tracks could be from anyone. Even if the deliveryman left them, doesn't mean he abducted Clarissa Scott. Heck, we don't even know if she came this way today."

Bell thumbed through the photographs and verified the images were crisp and clear.

"She came this way, Sheriff, like the neighbor said. I would have. Not many route choices in Golden."

"I suppose," Marcel said, unconvinced.

Across the street, the sidewalk crumbled in a deep state of disrepair. A pair of homes stood to either side. Wooden steps climbing up to the entryway of a white two-story drew her attention, though she couldn't say why.

"We're not getting anywhere," Marcel said, removing his hat and fanning his sweat-beaded face. "Best we head over to the school, don't you think?"

No, nobody at the school could tell them where Clarissa Scott disappeared to. But Marcel was insistent, and Bell climbed into the truck, sensing she'd lost Scott's trail.

CHAPTER FIFTY-THREE

As Bell presumed, Golden Central School turned out to be a dead end. Except for the dogged insistence by everyone from the principal down to the janitorial staff that Clarissa Scott loved her job and wouldn't abandon her kids, nobody offered an explanation for her disappearance. By all accounts Scott was a beloved member of the school, though the community treated her like a ghost. Like all teachers, she butted heads with faculty members, and Scott and Mrs Erst, the fourth grade science teacher, had a running dispute over teaching methods, but Erst was sixty-three, a hair over five foot, and walked with a cane. Not a likely suspect to overpower Scott and throw her in the back of a truck.

Bell and Gardy reconvened at the County Sheriff's office, a squat brick-and-mortar building with an American flag flying above a landscaped walkway. Through the break room window, Bell spied the blue shingles of the County Corner's Building. An unwelcome vision of Shelly LaFleur's pallid body came to her. What little information they had to work with suggested the killer kept LaFleur alive for two or three days before he murdered her, and that was based on nebulous accounts by witnesses who claimed they *might* have seen LaFleur in the village square earlier in the week.

Bell and Gardy exchanged only a few words, Gardy grunting instead of replying to Bell's questions. The intolerable conversation ended when a large, forty-something man wearing a gray Golden Parks t-shirt entered the sheriff's department with Deputy Rasovich.

Gardy glanced up.

"That Drake Quentin?"

"Must be. Marcel works fast. I'll give him that."

Earlier, Marcel phoned the parks department and spoke to Quentin, the man who'd delivered a bag of chalk and several wheelbarrow loads of soil to the field that morning. When Marcel mentioned the missing jogger, Quentin went quiet for a moment, then admitted a woman was in the fog.

The square interrogation room stretched a little longer than a postage stamp, and it took considerable effort for Marcel, Bell, and Gardy to wiggle into chairs across the scratched wooden table from Quentin. Quentin fiddled with his hands, eyes darting around the room.

Marcel chose the agents to lead the questioning, and Gardy deferred to Bell who'd become the de facto interrogator during the short time they partnered together. While Marcel leaned back in his chair, glare fixed on Quentin, Bell removed a notepad and began the interview.

"How long have you worked for Golden Parks, Mr Quentin?"

"Since summer of 1996."

Quentin's voice quivered, and he swallowed after answering.

"Summer of 1996? That's a long time. Have you lived in Golden your entire life?"

Bell had already learned the answer from Marcel. She wanted to get Quentin talking, establish trust.

"Yes."

"College?"

"No. Never saw much need for that."

"What made you want to work for the parks? Do you like being around children?"

Quentin's spine straightened as he glanced between the faces across the table.

"Now, hold on. You're trying to make it sound like I'm a sicko or something."

"Not at all, Mr Quentin. I want to understand why you chose your line of work."

He shrugged.

"I grew up playing ball on the town field. Cleanup hitter for Golden High in 1993, seven home runs my senior year." Quentin smiled at the memory. The grin faded when nobody reciprocated from the other side of the table. "Anyhow, I knew a little about how to keep the field in shape. Seemed like an easy job, unloading and loading supplies, drawing the chalk lines on a summer morning with no supervisor breathing down my neck."

"Sounds like relaxing work."

"It is except when you get a rainy summer like last year. Then you can't keep up with the mowing, and the infield turns into a swamp. You have to fill the holes and rake the field so it's smooth. Don't want somebody's kid tearing up his knee on account of your negligence. Besides, Golden is a small town. Everyone knows everyone. We all look out for each other."

Bell smiled.

"Did you deliver supplies to the baseball field on Oak Street early this morning?"

"Yes. Chalk and soil, just like I told the sheriff."

"You told Sheriff Marcel you heard a woman across the street. Is that accurate?"

"I *th*ink so. It sounded like she fell. You need to understand the fog was so damn thick I couldn't find the fence gate."

Bell narrowed her eyes and clicked the pen.

"Let me get this straight. A strong, good-looking man like yourself hears an injured woman, and he doesn't cross the street to help?"

Quentin gave Marcel a pleading stare before turning back to Bell.

"Listen, I'm not positive of anything. There was a sound like someone tripped, and then a voice. I called out to whoever it was. Three, four times, and nobody answered. So someone fell on the sidewalk. What's this about, anyway?"

Marcel handed Bell a staff photograph of Clarissa Scott. She passed it across the table to Quentin. Bell watched for his reaction.

"Do you recognize this woman?"

Quentin picked up the picture, his thumb and forefinger holding the photograph at the corner. He tilted it.

"Yeah, I see her around. She's a runner. Snow or rain, she's out there first thing every morning." Reality dawned on his face. "Wait, you don't think I did anything to her, do you?"

"You're not a suspect," Bell said, though Quentin was their best lead.

"Was it her? The woman in the fog?"

"That's what we're trying to find out. Her name is Clarissa Scott. She teaches third grade."

"Gee, I hope nothing bad happened to her. Hey, this isn't related to that murdered farmer, is it?"

"I never said it was, Mr Quentin. Consider this an information gathering session." Quentin nodded, but Bell noted the way he squirmed in his chair. "Did you know Shelly LaFleur?"

"Sure." Quentin waved his hands when Bell wrote on her notepad. "What I mean is I saw her in town at the general store and every Saturday at market, but I didn't *know her* know her."

"You're an intelligent man, Mr Quentin. Do you own a computer?"

"Why does it matter?"

"Please answer the question."

"Yeah. It's not a crime."

"Do you have a website?"

"I have a Facebook if that's what you mean. Never use it, though. I thought this was about an injured woman?"

Bell glanced at Gardy, and he shook his head. Quentin couldn't tell a server from a broccoli plant.

The man's brow beaded sweat. Marcel dug a handkerchief from his jacket and offered it to Quentin.

"No, I'm fine."

Bell set her pen down.

"You seem nervous, Mr Quentin."

"No…I, uh…well, you'd be nervous if two FBI agents and the county sheriff claimed you'd hurt someone."

"Calm down. Take a deep breath." Bell waited until Quentin composed himself. "Let's talk about Scott and LaFleur. You ever see them together?"

Quentin itched his head.

"Not that I can remember."

"Can you think why anyone would want to hurt them?"

"In Golden? No way. You ask me, the people who killed the farmer lady came from Syracuse. Nothing but criminals in that city."

"So a group of people murdered LaFleur."

Quentin lowered his eyes to the table.

"Could be. I'm not sure. But Golden is full of good people, not murderers."

"Something confuses me. Earlier you claimed everyone in Golden knows each other, and you look out for your neighbors."

"We do."

"Yet I mentioned Shelly LaFleur and Clarissa Scott, one murdered, the other missing and potentially injured, and you don't speak to either. And you care for each other, but if you spot an injured woman across the street, you leave her alone in the fog and drive off."

Wiping his brow on his t-shirt, Quentin sniffled, eyes watery.

"I don't know everyone, okay? Sometimes people move to Golden and they don't run in your circle. Besides, I figured the woman was fine because she left around the back of the house. I figured if she walked, she was okay, or maybe it was the woman who lives there picking up the newspaper. I might have misheard."

Bell pictured the house across from the park.

"The white two-story with the big porch?"

"Yeah…I mean, I guess. I couldn't see."

Bell caught Gardy's eye. He nodded at her to wrap up the interview.

After Quentin departed the station, Gardy pulled Bell aside in the break room.

"You think he's our guy?" Gardy asked, lowering his voice when Deputy Greene sauntered to the coffee pot.

Tempted to lay into Gardy for giving her the cold shoulder all day, Bell took a composing breath.

"No. He's the right size, and I don't buy the bullshit about painting Golden like Mayberry, but he didn't do this."

"How can you be sure?"

"The guy we're looking for is mentally ill. The crown of thorns suggests a religious aspect not unlike God's Hand. Quentin doesn't possess any of those traits."

"That's reasonable."

"It's not a shot in the dark that he heard Scott in the fog. She's the only person in town running the sidewalks at that time of morning."

Greene filled his cup slowly, probably listening in. Gardy folded his arms and leaned against the counter until the junior deputy moved on.

"A little obvious on the eavesdropping," Gardy said, reaching for a Styrofoam cup as he cocked his head at the departing deputy. "Take Marcel back to Oak Street. I'll call Harold and have him check Quentin's background, make sure we didn't miss anything."

Bell cringed at the thought of another investigation with the sheriff. Before she could protest, Gardy grabbed his coffee and left her alone in the break room.

CHAPTER FIFTY-FOUR

The dream dims, and she no longer stands before the children, the classroom vanished.

She blinks several times before the double vision clears. Her neck aches, and swallowing burns the back of her throat.

A confused scene surrounds her. Unlaundered clothing strewn about a tattered rug. Wood-paneled walls, circa 1975. Half-light borne of hazy sunshine through gray, translucent drapes as though day and night vie for supremacy before her.

Footsteps overhead jolt her awake. Clarissa Scott remembers running in the mist. Falling. A man yelling to her before a hand reached out of the darkness and cupped her mouth. Someone abducted her. Who?

Yet no one guards Scott. No ropes bind her. Daylight beckons, urges her to flee while she has the opportunity.

The ceiling groans. She struggles to her feet and crosses the room. Sees a green-tiled hallway. Muddy footprints track to-and-from the room.

Back to the wall, she slides along the hall. Past a kitchen with a dripping faucet. *Plunk, plunk, plunk*, then a louder creak above her head.

She continues down the hall. An empty room stands to the left. The stairway to the second floor climbs straight ahead. To the right, a foyer with an empty coat rack is tucked into the corner.

And a door.

Her heart pounds. It seems too easy.

Scott edges past the coat rack. Freezes when the hangers rock. Fate is on her side when the hangers don't clang together.

Something is wrong with the doorknob. What is out of place? No button. The knob requires a key to unlock.

Frenzied, she yanks on the door. Twists the knob against the locking mechanism. It won't budge. Scott pulls harder as though she can muscle her way to freedom.

A narrow rectangular window accepts a shaft of light. If she breaks the glass, he will hear, and undoubtedly the door won't open from the outside without a key.

Swallowing a sob, she retraces her steps and peeks inside the empty room. This was once a bedroom, she thinks. Scrapes mar the bare wood where someone dragged furniture across the floor. Bars cover the windows.

Again, the ceiling protests under the man's weight. He is at the top of the stairs. Listening for her.

She backtracks to the kitchen and searches for another door.

Now the stairs creak under the weight of a large, strong body. She scurries back to the room she awoke in, a trapped rat, as the footsteps come closer.

Scott searches for something to defend herself with. Considers the lamp but knows it will be ineffective. His shadow grows along the wall before she sees him, and she envisions a nightmare monster shuffling down the hall.

When he turns the corner, she sees he isn't demon or monster, but an ordinary looking man with no discernible facial features except for the eyes, which appear slightly offset, the left socket a fraction higher than the right.

He wears a red flannel shirt, blue jeans tucked into work boots, and a baseball cap over a nest of curly, brown hair. Somehow his normalcy frightens her more than a monster would, for she cannot believe one of her neighbors, a man she might have passed on the street, abducts women. The light catches him in side profile, and she realizes she's seen him before. Where? His facial features and shy mannerisms are familiar. Every time Scott tries to recall, the memory slips through her fingers, lost in a whirlpool between her aching head and pure terror.

Despite his placid appearance, hostile energy surrounds him. Volatility.

"Are you cold?"

She doesn't understand why the man would ask her such a thing until she realizes she's trembling. When she doesn't answer, he kneels before her, studies her the way one would a sick pet. While he glares, she discerns a strange sound in the distance. A constant *whump whump whump* repeating every few seconds. As she recognizes her abductor, she also finds the noise familiar. Attentive to the sound, she almost places it before he speaks and breaks her concentration.

"As I told you, no reason exists for your terror." Her skin creeps with the possibility he'd spoken to her while she slept. Leered over her. "Sin is a badge all of us wear. We're imperfect, flawed. Would you like something to drink? You must be thirsty."

His eyes light as though he'd invited her into his home for tea and cookies.

Scott's voice dies before she can say, "no," and she shakes her head as he glares at her.

Disconnected. That is the impression he gives her. As if two different men breathe behind his eyes. One kindly, the other insane.

Her attention drifts around the room, possibly a den,

as he speaks. So many items look out of place in the den. On the wall is a cross chained to a string of rosary beads. Inconsistent with the wood paneling, a modern lamp with an LED fixture stands in the corner. The chair, couch, and end tables appear mismatched, the furniture cobbled together from garage sales or low-end consignment stores. And a jumbled mess of sticks and twine spill off an end table.

No, not sticks. Prickers. Thorns.

Her eyes widen on the thorns, though she cannot say why. Swallowing, she finds her voice.

"Why did you bring me here?"

He crosses the room to the end table. Hunches over. Runs his hands along the thorns.

"Please, just let me go," she says, crawling into the corner and drawing her knees to her chest. "I won't tell anyone. I swear."

The man doesn't notice or doesn't care, so enraptured is he with the thorns. His gaze moves to Scott, and a shiver ripples through her body.

"It wasn't me she wanted," he goes on as if she hadn't spoken. "I thought it was at the time, but we are all imperfect. Who am I to pretend I am without flaw? Those were different days, though. No cell phones, no Internet. We played outside all day, and when our parents called us in at night, nobody locked their doors. We trusted. Maybe not strangers. You always had to be careful with them. But people we knew..."

Like a phantom, he floats out of the room without finishing his thought. Beyond the wall comes the sound of running water. The clink of a glass set upon the counter.

Her chin falls to her chest. Dark hair unravels and cloaks her face.

She looks down and sees the blood spots in the carpet. Not an arterial spray, but a scattering of droplets crust the fibers together.

Scott screams, and no hero comes to save her.

CHAPTER FIFTY-FIVE

Sheriff Marcel intimated his belief they'd wasted time with Drake Quentin as he escorted Bell back to Golden and along Oak Street.

"Is this one of those *visions* profilers get?"

Bell rubbed at her eyes.

"No visions, Sheriff. Just hunches based on evidence and logical conclusions."

"Evidence," Marcel huffed over a snicker. "We're chasing after rainbows for a pot of gold."

Bell ignored the comment.

"Anything on the missing dogs cases?"

Marcel nodded and rubbed at his chin.

"Now that's something worth pursuing. I sent Rasovich and Monteville out to interview the families again. Five households altogether. Is it the same guy?"

"Wouldn't be the first time a budding murderer cut his teeth with animals. But this isn't an ordinary killer. He's bouncing his website through multiple dark web servers. Taunting us, really."

Marcel's fingers tightened on the wheel.

The baseball field had a fresh look to it when they neared the park, the lines bright and striking against a green only seen during a rainy season, and it had poured for much of the last month.

Greasy black hair, dressed in a navy blue sweat suit, Reginald Schultz opened the door so quickly Bell figured he'd spied them through the window from the moment the big truck pulled curbside.

Marcel flashed his badge.

"Mr Schultz?"

In his mid-sixties, Schultz regarded the badge over his glasses as though he doubted its authenticity.

"Yes? Who wants to know?"

"I'm Sheriff Marcel, and this is Agent Bell with the FBI."

Schultz raised an eyebrow.

"FBI? What's she doing here?"

"Sir," Bell said, sliding her badge into her pocket. "Did you notice a woman outside your apartment between five and six this morning? She may have injured herself."

"Wasn't up that early. How she get injured?"

"We're looking into that. She's a jogger, and it's possible she didn't see the buckled sidewalk with the fog being so thick."

For a moment, Bell felt certain Schultz would spit.

"Been telling the village they need to fix that sidewalk for over ten years, and you think they listen? Someone was bound to get hurt." His eyes narrowed. "You best not be considering a lawsuit. That sidewalk is the village's responsibility. I got a good lawyer."

"Nobody's blaming you, Mr Shultz," Marcel said, waving his hands in appeasement.

"Sure, you say that now, then the woman decides she wants money and the village attorney sends me a notice. I know how this works. Someone's always looking to sue these days. I complained to your office last summer about the damn kids tracking across my yard. Just a matter of time before one of them falls and takes me to court."

"You called our office?"

"That's what I get living across the street from a park. They trudge through with their bats and gloves like my property is the only path to the field. I tell 'em, 'use the damn sidewalk. This ain't a highway.' But they keep coming. Walked through my garden this morning, they did. Right over the lettuce and chard. Damn vagrants."

Bell locked eyes with Marcel. She knew what he was thinking. School was in session this morning. Kids wouldn't head to the park at sunrise.

"Mr Schultz," Bell said. "Could you show us the footprints?"

Schultz grinned.

"Certainly. It's about time you caught those hoodlums."

Bell and Marcel followed as Schultz marched them around the house, past trellised grapevines curling up the side, then to a tilled garden. Various greens grew out of mounds at regular, almost military-perfect spacing.

"See what I mean?" Schultz knelt beside a crushed lettuce plant, lifting its leaves as if he meant to resuscitate the lettuce. "Walked through the garden without a care."

Bell bent to examine the prints. Marcel placed his foot beside the print to compare.

"Awfully big for a kid," Marcel said. "Looks like an adult, if you ask me."

"Nah, it's kids. I watch 'em through the back window. They don't care about nothin' but themselves."

Bell photographed the footprint. A broken line ran parallel through the dirt, and Bell pictured the heel of Scott's sneaker digging through the soil as someone dragged her away.

"That look like he pulled Scott along?"

Marcel glared at the pattern, then shook his head.

"It's possible. That mark could be anything."

Rising, she cupped a hand over her eyes to block out the sun and considered the prints. They arrowed toward a stand of trees.

"Figure out who did this?" Schultz asked Bell, interjecting himself into the investigation.

"What's on the other side of those trees?"

Schultz shrugged.

"Riverside Place and the old corset factory. Nothing else. Don't know what they'd want with an abandoned factory, but you can't figure kids these days."

Marcel opened his wallet and handed his card to Schultz.

"If you remember anything else, don't hesitate to call."

Schultz's eyes widened.

"That's it? I lost half my crop."

He continued to yell as Bell and Marcel stepped through the garden, careful not to tread upon the plants.

Marcel removed his hat and wiped his forehead.

"So your working theory is the unknown subject grabbed Scott, then escaped through Schultz's backyard with the fog as cover and headed toward Riverside."

"It's the only thing we have to go on. Did you just call him an unknown subject?"

Marcel's mouth curled into a smile, the first instance he'd regarded her without animosity today.

"I know a little jargon. Either that or I'm addicted to too many TV shows." A pricker bush blocked the pathway to Riverside. Marcel held the thorns aside for Bell. "What made you want to work for the BAU? A lot of darkness in that line of work."

Bell gave him a guarded look.

"You mean you didn't read *The Informer* articles?"

"Skimmed them. Figured I ought to learn more about Agent Bell after the Coral Lake murders, but I didn't want to wade through the muck to get answers."

Though Bell wished to put the God's Hand memory behind her, she retold the story of the serial killer who murdered her childhood friend and attempted to abduct Bell. By the time she finished, they'd reached the Riverside curb.

Marcel regarded Bell with a tight-lipped grimace, but he didn't reply.

As Schultz told them, an abandoned factory slumbered across the street, half the windows boarded or missing, the black holes like empty eyes peering over a parking lot of broken glass and garbage. Plywood boarded the doors from entry, and the windows were too far off the ground to lift a body through.

"So if someone kidnapped Scott across the street from the park, and that's a big if," Marcel said, hands on hips as he surveyed the street, "he'd need a getaway vehicle. Fog or no fog, you don't drag a screaming woman for a block without someone reporting a commotion."

Bell swiveled around and lined up the path from the garden to the street.

"If he parked along Piper, we should check with the neighbors."

One lone house, a red ranch with black shutters, stood across from the factory.

"You want to do the honors this time?"

Bell led Marcel up the porch steps. She pressed the doorbell, and it rang deep inside the home. After nobody responded, she rang again. Thirty seconds passed in uncomfortable silence, but when Marcel cleared his throat, the muffled thuds of footsteps approached the door.

A balding man with glasses and a llama face answered.

"Help ya?"

Bell read the name on the mailbox.

"Mr Ripple?"

"John Ripple, yes."

"Agent Bell, FBI," she said, removing the badge from her pocket. "And this is Sheriff Marcel."

Ripple stepped onto the porch and shut the door behind him.

"FBI, huh? This have anything to do with that farmer?"

"We're investigating a missing persons report. We have reason to believe she was near the park around sunrise this morning." Ripple crossed his arms and leaned over the rail so he could see the park. "Did you see or hear anyone outside your house?"

"No women, but somebody parked a truck outside the house before dawn."

Bell eyed Marcel, who pulled out a pen.

"Can you describe the truck?"

"Black. A big pickup, 4x4 type. Couldn't tell you the make, though. Nothing I recall seeing before."

"You didn't happen to read the license plate, did you?"

Ripple shook his head.

"No reason to. I thought it was odd, someone parking outside the house so early, but I assumed it was one of the park crews."

"And you didn't see the driver?"

"Well, no. I noticed the truck when I got up to make my coffee. By the time I showered, it had gone."

"And what time was that?" Marcel said, glancing between Ripple and his notepad.

"Six, six-thirty. The driver must have driven off while I was in the shower. I would have heard an engine that size, otherwise."

Marcel handed out another card, but Bell didn't expect Ripple to call. On the way back to the sheriff's truck, Marcel kept shooting Bell glances. At first, she surmised

Marcel was trawling for another argument, but the sheriff seemed troubled. Even haunted.

"Something on your mind?" Bell asked.

Marcel looked sheepishly at the ground.

"My apologies. It's just that..."

"What?"

"You remind me of someone."

Paging through the interview notes as she walked, Bell giggled.

"You work with a lot of FBI agents who chase gold at the end of rainbows?"

Marcel fumbled through his pockets for the keys.

"Not exactly."

"So who?"

He stopped at the truck, keys in hand, weighing whether he should reply or shut his mouth and unlock the door.

"Juliette Marcel. She was my sister."

The key fob unlocked the doors, and Bell climbed into the passenger seat. *Was* my sister. She chewed on the thought as the sheriff slid behind the wheel, the truck shaking under his girth. The engine rumbled. Marcel pointed them toward the county road which took them to the office.

He remained quiet for many minutes. No music. Only the pop and squawk of the police radio and the rolling hum of the tires. The silence almost made her think wistfully of conversations with Gardy. Almost. For the time being, she celebrated the silence and studied the endless patchwork of forest and meadow sweeping past the window.

When he broke the quiet, she jolted.

"She was only thirty-two." The words pulled her attention. She realized he spoke of his sister. "Good cop. Better than me, that's for sure. Said I was her inspiration." He chuckled without mirth and returned his concentration to the road. "She'd stationed in Rochester back then. Wanted to work her way back home, get away from the city, but I told her to hang in there. Make her mark, do things her way."

The silence returned. Marcel wrestled with a memory.

"A call came into the office. Domestic dispute in a bad part of town. They found the front door open, moths buzzing around the porch light. Juliette knocked. No one answered. Her partner was a rookie, green as algae after a flood. Juliette went in first. They always tell you the first thing you do…the very first thing…is you clear the corner. Your most vulnerable point is the one you can't see."

His mouth opened and clamped shut. The road pulled them forward, a double yellow line slicing past the truck as the first residences announced the next town.

"I'm sorry," Bell said as the station came into view.

Rather than replying, Marcel hit the gas and shot through a yellow light. Bell felt surprised to find herself trembling with pent up emotion when Marcel brought them to a stop beside his deputies' trucks.

She grabbed the door handle but sensed his stare.

"Always check the corners, Agent Bell."

CHAPTER FIFTY-SIX

Bell stepped out of the motel room and into the night. She wondered where Clarissa Scott was and if the woman had seen the land drag the sun down. If she was still alive. No, Bell wouldn't do that to herself. Time remained to rescue the teacher.

Since Gardy's blowup, Bell had felt alone on this case. Outside of a professional capacity, Gardy still wouldn't talk to her, and he'd remained stoic on the drive back to the hotel. Usually he invited her over to eat after work. Tonight, he took his sandwich and she hers, and they entered separate rooms without a word.

The peepers sang loud outside the motel. A silver mist crawled across the meadow and encroached on the road. She glanced around for signs of civilization beyond the motel lot and found none. Walking in the dark seemed like a worse idea by the minute, but she needed to clear her head.

And there was something she'd put off for too long.

After ensuring Gardy wasn't peeking through his curtains, Bell inserted the key and crept into her room. She snatched the holster and gun, concealing both beneath an over-sized sweatshirt. Digging through her bag, she closed her hand over the hidden phone. A moment of paranoia touched her like cold, dead hands in a graveyard. She spun around to an empty room, the curtains cloaking the window, night creeping around the edges.

"You're a little old to believe in monsters," she said to the face in the grimy mirror.

Bell pocketed the phone, one of three burners Logan Wolf had dropped on her kitchen table a week ago—she had no idea how he'd broken into the apartment, for she returned to find the door bolted as she'd left it—and opened the door with one anxious hand touching the Glock through her sweatshirt.

The parking lot appeared darker than it had moments before. She edged the door shut, careful it didn't click and alert Gardy. Then she turned the corner and jogged across the blacktop, casting glances over her shoulder until certain no one followed.

The phone reception improved near the road. A stand of trees provided cover. As she waded through a dew-laden meadow, a motel room door shut behind her. Instinctively, she pulled the gun from her holster and aimed it into the mist. Nobody followed. Probably just Gardy making a run for the vending machine. Feeling stupid, she holstered her weapon and dialed the number Wolf had programmed into the phone. She didn't take note of the number, knowing it was pointless to track him. The serial killer cycled through burners and would dispose of his phone.

The phone rang four times. Bell wondered if Wolf was asleep. Did fugitive murderers sleep? On the fifth ring, the call connected.

Wolf didn't say hello. Quiet followed through the speaker.

"Wolf? You there?"

No reply. Bell cursed the cheap phone. Then the eerie, musical voice of Logan Wolf, a Chopin piece played in a dark and somber key, spoke to her.

"What a pleasant surprise, Agent Bell. I see you located my gifts without issue."

"Get one thing straight, Wolf. You need permission to enter my home."

"Am I a vampire, Scarlett?"

"Don't test me tonight. I'm not in the mood."

Wolf snickered. She'd phoned him because, unlike Gardy, Wolf knew the hillside sniper was real and had taken a bullet in the shoulder the night Bell killed God's Hand. With Weber burying the truth, the serial killer became an unfortunate ally. But what good was Wolf if he played games with her?

"Cheap motel beds and fast food will do that to a body."

Bell lowered the phone and drew herself into the shadows. The silhouette of a silo grew out of the distant horizon, the sky sprinkled with stars.

"Are you following me? Show yourself."

"Easy, Scarlett. Just an elementary deduction. The news claims a murderer is loose in the little village of Golden. What a shame. Northern New York is quite pleasant this time of year. I see only one motel listing in Golden, and it isn't exactly the Four Seasons. Enjoying yourself?"

Wolf followed serial killer activity. One could come to the obvious conclusion Bell and Gardy were in Golden, but Wolf's guess was too close for comfort. Agitated by the wind, mist swirled through the tall grass and ascended like an angry ghost.

"I'll help you, Scarlett, if you allow. I'm following the case closely."

"All right, I'll play. What do you know about the killer?"

Wolf made a clicking sound with his tongue.

"Only what the newspapers report."

"You're bullshitting me."

"A better question: what have *you* ascertained about the Golden murderer, Scarlett? After all, it's up to you to catch him."

Bell hesitated, unsure how much she wanted to tell Wolf.

"Go on, Agent Bell. I won't bite."

The fog swirled around her knees as she glanced back at the motel. No Gardy, no prying eyes.

"A crown of thorns. What's the significance?"

A moment of silence, then…

"He adorns his victims with a crown of thorns? Intriguing."

"He might place the crown post mortem."

"Jesus's enemies placed the crown upon his head to mock him. Our killer has religious issues, but thorns signify many things."

"Sin and sorrow?"

"Very good. You've done your homework."

"Significant for the victim or the killer?"

"Without more information I cannot say. Tell me, Scarlett. How does he display the bodies?"

Display the bodies. Wolf knew more than he let on.

"He perched her in a cornfield in place of the scarecrow."

Wolf hissed. In the background, Bell heard another noise. Wind?

"Arms outstretched as though hung upon a cross?"

"Yes."

"Left for the crows to pick her eyes clean. Our killer's deep-seated anger bonds with religion."

"Like God's Hand."

"I doubt our man believes himself an avenging angel, Scarlett. No, he's more complex than that. You'll have to dig deeper. Displaying the body tells me he's making a statement. Needs attention."

Bell slumped against a tree and leaned her back against the trunk, her head submerged beneath the mist.

"He sent a photograph of the victim to the FBI."

"As you discovered her?"

"Yes."

"Bold. I wouldn't suppose Harold tracked the email."

"This guy's smart. He loaded the photo onto a website and bounced it through multiple servers. We're waiting for him to make a mistake, but I don't think we'll catch him that way."

"No, you won't. Understand why he displays the bodies as he does and you'll find your killer." A pause. "Scarlett, I could join you on this investigation. Our two minds together…he wouldn't stand a chance."

"I have a partner, Wolf."

"Do you now?"

The motel's outline disappeared and reappeared in the swirling mist. She couldn't see Gardy's room, only the glow of the vending machine outside his door.

"How could you know Gardy and I aren't on the same page? You're following me, dammit."

"Neil Gardy lacks your imagination and talent, Scarlett. He'll never live up to you."

"He's the senior agent."

"In name only. Tell me, Scarlett. When you broke the neck of Alan Hodge, where was Gardy? Wrapped around a tree, I believe."

Bell swallowed. There was an accident. But that information never made it to the press.

"And when you gunned down William Meeks in California, did you not save your partner's life in the process?"

"He took a bullet for me."

"Neil Gardy takes a bullet for no one. Carelessness got him shot. God's Hand. William Schuler. All your heroism. It was I who pulled Gardy to safety after Schuler knocked him unconscious. Should have left him to die. It would be one less anchor around your neck."

Biting off a sob, she dried her eyes.

"Don't say that."

"But it's true. The world would be a much simpler place if we spoke the truth more often."

"Gardy's a good man."

"Is he, Scarlett? Are you certain no skeletons lurk in Neil Gardy's closet? If you venture inside his empty apartment in the dead of night, trawl through his belongings and see the wolf without its sheepskin, you might not like what you find."

"Sure you're not talking about yourself?"

A dry cackle.

"If you wish to find the fair teacher alive, you'll accept my aid."

"How did you…we haven't released…"

"I'm coming, Scarlett. See you soon."

CHAPTER FIFTY-SEVEN

Night is at the window when an odd discomfort pulls Clarissa Scott awake.

She droops over. Bindings catch her before she falls. Ropes tied around her chest and legs clasped at the ankles, arms splayed to either side with her wrists pinned to a rough, scratchy surface. Wood shaped into an X. No, not an X, but a cross. The texture is rough through the bare skin of her back.

He stripped her. Left her naked except for her bra and underwear.

She yelps and wiggles her feet. Searches the gloom for the kidnapper and sees a video camera on a tripod aimed at her from across the room, a blinking red light above the lens signaling the camera is running. A cable snakes from the camera into a daisy chain of electronic equipment, one box she identifies as a computer. Drives whirl and grind as the machinery renders her in digital bits. And she thinks, where does the video go? Corrupt voyeurs enraptured by torture pollute the Internet. Now she's the star of their sick show.

Then she suddenly remembers where she'd seen the man before. Several months ago a man came to the school to fix her computer. Something about the network not connecting properly. He'd spent an hour inside the classroom, just the two of them, the children downstairs for physical education. When she tried to converse with the man, he averted his eyes and gave timid, one-word answers as he concentrated on the task at hand. Afterward, he left with barely a word, and that was the last she saw of him, though the computer worked liked new and no longer slogged through websites.

Did he target her? How long has he planned this?

Wind rattles the windows. She yanks at the bindings, but they hold her tight. In the dead of night, the *whump whump whump* sound repeats. Something she's heard a hundred times without giving it a second thought. Her mind races too fast to zero in on the source of the noise.

Scott gasps. She hadn't seen the man beside the window until now. He staggers out of the shadows and stands beside the camera.

"Please, whatever you want. I'll give you money. Don't hurt me."

Pleading will get her nowhere. Instinctively she knows this, yet she hopes she can appeal to him on a basal level, sway him to keep her alive long enough until…

Until what? Nobody knows she's here, wherever here is.

"I know you," she says, sniffling. Tears clog her eyes, turn the room blurry. "Golden Central School. You worked on my computer."

He studies her with increased curiosity, though he doesn't reply. Now and again he peers through the camera's viewfinder, makes certain the equipment is working, the focus razor-sharp.

"You were polite, I remember. Nice. You wouldn't hurt someone."

The lens rotates. Zooming in.

"Why are you doing this? I was kind to you."

He turns the lens to the wall. The floor shakes as he storms at her. She flinches, unable to move. When the maniac stops, they stand nose to nose, the man's breath puffing against her face.

"Now the world will watch you pay for what you did to me."

He reaches into the dark and yanks something sharp and spindly off the table. Thrusts it toward her face as she turns her head and clamps her eyes shut.

Cautiously she opens them. Recognizes the thorns, now shaped into a circle and woven upon one another. A crown, she thinks with a shudder.

He places the crown upon her head. Thorns yank her hair from the roots, scrape her scalp, dig into the thin layer of flesh. She moans, not wanting to give him the satisfaction of watching her cry. Warmth trickles down her cheeks and rides the curve of her scalp to her neck.

Unsatisfied with the fit, he jiggles the crown and sets it to his liking. Each twitch tears her head and invokes fresh pain. Pleased, he backs toward the camera, never pulling his eyes away.

He drops to a knee and types a string of characters. The computer responds with a green button prompt upon the screen. Moving the mouse, he clicks the button, and an adjacent monitor fires up with a live picture of Scott suspended and bleeding.

"They can see you now."

The maniac and camera divides Scott's attention, both leering at her out of the gloom. The ropes dig her wrists. Burn.

As she fights, the crown plunges down her tilted head and draws bloody streamers.

CHAPTER FIFTY-EIGHT

In her dream, Bell ran through a black forest of nightmare limbs, the branches claws that tore clothes and raked her eyes. A man pursued her through the dark. Her semi-conscious mind, the lone rational voice which understood this was just a nightmare, worried she'd never rid her dreams of God's Hand. He closed the distance with each step, and in the strange way of dreams, she realized her pursuer was not God's Hand but a new threat. One she hadn't considered.

I see you, Scarlett, the voice whispered against the back of her neck. But when she twisted her head around, the forest path was clear.

She broke into a meadow of switch grass and blue moonlight. The desolation exposed her.

Weaponless, Bell spun in a circle. The pursuing footsteps no longer followed through the forest, yet she sensed eyes watching her.

She took one step before the gunshot exploded down from the heavens and clipped her shoulder. The momentum twisted her around with a spurt of blood. She dropped to one knee, panting, scanning the night for the shooter.

She ducked below the second shot and felt the bullet

singe her hair. The shots came in rapid succession, forcing her face down against the muddy earth. The noise grew into thunder.

BOOM BOOM BOOM

She sprang awake with a gasp as the explosions followed her out of her dream. Reaching through the dark for the Glock, she checked the cartridge and aimed it toward the source of the sound. Logan Wolf? Her heart was a trip hammer through her chest and lungs.

"Bell, it's me. Open up."

"Gardy?"

Bell exhaled and lowered the gun. Her hand trembled as she flicked the table lamp on. She rubbed her eyes against the harsh light assailing her.

"Bell, open the door."

"I'm coming," she said, sliding into her sweatpants.

She padded across the room. Before she opened the door, she checked the peephole and saw Gardy standing in the walkway, his laptop cradled under one arm, his eyes scanning the parking lot.

She unlatched the bolt and let him inside.

"Why were you pounding so loud? You'll wake the dead," she said, checking the parking lot. Theirs was the only vehicle in the lot.

"I knocked for five minutes. You didn't hear?"

"No…I mean, I might have," she stuttered, remembering the nightmare gunshots.

"What?"

"Never mind."

"It doesn't matter. You need to see this."

Gardy swept the empty food wrappers off the table and laid the laptop in the center. She circled around to Gardy's side while he typed his password.

A cluttered room of light and shadow appeared on the screen. Bell couldn't take her eyes off the woman, head slumped over as though dead, arms stretched to either side. Camera lights pulled the woman's form out of the dark.

"Harold has been running scans all night," Gardy said, stretching the video window so it filled the monitor. "He followed a suspicious link to this site. Bell, there are over two thousand people watching this."

A counter on the bottom of the screen updated as viewers joined and departed the morbid presentation. With the picture zoomed in, Bell discerned a shallow rise and fall from the woman's chest. Stripped and degraded, but still alive.

"That has to be Clarissa Scott. She's suspended the way we found Shelly LaFleur."

"Like a scarecrow."

"I don't think he sees her as a scarecrow."

A crown of thorns angled from the top of Scott's head to her eyebrow. Dark streamers followed the thorns across the woman's face. They barely glistened in the light, suggesting the blood had dried.

"Why can't Harold find the source?" Bell asked, though she knew why. The killer covered his digital tracks.

"If there's a way, he'll find her. In the meantime—"

"There is no meantime, dammit. She's dying." Bell grasped the laptop and spun it toward her. She dropped to her knees and brought her face closer to the screen. "Is there sound?"

"It's on."

She clicked the controls and amplified the volume to its maximum setting. If the killer was inside the room with Scott, he remained silent.

Scott suddenly hitched. Bell jumped at the noise.

"Can you enhance the sound?"

"Not from here. They're working on it at headquarters. If they get anything, Harold will send us the audio files."

The likelihood the video originated within a ten-mile radius of Golden drove Bell to the edge of insanity. So close, yet he hid in plain sight. Zooming the video to double size, she studied the room, searching for anything that hinted at the killer's location.

"Why is it we can trace a goddamn phone call but we can't track a lunatic with a computer?"

She trembled with helpless fury. Gardy lowered the screen and touched her shoulder.

"We'll find her, Bell. I promise. Right now I need you to be calm. Focus on what we can control."

It was the first time he'd been civil to her since the Logan Wolf argument. She harbored pent up anger, yet the shared crisis and common goal of bringing Clarissa Scott home alive reunited them, if only for a moment.

The problem was Bell couldn't control anything. The killer taunted them, laughed in their faces.

Gardy opened the laptop, pausing until certain Bell wouldn't launch into another tirade. Placing her hands on her hips, Bell walked in a circle from the bed to the table, then back again. Perhaps they could trace the killer by bandwidth usage. Unlikely. Kids playing shooter games taxed the Internet more than one guy with a video stream.

Gardy lifted the phone to his ear when a familiar noise drew Bell's attention. It might have come from the hard drive as Gardy's laptop churned, except it grew and diminished as she played with the volume controls.

"Hold on for a second," she said, and Gardy clicked off the call and lowered his phone. "What's that noise?"

"I don't hear anything."

"It repeats in waves. Listen."

She raised the volume to maximum amplitude and stood back. There it was, plain as day. *Whump whump*

whump.

Gardy squinted and stroked his thumb across his chin.

"Weird. Maybe we're hearing the computer or servers."

"I don't think so."

She continued to listen, and she could see Gardy's curiosity growing.

"I swear that sounds familiar," he said, and she nodded. "Keep listening. I'll call the office and have them zero in on the pattern."

Bell knelt before the table and stared at the screen. Clarissa Scott's life hung by a thread. But for how much longer?

CHAPTER FIFTY-NINE

The briefing room inside the County Sheriff's Department was smaller than the break room. A running joke around the office stated you could fit two chairs and a card table into the room, but if you added the cards, you'd break the fire code.

Barely enough space existed for the deputies. A table outside the room featured coffee and three boxes of donuts. Deputies Rasovich and Monteville each grabbed a pair of glazed donuts, while Greene licked frosting off his fingers and sipped coffee, staying out of the way of the others.

Inside the briefing room, an LCD screen hanging over the podium simulcasted the video coming into Gardy's laptop. The feed died once per hour when the video switched to a different home on the dark web. Harold's skill allowed him to locate the new site within fifteen minutes, but to do so he needed to follow the path of detritus left behind by voyeurs on message boards. When he didn't find it, an anonymous email arrived, mocking him with a direct link.

Clarissa Scott hung limp on the video screen, a scarecrow close to death throes, gaunt ribs poking out below a spill of black hair. The crown crept over one eye, and Bell worried Scott would jolt awake and expose her eye to one of the wicked thorns. For now, the woman's chest swelled and receded, proof Scott still lived. Sheriff Marcel conferred with Gardy off to the side. They both gave Bell furtive glances as they spoke. She tried to ignore them.

When Marcel called his deputies into the room—they all carried coffee now, Rasovich's face sunken as though he'd gone on a bender last night—they shuffled inside with concerted effort not to look at the video. Greene pulled his gaze away, horrified and embarrassed, and sat with his head down and his hands clasped between his knees.

"You're all aware of the situation," Marcel said, adjusting the podium's microphone upward. "So I won't waste any time. The only goal is to find Clarissa Scott alive, so I'll turn it over to Agent Bell with the FBI's Behavioral Analysis Unit."

The deputies whispered as Bell took her place behind the podium. A step stool lay at her feet, but she chose to lower the microphone with her head poking over the podium.

"Good morning. The BAU lab obtained the link to a private video feed after midnight this morning. We have verified the woman in the picture is Clarissa Scott." Murmurs rippled through the room. Marcel drove his hands down to silence the room. Bell finished her introduction before transitioning to the profile. "The unknown subject is a large man. He'd need to be to prop Shelly LaFleur on the scarecrow post. The killer is intelligent, possibly a genius with computers, but in public he's a ghost. He goes out of his way to avoid conversation, keeps his head down, eyes on the floor. Based on an eyewitness account from yesterday morning, it's possible the killer drives a black 4x4."

Rasovich spoke up.

"You just included half the county."

Monteville laughed.

"Be that as it may, it's a lead, and we need to follow it. Back to our unknown subject. His anger ties with religion.

The crown of thorns is significant. In the bible, Jesus's enemies placed the crown upon his head to mock him for claiming to be the son of God. But some believe the crown of thorns symbolizes sin." From the shadowed corner, Gardy glared at Bell. This was the first time he'd heard a theory regarding the crown's symbolism. "Perhaps a religious figure victimized our unknown subject."

"We're checking into molestation cases involving area churches over the last twenty years," Marcel added.

"Good. The FBI is running their own checks. Between both our efforts, we should find something soon if the killer grew up in this area. Keep in mind we're grasping at straws, and parts of the profile don't add up. If a male priest molested our killer, it's likely he'd direct his anger at other males, particularly those in positions of authority. Instead, he's targeting women."

"Could be he's angry at his mother," Marcel said, itching his head uncertainly.

"Go on."

"Well, maybe a religious figure molested him as you suggested. First thing he'd do is go to his mother. What if she called him a liar?"

"Or blamed him. Very good, Sheriff." Marcel sat up a little straighter. "In addition to the religious angle, the deputies are following potential leads regarding the missing dogs. While we haven't identified a common thread between the families, one exists. It's up to us to find it."

Rasovich said something under his breath and brought a snicker out of Monteville. Something about wasted time and government incompetence. Marcel shook his head at them, and Bell continued.

"As for the video, our tech team is fighting to trace the link, but as was the case with the photograph of Shelly LaFleur, the unknown subject switches the pictures from one website to another while bouncing each website among different servers. He must be using an algorithm.

Otherwise, he'd need to stay awake constantly and wouldn't have time for the victim."

Marcel asked, "At any point, has the killer entered the shot?"

"No. He's either careful to stay out of the picture or content to stand back and let the world see what he's done. Already, a few video snippets leaked and went viral. The networks picked up the story as well."

More murmurs, this time laced with anger over the press sensationalizing a local murder and abduction. Marcel attempted to regain order so Bell could continue, but Monteville already had his hand in the air.

"Yes, Deputy Monteville?"

Monteville stood up from his chair.

"I'll acknowledge the elephant in the room. Are we sure this guy didn't already kill Scott? This might be a video playing on a continuous loop."

Rasovich nodded, and Greene glanced at Bell with the frantic hope the BAU could verify Scott lived.

"We considered that. The lab is compiling the video as it comes in. On time lapse, shadows receded through the room consistent with sunrise, though he blocks the light. We think the killer drapes the windows to keep the room dark. And to conceal his activities."

Bell opened her mouth when the burner phone buzzed in her pocket. It was dangerous to carry the burner with Gardy standing a few steps away, but if there was one thing she could say about Logan Wolf, the man didn't make idle threats. She looked out over the deputies' faces and half-expected to see Wolf staring back at her.

Bell cleared her throat and excused herself from the podium. Gardy raised an eyebrow and mouthed, "you okay?" The blood drained from her face.

The burner buzzed again. Insistent.

"That's all for now."

Confused banter followed Bell as she rushed for the hallway. Someone grasped her arm, and she swiveled around to Gardy staring at her.

"What's gotten into you?"

"Nothing, Gardy. You need to let go of my arm if you don't want me to puke on your shirt."

He released her arm and stepped backward. Marcel rushed into the hall beside Gardy.

The sheriff asked, "She okay?"

Bell locked the door to the women's room before Gardy replied.

The phone rattled like an angry hornet when she pulled it from her pocket.

"This better be important, Wolf. Do you know how many cops I'm surrounded by now?"

She assumed he knew the precise number of deputies inside the briefing room. Had the restroom possessed windows, she'd expect to glance through the glass and find him staring at her. A chuckle came from the phone.

"Time ticks away for Clarissa Scott, Scarlett. Our killer means to flay her in front of the world."

"If you're watching the stream, you're as guilty as the miscreants getting their kicks off torture porn."

"No more guilty than you, dear. How does it make you feel when you see her tied to a stake?"

"You're sick."

"And you're asking the wrong questions. Enter the killer's mind. Identify his motivation and anguish."

Bell checked her face in the mirror. Black crescent moons, the price paid for lack of sleep, formed beneath her eyes. She ran the faucet and splashed water on her face.

"If you know who he is and you're holding out on me —"

"Dear Scarlett, I would never hold out on you. I'll help

you catch him, but first you owe me a profile."

The profile of his wife's killer. She'd given the matter a great deal of thought during quiet times over the last month. Unconvinced a serial killer murdered his wife, Renee Wolf, Bell believed someone Logan Wolf knew killed her.

"Tick-Tock, Tick-Tock. Your answer, Scarlett?"

Placing her ear against the door, Bell listened for conversation outside the restroom. The hall was quiet, Gardy and the sheriff having moved on.

"Fine. Where shall we meet?"

"I'm inside your motel room now."

CHAPTER SIXTY

During her trip back to Golden, Bell fought to keep control of the wheel. The few vehicles she encountered on the desolate county road appeared to hurtle at her like shooting stars. She couldn't think straight when she imagined Logan Wolf inside her motel room.

After hiding in the restroom, she'd discovered Gardy in the break room with Marcel. Since they were due to break for lunch, nobody objected when Bell suggested she make a run to the drugstore. Medicine to settle her stomach, she lied. Gardy nodded and said he'd phone her with a meeting place after lunch, yet a strange fire burned behind his eyes. She never saw him blink.

Every several seconds she checked the mirrors. No one followed. She almost wished someone had so she wouldn't need to face Wolf alone.

When she pulled into the motel parking lot, another vehicle slumbered outside the last room on the right. But this was a minivan with banal stick figures adorning the rear window: a man, a woman, one girl, two dogs. Not the ride of choice for the nation's most wanted serial killer. Whatever transportation Wolf utilized, he'd hidden it.

She felt vulnerable, defenseless. Not just because

the serial killer waited inside her motel room. He'd found a way inside again. Doors didn't stop Logan Wolf, and the potential always existed for Bell to awaken in the dead of night and find him glaring down at her.

Stopping outside the door, she ran her eyes toward the manager's office and scanned the motel windows. Nobody spied on her. Satisfied, she removed the key from her pocket and turned the lock. She paused and touched the gun. Then she removed the weapon from her holster and moved beside the door, back against the wall.

She shoved the door open and swung the gun into the empty room. Her bed was unmade, the sheet and blanket tangled into a clump at the foot of the bed. The window shade moved. Shadows descended the walls.

Edging the door shut, Bell aimed the gun toward the bathroom. Darkness bled across the threshold. She dropped to one knee and checked beneath the bed. Boards fixed the bed to the floor and prevented anyone from hiding beneath.

"Good afternoon, Scarlett." She hissed and swung the gun. He stood at the entryway to the open bathroom, half in the light, half cloaked by gloom. "No need for weapons. You should know by now I mean you no harm."

"Then why the games? Why not announce yourself the second I opened the door?"

"I needed to be certain you weren't Neil Gardy. Or perhaps the young lady come to clean the mess you made. Have you seen her, Scarlett? I doubt she meets the age requirements, but who the manager hires isn't my business. She's quite young and fetching. She'd look stunning stripped of her clothes and hanging off a pike while crows picked at her eyes."

Bell swallowed the retch bubbling up her throat.

"Stop."

"Would the sight not excite you, dear Scarlett?"

"No."

Wolf glided out of the dark, silent upon the old carpet. A death adder. She motioned with the Glock, a warning for Wolf to keep his distance.

"That's no way to greet your partner. Put the weapon down."

"Gardy's my partner. Not you. Never you."

Wolf tutted.

"A partner is there for you always. A man who vanishes at the first sign of danger but gladly shares the credit for your heroism isn't a man. He's a tick. A parasite feeding off the success of others."

"Liar. He's a good man."

"That good man will run the BAU once Weber moves on. Imagine one of the most powerful men in the FBI, someone who knows your secrets, directing your every move. You'll be his puppet and dance for him."

Bell shook her head.

"What's stopping me from putting a bullet between your eyes? Nobody would question me after they found fugitive murderer Logan Wolf dead inside my motel room."

Wolf grinned.

"You wouldn't kill me, Scarlett. I gave you the name of God's Hand, and I'll bring you the head of Clarissa Scott's kidnapper if you'll allow me."

"Then start talking. How do I find him?"

"You must have leads. Tell me."

Bell leaned against the wall, exhausted from the fruitless search, on guard in case Wolf moved on her.

"Not much. Except a bunch of missing dogs from last year."

"And you think our killer started with animals."

"It's possible."

"No maybes about it. The question is, how did he know the families? This isn't a man who strikes at random. Our killer desired to murder those families and string them up for everyone to see. But he wasn't ready yet. He took the animals instead."

"That's a stretch. We can't find a single link between the families."

"You're looking past the obvious. Put the clues together, Scarlett. You're better than that—"

Wolf opened his mouth and froze. The air felt different, charged with electricity. The doorknob turned. Someone quietly slid a key into the lock.

He grabbed Bell's arm and yanked her back before the door burst open. Gardy shot through the entrance, gun fixed on Wolf's forehead.

"Freeze. FBI!"

Wolf laughed, his black eyes burning with hatred.

"Ah, if it isn't my old friend, Neil Gardy. We were just talking about you."

"Hands in the air, Logan."

Wolf's arms hung at his sides.

"No."

"Don't think I won't shoot. Do as I say. Put your hands in the air."

The room key dangled from Gardy's finger, and as Bell checked her pockets to verify she still had her key, Gardy pocketed his copy.

"What are you doing with a key to my room?" Bell asked, narrowing her eyes at Gardy.

"Not now, Bell."

Wolf edged closer to Bell, a movement so subtle Gardy hadn't noticed.

"You see," Wolf said, black coat dangling past his hips, hands poised beside the pockets. "This is what I meant about Neil Gardy. He procured a key to your room without your knowledge or consent."

The irony of Wolf's statement bristled her. Many times he'd broken into her apartment or hotel room while stalking her across the country. But that didn't excuse Gardy. She glared at her partner as though seeing him for the first time. Did she truly know him?

"Don't listen to him," Gardy said, reaching for handcuffs. "He might have fooled you, but I've known him too long. Wolf's a murderer. He killed his own wife."

Wolf growled and tugged Bell in front of him. Gardy touched the trigger and halted.

Too late.

Wolf slipped the weapon from his pocket and squeezed the trigger. Bell screamed.

Instead of a gunshot explosion, wires arrowed across the motel room and punctured Gardy above his chest. He dropped to the floor, twitching, drool tricking off his lips.

A Taser.

Bell swung her elbow back at Wolf and found nothing but air. The breeze on the back of her neck told her Wolf had escaped out the door.

She dropped down and yanked the wires off Gardy's body. He moaned and rolled to his stomach, trying to crawl toward the entryway, body refusing to obey. Bell swung the gun around the jamb.

The parking lot was empty.

CHAPTER SIXTY-ONE

Ambulance lights flashed across the motel room parking lot as Bell answered questions from Don Weber, the deputy director irate and screaming into the phone.

"Sir, that's not fair," Bell said, cupping a hand over her mouth for privacy. "We have more than enough bodies assigned to the Wolf case. What about Clarissa Scott?"

Arguing with Weber seemed as fruitless as kicking a mountain. He refused to budge before cutting her off mid-sentence and hanging up.

Over a dozen agents were en route to Golden. When they arrived, they'd fan out with local law enforcement and cast a net Logan Wolf couldn't escape from. But they'd never find the serial killer. You only found Wolf if he wanted you to.

Officers from three different police departments and the neighboring county sheriff's office had descended upon Golden by the time the EMT workers declared Gardy healthy. Despite their admonitions to rest a minimum of two days, Gardy strapped the holster around his hip and strode past Sheriff Marcel to where Bell was standing outside her motel room. No sooner did Weber's diatribe end than Gardy's began, and Bell stumbled against the wall from the onslaught.

"Don't give me that shit about being sick. Am I stupid, Bell? I smelled Logan Wolf the second you bolted from the podium."

"Then you followed me."

"You gave me no choice."

"Really? Is that why you made a duplicate of my room key?" Caught off guard, Gardy choked on his reply. "You're worse than an overbearing parent sometimes, Gardy."

"Because of me, you're still alive."

"I was never in danger."

"You're delusional."

"He wouldn't harm me. I realize that's impossible for you to understand, but I'm not his target. Gardy, Wolf was about to help me catch this killer."

"You're a fool for trusting him. Wolf would never aid —"

"He gave me God's Hand's name, or have you already forgotten? And by the way, who pulled you to safety after Warren Schuler knocked you unconscious?" Gardy's expression froze between shock and horror. "Yeah, Logan Wolf saved your life. Think about that tonight when the entire FBI is hunting him down for a murder he didn't commit."

Gardy puffed his cheeks and spun around. Marcel, Greene, and two EMT workers watched the argument. Gardy glared bullets into them until they went about their business. When he spun back to Bell, Gardy took a deep, composing breath, and the beet-red of his face lightened a touch.

"Wolf could have murdered us," Bell said, touching his cheek. Gardy flinched and turned his head. "He chose not to. A Taser. Are you kidding? Not exactly Logan Wolf's murder weapon of choice. If he wanted to slit our throats, he had every opportunity."

"No matter how many times you pet a rabid dog and try to nurse it back to health, eventually it bites."

"Not if I put him down first." Bell met Gardy's glare. "Oh yes, Gardy. The second Logan Wolf moves against me or someone I care about, I'll end this. Permanently."

Gardy strolled down the sidewalk, hands clasped behind his head. The father of the minivan family poked his head out of their motel room. When he saw Gardy approaching, he shut the door and latched the bolt. Gardy's eyes were closed in thought when he returned to Bell.

"Even if I believe this crazy theory about Wolf not killing his wife, I can't protect him. You know what the FBI will do once they track him down."

"Weber made it clear."

"Weber blames me, I take it."

"He blames *us*. I won't cover my ass if it endangers you, Gardy. I'll tell Weber I chose to meet Wolf."

"No. There's no reason to get yourself fired over this." Gardy tapped his foot and glanced around the parking lot. "Here's the story. Wolf followed us to Golden and broke into your motel room. You felt sick, came back to rest, and found him waiting. Every bit of information is truthful."

"Except the sick part."

"What Weber doesn't know won't hurt him. What did he say about the Scott case?"

Bell sighed.

"There is no Scott case as far as the FBI is concerned. It's back in the hands of local jurisdiction."

"So that's it? He redirected every agent to hunt Wolf?"

"Seems like overkill."

"It is, but we don't have a choice in the matter."

Noticing Marcel walking toward them, Bell shifted her body so the sheriff wouldn't eavesdrop.

"We're abandoning an innocent woman, throwing her to the butcher. Marcel's team doesn't have the resources to catch this guy."

"Then our only choice is to catch Wolf and catch him fast. As soon as he's in custody, we can jump back into the Scott case." Bell rolled her eyes and started away. "You intend to play this by the book. Right, Bell?"

"Whatever."

She hopped the curb and angled between two ambulances. Gardy called out to her, but she couldn't hear him over the engines. Damn Weber. If Scott died, her blood was on the deputy director's hands.

No, she wouldn't let Clarissa Scott die.

Their rental SUV sat beside the sheriff's truck. Gardy had taken the keys from her, leaving her without a ride. She surveyed the lot and spied Deputy Greene, sheepish and standing back from the others, hand resting on the gun hilt as if he expected Logan Wolf to explode out of the manager's office with a knife raised above his head.

"Afternoon, Deputy."

Greene touched the rim of his hat and returned to scanning the area. He shot her glances from the corner of his eye.

"I guess the FBI doesn't care so much about a small town teacher. Just another hick nobody in Washington cares about."

The deputy's words slammed hard into her belly. She figured Greene had read her face during the Weber phone call.

It wasn't fair. Life seldom was. If she had a vehicle…

Greene's truck sat a few parking spaces from Marcel's.

"Would you give me a tour of Golden, Deputy Greene?"

Greene smiled. They climbed into the truck.

CHAPTER SIXTY-TWO

It was difficult for Bell to hear Gardy over the roar of the engine. Greene swerved around a tree branch, almost causing Bell to fumble the phone.

"Relax, Gardy. I'm taking the route we followed into Golden. Deputy Greene is aiding the search for Logan Wolf."

The curse through the phone suggested Gardy wasn't buying it. She ended the call when the truck clipped a pothole.

"Sorry about that," Greene said, easing off the gas. "This road is a mess. What are we looking for, anyway?"

Bell peered out at the rolling country and wondered what drew her back to this location. A memory from their trip into Golden. A puzzle piece she needed to fit.

"He's out here somewhere."

"The killer?"

"Yes."

"How can you be sure?"

Bell pointed out the window.

"Two abductions in less than a week. That tells me he needs seclusion."

"Golden is small."

"But the neighbors are nosy. Everyone talks. No, this guy needs privacy to—"

She caught her breath. There. On the hill.

"Take me up there," she said, staring up the incline.

"What? It's just a windmill."

"Hurry, Deputy."

He pressed the gas and turned onto a dirt road, the brown and gray path twisting up the hill to where the sun merged with the horizon. The front of the truck pitched upward at the steepest point and rushed the blood to Bell's head. Then the road leveled out, and they drove beneath the great spinning blades.

"Stop the truck," she said, lowering the window. A storm of dust kicked up as he brought the truck to a halt. "And cut the engine."

Bell climbed out of the car and stared up at the white behemoth. As the wind moved the blades, they clipped the air with a distinctive sound. She immediately recognized it as the background noise in the killer's video. The same noise she'd discerned when they drove into Golden. Why didn't she remember sooner?

Greene climbed down from the cab and met her on the shoulder. Together they craned their necks up at the wind mill.

"Why are we stopping here?"

"There must be a house nearby."

All around them, empty countryside sprawled beneath a sea of blue.

"All I see is goldenrod and hay fever coming on. Should I radio this back to the sheriff?"

Bell chewed her lip. Greene was right. Nobody lived up here.

"Not yet. Let's follow this road and figure out where it takes us."

Greene gave an unconvinced shrug and climbed into

the truck. Then they started down the road again, the dust obscuring the way forward and forcing the deputy to run the wipers. Around the next bend, Bell spotted am opening between two trees. A driveway. Had she not glanced down at that moment, she would have missed it.

Deputy Greene backed the truck up and swerved onto the driveway. Bell's flesh prickled. A gray paint-chipped house lay at the end of the drive. No phone or cable lines trailed into the house, but a pair of high-tech satellite dishes extended above the roof. Poplar trees flanked the drive like giant sentries and concealed the back of the house. But Bell spotted the rear bumper of the black 4x4 peeking out from behind the trees.

"Shit, it's him."

Greene swallowed.

"The killer?"

"Call it in."

He fumbled for the radio with shaking hands. Then the bullet blew out the windshield and painted the backseat with Greene's blood.

CHAPTER SIXTY-THREE

Everything hurts. As if someone took a club peppered with broken glass and swung it against her forehead. Bell groans and tries to move. Finds her arms bound to either side, splayed, splintered wood digging into her back.

On a subconscious level she senses the danger she's in, but brain synapses misfire and leave her murky and confused.

When someone moans beside her, she remembers what happened to Greene. A gun blast. The accident when the truck hurtled against the side of the house.

Her eyes pop open to a nightmare. The den from the video feed. She twists her head, and knife-like talons from the crown of thorns rake her scalp and forehead, missing her eye by a fraction of an inch.

Keeping her head still, she rolls her eyes to the side. Toward where the moan came from.

And sees Clarissa Scott. Alive, but barely. Bound to the stakes as Bell is. Scott's blood is brown and crusted over like a Halloween disguise. Bell can already feel the warmth of her own blood trickling down her cheeks. A chill rolling over her flesh alerts Bell she's been stripped to her bra and underwear like Scott.

The camera fixes on her. Is the FBI and the world watching her die right now? Below, the computer equipment hums, while the windmill blades taunt her from the hill crest.

"Clarissa. Clarissa Scott, can you hear me?" Black hair clinging to her face like a dead husk, the other woman doesn't respond. "I'm Agent Scarlett Bell with the FBI. We're going to get you out of here."

The words sound ridiculous to her ears, false bravado and delusional. There's no escape. She's as good as dead, just like Scott.

A moment of hope glimmers. Help will come soon. Until she remembers the bullet ripped through the windshield before Greene radioed back to the office.

Greene is dead? The room spins as a wave of nausea clips her.

Maybe the sheriff's department can locate the truck via GPS. Some law enforcement agencies put trackers on their vehicles.

But blind faith will get her killed.

She tests the bindings. Strains. The ropes hold firm and dig into her skin.

A noise comes from above, the strain of floorboards as her abductor paces. Then a shadow descends the staircase.

He's coming.

CHAPTER SIXTY-FOUR

Gardy shouted into the sheriff's radio, but Bell apparently decided to ignore him. He'd defended his partner to this point. Bell stepped too far over the line this time. He set the radio down when his phone rattled. He glanced down and recognized Harold's number.

"Not now, Harold. I've got a rogue agent to deal with."

"Gardy, you need to open the link I sent you. It's Bell."

Harold's words didn't make sense. Clicking a link would connect him with Bell? As he flipped open his laptop, the cold reality struck him.

"No, no, no," he muttered as the video feed began to load. "This has to be some kind of mistake."

When the image of his broken partner appeared on the screen, Gardy stumbled and fell into a chair. Marcel threw down his radio and hurried to Gardy, the blood draining from the sheriff's face as he looked over the agent's shoulder.

Gardy swallowed. Touching the screen as though he could shield Bell and protect her from afar, he switched the phone to his other ear.

"How long, Harold?"

"The link came online minutes ago."

"You can confirm its live?"

What he meant was could Harold prove Bell was still alive.

"We think so…it might be a recording but…"

"It's not a recording! She's alive, Harold. I'm looking right at her."

Marcel placed a hand on Gardy's shoulder. The agent flinched.

"Yes," Harold said, fumbling over his words. "She's alive."

"And you'll trace the link."

"I'm doing my best."

"Trace it, goddamnit!"

Silence came from the phone.

"Harold?"

When Harold replied he spoke a hair above a whisper.

"Listen, Gardy. Weber wants everyone on the Wolf case. If he finds out I'm aiding Bell…"

"An agent is in danger. There are protocols."

"Right now Weber doesn't care about protocols. He's seen the feed, and he still wants all resources directed toward apprehending Wolf. I've never seen him like this. Nobody can get through to him."

"That doesn't make sense. Congress will eat him alive when they find out he did nothing to help an agent in danger. He's lost his mind."

"Maybe so, but he's got all of us running scared." Gardy growled under his breath, and Harold changed his tone. "But I'm staying on this case until we find Agent Bell. I promise."

"You'd better, Harold."

Gardy clicked the phone off and yanked his hair.

"You can't help her if you don't think straight," Marcel said, handing Gardy a cup of coffee.

Gardy pushed the cup away. He couldn't stomach the sight of food or drink.

"Why the hell can't we find this guy? There can't be more than a thousand people in Golden. If we have to go door to door..."

Gardy trailed off as Marcel snapped orders at his deputies. On the screen, Bell groggily lifted her head as though weights hung off her neck. She stared into the camera. At Gardy.

His fingers trembled as he reached for the mouse. The phone buzzed again, an electric jolt that pulled his attention from the horror movie playing out before him.

He didn't recognize the number and considered ignoring the call. The phone rang again. An angry sound. He answered the phone and barked at the caller for bothering him during a crisis.

"Easy, Neil. You're no good to her like this."

Stunned, Gardy stood up from the chair and paced to the corner. The others watched him curiously.

"How did you get this number, Wolf?"

"Focus, please. Before you rudely interrupted us at the motel, the wise Agent Bell mentioned missing dogs."

Wondering if he could trace Wolf's call before the serial killer cut the line, Gardy recalled the dead end leads. Marcel waved at him from across the room. Gardy shook his head. The sheriff went back to coordinating the search but kept shooting glances at Gardy.

"Yes. The leads hit dead ends. It's not important now. I swear, if you're holding out on me with Bell's location, I'll hunt you down."

"Enough bragadoccio, Neil. It's unbecoming, not to mention you're wasting precious time. The missing dogs, remember. Agent Bell was so close. You both were."

"Explain."

"While it's true none of the families knew our killer on

a personal level, they all brought him into their homes. Think, Neil. Name our killer's most impressive skill."

Finding it difficult to hear Wolf over the clamor, Gardy stepped into the hallway. The FBI would take his badge if they discovered the fugitive aided him. To make matters worse, Wolf spoke in circles, bombarded him with a barrage of confusing half-truths.

"Answer the question, Neil."

Gardy shook the cobwebs free.

"I don't know. He's learned to hide in plain sight."

"Simpler than that. Don't be a fool. What's his skill? Even budding serial killers need to pay the bills, Neil."

Helpless to prevent the haunting images from clouding his thoughts, he pictured Bell as he'd last seen her on the video. Bloodied. Close to death. Then it struck him. The killer taunted him with the video feed and pictures, bounced the website around the dark web and eluded the BAU.

"You're saying he's a technology specialist. Someone who repairs computers or sets up networks."

"Very good. But Neil?"

"Now what?"

"If you fail Agent Bell, I'll gut you myself."

Ignoring the threat, Gardy hurried into the operations room.

"Sheriff, the families the deputies interviewed. Give me a name."

Marcel looked at Rasovich. The deputy pulled a stack of papers off his desk and read the first name.

"The Mariano family, Harrington Street."

"Call them," Gardy said, covering the phone with his hand. "Ask them who set up their home network or if someone repaired their computer last year."

As Rasovich dialed, Marcel grabbed the notes and read the next name on the list.

"Adam Ortiz, Elmwood Avenue." Marcel read off the phone number.

Hustling back to his desk, Deputy Monteville recited the number back to Marcel, and when the sheriff gave him a thumbs-up, Monteville picked up the receiver.

As the deputies phoned the other families, Gardy swung outside the door. When he uncovered the phone, the line died.

"Wolf?"

The man Gardy worked beside at the BAU, the country's most dangerous killer, gave him no opportunity to trace the call, and Gardy assumed Wolf was on the other side of the state by now. As he muttered a prayer for Bell, Gardy returned to the operations room and shut the door.

Rasovich snapped his fingers and waved a sheet of paper in the air. Marcel grabbed it from him and read the name.

"Charles Schow," Marcel said.

Gardy repeated the name. "That's our guy?"

"It has to be him."

Gardy typed the name into Marcel's workstation. The address came back a second later.

As Marcel picked up the radio, Gardy ran for the parking lot.

CHAPTER SIXTY-FIVE

Each ticking second took a year off Gardy's life. He hit ninety mph on the back roads and nearly lost control on a blind curve. In the mirror, the red and blue lights flashed atop Marcel's truck, the sheriff falling back and surging forward in a desperate attempt to keep up. With Monteville beside him, Rasovich drove another truck a few hundred yards behind Marcel. Several police cruisers rushed toward the hill from across the county, too far off to wait for. Gardy hoped they were smart enough to cut the lights when they neared Schow's home. More than anything he prayed Bell was alive.

At Golden's outskirts, a road branched off and climbed one of the county's loftiest ridges. Gardy stomped the brakes and swerved up a dirt-and-stone incline flanked by overgrown weeds and a throng of buzzing insects. Looming over the SUV, the windmills spun, the blades sweeping down from the sky. He felt very small in their presence. Infinitesimal. He didn't see any houses. Schow's was just around the bend. A good place to hide.

"Got some info back on Schow," Marcel said over the radio. "He grew up about twenty miles from here in Fairdale. Age of eleven, the kid got caught up in a sex scandal at his church."

Gardy slowed the vehicle, aware he was close to the turn.

"Priest?"

"No, one of the sisters. Never heard of such a thing. The human race creates its own monsters, Agent Gardy."

"Flashers off, Sheriff."

Marcel doused the flashers behind Gardy, then it was just the two vehicles creeping down a road devoid of human life. He caught sight of the driveway at the last second and stopped short of the entrance.

Gardy scrambled out of the SUV, gun in hand as Marcel fell in behind him.

Seeing the determined look on Gardy's face, Marcel agreed, "We aren't waiting for backup."

***

To Bell, the man is unnervingly normal in appearance. Taller than the average man, yet indistinguishable otherwise. A deadly chameleon.

He checks the camera, the computer, the network feed, then types a command. His eyes follow the swarm of characters scrolling down the screen.

Bell hangs on the posts, arms bound and splayed to either side.

"She's dying, can't you see?"

He ignores Bell's pleading. Clarissa Scott murmurs something indistinguishable. It's the first sign of life from the woman.

"Get her a glass of water. There's no reason for her to suffer." When he doesn't react, Bell glares into the lens. "If you are watching this, my name is Scarlett Bell. I'm an FBI agent. Tell the police I'm somewhere outside of Golden, New York, with Clarissa Scott, a local teacher. We're held prisoner by a white male, approximate age thirty-five years.

Brown, curly hair. Height six feet, average build—"

He yanks a patch cord out of the computer. He's killed the audio.

"Nice try," he says, grinning, and types another command. "The audio works on a ten-second delay. Nobody heard you."

His face twitches, and Bell knows she rattled him. He might be bluffing. And even if he isn't, a good lipreader can pull the information off the video feed.

Scott moans, anguished. Against her bindings, the woman stirs.

"You're not alone, Clarissa. I'm not leaving without you."

A shadow rolls down Bell's face, and she turns her attention back to the maniac. He's stalking toward her, the camera lens pointed down at the rug. This is it, she thinks. He'll murder them now. Suffocate them the way he did Shelly LaFleur, then string up their carcasses outside Golden and let the vultures feast.

"Stay away, you son-of-a-bitch."

Bell yelps as he clamps his palm over her mouth, the other hand pinching her nostrils shut. The loss of oxygen is sudden and shocking. Her body writhes, eyes bulge as the maniac smothers the life out of her. He cannot kill her instantly. It will take four or five minutes for him to suffocate her. This knowledge cannot stand against the explosion of panic rippling through her body. Her eyes meet his, and she sees no remorse, no sadness, only an insane need to watch her die at his hands.

She bucks her body against the ropes. Squeals as the splintered posts dig into her flesh.

How long has it been? One minute? Already her strength saps. Along the periphery of her vision, Scott twitches as she awakens.

Emboldened, the killer becomes careless. He turns his back on Scott and shuffles too close to her bound hands. With the man's shirt riding up his belly, Scott claws his exposed back. Nails dig deep and draw blood.

The man spins and smashes his fist against Scott's jaw. Her head rocks back. Blood spurts from her mouth and sprays a red, dripping slash against the wall. But Scott is awake now and screaming into the maniac's face as Bell dry heaves from sucking air back into her lungs.

The hands clamp over Bell's mouth and nose again. He's positioned himself to the opposite of Bell so Scott cannot reach him, and when he shoves his palms down, something cracks in Bell's nose. Blood fills her nostrils and flows down her throat.

Defenseless, Bell quivers. Her vision darkens, sounds grow muted. Even Scott's screams seem to come from a great distance.

Then all she sees is the red hatred of the maniac's eyes. Bell no longer struggles. She'll die at his hands.

An explosion she cannot place jars her. Her face drips with blood.

But the blood is not hers.

CHAPTER SIXTY-SIX

Bell gasped when the killer's grip weakened and slipped off her mouth and nose. His hand touched his side and came away red. As he stared into his palm in disbelief, legs trembling to hold his weight, another explosion rocked his head sideways and crumpled him.

The camera crashed to the carpet as Marcel rushed to stand over Schow. At the entryway, Gardy lowered his gun, arms hanging at his side like they were stapled at the shoulders.

The sight of Bell shocked Gardy into blinking twice. Sirens approached from the distance, and two additional figures—Monteville and Rasovich—waded into the house of horrors.

"For Pete's sake, is someone going to untie them?" Marcel said, the gun poised over the still breathing killer.

Unfrozen, Gardy ran to Bell as Rasovich aided Clarissa Scott. Monteville joined the sheriff. The tension on Monteville's face promised he'd squeeze the trigger if the killer moved.

"Nice shot, Gardy. I always said you were the second best shooter in the FBI."

As though he missed the joke, Gardy concentrated on

untying the bindings while trying to ignore her exposed body.

"I thought I'd lost you and…"

Gardy's throat closed up while he unraveled the ropes. She shivered, and he removed his jacket and placed it over her blood-smeared chest.

"You'll ruin it. That's an expensive jacket."

A smile curled his lips. He glanced surreptitiously over his shoulder, then leaned in to whisper in her ear.

"Bargain rack at Target."

He pronounced Target as *tar-jay*.

The last binding unraveled, Bell slipped off the wooden posts. Gardy caught her before she tumbled over, and as she found her sea legs, he helped Bell to her feet.

"Goddamn cop killer," Monteville scowled.

The deputy begged for an excuse to pull the trigger and avenge Greene, whose body lay outside, slumped over the wheel in the crumpled truck. He didn't need an excuse. Schow's breathing ceased. The maniac lay still beside the purring computer equipment with the camera aimed down at his head.

"Deputy Greene?" Bell asked, praying the gunshot was only a nightmare, her mind playing tricks on her.

Gardy shook his head. Bell slid down the wall and came to rest on the floor, knees drawn up.

Two police officers, strong-looking males not long on the force, arrived next. Three paramedics joined them seconds later. As the officers led a bloodied Clarissa Scott outside, Marcel knelt beside Gardy and Bell. The sheriff's eyes misted over, and Bell knew he was thinking about his sister.

"Here you go," Marcel said, dropping Bell's clothes in her lap. "The boys found them in the next room along with the teacher's."

The perfect gentleman, Marcel pulled his eyes away,

though Gardy's jacket only left Bell's legs exposed.

"Thank you, Sheriff. I'm sorry about Deputy Greene. He died a hero."

Marcel removed his hat. He ran his hand through hair which seemed to gray by the minute.

"That he did, Agent Bell. That he did."

The sheriff excused himself and walked outside.

"Maybe you should get dressed," Gardy said, offering his hand.

Cupping her clothes to her chest, she took his hand and followed him into the vacant bedroom toward the end of the hall. He turned his back when she handed him his jacket. When he started for the door, she grabbed his arm.

"Hey, Gardy."

"Yeah?"

"I'm sorry for the way I've been acting."

He lowered his head.

"Don't be sorry. Seems I should be the one apologizing."

A moment of quiet fell over the room. Murmurs from the den drifted through the home like memories.

"Yeah, you really should. You've been one hell of an ass-hat lately."

He stumbled at the door and grimaced. A grin broke across his face.

"Takes one to know one," he said, stepping outside and edging the door shut.

It was then she realized she was alone in Schow's house. Goosebumps covered her body.

"Gardy, can you leave the door open a crack?"

"Sure thing."

"And stay outside the door?"

"Of course. Ass-hat on guard."

She chuckled, and for a brief second the levity helped

her forget where she was and how close she came to dying.

But as she pulled her clothes on, she pictured Greene. So young. Certainly his parents brimmed with pride over their deputized son. Their boy died today. Someone would have to tell them.

Bell thought it should be her.

CHAPTER SIXTY-SEVEN

The sun hovered low in the sky when the last of the crime techs filed out of Charles Schow's little home. Gardy waved to Marcel as the sheriff drove off. They'd meet him at the office in an hour.

Yellow police tape covered the door. The tape flapped whenever the wind blew, and that made Bell think of the windmill and why she hadn't identified the sound sooner. She realized such thinking was the path to madness, and no guarantee existed a deputy wouldn't have lost his life storming the house if she'd figured it out sooner.

"Don't go there," Gardy said, reading her mind. "Schow would have seen us coming. He rigged cameras around the property and monitored everything from his den. Only reason he didn't spot me running up the porch was—"

"Yeah, he was busy killing me." Bell shrugged. "I led Deputy Greene into an ambush."

Gardy set his jaw and looked away. She could tell he was frustrated. Yet he let her vent and purge her guilty mind, and she appreciated him for it.

When Bell gathered herself, Gardy had his hands on his hips, staring off toward the rolling hills, everything tinted red beneath the sun's last stand.

"You know why we found you, right?"

Bell walked over to Gardy.

"No."

He opened his mouth, stopped, and licked his lips.

"Wolf called me."

"How did he get your—"

"Don't ask. It's probably best I never find out. He connected the dots when I couldn't. The missing dogs, in particular."

"I remember. The deputies didn't find anything when they followed up with the families."

"We didn't ask the right questions. The video feeds and server bounces should have clued us in. Schow was a genius with computer technology."

Nodding with understanding, Bell said, "He worked for the families. Around here, Schow was the only choice if you ran into trouble with your PC."

"Turns out he fixed Clarissa Scott's school computer. Scott remembered him."

"Jesus."

Gardy gave her a knowing look. "Marcel sent Monteville back to LaFleur's house. Inside the bedroom, he found a laptop with a sticker affixed to the shell."

"Let me guess. Schow configured her computer, too."

"That's how he chose his victims."

The light began to fail. Shadows crept across the lawn, claiming Schow's murder house as their own.

Gardy kicked at a rock. "You know I can't protect Wolf."

"I know."

"Between local law enforcement and the FBI, they sealed the perimeter air-tight."

"And yet they won't catch him," Bell said, peering out over the silhouetted hills. "We tried for over a year."

Gardy looked doubtfully at Bell, seemed to

reconsider, and nodded his agreement.

"You really don't believe he murdered his wife."

"I don't. Nor did I imagine the special ops shooter who tried to kill us outside Bealton. I never told you this, but the sniper shot Wolf that night."

Gardy followed Bell's gaze to the horizon. His jaw shifted in thought. Soon they'd need to explain to Weber why they chose to rescue Clarissa Scott after he ordered all agents to contain Logan Wolf.

"What are we going to do, Gardy?"

"I don't know. But whatever happens next, know I'll be by your side."

DEAD WATERS

CHAPTER SIXTY-EIGHT

Darkness shrouded the woman and rendered her as a silhouette beneath the midnight sky. Special Agent Scarlett Bell approached the figure, walking through the grass to mask her approach. She bent low against the vacant building and stuck to the shadows. Behind the agent, the surf pounded the Chesapeake Bay. Each time the wind shifted onshore, the spray touched the back of her neck and wet her clothes.

Bell didn't like this. Too much darkness, no witnesses. Her partner, Neil Gardy, monitored Bell's movements through the wireless microphone taped to her chest, but if the meeting went badly, or the woman awaiting her approach turned out to be someone dangerous, she'd be out of luck. Gardy's van idled a block away. He'd never reach her in time.

She touched the Glock-22 holstered on her hip and prayed she wouldn't need it. Bell edged along the wall and closed the distance on the woman. An overflowing dumpster lay between Bell and the end of the alley. It stunk of oil and spoiled meat. Deep fried food scents slid through the air vents of a seafood dive restaurant.

By the woman's impatient pacing, Bell knew her target hadn't registered her approach. Not yet. Still time to turn back if Bell sensed something was out of place. She crouched beside the dumpster and peered around the corner.

One small notch of tension released from her shoulders when she recognized the woman. Congresswoman Lana San Giovanni: leader of Washington's new class of democrats. She'd met the controversial politician several months ago when Vincent Hooper, the God's Hand killer, kidnapped San Giovanni's daughter, Joelle. The night Bell took down God's Hand and rescued Joelle, San Giovanni phoned Bell, claiming God's Hand had written her, and directed Bell to a derelict farm outside of Bealton, Virginia, where the killer supposedly held Joelle. A hidden sniper fired at Bell and serial killer Logan Wolf, a former FBI agent, and the sniper clipped Wolf in the shoulder. Bell shot and killed the sniper, a man she believed to be special ops after recognizing the pendant around his neck. But someone removed the body before the authorities could identify him, and Bell continued to suspect San Giovanni had set her up and wanted her killed.

Dark hair curled down San Giovanni's shoulders to the small of her back. The wind kicked up, and the congresswoman wiped the locks from her eyes. Bell edged out from behind the dumpster, and San Giovanni hitched in surprise. She placed her hand over her heart and took a deep breath.

"You scared the hell out of me, Agent Bell."

"Hands where I can see them, Congresswoman."

San Giovanni's eyes narrowed.

"No thank you. I'm not under arrest. You're fortunate I agreed to meet you at all."

"All the same, I'm prone to inconsistent behavior.

Read my personnel notes if you don't believe me."

"Oh, I've read every line," San Giovanni said as Bell patted her down. "But this isn't necessary, Agent Bell. I don't carry a weapon, and I'm not wearing a wire."

Satisfied, Bell straightened and positioned herself in front of the alleyway to block San Giovanni. The congresswoman wore sneakers instead of her trademark Stilettos tonight, but her body was soft, unathletic. If she turned and ran, Bell would catch her in an instant.

"Maybe you should. Carry a weapon, that is. An alleyway at midnight is no place for a congresswoman to come unarmed and alone."

"Who said I'm alone?"

Something shifted inside a dark entryway about twenty paces behind San Giovanni. Bell caught her breath and reached for her weapon.

"Don't bother," San Giovanni said, the starlight glinting in her eyes. "He trained his weapon on you the minute you stepped out of hiding. You'll be dead before you pull the trigger."

The woman might have been bluffing, but Bell didn't think so. She was an idiot to believe San Giovanni would come here alone.

Bell touched the Glock for a split second and pulled her hand away. For a brief moment, she'd spotted the enemy's gun gleaming in the doorway, though she still couldn't discern a face.

"Now that we have an understanding, Agent Bell, you'll hand me your weapon."

The tenor of San Giovanni's voice made her an expert debater and propelled her to a landslide victory over a popular incumbent during the last election. The voice brimmed with hostility. San Giovanni could read a grocery list and make it sound insulting. In recent weeks she'd engaged in a much publicized argument with Virginia Senator Chet Ewing over the president's budget proposal.

Bell had followed the debate on Twitter and CNN. She respected the congresswoman, but she wasn't about to hand over her gun.

"Over my dead body."

"That's exactly what it will be if you don't do as you're told." When Bell refused to budge, San Giovanni squeezed her eyes shut and closed her hands into fists. After a steadying breath, San Giovanni refocused. "Be reasonable. You contacted me and set up this meeting. I was under no obligation to comply, and I'm the one taking the risk. You want to talk, so we'll talk. But first, you're handing over your weapon."

Bell imagined Gardy screaming into his hands over Bell's compliance. He might already be out of the van and on his way, trying to get a bead on the hidden gunman.

She had no choice. Bell handed San Giovanni the weapon, and the shadowed figure stepped out of the doorway and paced toward the congresswoman. The man lowered his own weapon, though he didn't holster the gun until San Giovanni handed him the Glock. That was the moment Bell recognized him. Agent Jack Kerr. Former agent, she corrected herself. Kerr had provided the Secret Service detail for Joelle San Giovanni on the night God's Hand kidnapped her, and a few days later, the Secret Service fired Kerr, citing incompetency. To Bell's eyes, he looked broken, wary, though he moved with the precision of a trained agent. What shocked her most was Giovanni's reliance on Kerr tonight. She'd been furious with the agent after the abduction and likely influenced the Secret Service's decision to let him go. Why put her life in Kerr's hands?

San Giovanni read the question on Bell's face as Kerr stepped back into the doorway.

"Agent Kerr contacted me a week after the FBI returned Joelle." Bell noted the congresswoman failed to credit her for rescuing her daughter. She didn't seek the spotlight, but this oversight seemed purposely antagonistic, a slight meant to throw Bell off balance. "After speaking with Agent Kerr at length, I came to trust him. More so than the other agents I encountered during that nightmare, yourself included." San Giovanni paused and pursed her lips. "After we compared notes…let's just say a lot of things didn't add up."

Showing no concern for Kerr, Bell edged closer to the politician and fixed her with a glare that would have melted most women. San Giovanni was no ordinary woman, Bell grudgingly acknowledged.

"Let's cut to the chase, Congresswoman. You set me up, but I'm a survivor, and I killed your sniper. What I want to know is why. Who wants me killed, and what kind of mother risks her daughter's life to take part in a conspiracy?"

Even in the dark Bell saw the woman's cheeks bloom with red.

"I don't know who wants you killed, Agent Bell, but if you think I'd sacrifice Joelle—"

San Giovanni put her hand to her mouth, and a tear stroked her cheek. The political world knew well the congresswoman's talent for producing crocodile tears on command, but the hurt appeared real this time. After a long moment, San Giovanni continued.

"I told you the truth. A man claiming to be the God's Hand killer sent me those coordinates."

"And you never once questioned the letter's validity?"

"No, did you?"

In truth, Bell had. But with the clock ticking against Joelle, Bell followed the only existing lead.

"Start over. Tell me everything you remember about that night. How did you find the letter?"

San Giovanni recounted the events of the night she phoned Agent Bell. She was sitting in bed, sifting through a stack of correspondences. Anything to stay sane while she prayed for the FBI to recover Joelle before the unthinkable occurred. The letter lay stuffed within the stack of notes and official documents, unlabeled, white as winter. And that made no sense. The Secret Service and FBI maintained round-the-clock presences at the San Giovanni estate, and agents checked all letters before the congresswoman read them. They tapped the house phone, and a nondescript vehicle watched the estate from the neighborhood.

Bell thought for a moment and nodded.

"If what you say is true—"

"It is."

"—then this sounds like an inside job. No way that letter gets to you unless an agent lets it through."

"Or one of your people placed it himself."

Bell glanced toward Kerr. The former agent watched them from the corner of his eye as he searched for intruders.

"Yes, that's possible. Do you recall the detail working the estate that night? Any particular agent you didn't trust?"

"If you're referring to Agent Kerr, he was nowhere near the estate."

"No, it couldn't have been Agent Kerr. That's true. Agent Gardy and I were among the many who questioned Agent Kerr in the hours following the abduction. I'm certain he never escaped FBI supervision until we took down God's Hand."

"What are you saying?"

Bell figured Kerr was eavesdropping.

"If I am to trust you, Congresswoman, we're both in danger. It's apparent someone wants me dead, and they used you as a pawn to get to me."

San Giovanni straightened her back, angered.

"I'll phone the office and obtain records of everyone present that night."

"That's a good start."

Agent Kerr hissed and swung the gun down the alley.

"Freeze!"

"FBI! Put your weapon down, Kerr." Gardy stepped out of the darkness, his weapon fixed on Kerr. His eyes swiveled to Bell. "You all right?"

"As well as can be expected."

Kerr still aimed his gun at Gardy, and Bell could see he meant to shoot for the head and end the battle with one pull of the trigger.

"Drop your gun, Agent Gardy. You're not on official duty."

Gardy took a half-step forward.

"You first, Kerr."

"Jack," San Giovanni said, touching her protector's arm. "It's all right. It seems we're all on the same side here. Lower your weapon and give Agent Bell her gun."

Kerr gave her a questioning look, and when he saw she was serious, he huffed and handed Bell the gun. Gardy brought his gun to his side, lessening the tension in the alleyway, but he didn't pocket it. Instead he kept watch of Kerr, who stayed a few steps behind San Giovanni where the darkness lay thickest. The former secret service agent remained edgy, eyes flying over the storefront windows and bisecting alley, always vigilant.

"We good here, Bell?" Gardy asked, moving to her side.

"Almost. Congresswoman, I'll need that list of agents as soon as you get it."

San Giovanni quirked the corner of her mouth.

"Pushy, aren't we? Politics would have suited you well, Agent Bell. You missed your calling."

"Just get me the list. In the meantime, if you remember anything about the on-duty agents which struck you as suspicious..."

"Yes, yes. You'll be the first to know. Now can we

please get the hell out of this godforsaken alley?" The congresswoman scrunched her nose at the sewage stench wafting out of the dumpster.

The two groups parted. Gardy and Bell backtracked through the maze of alleyways bordering the coast, while Kerr and the congresswoman disappeared in the opposite direction.

"Dammit, Gardy," Bell said, clutching her jacket together as the ocean spray found her again. "I told you to stay in the van."

"And I would have if you hadn't surrendered your weapon to a fired secret service—"

The gunshot exploded out of the darkness.

CHAPTER SIXTY-NINE

After nightfall, the monster that is the lake sheds its blue veneer to expose the black abyss rising up from its depths. It is a beast that drowns, consumes. A phantom mist forms over its surface as he pushes the boat off the launch and motors toward the fleshy center of the lake, careful to keep the lights off so he doesn't attract attention.

Initially waves cause the boat to buck and slap the water, then the lake smooths, and the watercraft puts the shoreline behind him. Water droplets soak his shirt. Dribble like blood from the perch of his nose and over his lips.

Cottages circle the shore. The lights at the windows are little burning flames that become pinpricks the farther he moves offshore. The docks are no longer visible, nor are the myriad of vessels anchored near the shoreline. He kills the engine and lets the boat coast, allows the water to plot his course. The water is calm here. Motionless and dead. Now and then it sloshes against the hull, hungry with anticipation.

Above him, far from the village lights, the sky is endless. Stars extend from one horizon to the next and cup the world. He lies back on the seat and intertwines his fingers behind his head. Drinks in the universe. Few sights invoke a greater sense of awe than the night sky, and he wishes dawn would never arrive, that he could sleep here tonight and forever. Nowhere in the world does he enjoy a greater sense of security or solitude than he does at the lake's dead center after dark. A crater opens between him and the village, the world, everyone. A chasm none may pass.

The girl shifts her legs and moans. The plastic lining the bottom of the boat crinkles, breaking his trance. He slides up in his seat. Watches her bulk come awake as she sprawls onto her elbows. Her name is Deirdre Rice. He followed her out of Paulie's Pub last evening. She wouldn't tell him her name, though he'd asked kindly. Instead she scoffed and hurried through the unlit parking lot toward her car, fumbling for her car keys while he slid between vehicles. The woman never heard him come up from behind until it was too late. He struck the back of her head and jammed her face against the hard aluminum beside the window. He recalls the expression in her eyes before they rolled back in her head. Confusion. Shock. A sudden understanding that he was master of her world now.

After he dumped her in the basement, he pilfered her belongings and found her driver's license along with almost a hundred dollars in cash. He likes to know their names. He once learned, probably from a television show, that serial killers didn't want to know their victims' names. It humanized them. Forced the killer to empathize.

Bullshit.

Deidre Rice. He'll remember her name forever.

The starlight catches her long, black curls, and he's confused again. Where the dark hides her features, his mind fills in the details. And she is Leigh, not Deidre. For years he suffered at his father's hand. Leigh could have helped. Could have saved him. She chose not to. Abandoned him like all the rest.

His hands shake with tremors. The woman slogs up to her elbows, slowly coming awake. He can't have this.

She'll try to escape again, and the abandonment needs to end now.

From the toolbox under the seat, he removes a hammer and thunders toward her prone form. She cries out, comprehending his intentions. He swings the hammer. The face strikes the back of her skull, and the woman collapses onto the plastic. The material grows slick where her blood spills. Oily and black. Now there is work to do.

Along the distant shoreline, a man shouts in laughter and others join in. A truck door slams, and an engine revs. These sounds echo back to him and fly off toward the distant hills. A pair of headlights cut down a winding road. They are all unaware of the man's presence. Quiet returns to the lake.

Wet droplets fleck his chin. He wipes the blood on his palm and rinses his hand in the water off the port side. After drying his hands on his pants, he places the tips of his fingers against her neck and feels for a pulse. Can't find one. This clock no longer ticks.

To be certain, he pummels her head again with the hammer.

Satisfied, he reaches underneath the seat for the toolbox and removes the knife and cleaver. Then he chops and throws the pieces overboard. Listens as the bits plunk and splash.

And sink toward the bottom of the lake.

CHAPTER SEVENTY

What little sleep Bell got concluded at four in the morning. She woke and stared at the phone on her nightstand, unsure where she was.

The memory of the gunshot played on an infinite loop inside her head. She could still smell the salty tang of the nearby ocean as she recalled sprawling face down on an access road between the commercial district and a vacant beach house, Gardy covering her as he scanned the rooftops for the shooter.

She'd immediately called San Giovanni after Gardy determined the shooter was gone. Kerr and the congresswoman remained holed up inside a restaurant but safe, thank God. Neither could say who the gunman shot at, though Bell had a good idea the shooter aimed for her.

Between the two of them, Bell and San Giovanni decided the congresswoman would report the gunshot. As far as anyone was concerned, Bell and Gardy weren't in the alleyway. Too much explanation required otherwise. San Giovanni would concoct a reason for being on the Chesapeake Bay in the dead of night, though Bell wondered how she would explain Kerr's presence.

Bell's head cleared. She placed the phone to her ear.

Her spine stiffened upon recognizing Deputy Director Don Weber's voice. Through her short career with the FBI's Behavior Analysis Unit, she'd had a cantankerous relationship with Weber. She deemed him unfit for his job, a politician more than a leader, and a man who placed his own aspirations above the mission.

There was only one reason Weber called his agents in the middle of the night. Another serial killer.

Weber filled her in on the details. Three women missing in less than a month. All in their twenties, petite, with long, dark curls. It sure sounded like a serial killer case.

The latest woman to vanish, Deidre Rice, went missing two evenings ago. Bell's intuition told her the woman was already dead.

She opened the patio doors to the deck and invited the Chesapeake Bay sea breeze into her living room. The wind rousted her better than any amount of caffeine could, and she raced about the apartment, gathering up her overnight bag.

Stars lit the sky, and a half-moon reflected in roadside puddles as she drove toward the interstate. Bell hit seventy-five mph on the open highway, aware she was working on less than two hours sleep. She kept the windows open. Wind thundered into the car and threw her blonde hair around the headrest. She cranked a classic Ramones album on the stereo, though she barely heard it over the wind.

Gardy was already at the police station when she arrived. He clutched a cup of coffee and yawned as she pulled to the curb behind him.

"I take it you slept as well as me," he said, tossing the empty cup into a garbage container.

"Am I that bad?"

"You look like you're working on an hour of sleep over the last twenty-four."

"Two, but who's counting?" She glanced around Gardy's shoulder at a pair of uniformed officers convening outside the Blackwater Police Department. "So what do we know about Deidre Rice?"

Gardy cocked his head at the younger officer, a slight man with a shaved head and goatee.

"Officer Bridges is several steps ahead of us. He checked around, and a few people claimed they saw Rice at Paulie's Pub around nine o'clock two nights ago. She kept to herself, drank one beer, spent most of her time texting at the bar."

"Kinda specific."

"Yeah, well. More than a few guys paid her attention."

"But none of them made a move."

"The way Bridges put it, she intimidated them."

"Nobody saw her leave with anyone?"

"No. She came in alone and apparently she left alone, or someone would have noticed. Small town like Blackwater, everyone talks when a pretty girl gets a new boyfriend."

Eustis Tanner, Chief of Police, greeted them inside the police station. Gray flecked his crew cut. Despite being on the wrong end of fifty, he appeared as fit as a rookie with strong arms and a granite jaw. He accomplished tasks at double-speed as he raced between his office and the briefing room, a blur of motion and energy. Immediately the Blackwater Police Department impressed Bell. For a small village, they utilized modern technology and worked with efficiency, though Tanner's department appeared understaffed.

Officer Bridges tapped a pencil against his thigh while he waited for Chief Tanner to begin the meeting. His partner, a veteran officer with gray hair named Yardley, leaned against the wall and nervously worked at his incisors with a toothpick.

"First, I'd like to thank Special Agents Gardy and Bell

for lending their expertise on this case," Chief Tanner said, pacing the front of the room. "They've already received an electronic briefing on our situation in Blackwater, so I won't waste everyone's time with a long presentation. At present time we have two patrol cars canvassing the village. These are the missing women." He projected three photographs onto the wall. "Carla Betters, Trina D'Angelo, and now Deidre Rice, last seen at Paulie's Pub. Eyewitnesses claim she was alone and dressed in a blue-and-white polka dot sundress. From all accounts Rice fell off the map two nights ago, and with three missing women in less than thirty days, we need to assume the worst."

The Chief recited the dates they'd vanished. Rice was the first woman inside the village border to disappear, but all three potential victims lived within a short drive from Blackwater. Tanner maintained a close working relationship with the county sheriff and would share meeting notes with him when the sheriff came on shift this morning.

When called to the podium to offer her opinion, Bell clicked the case notes together on her knee and stood. Tanner took a seat beside Bridges.

"The similarities between the three women make me believe a single perpetrator, likely a white male, abducted these women," Bell said, turning to look at the three projected photographs behind her.

"How can you tell it's a white male?" Bridges asked, leaning forward with his elbows on his knees.

"Statistics show serial killers rarely cross racial lines, though we're always vigilant for exceptions."

Officer Yardley, who'd tossed the toothpick and slid onto a seat at the start of the meeting, squirmed uncomfortably. The entire department must have considered the possibility, but hearing a Behavior Analysis Unit agent confirm the likelihood of a serial killer hunting the village made the nightmare real.

"More striking are the similarities between the three

women," Bell said, continuing. "All in their twenties, pretty and petite, dark hair with curls. Three abductions over a short period suggest escalation. Something set our unknown subject off. Some life event that acted as a stressor. Think a messy breakup, loss of a job, something that pushed him over the edge."

"So he's going after a certain type," Tanner said, squinting at the pictures.

"Almost certainly. Figuring out why he hunts these women will be our key to catching him."

"Are you ready to release a profile to the public?"

"Not yet. These are first guesses, and we don't have a single body to prove he's a killer. For all we know, he's holding these women somewhere, all still alive."

"But you don't think so."

Bell pursed her lips and shut the folder.

"No, I don't."

The meeting concluded a few minutes later. Bell noted the entire briefing took only fifteen minutes. She liked Chief Tanner even more. No wasted motion, no time wasted in meetings when his officers could be actively searching for Deidre Rice.

There was only one problem. Bell knew Rice was already dead.

CHAPTER SEVENTY-ONE

The sun ascended from the nearby Atlantic when Bell followed Gardy out to the parking lot and the black FBI Jeep. She climbed into the passenger seat and rubbed her eyes.

"You don't have to come," Gardy said, touching her shoulder. "I scored us two rooms at a bed-and-breakfast on the lake. No problem if you want to grab a couple hours and meet me back at the station around lunchtime. It only takes one of us to interview the families."

Bell stifled a yawn with her hand and blinked twice.

"I'm good to go."

"You look like death warmed over."

She cocked an eyebrow.

"Says the zombie in the ruffled suit. Walk into these people's homes without me, and they'll chase you from the village with pitchforks."

Gardy turned the key in the ignition.

"Don't say I didn't ask."

They followed a humpbacked hill out of the village, slashes of early morning light and shadow throwing a picket fence pattern across the roadway. Dew hung thick and dripped off the trees. But what began as a hopeful expedition ended in disappointment. After speaking with the families of Carla Betters and Trina D'Angelo, it was obvious the two women had nothing in common except they lived in the same area code. Betters had recently returned to graduate school to study finance. D'Angelo worked night shifts as a nurse at a children's hospital. They didn't know each other, and apparently neither had contact with Deidre Rice. Still, a clear pattern existed. The killer stalked a tiny geographic area for women who fit his type. Now they needed to determine the connection, the unseen thread that bound all three women together.

By noon, Paulie's Pub began serving suds and fried food to the lunch crowd, and Gardy and Bell stopped to interview Jeffrey Romonowski, a lanky, bald-headed barkeep nursing a sunburn.

"Yeah, I saw Rice come in around seven or so," Romonowski said, wiping down the counter.

He slid an assortment of salty snacks in front of the two agents. Patrons filled every seat in the establishment. A Bruce Springsteen song pounded out of the jukebox.

Gardy popped a pretzel into his mouth.

"Was she with anyone?"

"No. She entered alone and sat on that barstool."

Romonowski nodded at the stool at the far end of the bar beneath the Coors sign where an overweight man in a jean jacket nursed a beer.

"What about the other patrons—anybody pay her an unusual amount of attention?"

"It's like I told the other officers. Rice wasn't just a pretty face, we get lots of those. She carried herself like a professional, always had a smile for the staff. Classed up the joint. She intimidated some of the guys. Made her feel unapproachable. But don't get me wrong. She was easy going once you met her."

"Sounds like you knew her well."

"Nah, I wouldn't say that. Never spoke outside of

Paulie's, and here we just chewed the fat about the Redskins and Nationals."

The pumping rock beat energized Bell, made her forget how much she needed to sleep.

"You told the officers Rice left around nine," Bell said as she swiveled on the barstool. "That accurate?"

"What I told them is I didn't see her after nine. That was my break, and she wasn't at the end of the bar when I returned."

"Mr Romonowski, did Rice mention a boyfriend?"

The barkeep paused in the act of sliding a beer down the bar.

"Yeah, she mentioned it in passing a few weeks back. He's some kid out of DC who probably didn't deserve her."

"She give you a name?"

Romonowski shrugged.

"No. She only mentioned that he's always flying around the country doing this or that. He's big into that EDM shit."

"EDM music?"

"Yeah, if you call standing in front of a computer music."

"I kinda like it."

"To each their own. Give me classic Led Zeppelin any day of the week."

They left the bar with little knowledge gained. Tanner had told them Rice didn't have a boyfriend. Gardy called the chief with the new information.

Bell's ears still rang from the jukebox while Gardy fiddled with the air conditioner.

"I'll take you up on the offer to drop me off. I'm lucky I didn't face-plant off the bottom step."

Gardy looked over his shoulder as he backed the Jeep out of its parking spot. A truck beeped, and he braked until the vehicle passed behind him.

"Truth be told, I shouldn't be driving, I'm so damn tired. Tell you what. Let's grab sandwiches on the way back and take the afternoon off. Until Tanner finds the boyfriend, not much we can do. He'll let us know when he has a lead."

"I'm down with taking the afternoon off, but I'll skip the sandwich."

"It's not like you to skip lunch. You sick, Bell?"

"I'm just not hungry," Bell said. He gave her a sidelong glance as he turned onto Main Street. "Come on, Gardy, I'm too tired to eat."

"Understood, but I worry about you." Turning toward the lake, Gardy went silent. His jaw shifted, a mannerism he displayed when he wrestled over what to say. "If that bullet had hit you last night…"

"It didn't. For all we know, some yahoo fired his gun on the beach."

"The shot came from the rooftops."

"And maybe the shooter targeted San Giovanni."

"You think that's true?" Gardy took a deep breath and turned up the air conditioning. "Listen, Bell. We've teamed together for the better part of the last two years and experienced a lot. Not all of it good. These cases changed us…or me, I guess."

Bell shot awake and glanced over at Gardy. He drove deep in thought, unaware she was looking at him.

"What are you saying?"

"What I'm trying to say is I worry because I care. I think about all you've gone through, especially over the last year…the long months with the counselor…and I don't like that you're alone in that apartment."

Her throat constricted. She swallowed the lump.

"The FBI watches my apartment all day and night."

"And I'm thankful they watch with an obsessed serial killer following you across the country. But you're still… alone."

Bell caught him glancing in her direction. He looked away.

"What are you proposing, Gardy?"

"It's just that…there's no reason for you to live alone."

Her heart raced.

"Gardy?"

"What I'm asking is—"

The phone rang. In her cloud of confusion, it took a second ring before Bell realized it was her phone, not Gardy's. Her mother's name appeared on the screen. Though they still lived in Bealton, Virginia, Sean and Tammy Bell had closed a deal on a condo in an Arizona retirement community. A part of Bell believed she would always be able to visit her childhood home, though consciously she realized time always moved on, ready or not.

She shot one last exasperated look at Gardy, who'd zipped his mouth shut and seemed to regret the last few minutes. Then she answered the call.

"Mom? Everything all right at home?"

Bell braced herself. Her father's false alarm with cancer last year still kept her off kilter. To Bell's surprise, her mother was mid-laugh, the phone held away from her as though she carried a conversation and didn't realize Bell had answered. She heard the low baritone of her father's laughter, then someone else's. Was she having a party?

"Mom?"

"Oh, I'm sorry, dear. I haven't laughed this much in years."

"Who's at the house?"

Someone spoke in the background and elicited another round of laughter. Tammy Bell fell into hysterics, then the reception faded amid the high terrain leading toward the lake.

"Mom, I'm losing you."

The next thing Tammy said came through in bits and pieces. The garbled laughter sounded unsettlingly like screaming. Bell's heart froze when the call resumed.

"...but where have you been hiding this partner of yours all these years. This Agent Wolf."

The call cut off. Serial killer Logan Wolf was inside her parents' house.

CHAPTER SEVENTY-TWO

Gardy drove as fast as the Jeep could handle, cutting hard on hairpin turns and speeding up on the few straightaways the country route offered. He couldn’t speed fast enough for Bell. Not with a murderer inside her childhood home. A mantra repeated in her head. Wolf had no reason to butcher her parents, not when he depended on Bell to profile his wife's murderer. That didn't slow her racing pulse.

“You're sure you don't want me to call the locals?” Gardy yelled over the roar of the engine. “They can get there a lot quicker than us.”

Bell shouted at him to drive. Whatever game Wolf played, he was more likely to kill everyone in the house if the police burst through the front door. Besides, cell coverage was negligible in the countryside and would remain so until they reached Bealton.

“Christ, Bell. If this doesn’t prove you can’t trust this psychopath—”

“Dammit, Gardy. Just get us there!”

Traffic thickened inside Bealton. Bell navigated Gardy down side streets and avoided the most congested areas. On one occasion she had him swerve into a shopping plaza with a vacant K-Mart building and cut across the parking lot.

What should have been an hour trip took only half an hour. As Gardy pulled the Jeep to the curb outside the little white home Bell grew up in, little more than a stone's throw from where the God's Hand killer tried to abduct a younger Bell, she tried to phone her mother again and received no answer. A Range Rover with Virginia plates sat in the driveway.

Gardy snagged her arm when she ran for the door.

"We'll check the place out first," Gardy said, placing a finger to his lips. "Then we go in nice and slow."

Both agents drew their guns on the suburban sidewalk. Gardy raced for the corner of the house and moved along the wall toward a picture frame window that offered a view into the living room. Bell circled around the left side of the house.

Her breaths flew in-and-out of her chest as she crouched below the glass. The casement window stood halfway open. If anyone was inside the kitchen, she couldn't hear. A dead silence poured out of the window. A horror show of images passed through her head—her parents dead on the floor, throats slashed, blood pooling and trickling under the refrigerator. And when she looked, she'd see Logan Wolf holding the gore-streaked blade and smiling a Cheshire cat grin at her.

But when she exploded out of her crouch with the gun aimed into the kitchen, she saw an empty room.

She squeezed her head between the casement window and screen and listened. Perhaps the strange trio had moved to the living room. Except for the ticking clock, she heard nothing.

A figure came around the corner of the house. Bell swung the weapon at Gardy, who raised his hands and shook his head to indicate he hadn't seen anyone inside. That's when her mother's laughter started again. From the backyard.

Gardy silently nodded and took off around the other side. They'd come at Wolf from opposite angles, take him by surprise if they were lucky.

Three distinct voices rang out from the backyard. She recognized Sean and Tammy Bell's, and the dark, sing-song voice of the nation's most wanted serial killer. She crept along the wall, the hot siding burning her shoulder through her shirt. Though she couldn't make out words, the conversation sounded amicable, replete with giggles. If the tenor changed or someone screamed, she'd put a bullet in Wolf's forehead and end this nightmare for good.

Wolf was the first to notice Bell when she emerged around the corner. As if he'd expected her arrival.

And he had, of course. Pointing the Glock meaningfully, she questioned his motivation with her eyes. He grinned back at her.

Tammy Bell followed Wolf's attention and saw her daughter. She clutched her chest upon noticing the gun.

"Good lord, dear. What's wrong?"

"Stay where you are, Mom."

"What's the meaning of this?"

Sean Bell stood up from his chair and stared wide-eyed at Bell. Dammit. He was in the line of fire.

Before Bell could answer, Gardy came around the other wall. He held his gun, too.

Now the two parents glanced between Bell and Gardy in confusion, a hint of terror in their eyes.

"Dad, sit down."

Gardy looked prepared to fire on Wolf, though the serial killer sat several feet away from the parents, one leg crossed as he leaned back in a lawn chair. Wolf's hands cupped behind his head, the fugitive oddly casual in blue jeans and an aqua-green t-shirt with a palm tree on the front.

Now Tammy Bell appeared angry at the unexplained intrusion. When she opened her mouth to question her daughter, Wolf carefully urged her down with his hand on her shoulder. Then the dark-haired killer walked a few steps forward.

"No need for alarm, Mr and Mrs Bell. I didn't wish to frighten you earlier, but I received an FBI text notification of a fugitive on the outskirts of Bealton. Obviously my esteemed fellow agents had reason to believe the criminal was nearby and wished to protect us. Isn't that right, Scarlett?"

Bell met Gardy's eyes. He shrugged.

"You may put your guns away," Wolf said, smiling as he edged closer to Bell. "Your parents are in good hands."

"Thank you, Agent Wolf. How may I ever repay you?" Bell bit off each word.

Sean Bell eyed his daughter, then swung his gaze to Gardy.

"Don't you think you should put your guns away? No need to frighten the neighbors."

"Yes," Wolf said, resting a hand on Sean Bell's back. "Listen to your father before we raise unnecessary alarm."

Bell's mouth twisted. She wanted to yank Wolf's hand away and break it for touching her father.

"The authorities haven't caught the fugitive yet," Bell said. "While it's wonderful Agent Wolf took precious time out of his day to introduce himself, I'm afraid we require his services. Immediately."

Much to Bell's horror, her mother gave Wolf a long hug and invited him to visit again. Alongside Gardy, Bell watched incredulously while her father shook hands with Wolf and slapped him on the shoulder as if they were pals from the bowling team.

"We need to go. Now."

Wolf acquiesced and followed Bell and Gardy, both

still armed, out of the yard. Her parents called their goodbyes from the backyard, and there came a stern warning from Tammy Bell for her daughter to phone her later. Yes, Mom was unhappy with her intrusion.

As Wolf opened the door to the obviously stolen Range Rover, Bell slid into the seat ahead of the serial killer.

"And here I thought we finally had an understanding," Wolf said, tossing Bell the keys.

"Get in the passenger seat," Bell said.

Gardy narrowed his eyes.

"Is this wise?"

"I can handle Wolf. Follow me to the lot we cut through before. The one with the empty K-Mart. Mr Wolf has some explaining to do."

Bell knew Gardy didn't trust the situation and felt he should drive Wolf. While Bell backtracked through familiar neighborhoods toward the center of town, her partner hugged the Range Rover's bumper with the Jeep. Wolf watched her from the passenger seat, an amused look on his face.

The drive took five minutes. Bell brought the stolen vehicle to a stop in the middle of the lot, far from the fast food burger joint and vehicle repair shop girding the blacktop. Gardy pulled the Jeep into an empty space behind her and hopped out, his hand poised over the holstered Glock.

"Get out," Bell said, killing the engine.

The three convened beside the Range Rover. Neither agent made an effort to cuff Wolf, but they stood to either side of the serial killer, blocking him in between the vehicles.

"What shit are you trying to pull showing up at my parents' house like that?"

"You worry too much, dear Scarlett. I hope you realize

you broke up a wonderful conversation. I dare say your mother was none too pleased." Wolf cocked his head at Bell. "You really believe I meant to murder your parents?"

"Where did you get the ride?" Gardy asked, nodding at the Range Rover.

"None of your business, Neil."

"Oh, this guy is precious." Gardy placed his hands on his hips and walked in a circle. "Why in the hell should she trust you?"

"Perhaps I came to fair Bealton because I wished to meet the man and woman responsible for the great Scarlett Bell," Wolf said, ignoring Gardy. He turned his head toward a car driving out of the repair shop, but the vehicle swerved out of the lot and accelerated down the thoroughfare. "Or maybe I sought human companionship. It's quite lonely moving from town to town."

"Shit happens when you leave a body count wherever you go."

Wolf rolled his eyes.

"Please, Neil. You're tedious."

Bell shifted in front of Wolf and stood chest-to-chest with him.

"In the driveway, you said you thought we had an understanding. I should be saying the same to you. I protected you when the entire BAU was searching for you. So you owe us…you owe *me* an explanation."

Wolf's grin was absent in his eyes.

"How long must I wait until you profile my wife's murderer as promised?"

"You thought the best way to call me out was to barbecue steaks with my Dad?"

"You're not an easy person to reach, dear Scarlett, not with the extra vigilance on your apartment and the entire BAU trying to reign me in. But you'll make good on your promise. In the meantime, you can't blame me for spending a beautiful Virginia afternoon with your charming parents."

"Don't you ever pull a stunt like that again."

"Sean and Tammy expect me for game night next Wednesday. They're playing Pictionary with the Bensons." As though a light flicked off, the smile suddenly slipped off Wolf's face. "Had you accepted my assistance in New York, you wouldn't have ended up suspended like a scarecrow, seconds from death. You should know by now to accept my assistance. We have another murderer on our hands, Scarlett."

"There is no *we*," Gardy said, nearly spitting the words. "Stay out of our investigation."

"I'll help you catch him, and the world's most gifted profiler will hand me Renee's murderer. Who can stop us if we work together?"

"No deal."

"I didn't ask for your permission, Neil."

"Fine," Bell said.

Gardy whirled on her.

"What?"

"You're both responsible for saving my life in New York. In my estimation, Wolf earned our trust, and we should listen to what he has to say."

"We can't very well parade Wolf into Blackwater and put him to work. 'Hey, Chief. A national fugitive is leading today's briefing. Who's making the popcorn?'"

"No, we can't." Bell stared at Wolf. "He'll remain out of sight and offer his expert opinion based on the information we choose to share with him. In return, I'll make good on my promise."

Wolf brushed the hair off her face.

"Thank you, Scarlett."

"But we're done after this, Wolf. Forever."

CHAPTER SEVENTY-THREE

A screaming noise awoke Bell. She hurled off the blankets and sat up, short of breath, and realized her phone was ringing. She was in her room at the bed-and-breakfast. A quick scan of the light falling through the translucent drapes told her the end of day grew close. Her mind raced through the last twenty-four hours—the meeting with Congresswoman San Giovanni and the attempt on their lives, the bleary-eyed drive to Blackwater, the panicked rush to Bealton. Gardy dozed in the next room. Incredibly, Logan Wolf occupied the room above hers under an assumed name.

The phone shrilled again, and Bell grabbed it off the nightstand. Her stomach turned seeing Candice Briggs was the caller. Deputy Director Weber's Administrative Assistant never hid her distaste for Bell and watched over her like a hawk inside the office. Bell bit her tongue and answered.

"Yes, Candice."

"Hold for the deputy director."

Candice put Bell on hold before the last syllable left her mouth. The line went quiet as though it cowered, anticipating Weber's arrival. No canned *please-hold, your-phone-call-is-very-important-to-us* message, no muzak. Bell couldn't decide why Weber wanted to speak with her. Whatever the reason, she felt sure it wasn't good. It never was when the deputy director phoned her.

Bell jumped when his voice boomed through the phone.

"Agent Bell, what's this I hear about you harassing Congresswoman San Giovanni?"

So San Giovanni had sold her out after all.

"Sir, I did no such thing."

"Do you deny meeting with the congresswoman?"

"No, of course not. We spoke at length about a personal matter. The conversation ended amicably."

For the next minute, Weber bellowed over how he'd come close to firing her. This transgression would go on her permanent record. Finally the deputy director allowed her to speak.

"Sir, there was obviously a misunderstanding. Let me speak to her. I promise we'll clear this up."

"You'll do no such thing. From this moment forward you will have no contact with Congresswoman San Giovanni. If I find you disobeyed my order, I'll suspend you indefinitely and fight like hell to take your badge. Have I made myself clear, agent?"

He had.

Bell collapsed against the headboard. Half of her shook with the pain of a child whose parent had screamed at her for no reason. The other half wanted to explode. She eyed the phone. San Giovanni's name sat at the top of her recent contacts. Not yet. She couldn't hold a rational conversation given her state of mind.

As the sun's colors grew richer and darkened, she slipped into her clothes and ran a brush through her blonde hair. Chief Tanner wanted Gardy and Bell back at the station for the second half of the swing shift which ended at midnight. There were no family members or friends left to interview, and unless the police uncovered a new piece of evidence, they remained at the killer's mercy until he took another victim.

After she brushed her teeth, Bell grabbed her room key and took the short walk along the balcony to Gardy's door. He answered on the first knock. Instead of greeting her, he strutted into the kitchen.

"Well, good evening to you, too."

He didn't reply. A wall separated the small kitchen from the bedroom and blocked her view. His travel bag sat neatly in an open closet. Ruffles in the bedspread marked where he'd napped. She was about to write off his irritation to lack of sleep when her skin prickled. Someone else was in the room.

In the kitchen, she found Gardy staring across the table at Wolf, whose lips quirked upward as he stared down Gardy. If either blinked, Bell didn't notice.

"Decided the playful banter couldn't wait until tomorrow?" Bell asked, arms folded over her chest.

"Special Agent Gardy believes I'm up to no good," Wolf said, folding his hands together. "He thinks I'm a bad influence on you, Scarlett."

Gardy growled.

"Former Special Agent Wolf needs to understand the ramifications should he bring you harm."

Wolf reached for a gratis coffee packet on the table and examined the back. "Barely edible." He tossed the packet to Gardy, who caught it with one hand. "This grows tiresome, Neil. If I meant Scarlett harm, if I wished to hurt either of you, I would have already done so. I've had numerous chances."

"Let's say I accept Bell's assertion that you didn't murder your wife."

"Yes, let's."

"You don't deny the countless murders you've

committed since."

"Serial killers, Neil. Men who deserved to die."

"Killers or not, you'd face the death penalty. The law frowns on vigilante murderers. I should bring you in right now."

"What's stopping you then? Afraid what might happen if you move on me, Neil?"

"Don't test me."

"Or what?"

Bell slapped the table, forcing them to look away.

"What is it with men? Do all of you think with your biceps?"

Gardy looked at her cockeyed. Wolf seemed amused.

Bell leaned her arms on the table.

"Tell you what, Gardy. You need to wash your face and shave so Tanner doesn't think I pulled you out of the local taproom. And hurry your ass up, because you're making us late. And Wolf? Trust isn't gained overnight. You're damn lucky we've given you the benefit of the doubt to this point and haven't dragged you to the authorities. Get back to your room, lock the door, and don't even consider snooping around tonight."

Wolf pushed back in his chair and swiveled to face Bell.

"How will I help you find the killer if I'm locked away?"

"Gardy and I will decide what information to share with you, and then I'll listen to your opinions. Your profile for mine. Until then keep your head down before one of us takes it off. I'll be in the goddamn Jeep."

Bell snagged the keys and stomped out of the kitchen. The walls rattled when she slammed the door behind her.

Wolf sneered at Gardy.

"Oh, Neil. Now you've gone and made her angry."

CHAPTER SEVENTY-FOUR

The newspaper article about the county-wide abductions concerned Pam Teagarden, and she'd taken precautions since the Rice woman vanished from Blackwater. Since then, she'd cut down on the small talk with the male patrons at Mulligan's Lakeside Restaurant where she waitressed. Less talk meant lower tips, and she needed the money to go back to school for her Masters, but she felt paranoid. She also stopped walking to work and relied on Uber, though it ate into her wages.

The problem was her ride never showed tonight. The clock read eight. Thirty minutes until her shift began.

Shit.

She punched her destination into the app again and waited for a vehicle to respond. The Lincoln should have arrived fifteen minutes ago but had vanished from the map. Probably some lazy kid who blew her off and went home to play Xbox. Chewing her lip, she eyed the setting sun. If she started walking now, she'd arrive on-time, and she wouldn't be searching for another waitressing job tomorrow.

Teagarden pulled her black, curly hair into a ponytail and descended the apartment steps. The old money wealth of Blackwater lay only minutes away, but she couldn't see the neighborhood yet, only a shadowed tunnel of trees at the end of the block. An abandoned warehouse stood between her and the wealthy neighborhood. Even before the missing girls, the factory had given her a bad case of the willies. Selena claimed squatters lived inside the derelict building. Teagarden couldn't imagine someone living in that filth of broken glass, dust, soiled insulation, and rat droppings. Junkies, Selena said. Junkies in Blackwater. What had become of their sleepy lake community?

The day's heat lingered into evening, and a sticky warmth choked her lungs and clung to her clothing. Teagarden walked with her head down, hands cupping elbows to stave off the chill creeping down her skin. When she reached the edge of the warehouse, Teagarden quickened her pace. She sensed the empty eyes of the windows following her. A thud brought her head around. Something moving in the darkened rooms where the sun never reached. It seemed cliche. Like in the horror movies she loved to watch, there was always a crazed murderer watching.

Teagarden convinced herself the thud inside the warehouse had been her imagination. Then glass shattered. That was most definitely not her imagination. She cursed the tardy Uber driver and stared straight ahead, afraid if she turned her head toward the building, she'd see some nightmarish horror shambling toward her with black, jagged teeth and bloody claws. She tripped over a rut in the sidewalk. Pinwheeling her arms, she caught her balance and hurried on.

In college, she'd learned a trick to manage stress. Count three calming things you can hear. The Sheridan's puppy yapping behind her in the apartment complex. A jet tracking through the eastern sky, maybe on its way to some place tropical. What else? The fresh scent of the lake on the wind. That counted, right? It was a smell, not a sound, but this was her panic attack, and she could change the rules anytime she wished.

Teagarden passed the warehouse without further incident, though she refused to look over her shoulder. How do we acknowledge the monster creeping up from behind? We don't, if we know what's good for us.

Through the tree tunnel, she raced. By the time she arrived at Mulligan's, she'd be sweaty and exhausted. Teagarden pondered how she'd survive until the bar shut down at two.

To her relief, the crosswalk appeared. Harper Street was quiet this evening, just a few vehicles puttering down the block. Now she was in the high-rent district. The houses grew progressively larger and more lavish as one approached the lake. Already she heard a motorboat, though she wouldn't see the water for another two blocks.

Another vehicle appeared on her app, and she toyed with the idea of ordering a ride to take her the remaining distance. But it was only another fifteen minutes to Mulligan's, and she was safe now. Better to save her money. She killed the app and continued down the sidewalk, checking her messages as she passed a white Greek Revival with a Japanese maple in the front yard.

The shadow lurched out from behind the fence. One arm wrapped around her neck and squeezed. A hand clamped her mouth shut and cut off her cries for help.

Then the man threw Teagarden to the grass and slammed her head against the ground. She lay unconscious while he dragged her into his car.

CHAPTER SEVENTY-FIVE

"I found the boyfriend," Tanner called over his shoulder as Bell followed the chief into his office. She jogged to keep up with him, marveled as he cut between desks, shocked he didn't clip his hip on the corners. His hustle infected the on-duty officers who moved between rooms as if shot from canons. Bell chalked the influence up to inspiration, not intimidation. The latter ran rampant in Don Weber's BAU.

Chief Tanner's desk was military-neat. A small stack of papers perfectly aligned on the right corner of his desk. One stapler and tape dispenser. No stray pens or pencils. A framed photograph on the left corner pictured a middle-aged blonde woman with a radiant smile beside Tanner. Someplace warm. Bell noticed palm trees and coral water in the background.

"Deidre Rice's boyfriend?"

"He'd been at a music festival in the California desert. No cell coverage, so he had no idea there was an issue until he got back to LA and his missed calls came in."

"He flew out of LAX. I take it you double-checked his boarding passes."

"Yes. His alibi is airtight." Tanner exhaled and sagged

into his chair. "We're not going to find her alive, are we, Agent Bell?"

Bell's jaw shifted. She reached around the corner and filled a cup of water from the dispenser outside Tanner's office. In the next room, Gardy conferred with Bridges, the young officer seated on the edge of his desk with a manila folder in his hand.

"Keep the faith."

"I don't know how you guys do it. The Behavior Analysis Unit agents, I mean. So much darkness. I'd picture murder whenever I closed my eyes at night."

Bell nodded grimly and slipped into a chair across from Tanner's desk.

"Our jobs aren't so different. Each have their horrors."

"I still don't want to believe it's a serial killer. In my head, I keep making rationalizations for the three disappearances. They all vanished from different towns, none of the women knew each other, and maybe they had personal reasons for taking off without telling anyone. A jealous boyfriend. Debt issues. Or one of them decided to backpack across Europe for the month." He paused and tapped his pen on the desk. "But then I see how similar all three women are. Size, age, facial features, hair. And my stomach falls like I just pulled the cord on my 'chute and nothing came out."

Tanner's feelings mirrored her own. She always felt the same early in a case when the evidence that a serial killer hunted the region was spotty and open to interpretation. You wanted to derive reasons why it wasn't a murderer, but the dread snaking up the back of your spine told you otherwise.

"It drives me nuts that there isn't anything to do but sit and wait," Tanner said, clicking the pen off and tossing it into his desk drawer. "The search crews haven't found any sign of Rice. It's like the world swallowed her whole."

Out of the corner of her eye, Bell spied the map

fastened to the wall in Tanner's office. Three colored tacks indicated where the women vanished. A red tack marked the last known whereabouts of Carla Betters fifteen miles north of Blackwater. Ten miles to the northeast of the village, a blue tack stuck into the map where Trina D'Angelo had disappeared. A green tack jabbed out from the village's edge where Paulie's Pub sat.

Bell walked to the map and peered at the tacks. She rocked back and forth on her heels as she rubbed her chin.

"He's becoming bolder."

Tanner pushed his chair aside and met her at the map.

"The unknown subject? Why do you say that?"

She pointed at the first two abduction sites.

"There's a strong chance this guy lives in Blackwater or close by. If I'm an aspiring kidnapper or killer, I'll want to start somewhere where I'm comfortable. Close to home, but not in my hometown."

"You don't want anyone to recognize you."

"Right. Also, the population thins north of the village. Fewer police, more opportunity to grab someone without anyone noticing."

Tanner nodded and rubbed his hands together.

"But eventually you get bolder and start to believe nobody can catch you. You're bulletproof."

"Because I've gotten away with it with both times. Nobody's talking about me. I live in a vacuum, my own little paradise. Chief, what was the media coverage like after the Betters and D'Angelo abductions?"

Tanner shrugged.

"In Blackwater? I'm sure the local newspapers mentioned it in their towns, but nothing here. Just a few missing persons posters scattered around the village. We didn't get involved because it fell under the county, and even after the second disappearance, nobody connected the cases."

Bell ran her finger along the Blackwater village perimeter. From his office, she could see the red heat of last light touching the windows in the operations room. It looked like blood.

"He'll strike again soon. He's confident now."

CHAPTER SEVENTY-SIX

The local authorities considered BAU profiles as conclusive, definitive maps with GPS directions which would lead them to their killer. But to Bell, the profile was more like a water painting with plenty of white space on the canvas. Add another splash here or there and the meaning of the painting changed drastically. It often wasn't until days after the initial profile that Bell had a full picture of the unknown subject. Until that point she relied on intuition to guide her down dark paths.

It was after midnight when Gardy drove them back to the bed-and-breakfast. The water reflected the moon, and all around the lake, the last remaining lights flicked off as Blackwater fell asleep. She was irritated with Gardy over the constant griping with Wolf. The situation was a powder keg, a bomb that was a match flare away from blowing up in her face.

She believed the FBI wrongly accused Wolf. He hadn't murdered his wife. But that didn't make him any less dangerous.

And she had no idea how she'd convince Gardy and Wolf to work together.

Moths and June bugs ricocheted off the light fixtures

of the bed-and-breakfast while they made their way to their neighboring rooms.

"We'll close in on this guy tomorrow," Gardy said at the door, his jacket slung over his shoulder. "Tanner and his team are good. They'll get us another lead."

"I know."

"And I can see you're beating yourself up inside, so stop it. We came into this situation blind. We don't have so much as a body, not even a crime scene."

She braced her arm against the door jamb and ducked as a moth darted at her face.

"Gardy, about what you said before my mother called."

He turned his back to her and dug through his pocket for the room key.

"Let's not discuss it right now."

"Wait, what? We should definitely talk about it, Gardy."

"You're angry."

"No, I just think we should be clear about what you were about to ask me."

He exhaled. The key wasn't opening his door.

"Don't read into it. I shouldn't have said anything. Forget it."

"Gardy, come on. Hey, Tanner doesn't want us at the office until noon. Come inside so we can discuss this like adults."

The locking mechanism finally clicked. Gardy opened his door.

"Go to sleep, Bell. See you in the morning."

With that, he shut the door. Though he'd closed the door softly, it felt as if he'd slammed it in her face. Bell stood on the walkway, torn between her door and his. She lifted her hand to rap on his door and pulled it back at the last moment. With a flustered sigh, she opened her room and stepped into the air-conditioned oasis.

She tossed her bag on the floor and flopped onto the bed. A calming off-white ceiling, the shade of cumulus clouds on a sunny day, offset the ocean blue walls. Above the bed, a vintage black-and-white picture from the 1930s showed Blackwater Lake in its glory. Several large boats floated beyond a long pier lined with men and women wearing their Sunday best. Bell stared up at the ceiling fan as the blades pushed cool air over her body. She attempted to force Gardy from her mind. She was successful for a while, then she heard the television in his room.

Footsteps shuffled past the door as another couple walked by. Their laughter reminded Bell of her loneliness and the long stretch of time she'd avoided dating.

She thumbed her phone on and tapped it on her leg. Biting her lower lip, she swiped to her contact list and glared at the congresswoman's phone number. Another betrayal.

Weber would fire Bell immediately if she contacted San Giovanni again. To hell with it. She called.

The congresswoman answered on the second ring. Bell expected anger, yet the woman sounded relieved to hear from her.

"Why in the world did you claim I harassed you? I thought we left things on a good note."

San Giovanni went quiet for a moment.

"Congresswoman?"

"This is news to me. I never made such a claim."

Bell shifted the phone to her other ear and rolled onto her stomach.

"Are you saying you didn't contact Don Weber to complain about me?"

"Weber?" San Giovanni snorted. "He's a little pissant. If I had a problem with a BAU agent, I'd go above Weber's head."

"Is that what you did? Climbed the corporate ladder?"

"Absolutely not. We're on the same side, Agent Bell. I'm confused. What's happening?"

Bell filled her in on the harassment complaint and Weber's phone call.

"I made the FBI aware of the gunshot, but as far as anyone knows, I was alone at the time. No Agent Kerr, and certainly nobody from the BAU."

"Someone saw us together," Bell said, sitting up against the headboard, legs crossed at the ankles.

"Yes, someone who wants you out of a job. So Agent Bell, who have you pissed off lately?"

"You want a list?"

The congresswoman snickered.

"If I charged you with harassment, I'd put it in writing, not call like an insolent child. Tell Weber you want to read the official complaint. And have him CC me a copy. I'd like to know who I'm suing these days."

The phone call ended with Bell more confused than when she'd dialed. She slumped down to her back and tossed the phone aside.

Past the kitchenette, a sitting area led to a sliding glass door and a private balcony. The lake lay beyond, scattered glints of moonlight rippling the surface. A small sand beach shrouded by the night divided the resort grounds and water. As she blinked, something moved on the beach. A single shadow.

It might have been a guest admiring the lake. No. This figure stared into Bell's room.

She bolted off the bed and crossed the floor to the patio door. Ice trickled through her veins. Logan Wolf looked up at her. She grabbed hold of the door and started to slide it back. She stopped. The night drew shadows down from his eyes and cloaked his intentions. She touched the Glock, still holstered at her hip, and ran a trembling hand over the weapon. Then she threw the door open and stepped onto the balcony.

The wind surprised her when she entered the night. It had been calm inside Blackwater, but a chilling breeze rolled off the lake toward the shore. Though an iron gate enclosed the patio, it was easy to scale the waist-high barrier and drop the last few feet to the sand. Bell turned, and he stood face-to-face with her, his eyes black holes that seemed to draw the night.

"You were watching me," Bell said, her throat parched.

"I wanted your attention, dear Scarlett."

"So you could have knocked."

He shook his head.

"Wouldn't want to disturb the guests. Besides, Agent Gardy warned me not to speak to you without him present." He turned his head toward Gardy's patio and smiled at the drawn curtain. "We won't tell him, will we, Scarlett? It would crush him, I fear. Neil is rather smitten with you."

"Don't say that. He's my partner, nothing else."

"As you wish."

"What is it you want with me, Wolf?"

"Walk with me. Let us enjoy all the secrets the night has to offer."

He lent her his hand, and she tutted. When he started down the beach, she considered letting him walk off on his own. Something drew her to follow. Curiosity, perhaps. It killed the cat, after all.

The bed-and-breakfast offered a hundred feet of sandy lake frontage, then the sand turned to stone. Water lapped at the shoreline, gentle compared to the way the ocean lunged when you least expected. The oscillations might have been calming had it not been for the serial killer's presence.

"How deep do you suppose Blackwater Lake is,

Scarlett?"

The breeze cut into Bell's skin and made her wish she'd worn a sweatshirt.

"A few hundred feet?"

"Six hundred feet at its center. Rather unusual for a small lake. One could disappear in those depths."

Bell stopped in her tracks and glared at him.

"If you know something about this case you're not sharing—"

"Nothing more than a theory, understand. No need to bite the hand that feeds you. Our killer is either a magician or he's found a special place to stash the bodies."

"A six-hundred foot grave would do."

"Quite. I don't wish to teach you how to do your job, but if I were in your position, I'd watch the lake closely. See if anyone likes to row out to the deepest waters under the cloak of darkness."

Bell stumbled where the sand transitioned to rock. Wolf caught her. Shrugging him off induced a smile out of the serial killer. The few times he'd aided her in cases, his speculations proved eerily accurate.

"Now that I've helped you again, dear Scarlett, it's time for me to be going. Though goodbyes are never easy, you will understand it isn't a good idea for me to grow roots."

"Where are you going?"

"It's best for us if I don't reveal my plans."

"I trust you'll stay away from my parents."

"If that is your wish, I shall comply. But I've waited too long for the profile you promised. I must have it, Scarlett. Now."

Something changed in the serial killer's gait. His pace quickened, became aggressive, made Bell worry over her answer. She knew he wouldn't like it.

Bell scanned the lake shore homes, most of which sat

far enough up the beach so nobody would overhear. Lights shone like cat eyes through the windows. Shadows passed over drawn curtains as people went about their lives unaware the nation's most wanted serial killer walked outside their doorways.

"I'm waiting, Agent Bell."

Bell spat her theory before fear stifled her.

"The man you stalk, the man who murdered Renee, is not a serial killer. That's why you can't find him."

Wolf stopped in his tracks. Beside them, the lake slithered beside their shoes, the water the color of blood in the moonlight. He slipped his hand into his jacket pocket, and she reached for her hip and brushed her fingers against the gun. But he didn't pull a knife from his coat. Instead, his hands dropped back down to his sides where his fingers twitched.

"Explain."

Exhaling, Bell reversed course and led them back toward the bed-and-breakfast. Back toward Gardy and familiarity. He stood watching her for a heartbeat, his stare digging holes into her back. Wolf caught up to her. She half-expected him to snag her arm and spin her around. Instead, he matched her stride, the intensity clear in his eyes.

"Understand I'm building the profile without benefit of forensic evidence and following a trail that turned cold years ago."

"You've read the police and FBI reports."

"I have."

"He sliced her throat from ear-to-ear and draped a bag over her head. If that isn't a serial killer's calling card —"

"It is," she said, turning to block him. He stopped before her, fingers continuing to twitch as if he might strangle her on the beach and leave her for the gulls. "The calling card is too perfect, like something you'd see in a movie."

"As you admitted, your profile is little more than a guess."

"Not a guess. The evidence suggests you're chasing a nonexistent phantom."

"What evidence?"

"The only person to leave that calling card since Renee's death is you. Think about it. You called him out, and he never answered, nor did he murder anyone else."

"You can't know that. Perhaps he changed his—"

"His calling card? You don't believe your own words, Wolf."

Wheels turned behind his eyes. As they spun, they chipped away at walls he'd constructed, walls that held the monsters at bay and kept Wolf from thoroughly descending into insanity. She discerned brittleness and hurt beneath the hard shell.

"Who would kill my wife, and why?"

The wind blew Bell's hair across her face. She brushed it back and buried her hands in her pockets, walking again.

"I'm not sure. But it feels like a professional hit."

"That doesn't make sense," he said, the break in his voice belying his conviction.

"In the current context, no. It doesn't. Perhaps we need to look at the murder from another angle."

"I'm intrigued, Scarlett, but understand you tread on dangerous ground."

The venom returned to his stare. It was fair warning, a cobra guarding his nest. She couldn't fail him.

"So here is my theory. Someone wanted you out of the way, but attempting to murder a man with your skill set would be dangerous. Too much potential for you to turn the tables. What better method to eliminate a decorated agent than frame him for murder?"

"I cannot follow this line of logic. The only people who wanted me dead were the killers I put behind bars, and they were in no position to act upon their wishes."

Yet the vein in his neck throbbed. Something in her profile threw him off balance.

"Then you're missing something, an incident you forgot after you lost Renee. The person who framed you isn't an ordinary killer. He's someone powerful, a man who believed you could hurt him."

Now Wolf rounded on her.

"Do you realize you just described Neil Gardy to a T?"

"Stop it. I swear, the two of you are worse than a couple of kids fighting over the last bucket in a sandbox."

"Fine. I'll take your profile into consideration. You'll promise me to be cautious while I'm away, dear Scarlett. Trust nobody, your partner included."

"At least tell me where you're going."

Wolf grinned.

"If I let my imagination wander, I might begin to think you'll miss me. Fear not. You'll see me again soon."

She grabbed his shoulder.

"You know who it is. The killer. And now you're going after him. Tell me who it is, and I'll help you bring him down."

"The game has become far too dangerous. Remember what I said. Farewell, Scarlett. Until the next time."

CHAPTER SEVENTY-SEVEN

Nicholas cannot hear the wind over his slamming heart. The humid night grasps him as he crosses the street, and he is heedless to the headlights washing over his face. A horn honks. Brakes slam. The driver yells a lewd slur out the window as Nicholas hops the curb and crosses the lawn. Brittle from the long summer, the grass crunches below his feet.

Despite the heat, his teeth chatter. And then he's a child again as he climbs the porch steps. Fears the beating he'll receive for coming home late.

Or coming home at all.

Cigarette smoke assails him at the screen door. He grabs the handle and pulls it open, no need to knock. The walls of the yellow-stained hallway seem to fly at him. As though the house pulls him inside. A conveyor belt beneath his feet.

The kitchen stands off to his right. Dirty pots and dishes spill in an overfilled sink. Flies buzz on the counter and at the window. The hallway pulls him past the dining room toward the living room. Against the wall, the blue light of the television flickers, and he hears the laugh track of some pretentious sitcom.

The phlegm-choked cough freezes Nicholas before his shadow breaks the threshold and enters enemy territory. If he turns and runs, the enemy won't know he's here. In seconds he can be back to the safety of his own home across the street. But his legs walk on their own accord, that feeling once again that fate forces him forward.

Inside the room, the elderly man slumps on the couch. Emaciated. Greasy hair strands clinging to peeling scalp. The man wears a stained wife beater tank. A lit cigarette curls smoke from an ashtray to the ceiling.

As Nicholas edges around the wall, the man spits a chunk into a napkin, wads it up and tosses it on the floor. Nicholas stands watching the man from the edge of the room. Knows the old man can see him, though he never pulls his eyes away from the idiot box.

"You just gonna stand there like a dullard?" The words make Nicholas jump as though a jolt of electricity shocks him. "Well?"

After Nicholas fails to reply, the man shakes his head and picks a can of beer off the coffee table.

"Good for nothing. Just like your sister. Make yourself useful and get me a beer."

Nicholas nods and turns back toward the kitchen. His shoulders relax now that he is out of his father's vision. Still, he senses the old man's eyes following him through the walls, piercing and cutting. Two Budweisers chill in the refrigerator. He grabs one, ensures it is cold lest he raise his father's ire, and walks it back to the living room.

Nicholas hands the beer at arm's length to his father. Up close he sees how scrawny the old man is, bone shapes poking against old parchment flesh like stakes through a tent. The logical lobe of his brain understands he is stronger than his father now. If he chooses, he can reach down, grab the old man by his scarecrow neck and squeeze, squeeze, squeeze until bones crack and his father's tongue turns purple and protrudes between his lips.

Nicholas has the strength to hoist his father halfway up the wall and bash his head against the plaster.

But the lizard brain is stronger. Always stronger. It remembers when Nicholas was the weaker one, only a child, and this portion of his brain will never climb out of that hole.

The old man snatches the drink from his hand. Pops the top and chugs a quarter of the can before slapping it down on the coffee table. Nicholas instinctively flinches, expecting the back of his father's hand. When it doesn't come, he releases his breath.

"What do you want, boy? Can't you see I'm busy?"

Nicholas shuffles his feet and crosses his ankles. His father's raised voice always makes Nicholas feel like he needs to pee.

"Punk kid. Tell me why you're here, or get the hell out of my house."

Nicholas swallows, wets the back of his throat.

"I wanted to see if you're doing okay."

"Why wouldn't I be doing okay? Stupid shit. You're worse than your mother was."

This causes Nicholas to tremble. He never knew his mother, the woman who succumbed to an aneurysm when Nicholas was one. Yet he often wondered how different his life might have been had his mother lived. Would she have saved Nicholas from his childhood hell and taken him to a better place? A place where his father couldn't hurt him?

And that causes his neck to redden with sweat as he thinks of Leigh. His sister. She witnessed the abuse and could have saved him. But she left Nicholas, abandoned him like everyone did.

"Fuck off, kid. The best day of my life was the day you finally moved out. Get out of my house and let me be."

Furious, Nicholas steps toward his father. For a moment, the confidence drains off the old man's face. He looks uncertainly at his son, the younger male towering over him. A few tense seconds pass, then the father grins his black-and-yellow teeth and picks up the beer can again.

"All right then. Spit it out, boy. You want to talk? We'll talk. How's the new job?"

Nicholas's pulse quickens when he thinks of the women. Of late nights on the open water with no one but God to bear witness.

"Good. Better than I could have imagined."

"Well then. I'm happy for you, I suppose." The father wipes his mouth on the wife beater and scratches behind his ear. "Your boss a prick? They usually are."

"I…work alone."

"Alone?" His father sniffs. "No one looking over your shoulder all day? Sounds like a dream job. Where you working?"

Nicholas looks off toward the window where night meets the glass. Eyes wander down the quiet road to his gray Cape Cod behind the old elms. And what he sees makes his heart skip.

The basement door is open.

Open!

How? It's impossible. The new girl, Pam Teagarden, is unconscious and bound to the beam. He checked before he left, dammit. He's careful and always checks. In his mind, he imagines the girl halfway across Blackwater, legs pumping as she races to the police station. She left him like Leigh and Mom and—

"You slow, boy? I asked you where you work?"

"On the water," he whispers through chapped lips.

The comedy prattles incessantly from the television. He strides to the window and places both hands on the sill. Leans and cranes his neck, believing a change in angle will reveal the open door was nothing more than a trick of the light. But it wasn't. The door hangs like a gaping wound. He searches the dark with growing desperation, listens for shouting or the scream of sirens approaching from the village center.

"The water? You a fisherman for Charlie Eggens or something?"

"I gotta go, Daddy. Gotta go now."

"Huh? Thought you wanted to talk. You haven't told me nothing yet. If it's Eggens, there are things you should know—"

Nicholas shoots down the hallway with his father's phantom bellows chasing him. The screen door bangs open and whacks against the siding, and he stumbles half-blind through the night and crosses the street.

The open basement door taunts him. When he reaches the yard, he swings around and checks the neighbor's house. Nobody watches through the window. Nothing makes sense. People should fill the streets, talking about the abducted woman who broke out of Nicholas Winston's apartment. Why doesn't he hear sirens? The police must know.

A black hole leads down to the basement. From where he stands, the open door looks like the fanged maw of a monstrous beast. He cautiously approaches the opening, sneakers making little swishing noises through the grass. His heart hammers. Too fast. Leaves him short of breath and dizzy.

The steps creak and groan as he clutches the rail and descends into darkness. Reaches the concrete floor and stands motionless, listening to the wind keen around the old house. It takes time for his vision to adjust to the pitch black, and even then red spots fly across his eyes and obscure the shadowed shapes of the cellar.

The first thing he sees is the gray hulk of the water heater. Nausea gurgles from the pit of his stomach when he doesn't see the woman. Then a noise comes from behind the water heater. A weak, shivering cry. As he pushes past the tool bench and rounds the water heater, he sees Teagarden curled on the cold cellar floor, hands tied to the beam as he'd left her.

The sound that comes from him is almost a whimper. Relief hits him at-once. Nicholas slumps against the post and sits beside her, legs bent at the knee, head softly banging against the rough wooden beam.

Did someone break into the basement? Unlikely. They would have discovered the woman. No, it must have been the wind. Never before had he appreciated the danger the flimsy cellar door put him in. He must replace the lock set, perhaps the entire door. He averted disaster but won't be so lucky next time.

Exhaustion grips Nicholas, but more work awaits. Behind him, the ancient freezer murmurs. He imagines Carla Betters inside, caked with frost, bloody icicles jutting off the racks. The lake is better. Bodies vanish there. But when he'd captured Betters, he hadn't honed in on this methodology. Thought he could keep her forever in the freezer, ensure she never left.

He strokes the sleeping woman's hair. Touches her face, almost lovingly. When Teagarden awakens she will need to eat, but he has time.

Nicholas reaches up to the shelves and pulls down a fresh roll of clear plastic. Slices it to size with his knife. Tonight, Carla Betters will finally leave him as Leigh had. But the new woman is here to take their places.

CHAPTER SEVENTY-EIGHT

The dark water lapped against the canoe with squishing noises that made it sound as if something black and rotten crawled toward the two men.

With Trent's help, Perry Wetlaufer pushed the canoe off the shore and high stepped into the shallows. Police ordinance forbade vessels on the lake without a boat light after sunset, but patrol boats didn't search these waters at night, and he'd always reeled in more trout after dark than he did during the day when half the community motored up and down the lake, scaring all his fish away.

The boat rocked and tipped when he climbed inside. Trent sat across from him in his waterproof waders, overkill to Wetlaufer who somehow managed to catch fish in cargo shorts and a tank. What good did waders do in a six-hundred foot deep lake? If you were stupid enough to fall in, you got wet. Oh well. One of them would be complaining about the humidity when they reached the center of the lake, and it wouldn't be Wetlaufer.

He liked Trent and enjoyed the man's banter, even though his friend couldn't catch a fish if it crawled into the canoe and threw itself at his mercy. Currently Trent, stringy red hair that had long receded from his forehead, shifted in his seat, twisting his upper body to observe their progress.

He scanned the water for other boats and smiled. They had the lake all to themselves.

"Someone will report us."

"Will you relax?" Wetlaufer dug the fishing rod from under his seat and touched the Styrofoam container. The red wigglers pushed through the soil inside. "Chief Tanner has bigger things to deal with than a couple guys breaking curfew on the lake."

"But all those abductions. That's gotta mean more cops on the street."

"On the street, yes. Not on the lake."

Anxious to escape the shallows, Wetlaufer put his shoulders into the rowing, rocking back to amp his heart rate. The farther they drifted from the cottage lights, the sharper the stars became. He could reach up and touch the heavens, the stars shone so brightly. The vast night sky made him infinitesimal and left him awestruck.

Though he enjoyed nothing more than fishing Blackwater Lake at night, the humidity always took his breath away, and tonight it was unusually thick. The moisture seemed a part of him. It wicked through his shirt, turned his skin clammy.

"I wonder what he does with the bodies."

Wetlaufer glanced up at Trent, his friend's face pale in the moonlight.

"Who?"

"The guy we were talking about. The one who kidnapped all those women."

Wetlaufer sneered. That was another problem with Trent. Damn guy was freaking morbid. If he could've put two words together, he might have been another Stephen King or Dean Koontz. Instead, he came off like a loudmouth simpleton with a death fetish.

"Hell, why are you asking me? Probably handcuffs them to the bed and gets his jollies. Let's talk about something else."

"You know what?" Clearly Trent didn't want to talk about something else. "Perry?"

"I'm afraid you're gonna tell me."

"I bet he kills 'em. Buries them in the swamp, or dumps their bodies in the mountains."

"Jesus, Trent. You must be great at parties, all that shit running around inside your head. Anyhow, you're jumping to conclusions. Could be kidnappings, or the women ran off. No reason to assume there's a killer in Blackwater."

Trent's eyes widened, his mouth bouncing amid a sea of red whiskers that made him look muppet-like.

"No? Why is the FBI here? I overheard Tom Bridges —"

"Officer Bridges to you."

"Yeah, Officer Bridges at Paulie's last night. Overheard him say the Behavior Analysis Unit agents are in town. They only get called when there's a serial killer like that psycho that was killing people around Bealton."

They were almost to the center of the lake. Wetlaufer pulled up the oars and let the canoe coast to a stop.

"Geez, Louise," Trent said, slapping his forehead. "Why didn't I think of it already?"

Wetlaufer glanced at Trent through the tops of his eyes as he slid a wiggling worm onto the fishhook.

"Now what?"

"The lake, you big dummy. What if he dumps the bodies in the lake?"

"Tell you what. I'm gonna cast this line, and then I don't want another word about serial killers or dead women or some crazy bastard dumping people in the lake. Besides, all that yapping is frightening the fish away."

The exclamation on Wetlaufer's rant was his rod smacking the side of the canoe when he botched the cast.

By dumb luck, the hook plunked into the water in the vicinity of his target. Concentric rings expanded outward in tiny waves.

"You're a grumpy bastard tonight," Trent said, itching his beard.

Wetlaufer ignored the comment and mulled over his friend's ridiculous theory. But as he waited for a fish to tug at his line, he wondered if Trent was onto something. He spun his head toward the shoreline, paranoia creeping up the back of his neck. Stupid Trent. Now Wetlaufer would spend the rest of the night fearing every boater was the crazed psycho of Blackwater Lake.

He realized the cottages were slowly disappearing into the night. A mist curled off the water, the humble beginnings of a London moors fog that would soon blanket the lake. He'd gotten himself stuck on the water in thick Virginia fogs and knew boating became dangerous. What if a larger vessel crashed across the center of the lake and didn't spot his little canoe? In the dark they'd be invisible until the last possible second.

Trent swatted at an insect.

"Anything?"

"It's been all of five minutes. If you didn't want to come, you should have stayed home. Maybe you could've watched one of those Hannibal Lecter movies and saved me the grief."

"Dick."

"Your mama's dick."

Trent glared at him. They both broke into a rousing laughter that rocked the canoe.

"What the hell does that even mean?"

The laughter sputtered to hitches, then all was quiet. Just the deep waters of the lake sloshing against the side of the canoe. Off in the distance, cottage lights winked through the thickening fog.

"Getting dense," Trent said, cracking his neck.

"Came up pretty fast, I'd say."

"We should head back while we can still see the shore."

"Shit, I just rowed us out here. Now you want me to turn around?"

Trent shrugged.

"What's the harm? The lake will still be here tomorrow night and every night thereafter."

"The harm is that I rowed to the middle of the lake for nothing. I haven't gotten a single bite."

In a moment of irony, the line tugged. Wetlaufer reeled in the slack while the fish chased through the water toward the canoe. It was a big one, and Trent needed to shift his weight to the other side of the canoe to keep it from tipping as Wetlaufer leaned back and reeled the fish in. Another minute of struggling ensued before a foot-long bass splashed out of the lake with Wetlaufer cursing as he pulled him in.

"You see, you see? And you wanted to go back. They're all around the boat just waiting for us to haul their asses in."

Trent excitedly grabbed his own rod and baited the line. He cast away from Wetlaufer's line, and the waiting game began anew, their optimism blinding them to the fog. A half-hour passed with little tugs that turned out to be false alarms. By the time Wetlaufer realized he'd lost sight of the shore, it was too late. They were screwed.

He barely saw Trent, and that was fine because Wetlaufer figured his friend wore an *I-told-you-so* scowl. One bass wasn't worth getting stuck on the lake over.

"Come on, Perry. Pull your line in and let's call it a night."

Wetlaufer opened his mouth to argue and clamped it shut. He worried, too. He kept listening for a big boat heading at them. Someone who'd downed a few too many beers and wouldn't notice the little canoe before he cut them in half. Strange that the fog made it difficult to hear. As if the gray cloak snuffed out sound.

"Sure," Wetlaufer said, winding the line. It was a struggle to keep his voice from breaking. "While we can still see."

Mist consumed the shoreline and the lights circling the lake. Where were the docks? He couldn't pull the canoe onto any old shore. The truck was back at the docks. Shit, this wasn't good.

He shoved the fishing rod beneath the seat. Then he turned the canoe around and rowed, a calculated guess at best.

"I don't think this is the way."

"If you keep second guessing me, you can swim back to shore."

The oars cut through the water and propelled the canoe into the unknown. The fish stench thickened, and anxiety tempted him to open the ice box and toss the bass into the lake. Ethereal silence swam around the canoe, a deathly quiet that reminded Wetlaufer of a scene from that Stephen King vampire movie, the one where the undead children raked their fingernails against the windows of the living and demanded entry.

He shook off the memory before a noise came out of the night…the murmur of water, like an advancing stream. Something in the lake heading at the canoe.

Wetlaufer met Trent's eyes a moment before they heard the motor. The nightmare scenario of a vessel smashing the canoe into splinters became real. As he searched the fog, he didn't see a light.

"Bastard doesn't have his light on," Trent said, swiveling in the canoe, trying to find the source of the motor. The rumble seemed to bounce off the fog and come at them from all directions. "Shit. He'll blow us to smithereens."

The moment Wetlaufer swung the canoe to the right to avoid destruction, the motor cut off. They stared at each other from opposite ends of the canoe, eyes unblinking.

"Don't make sense. He just stopped."

"You figure he's fishing and doesn't want to get caught? Like us?"

"He's driving a motorboat. Why no light?"

"Might be busted."

Wetlaufer nodded, unconvinced. Whoever was on the lake with them, he was a ghost. The canoe rode gentle swells agitated by the larger vessel, both men gripping the sides of the canoe and feeling very small. Trent opened his mouth. Wetlaufer cut him off and placed a finger to his lips.

Another sound. A metallic rattle like someone dug through a toolbox. Perhaps it was like Trent said...just another guy fishing in the dark. But why didn't the fisherman cast?

The crinkle of plastic brought his head around. He could almost see the boat, a nebulous silhouette behind the veil of mist. Several seconds of quiet, then a splash.

The canoe rocked. Wetlaufer swallowed and reached for the oars, wanted to get the hell out of there. But instinct froze him. A warning not to announce their presence.

A second splash, this one louder. Wetlaufer jumped as Trent materialized out of the fog in front of him. His friend had crept across the canoe without thinking, and now the narrow boat tipped and pitched, threatening to toss them into the lake.

The jowls on Trent's face trembled as Wetlaufer eased him back toward the center of the canoe. They sat beside each other and shivered while waiting for the canoe to reach equilibrium. Shaking his head at Trent, Wetlaufer pointed at the shadowed boat before a third splash rippled the lake.

At that moment, all of Trent's paranoid fears spread to Wetlaufer. What if the serial killer dumped his victims into the lake under the cloak of darkness? What if the madman floated fifteen yards from their canoe? They'd never outrace a motorboat if the psycho came after them.

The unseen person continued to toss objects into the lake. As they waited in the quiet, a death stench reached Wetlaufer's nostrils. Surely that was his imagination running on overdrive. Yet there was a smell on the wind, a stench like carrion baking on the side of the road.

Silently, Wetlaufer dunked the oar into the water and pulled. Enough to point the canoe away from the boat and get them moving. Trent grabbed the second oar and rowed on the other side of the canoe.

Good. They began to drift into the fog, unsure where they were heading. It didn't matter provided they put distance between them and the phantom figure on the lake.

As they pushed through the mist, Wetlaufer feared the killer would spy the canoe and come after them, but the splashes became softer, distant.

Five minutes later, the canoe skidded blindly onto the shore fifty yards from the docks.

CHAPTER SEVENTY-NINE

Along the dark shoreline, Bell yawned beside Gardy and shook her head to jostle herself awake. The police motorboat, fitted with two adjustable spotlights, docked at the end of the pier, two officers already on board. She recognized Tanner and Bridges, the chief conferring with another officer on his radio. A second boat took off from the docks and headed toward the center of the lake.

Two fishermen, one in shorts and a tank top, the other wearing waders a size too large for him, clutched their elbows and shivered. Both were soaked from stomping through the foggy waters toward the docks, though the redheaded man in waders appeared far more comfortable than his drenched friend.

Tanner hopped out of the boat and jogged toward Bell and Gardy.

"Sopping wet guy over there is Perry Wetlaufer," Tanner said, tilting his head toward the fisherman in cargo shorts. "His buddy is Trent O'Malley. Looks like they were out fishing in the dark."

"Is that illegal?" Bell asked. She caught Wetlaufer looking at her, and the man lowered his head.

"There's an ordinance against boating without a light

after sundown, not that it matters at this point. I couldn't care less. Wetlaufer says there was another boat on the water, a motorboat of some sort. Sounded like whoever was on board kept tossing objects into the water."

"But they couldn't see?"

"Not in the fog, no. For all we know, somebody tossed their garbage overboard. We're grasping at straws."

"Where were they?"

Tanner cupped a hand over his brow as though doing so would help penetrate the fog. At the same time, Wetlaufer and his friend climbed into the boat with Officer Bridges.

"Toward the center of the lake," Tanner said, pointing toward the second boat, already halfway across the lake.

"Six-hundred foot depths."

Tanner raised his eyebrows.

"Impressive. Sounds like someone did her homework."

"Wikipedia knows all," Bell said, recalling her discussion with Wolf. "If someone wanted to get rid of a body, I can't think of a better place."

Tanner nodded.

"The divers will be there in a second. If our killer was out there tonight..."

Tanner trailed off as he ran his eyes across the gravel parking area. Several sets of tire tracks sliced across the lot. Any of them might have belonged to the unknown subject.

Gardy moved to Tanner's side and looked out at the water.

"What about all these boats floating off the docks? You know who they belong to?"

Tanner did. He rattled off the owners' names. In the chief's opinion, none of them matched Bell's profile. Bridges shouted from the boat.

"We're ready to roll," Tanner said as Bell and Gardy followed him down the pier.

A moment later, Bell and Gardy sat beside Tanner, the boat skipping over waves and turning her stomach as they rumbled toward the center of the lake. Captaining the boat, Bridges peered into the mist. Now-and-then, he twisted his head toward the two fishermen for directions.

Each time the boat bucked over a breaker and landed, the lake sprayed Bell and soaked her pants. Should have worn shorts like the fisherman, Bell thought, wringing out her jacket. When it seemed the trip would never end, Bridges eased them to a stop and killed the motor. The second boat floated about fifty feet away. Spotlights stroked the surface of the water like alien suns, their beams catching the divers.

Gardy stood and leaned over the side, scratching his head.

"What do we expect to find? The evidence is at the bottom of the lake by now. Hell, we might not even be in the right spot."

He glanced at the fishermen. They shrugged, hardly a vote of confidence.

"Let's hope he made a mistake," Tanner said. "If he did, we'll find it. You won't find a better diving crew."

A female diver surfaced and removed her mask, catching her breath. An officer in the second boat swung the light over her and called down.

"You okay?"

She raised her thumb.

"I saw something below the surface. It's about fifty feet off your starboard side."

"Give her some light!" the officer shouted, and Bridges aimed the beam.

The diver replaced her mask and disappeared into the lake's depths. Bell followed the beam, trying to discern what the diver had seen. Swinging her eyes to Gardy, she lowered her voice.

"Wolf left again."

"I doubt it. He's probably hiding in my closet," Gardy said, wincing. "He'll jam a knife into my back when I open the door."

"I hoped we were past that by now. Insane or not, he theorized the killer deposited bodies in the lake."

"Really? When did this conversation occur?"

Bell shot Gardy a warning glance as Chief Tanner shuffled toward them.

"Someone else thinks our killer is using the lake?" Tanner asked.

Gardy rolled his eyes, unhappy Bell nearly gave them away.

"Another agent at the BAU," Bell said, crossing her legs. "We collaborate whenever possible, especially on difficult cases like this one."

"It's a good theory. Starting tonight, I'm putting an undercover officer on the water. If anyone sneaks onto the lake under the cover of darkness, we'll get a bead on him."

Gardy wandered to Tanner's side and watched the diver below the surface as she circled through the beam radius.

"You need more people," Gardy said. "Set up a perimeter around Blackwater. Check every vehicle trailing a boat just in case this guy makes a run for it. He must know you're onto him by now."

"I'll radio the sheriff and get extra bodies." Tanner popped a piece of gum in his mouth. To Bell, the chief looked like a compressed spring. "But my gut tells me Agent Bell is correct. This guy is local to Blackwater."

Bell stopped short of replying when the female diver surfaced, water pouring off her suit as Bridges brought the boat around. Good God, she held something in her hand.

Tanner bolted to the side of the boat and leaned over.

"You get something, Devers?" Out of breath, the woman nodded. "Bring her in, Bridges."

Gardy chewed his lip beside Tanner as Bell maneuvered around the men to get a better look. She could see the object now. Torn fabric.

A piece of a woman's dress.

CHAPTER EIGHTY

The sun descended over the Blackwater Police Department after a long an frustrating day. Throughout the afternoon police and sheriff deputies had stopped boaters leaving Blackwater to no avail. The killer had slipped through their fingers.

Unless he was here all along, hiding in the shadows.

Tanner's team contacted the victims' families and confirmed the red plaid fabric matched a dress worn by Carla Betters. For Bell, the verification confirmed her worst fears. The killer dumped the bodies into the lake. When Bell and Gardy had floated on the lake during the early morning hours, Carla Betters's bloated body parts had lain beneath them, fish picking at her flesh. This one time, Bell wished she'd been wrong.

Gardy traced his finger over the wall map inside the chief's office. Bell set her coffee down and nodded at the map.

"Right now our target's confidence is at an all-time high," Bell said. "He no longer believes you can catch him. Use his overconfidence against him. He'll slip up."

Tanner leaned back against his desk and folded his arms, chewing on a fresh piece of gum.

"What about the boat patrols? You still in favor?"

"Patrol the lake, but make sure your officers keep a low profile. This killer is a loner and easily spooked. If he figures out you're closing in on him, this will go one of two ways. Either he bolts and leaves the area for good, or he escalates and makes a final stand."

"How so?"

"Think back to the women," Gardy said, pointing at the tacks. "All brunettes in their twenties with similar features. They're substitutes for someone important in our target's life, a woman who emotionally broke him. With each victim he captures he's building up to this one woman. If she's still in the area, he'll go for her next."

Tanner paced the room.

"Dammit. I should have kept a patrol on the lake all along. We'd have him by now."

Bell wanted to tell Tanner it wasn't his fault. She'd offered the theory only hours ago. Before she could, Officer Bridges slammed the phone down in the operations area and ran into Tanner's office with a sheet of paper in his hand.

"We got another one."

"Shit."

"Pam Teagarden, age twenty-six. She waitresses at Mulligan's and didn't show up to work last evening, and now she isn't answering her door. It's been twenty-four hours since anyone last saw her."

The new disappearance might have been coincidental, a woman who decided she'd had enough of waitressing and blew out of town for the night. Any hope Bell harbored vanished when Bridges handed Tanner the printout of Teagarden's license. Black curls to the shoulder, young and pretty. According to the license, Teagarden fit the other girls' heights.

"Where's Water Street?" Bell asked, tilting the photocopy away from the glare of the florescent lights.

"East side of the lake," Bridges said. "A twenty-minute walk to Mulligan's, but the owner claims Teagarden usually took an Uber. Says she worried about the abductions."

Tanner handed the sheet back to Bridges.

"I want the area between Water Street and Mulligan's canvased. Somebody must have seen Teagarden."

"Right away."

When Bridges hurried out to the operations area, Tanner deflated as though pricked with a pin. The chief slouched in his chair and ran a hand through thinning hair.

"He's playing games with us. I don't know where to begin looking."

As Tanner rubbed his eyes, Gardy nodded at Bell.

"Gardy and I have been in this predicament more times than I care to mention," Bell said, pulling up a chair across from Tanner. "As the killer escalates, he loses control and makes mistakes. The dress might be the first big one we've found, but it's the tip of the iceberg."

Tanner blinked his tired eyes and rocked back in his chair.

"We know he uses the lake."

"Yes."

"And the last two abducted women lived in Blackwater. He's hunting closer to home, exactly as you predicted."

"Which means he's a village resident. Chief, how soon can you compile a list of boat owners in Blackwater? Keep in mind we're looking for a man in his twenties or thirties, and we'll want to cross-reference with childhood abuse victims."

"I can get you that list, but my staff is stretched to the point of breaking as is. It might take a while to narrow it down to abuse cases."

"Don't worry. Keep your men on the streets. I have someone at the BAU who can help."

"I'll call Harold now," Gardy said, exiting the office.

Tanner shuffled the case notes on his desk. The chief was jostled but unbroken, and Bell could see the man pulling himself together by sheer will.

"I hope you're right about the profile."

"I am, Chief. We'll corner this guy. If he's still in Blackwater, he's not getting out."

CHAPTER EIGHTY-ONE

Nicholas jolts awake on the basement floor. Back aches from where the crumbled surface dug into his spine and tore his flesh. It takes a moment to remember where he is, and then he grabs the beam and yanks himself to his feet, electric panic surging beneath his skin.

How long had he slept?

He digs the grit from his eyes and blinks. Dying sunlight beams into the cellar through a dirty, cobweb-encased window. Almost evening. That means he'd dozed for two or three hours.

Fool!

In his mind, his father screams in his idiot face, spittle hot against his cheeks. He'd seen the police boats on the lake, knew where they were heading and what they'd find. Tearing the dress and throwing the pieces overboard was a mistake, for he'd known they might float near the surface before the lake pulled the evidence to the bottom. Now the police have more divers and equipment which will uncover the bodies at the lake's bottom.

He needs to leave. Now.

It wasn't supposed to end like this. Not before he completed his work.

His jaw shifts, hands curl and uncurl. The Teagarden woman lies at his feet. Unconscious, she looks like an angel except for the crease of worry furrowing her brow.

The cleaver, crusted red and brown with old blood, sits atop the workbench. He can spread the plastic across the floor and pull Teagarden onto its center. Murder her. But he can't prevent the splatter. It took him two full days to scrub the walls after he killed Carla Betters, and even now he can't guarantee he removed all the evidence. The police have methods for identifying blood invisible to the eye. He should have known better.

"Why are you doing this?"

Nicholas catches his breath. The woman is onto her elbows, face smeared by grime, shirt torn down the neckline, though he never tried to rape her. The fabric tore during the struggle.

"I know you. I've seen you in town, right?"

Her words are meant to humanize. Though Nicholas understands this, she confuses him. Makes him question why he would want to hurt her.

"Let me go, and I swear I won't tell anybody. I'll say I never saw your face."

He turns his back to her and chews his thumbnail. Shifts away from the sun as though the entire village trains lights on him.

"Damn you! Aren't you going to answer? Let me the hell out of here!"

He winces at her screech. The words remind him of his father.

Rounding on her, he snatches the cleaver off the table. Teagarden's eyes widen, jaw slackens. Her face twists in horror as he runs his fingertip along the cutting edge.

And as he crosses through the light and disturbs the shadow, her facial features shift. Teagarden doesn't simply look like Leigh. She *is* Leigh now.

A siren in the village breaks his trance. Are they coming for him already?

The woman's eyes never blink as she follows the police siren. The noise rises to a fevered pitch and draws nearer as Nicholas runs to the window and peers out.

But the police don't come. After several heartbeats, the pitch of the siren shifts and fades. He's safe. For now.

Decided, Nicholas drops the cleaver and gags Teagarden's mouth with the same dusty, blood-stained cloth he'd used on the others. The woman thrashes and shrieks into the gag. The cloth stifles her cries for help.

She is still screaming and writhing along the floor while he climbs the stairs to the kitchen. He needs his keys. They must leave before the police come.

CHAPTER EIGHTY-TWO

Outside Leigh Winston's window, the drainage creek turned the color of blood beneath the setting sun. Her eyes followed its curves down the hillside and through the woods, the water growing ever darker as it plunged two hundred yards off the ridge and into the lake. A steep gravel road, treacherous when it poured or snowed, slithered through the trees and dead-ended beside her A-frame.

She rinsed the suds off the last of the dinner dishes and set the plate in the rack. While she dried her hands, her eyes flicked back to the road. Shadows lengthened, the ancient trees monstrous in the dark. Somewhere an engine revved…a truck, she thought, as she stood on tiptoe and peeked down the hill, wondering who it might be. The Kensey family ranch stood halfway down the slope, the only other home the gravel road served, and they were in Florida for the month. Though she preferred the hillside over the village traffic, solitude was sometimes dangerous. Last winter, a freak ice storm knocked out the phone lines and left the road impassable for three days. By the time the ice melted, she was subsisting on dry oatmeal and bread.

There was another reason she felt at home amid the trees. The leaves blotted out her old neighborhood across the lake and the monster she'd escaped from. She still carried guilt for leaving Nicholas behind. At the time, she'd pleaded with her father to give her custody—Burt Winston despised his son and would smile at Nicolas's funeral if some tragedy befell the boy—yet he refused to give Nicholas up. After all, who would he have left to abuse?

But living alone on the ridge gave her a greater sense of anxiety after news of the abductions broke. To further increase her paranoia, she'd run into Juliette at the grocery store this morning, and Juliette laughed about Leigh being the spitting image of the D'Angelo woman. And didn't she bear at least a passing resemblance to Carla Betters?

"She could have been your *sistah*," Juliette had joked in her thick Bostonian accent, referring to D'Angelo.

God, what if someone in Blackwater was kidnapping women who looked like Leigh?

She dried her hands on the towel and stepped away from the sink. Halfway across the kitchen, a truck motor brought her head around. This time she was sure she'd heard it. Was it climbing the road to her house?

Leigh kept a Remington rifle in the hallway closet. She started for the hallway when the phone rang. Not her cell, but the land line affixed to the kitchen wall. The caller didn't respond when she answered. Yet she discerned the truck motor in the background. The same motor coming up her driveway.

Instinct told her the call had been a distraction meant to slow her down before she grabbed the rifle. Slamming the phone down, she raced for the hallway as the front door imploded and a dark figure blocked her passage.

She dug the cell phone out of her pocket. The figure rushed through the slashes of shadow and fiery light, and as the beam caught his face, she recognized Nicholas. Seeing her brother was enough to stop her from calling the police, yet she held the phone at her chest as he advanced. Nicholas carried what appeared to be a tangle of rope. He ricocheted off the walls in a frantic, drunken gait. And something was wrong with his eyes. They were too wide, crazed.

The ropes snaked around her and squeezed, locking her arms against her sides. She screamed for him to stop a moment before he struck her head with his fist.

Then the hallway tilted. She pitched backward. Plaster clubbed the back of her head.

Leigh lost consciousness as her little brother gripped her ankle and pulled her into the dark.

CHAPTER EIGHTY-THREE

Gardy lowered the binoculars and handed them to Bell. Dusk fell over the village and reflected off the water. Scanning the lake, Bell centered on the vessel resting over the deepest depths, visibility falling as night crept down from the hills.

"They're using sonar, I take it."

Gardy nodded.

"And ground penetrating radar in case the bodies are below the sediment."

Intellectualizing the search party's technique was a coping mechanism, she realized, a curtain to draw between the hunt and the grisly truths they'd soon uncover. Yet she couldn't stand still waiting for Harold to call back with the search results. She bounced on her heels until Gardy set his hand on her shoulder.

"Easy now. Harold always comes through."

Gardy was right. The BAU's technology specialist was an alchemist at dreaming up new ways to manipulate databases. But while they waited, the killer might murder Pam Teagarden and flee Blackwater.

"Question for you," Gardy said, twisting around to study the parking lot.

Bell followed his eyes but noticed nothing unusual.

"Go ahead."

"Can you think of a reason for Agent Flanagan to be in Blackwater?"

Flanagan was the junior FBI agent assigned to guard Bell's apartment on the Chesapeake Bay if Wolf appeared. Bell's fellow agents considered Flanagan Weber's puppet, his eyes and ears outside the office.

"Not unless the FBI sent him to help."

"That's just it. He would've contacted us by now."

"What makes you think he's here?"

Gardy scratched his head and scuffed his shoe through the stones.

"I'm probably losing my mind. A black SUV cut through the police station parking lot while I was making a call. It happened quick, but it sorta looked like Flanagan driving, and the vehicle had government plates."

Bell considered the possibility for a second before shaking her head.

"Government plates prove nothing. The driver might have been FBI, DEC, NOAA, any organization. Why would Weber send Flanagan to spy on us?"

Gardy dug his hands into his pockets.

"There's something else."

"Wonderful."

"I don't suppose you checked the gossip news this afternoon?"

"I've been a little busy," she said through clenched teeth.

"You're a star again, Bell. Well, we both are now."

"Hayward."

Gavin Hayward. The lead reporter for *The Informer*, a tabloid newspaper obsessed with serial killers and the female FBI agent who hunted them, had hounded Bell, stalking her across the country.

"The same."

"He took pictures of us? When?"

Gardy glanced at his shoelaces.

"Gardy, tell me."

"During the meeting with San Giovanni."

Bell hissed through her teeth. Now her alliance with San Giovanni was compromised. Not to mention a sleazy tabloid reporter followed her every move.

"How is that possible? There was nobody in that alley. We checked."

"Except for a gunman on the roof, of course. Face it. It wasn't our most thorough search. The good news is the congresswoman's face isn't visible in the pictures, nor is Kerr's. The article doesn't mention them."

"Good lord. Talk about a lucky break."

"I'd make a joke about Hayward missing his shot, but…"

"Yeah. It's a little too soon."

Gardy looked like he wanted to say something else when the phone buzzed in Bell's hand. She answered before the first ring ended.

"Tell me you found him, Harold."

The specialist stammered for a moment before steadying the ship.

"I found three licensed boaters living in Blackwater who fit the profile. One stands out."

"Give him to me."

"Nicholas Winston of thirty-nine Water Street."

Bell snapped her finger, and Gardy handed her a pen and notepad. She scribbled the name and address and handed it back to Gardy with a thumbs-up as Harold continued.

"White male, twenty-six years of age. He worked at the marina until they fired him last month." That was the stressor. "Father, Burt Winston, resides at thirty Water

Street. No official abuse charges, but child services visited the home when Nicholas Winston was seven after a boater witnessed the father throw his son into the lake. Said he was teaching the kid to swim."

"Let me guess. The dead center of the lake."

"The report indicates deep waters."

"Christ. Okay, what else?"

"Numerous police visits over the years. Neighbors heard screaming and Burt Winston beating his son. But the charges never stuck."

Gardy was already on the phone with Tanner and feeding him the information. Bell's gaze jerked over to the search boat, observing the macabre excavation and struggling to compartmentalize, all emotions hidden behind her stoic glare.

"What about the mother? How does she play into this?"

Harold paused.

"She doesn't. According to the records, Betsy Winston died when the kid was a year old."

Bell bet the mother fit the abducted women's descriptions, but even if she'd hurt her son, he wouldn't have remembered at such a young age. She'd felt certain the killer hunted women who reminded him of an abusive mother. Was she way off base with the profile?

"Records indicate a sister in the home. Leigh Winston, age twenty-eight. Still lives in Blackwater. Forty-three Dorian Hill."

The sister. Yes, it had to be her.

She ended the call as she jogged back to the Jeep beside Gardy. Gunning the engine, he waited for Bell to clip her seatbelt while he relayed their position to Chief Tanner. A siren wailed through the village, a panicked sound.

As they weaved through the parking lot, Bell missed the black SUV parked beside the exit. Agent Flanagan pulled out and drove off after they passed.

CHAPTER EIGHTY-FOUR

"I repeat, the house is clear," Gardy barked into the radio as he and Bell clambered out the door and onto the stoop.

Full dark blackened the sky and made it difficult to hunt for evidence beyond the perimeter of the porch light, but Bell spied footprints leading toward the driveway, too large to be Leigh Winston's. The front door wouldn't close, the hinges warped from impact when the intruder broke in.

They'd checked every room in Leigh Winston's home and found nothing except a small plaster indentation in the hallway. It might have been a sign of a struggle, or the woman could have dented the wall in any of a hundred ways. Beside the broken door, the most damning pieces of evidence pointing toward an abduction were the keys on the kitchen table and the Kia outside. One might have argued Leigh Winston had left her vehicle and gone for a walk, but the house keys were attached to the chain on the kitchen table.

Behind the house, Officers Yardley and Bridges threw flashlight beams around the property.

Bell cast her own light where the gravel road and driveway merged. Divots marked where someone had backed out in a hurry and trampled the grassy border with truck tires. Nicholas Winston drove a Ford Ranger. The APB for Winston had the entire county hunting him. He was running out of places to hide, and they'd catch him soon. Bell hoped they found Pam Teagarden and Leigh Winston alive.

Chief Tanner's voice boomed over her radio.

"Winston's house is clear. We found ropes around a support beam in the basement and a bloody fingerprint on the floor. Sheriff McNaney just left the father's house—sounds like that guy is a piece of work—and we'll put officers on each house in case Winston returns."

"Good work, Chief," Bell said, clicking a photograph of the tire tracks.

"That thing you said earlier about Winston escalating and making a final stand."

"I remember. Leigh was the ultimate target all along, and now that he's taken her, there's only one thing left for him to accomplish."

"To murder his sister."

"Right. And there's a fighting chance he'll take her out to the lake."

"That's insane. We have a patrol boat waiting for him."

"I don't think it matters to him. He's not considering his wellbeing or what happens after he murders his sister."

A call came in on Bell's phone. She intended to ignore the caller, but Gardy started walking toward her, his face drained of blood.

"I'll get back to you," she told Tanner, lifting the phone to her ear.

Gardy shook his head and stopped dead in his tracks as Bell answered. He waited while she listened to Deputy Director Weber, whose words made little sense.

A minute later, she hung up on her supervisor and

swayed on her feet. How had this happened?

"She's strong," Gardy said, touching her shoulder. "And she has the best doctors in DC."

"This can't be happening. Why her?"

A surge of nausea dropped Bell to her knee. Gardy supported her and offered to help her up, but she waved him off.

How could she think straight knowing Lana San Giovanni lay in critical condition with a gunshot wound?

CHAPTER EIGHTY-FIVE

A metallic crash startled Pam Teagarden awake. Her skull throbbed, and when she touched her forehead, her fingers came away with blood.

She blinked at the dead woman beside her, both women stuffed between the dash and seat on the passenger side of a truck. The gag swallowed her scream.

She sat on bare knees, stray sediment on the truck floor digging and scraping. A zip tie bound her wrists behind her back, while ropes held the other woman.

It made her wonder why the psychopath would tie up a dead person, but then she saw the woman's chest rise and realized she was alive. Barely. The breaths were shallow, labored, the oxygen dragged over broken glass.

Beside her, the madman pounded his sneaker down on the gas pedal. The truck lurched forward and hit a bump, causing the smashing noise behind them again. A trailer, she thought.

A sharp turn swung her sideways. The woman slouched onto Teagarden and pressed her against the door. At that moment she got a good look at the unknown woman and realized she'd seen her in town. A pretty woman, about Teagarden's age. For a heartbeat, Teagarden thought she resembled the woman, if only vaguely. Fighting to clear her head, she remembered the photographs of the missing women on the news. They all looked the same. Like the woman pressing into her. Like Teagarden. Now she understood.

She moaned and tugged at the zip tie. The sharp plastic cut the flesh around her wrists. Pulling her knees inward, she felt a second tie around her ankles.

The truck weaved in the opposite direction and pulled the other woman into the gear shifter with Teagarden atop her. An idea formed. A last-ditch attempt to escape the lunatic who'd imprisoned her in his basement. Though Teagarden lacked use of her hands and legs, she thought she could shove the woman sideways and into the gear shifter. Cause the man to lose control over the truck.

The idea was risky. A violent crash might kill all of them. But it was better than surrendering to fate and allowing the maniac to murder her.

As though he sensed something was wrong, he swung his head toward Teagarden. She shut her eyes and feigned sleep, head lolled onto the unknown woman's shoulder. Inside her self-imposed darkness, she cringed as his fingers caressed her hair. A chill rippled through her skin as he slid his hand down her shoulder and toward her breasts. His hand receded as though he knew what he was doing was wrong, that his twisted conscience justified butchering Teagarden but not violating her sexually.

After his hand left, she counted to thirty in her head, convinced he knew she was awake and wanted to catch Teagarden opening her eyes. When she reached thirty, her heart thumped. All her senses reached high alert. She cracked her eyes open to thin slits and watched him through the gauzy veil of her eyelids. If the madman suspected her, he hid it well. He navigated the truck around another curve that tossed Teagarden and her abducted partner into the dash, then they were falling, descending a steep hill, the worn brakes squealing as gravity forced her toward the console. All routes descending off the ridge led to the water. He was taking them to the lake.

A pothole rattled her teeth. Her eyes popped open, and the trailer echoed the impact of the truck. The killer was too focused on the lake to notice.

If she wanted to roll the dice and shift the gear, now was the time. Shoving hard enough might push the woman against the steering wheel. Given his speed, too fast for the narrow roads along the lake, he'd wreck the truck. Possibly hit a tree or smash into a cottage. A cottage with a family inside.

Before she could second guess herself, Teagarden kicked her heels against the door and burst shoulder-first into the unconscious woman. The gear clicked into neutral, engine over-revving as her body struck the steering wheel.

A squeal of brakes.

The truck ramped the ditch. Then the horrible shriek of metal and broken glass when they barreled through a cottage.

CHAPTER EIGHTY-SIX

Bell clutched the interior handle while Gardy cut down an unmarked road halfway down the ridge. It was near impossible to pick the turns out in the dark, but somehow Gardy guided the Jeep at highway speeds without crashing.

Though the horror of the San Giovanni shooting still chewed a hole in her belly, the adrenaline of the chase coursed through her veins like a speed hit.

"Where on the lake?" Gardy yelled over the Jeep's engine. "There are more than a hundred docks."

"Just get us there. We know where he's headed. He'll be easy to find on open water."

The trees parted and lent a picture of the lake. Bell could understand where the Blackwater name came from. At night, the water was syrup-thick and black as midnight. Emergency vehicle lights flashed along the opposite side of the lake as they angled onto the main access road. Gardy headed in their direction until Bell shouted at him to stop.

Halfway down a shadowed avenue that led to a row of lakeside cottages, a man and a woman stood in a yard, waving their arms.

"Back up," she said, tilting her head out the window to get a better look.

Then she spotted the backside of the truck jutting out of the cottage. An entire wall was missing, smoke billowing from the back of the truck.

Gardy swung the Jeep to the shoulder, and Bell bounced out, running full-speed toward the wreckage as she radioed the crash to Tanner's team.

"Slow down, dammit!"

Bell shot a glance over her shoulder at Gardy and kept running, propelled by her duty to rescue the injured. And to check the license plate.

But she already knew the truck belonged to Nicholas Winston. His escalation had taken a tragic turn, and she prayed none of the innocents had died when the truck smashed through the little home by the lake.

Holding up her badge, she angled past the sixty-something couple who'd flagged them down. The woman wore a bathrobe and slippers, black hair dripping wet. The thin, tall man beside her, most likely her husband, held the woman by the elbow as if the terror which struck the waterfront neighborhood might rip her out of his arms.

"Anyone hurt inside?"

The woman shook her head.

"No, they're in Texas for their grandson's wedding."

"Where's the driver?"

"I…I didn't want to look. Should I call 911?"

"They're already on the way," Bell said, leaving them behind as she sprinted for the truck.

Behind her, the woman tried to tell Gardy the crash sounded like a bomb. When he raced past and drew his gun, the couple turned and hurried for their yards.

The truck bed stuck out from the cottage, taillights glowing like demon fire. Off one side of the truck, a mangled trailer lay on its side. Winston's boat had flown across the lawn and crushed a small grove of fruit trees. But the cottage had taken the worst of the impact. A jungle of sparking wires snapped and hissed in the open wall, driving Bell back.

She could see into the truck's cab but couldn't tell if anyone was inside, possibly slumped over on the seat. With no way to squeeze between the truck and wall, she tested the front door. Locked. She kicked the door open and swung her gun across the living room, Gardy following her into the cottage.

The grille chewed into a wall-mounted television, the truck's front end collapsed like an accordion and the windshield shattered. A glass coffee table lay in pieces at her feet, the glass crunching as she walked over the mess.

Back against the truck, she nodded at Gardy and yanked the driver side door open. Gardy swept his gun across the empty cab. Blood smeared the windshield, seat, and dashboard, but there was no sign of Nicholas Winston or his sister. Had Winston brought Teagarden with him? Bell hoped so. The alternative was the woman already drifted along the bottom of the lake.

Bell eyed the staircase. Gardy pointed at the floor, and she spotted blood drops trailing through the dining room and a crimson hand print on the back door. They followed the trail and pushed the door open to a small backyard with a picnic table. The yard ended at a pebble beach, a dock and boathouse to the left.

"It's empty," Gardy said, peering into the boathouse.

The stolen motorboat coasted toward the center of the lake.

Bell followed the boat lights across the water.

"I see him. He's heading toward the west end of the lake, not the center like before."

Tanner had two boats on the water, but the lake stretched fifteen miles, too much ground for a small fleet to cover. Did the police see him?

As Gardy transmitted Winston's location, Bell's gaze traveled to the next cottage, a brown shingled home with a pair of jet skis tied to a dock. Gardy met her eyes.

"Don't even think about it."

"I won't stand here with my hands on my hips while he murders his sister."

"Tanner has a boat heading toward Winston right now."

Bell nodded to herself as she calculated the distances in her head.

"I can get to Winston faster. At least three minutes before the police arrive."

She kicked off her shoes and padded across the lawn toward the neighbor's dock. Gardy followed, his jacket flapping in the wind.

"Think for a second, Bell. You aren't stealing someone's jet ski. And anyhow, I don't think you can hot-wire one of those things."

Bell leaped onto the deck and pounded toward the first jet ski, a sleek red-and-yellow beauty with flames along the side. Ignoring Gardy's protests, she dug the keys from her pocket and flipped open the folding knife she kept attached to the chain. As a mortified Gardy looked down at her, she jammed the knife into the key slot and wrenched it to the right.

The engine didn't fire. Gardy exhaled.

"All right, that didn't work. Let's forget this nonsense and take the Jeep to the other side of the lake."

Bell yanked the knife out and slammed it back into the key slot. This time she twisted the blade until she heard the lock pins snap. The jet ski roared to life.

"Unless you have your own knife, you'll have to watch this one from the sidelines."

"Like hell," Gardy said, grinning. He stepped out of his shoes, threw his jacket on the beach, and climbed onto the back of the jet ski, wrapping his arms around her. "If you dump me in the lake, I won't be happy."

"Then I suggest you hang on."

CHAPTER EIGHTY-SEVEN

Every inch of Pam Teagarden's body pulsed with white-hot agony. The only saving grace was her abductor removed the gag so she could breathe. And scream. He didn't seem to care now that they were on the open water and hurtling across the lake.

She'd survived the crash by dumb luck when she fell beneath the seat with the other woman sprawled atop her back. Now the other woman stirred beside her on the floor of the boat. The woman pushed herself up on her elbows and coughed. Blood drooled out of her mouth.

A fine spray wet Teagarden's hair as the killer navigated the boat into the dark night. The two women locked eyes, and Teagarden tilted her head toward the man at the wheel, his back to them.

"Why, Nicholas?"

Nicholas. The woman knew him. Teagarden glanced between the killer and the woman, but the killer remained stoic, hands gripped to the wheel. Where the hell was he taking them?

"God damn you, I did everything I could to protect you from Dad."

The woman's words sounded slurred and garbled.

Nicholas swung his head around, face twisted with rage.

"No. You left. You saw what he did to me, and you left me alone."

"No, Nicholas," she said, forcing her drooping eyes to stay open. "I love you. I tried to bring you with me, but he wouldn't allow it."

Teagarden saw the woman anew. His sister? She struggled against the zip ties, every nerve in her body flaring with pain.

Sirens called from across the lake. In the distance, a motorboat raced westward with a spotlight throwing light across the water.

"It's over, Nicholas," the sister said, pushing herself into a sitting position. "Don't you hear the sirens? They're surrounding the lake, and there's a boat coming. Give up now before they hurt you."

Eyes glossed over, the woman winced as she leaned against a seat. Lifeblood stained her shirt. The woman had lost too much blood and needed to get to a hospital. They both needed to. Teagarden doubted the madman's sister would survive the hour.

A hand slammed down and snapped Teagarden's head up. Nicholas walked away from the wheel, the boat still arrowing through the night on unspent momentum.

"You think the police can hurt me, Leigh? There's nothing left for any of you to take." A strange grin curled Nicholas's lips as he stalked toward the two women. "But they're too late. I'm keeping both of you, and this time it's forever."

Teagarden cried out seeing Nicholas pull the knife from his back pocket. Leigh's eyes lit with sudden understanding. Her brother meant to butcher the woman.

An inhuman screech came from Nicholas. He bounded across the boat, knife raised above his head as Leigh toppled backward and lifted her knees to her chest.

The knife began its deadly plunge. Without thinking,

Teagarden leaped between Nicholas and his sister and threw herself atop the helpless woman. The blade swept down and dug into her back, tearing from shoulder to spine. She screamed and bit her tongue, feeling the boat rotate as convergent flows caught the vessel.

Though instinct begged her to roll away, she lay protectively across Leigh, her wrists and ankles still locked by the ties. In her mind, she pictured Nicholas raising the knife again. Sobbing, coughing blood, Teagarden noticed a buzzing noise flying toward the boat.

A rough hand gripped one of her bound arms, wrenching her shoulder out of socket, and tugged her off Leigh. Teagarden skidded across the boat and slammed against the side. The killer came at her with the knife. When he was within reach, she drove both feet against his knees, buckling his legs and buying time. Nicholas screeched again and fell to his hands and knees. The knife dropped between them.

Now it was a race for the knife. Teagarden didn't know what she'd do with the knife with her hands tied behind her back, but if she trapped the knife beneath her, it would give Leigh and her a fighting chance.

She threw herself atop the open blade. The tip cut into her chest and opened another gaping hole in her battered body.

Nicholas clutched her ankles and pulled, but the knife slid with her. Frustrated, he booted her in the ribs. Pain exploded through her midsection.

His knee drove into the small of her back. But there was no force behind it. As if he'd toppled onto her and caught his balance at the last moment. She twisted her head and saw Leigh. He'd roped her arms together, but her legs were free. Wobbling on her feet, she drove a heel into his shoulder.

Yet all she did was postpone the inevitable. Eventually he'd wrestle the knife free and kill them. His weight eased off her. A smack of hand against flesh informed Teagarden he'd struck Leigh. The boat rocked as the woman's body hit the floor.

Then his hands encircled Teagarden's throat. Squeezed. Her eyes bulged, oxygen cut off. And she had no leverage to fight with.

Her vision darkened as the buzzing sound increased tenfold.

Water doused Teagarden a moment before a weight slammed against the boat.

CHAPTER EIGHTY-EIGHT

"Slow the hell down. You're gonna crash right into it!"

Bell barely heard Gardy over the engine and the wind. Floating at the west end of the lake, the vessel appeared abandoned. A ghost ship.

"I know what I'm doing. Hold on."

But the boat she targeted began to rock and sway, signs of a struggle on the floor.

The jet ski blasted toward the boat, closing the distance at an alarming rate as water kicked up behind them. She should have pulled up by now. Too close. If she smashed into the side of the boat, the impact would injure them both. Or worse.

Bell read the registration number and name of the boat—The Islander—as she released the throttle. Yanking the jet ski sideways, she slid them toward the side of the boat. But she'd misjudged her speed. They would slam into the boat. Hard.

Gardy tugged her sideways. Together they toppled off the jet ski and into the cold lake waters. Bell dipped beneath the surface and flipped over as the jet ski collided with the boat.

Oxygen bubbles exploded toward the surface as the

lake pulled her down and down. Six hundred feet, she thought. For a terrifying moment, she couldn't tell which way was up. Where was Gardy? She twisted her head around and saw only black.

Panicking, she opened her mouth. A mistake. Water surged into her lungs. She kicked her legs and spun, no idea if she lay just below the surface or a hundred feet down. Then Gardy clutched her arm and hauled her up.

She burst out of the water, coughing. Gardy hooked an elbow around her chest and swam with his free arm, dragging her until he reached the overturned jet ski. As her ears unclogged, the screams inside the boat became loud. Gardy put his finger to his lips. Bell couldn't imagine the killer hadn't noticed the collision.

They reached the boat and grabbed hold. No time to catch their breath, Gardy leaped and pulled himself up, Bell scaling the boat beside him. They would reach the top, she thought, and the killer would be waiting for them with a cleaver. Arms straining, Bell fought her way up the side with Gardy, and as they reached the top, she saw Nicholas Winston astride Pam Teagarden, the woman's legs flailing as he choked her. Leigh Winston curled in a ball on the floor and clutched her stomach. Blood welled through her fingers.

"FBI, freeze!"

The killer spun around at Bell's voice. One hand pinning Teagarden's neck to the floor, he produced the knife in his other hand, the tip dripping with fresh blood.

The knife descended toward Teagarden's face. Bell and Gardy fired their guns.

Nicholas Winston whipped around from the impact as the blade struck the floor beside Teagarden's head. Bell fired again. The bullet blew a chunk off Winston's forehead, and the killer collapsed in a spray of blood.

While Gardy stood over the dying killer, Bell dropped beside Teagarden. Covered with blood, only some of it

Winston's, Teagarden hyperventilated.

"Slow down. You'll be all right."

Wrists bound by zip ties, Teagarden motioned at Leigh Winston.

"He stabbed her. You have to get her to a hospital."

Bell scurried over to Leigh. She felt the glare of a spotlight brush the back of her neck as the police boat closed in. The sister's face looked like December snow. Bell tried to convince herself the boat lights washed out the woman's skin tone, but she knew better. She struggled out of her t-shirt and pressed the drenched cloth against the stomach wound. Leigh's eyelids fluttered shut.

"Stay with me, Leigh. Help is coming."

The boat rocked. Heavy boots thumped onto the floor. Chief Tanner hurried to Teagarden and Gardy as his eyes flicked between the fading killer and Leigh Winston.

"I need a paramedic, dammit," Tanner called back to Bridges.

Officer Bridges glanced over his shoulder at the next boat approaching.

"She's here now."

Bell touched Leigh's shoulder.

"You hear that, Leigh? The doctor's coming now." But Leigh's eyes kept closing, the final sleep trying to pull her under. "Leigh! Leight! Look at me."

Bell smiled down at Leigh, and the woman returned the smile. Then her mouth fell open and froze.

"Shit! Where's the paramedic?"

Tanner yelled off the starboard side, willing the next boat to arrive faster.

But there was nothing left for the paramedic to do. Leigh's unblinking eyes stared into the dark heavens.

CHAPTER EIGHTY-NINE

The sickly sweet disinfectant smell and the murmurs down the corridor. These were the things Bell noticed while she doddered down the hospital corridor in a trance-like state.

It seemed she'd been in hospitals all night, and she had.

With Gardy beside her, she'd followed the ambulance to the hospital in Blackwater. Leigh Winston had died before the paramedic dropped into the boat, but the doctors had given Pam Teagarden a puncher's shot to recover. The woman lost a lot of blood in the crash and on the boat. She'd received a transfusion. The stab wounds required multiple stitches, and her lung was on the verge of collapse by the time the doctors got her on the operating table. Teagarden needed plenty of sleep now. No chance the FBI or police would talk to her until tomorrow afternoon, and that was assuming Teagarden didn't experience complications.

Nicholas Winston had gotten his own ambulance ride. Like his sister, he was dead before he reached the gurney. Brother and sister, both dead. And the monster who created them wouldn't shed a tear for either.

Bell insisted she drive to DC to visit San Giovanni. Gardy rode beside Bell, refusing to let her go alone. Now they meandered along the corridors of the sick and injured, an army of police and government agents patrolling the halls.

Bell had forgotten Gardy was with her until he put his hand on her back and turned her to face him.

"They won't let you see her. At least let me take you to the waiting room. Grab an hour of shuteye."

"The first bullet was meant for me, Gardy."

"Or me."

"I think you know better."

An imposing agent with a bald head and an ear piece held up his hand to stop them in the next corridor.

"FBI," Gardy said as they flashed their badges.

The agent glared at the badges, then he turned his shoulder and spoke into his microphone. After a few tense seconds, he motioned them through.

Bell recognized an olive-skinned female FBI agent from Quantico. Cataris was her name, though the two rarely crossed paths. Recognizing Bell, she crossed the hall to them.

"Agents Bell and Gardy."

"Agent Cataris," Bell said. "How's she doing?"

Cataris shot a glare back at the doorway. Lowering her voice, she pulled Bell and Gardy aside.

"The doctors say she's got a day left at best. Nobody can see her but the family."

It felt as if someone struck Bell in the belly with a sledgehammer. She closed her eyes and tilted her chin toward the ceiling. When she opened her eyes, she spotted a young girl with dark hair outside the room. Joelle San Giovanni, the girl Bell rescued from the God's Hand killer. Joelle leaned into the arms of a woman Lana San Giovanni would look like if the heavens intervened and allowed her to live another thirty years. The grandmother. Bell remembered her from the San Giovanni estate. Seeing Joelle worsened the pain. Lana San Giovanni was more than a respected congresswoman and ally to Bell. She was a mother and a daughter. A loved one who many would grieve.

Gardy leaned toward Cataris and whispered.

"Did San Giovanni say anything about the shooter?"

"She never regained consciousness. Traumatic brain injury. It's a wonder the woman is still alive. Hell of a fighter, that one. But you should know, and this stays between the three of us, the shooter was a professional. Ex-military."

A chill ran down Bell's spine as she recalled the sniper she killed outside Bealton and the gunshot from the rooftop.

She threw her eyes over the corridor and ensured no one listened in.

"What makes you think the shooter was ex-military?"

Cataris cocked her eyebrow.

"From 1200 meters at the exact moment she walked past the bedroom window? Even with a light wind and an unobstructed view, that's not a shot Joe from the gun range makes."

"Where did he fire the shot from?" Gardy asked.

"There's a wooded park on the edge of town. We think he fired from the hill. No footprints. Cleaned up after himself real well."

Bell sensed someone staring in her direction. Over Cataris's shoulder, San Giovanni's mother, caressing Joelle's hair while the girl sobbed, met Bell's eyes.

"Excuse me for a moment," Bell said as Cataris and Gardy continued talking.

She squeezed between two police officers. The agent guarding the congresswoman's room watched Bell as she passed.

Before the two women spoke, Joelle threw herself at Bell and hugged her.

"Why is this happening? Why would someone want to kill my mommy?"

Mommy. Most girls stopped referring to their parents as Mommy and Daddy at a young age. Joelle had regressed into a terrified child. Bell felt her heart crack in half as she tried to console the girl she'd rescued. After the girl finished crying, the grandmother touched her shoulder.

"Joelle, dear. I want you to go sit with your mother for a little while so I can talk to Agent Bell."

The girl nodded and slouched past the guard into the hospital room. The lights were off inside. Greens and reds from the life monitors reflected off the floor.

"I'm so sorry—"

The grandmother held up her hand.

"Lana never subscribed to sympathy when a job needed to be done. And as this affects you as much as it does my daughter, you can't waste time crying over things none of us can change. Especially when the killer is still out there."

Bell slipped into an uncomfortable plastic chair beside the grandmother.

"Can you think of anyone who would want to hurt your daughter?"

The woman pursed her lips as though she'd bitten something bitter.

"My daughter made many enemies. I suggest you look into the government corruption task force she headed up."

San Giovanni and her team had targeted Chet Ewing, the senator the congresswoman warred with over budget proposals.

Corruption. Did San Giovanni have something on Ewing that went beyond partisan politics? Even if she did, why would Ewing want both San Giovanni and Bell killed? Bell had never met the man.

"And Agent Bell."

"Yes?"

"You're the only one I trust to do my daughter justice. When you catch the man who did this, remember there's a little girl who will grow up without her mother. An eye for an eye."

Bell nodded. This was a promise she meant to keep.

Gardy broke off from Cataris and awaited Bell at the end of the hall. She could see the worry on his face, knew he disapproved of her sleep deprivation. He pointed at his watch, and she said goodbye, knowing there was no chance she'd get to see the congresswoman.

"Everything okay?" Gardy asked.

"Nothing is okay."

"What did the mother tell you?"

"I'll fill you in on the way home."

A weight fell off his shoulders.

"Now you're finally listening to reason. I'll pop for the hotel. You shouldn't drive back to the coast."

She opened her mouth to protest and chewed her lip.

"Sounds wonderful."

He stammered, shocked she hadn't given him an argument.

"All right then. Anyplace in particular?"

"Nope. Just one with a ridiculously oversized breakfast buffet."

He grinned.

"You must be starving."

"Nah. I just want to make sure I have enough energy when I put a bullet in the bad guy's head."

His mouth hung open. Bell was already halfway to the exit doors.

THE REDEEMER

CHAPTER NINETY

Vengeance is the progeny of maltreatment and corruption.

The weather, fair and warm for October along the Chesapeake Bay, should have put Scarlett Bell at ease. Yet something dangerous prowled inside the FBI agent as she paced the beach. Her partner, Neil Gardy, the Behavioral Analysis Unit's dark-haired senior agent, spotted Bell's anger the moment he arrived. Dressed in his work clothes, black suit and shoes with his hair neatly combed, Gardy's clothing was ill-suited for a walk on the beach. Gardy had visited Bell's bay side apartment on her day off, concerned over his partner's wellbeing.

"Any word from Weber on the San Giovanni assassination?" she asked, skipping a smooth-sided rock across the waves.

"Weber doesn't want BAU involvement."

Ever since a sniper gunned down star congresswoman Lana San Giovanni, Don Weber, Deputy Director of CIRG, had lobbied against BAU involvement in the investigation. The murder of political figures fell upon the FBI, and the BAU typically contributed to counter-terrorism and corruption cases, so it confused Bell and Gardy why Weber remained steadfast against the BAU investigating the assassination.

"Weber claims we're stretched thin," Gardy continued, stumbling when the sand engulfed his dress shoes. "His number one priority is catching Logan Wolf, and he wants all available resources devoted to bringing Wolf to justice."

Gardy's words were fuel to the flame, and Bell grew irritable as Gardy justified Weber's decisions. Bell believed Wolf, the former BAU profiler accused of murdering his wife in 2013, was innocent. The murder felt too perfect, too planned for a disorganized, violent serial killer. Wolf had found Renee on the kitchen floor of their Virginia home, throat slashed with a sack placed over her head. Forensic evidence pointed an accusing finger at Wolf. The crime scene investigators uncovered Wolf's prints and hair fibers at the scene, but it was expected. Wolf lived there. The lack of DNA evidence for a third person implicated Wolf, and the profiler had been a fugitive ever since, murdering serial killers across the country to avenge his wife. Worse yet, Wolf adopted the unknown murderer's modus operandi, slicing his victim's throats and placing sacks over their heads to draw his wife's killer out of hiding. But since then, no other killings mimicked the 2013 murder, further proving Wolf must be guilty.

"Nothing changes. It's a waste of resources. Weber can't catch Wolf."

"He will," Gardy said, studying the breakers as the ocean dragged a string of kelp over the beach. "Wolf keeps taking chances by involving himself in our cases. One of these days, he'll walk into an ambush."

Though Gardy had come around to Bell's belief that Wolf might be innocent, she didn't trust her partner to keep their collaborations with Wolf secret. While the fugitive had helped Bell and Gardy track multiple serial killers over the last year, Gardy put honor and duty first. Eventually, Bell theorized, Gardy would lay a trap for Wolf and turn the mass murderer over to the FBI.

"There's something San Giovanni's mother told me at the hospital," Bell said, ducking when a wind gust hurled sand at their faces. She stepped through the waves, prompting Gardy to follow, the agent maintaining a safe distance between the tide and his expensive shoes. "San Giovanni had powerful enemies. The congresswoman headed the task force targeting government corruption. What are the chances she uncovered evidence that got her killed?"

"It's a logical theory, except the FBI couldn't find a connection. Most of the task force's targets were small time offenders: government officials accepting bribes, overzealous lobbyists influencing elections. Nothing particularly juicy."

"Doesn't it concern you Weber kept us out of the loop? It makes me wonder about his innocence."

Gardy stopped along the shore and grabbed her arm.

"Wait a minute. Are you suggesting Weber masterminded an assassination?"

"Weber is involved. He didn't pull the trigger, but I bet he knows who did."

"Listen to yourself. Bell, regardless of your personal issues with the deputy director and the amount of hurdles he puts in your way, you can't possibly believe he's behind the murder."

Bell chewed her lower lip, unconvinced. The sun dropped low, the water turning red as light seeped out of the sky.

"I'm certain Weber would do anything to accelerate his career." Gardy started to protest, and Bell raised her hand. "Let's assume San Giovanni's task force gathered damning evidence against an elected official, someone powerful enough to push Weber up the food chain."

"But they didn't. We saw the notes. The task force investigations are old news."

"Let me finish. The congresswoman was a bulldog, but until she had evidence against an opponent, she played the hand close to her chest."

"So you're suggesting San Giovanni wouldn't bring the case to the task force until she knew it was strong."

"That's exactly what I'm thinking. The FBI hasn't turned over enough stones. I'd check the congresswoman's computer files for—"

The gunshot echoed down the beach. At first, Bell thought the naval jets flying out of Norfolk caused the sound. Then a red streak formed across Gardy's pant leg, and he dropped to his knee, clutching his thigh.

When the second shot tore over the sand, Bell knocked Gardy flat and covered him amid the sloshing water and frantic gulls. She glanced around the beach, searching for cover. The nearest dune lay fifty paces away. Then she saw it. A trench dug around a crumbling sandcastle, just enough space for the two of them to lie flat inside.

Tugging Gardy's arm, Bell coaxed the injured agent toward the trench as another gun blast flew over her shoulder, close enough to raise the hair on her head.

"Stay low," Bell said as the gunfire kept them pinned. "How's the leg?"

"It grazed me. I'll be okay if I can—"

The next shot barreled into the sand, cutting Gardy off. Grit sprayed her face while she covered her head. Protective of her injured partner, Bell shifted her body to shield Gardy's, earning her an irritated groan.

Sirens approached the coast. The gunfire ceased, the sniper fleeing.

Carefully, Bell emerged from the trench, convinced the shooter would pull the trigger now that they'd come out of hiding. Gardy's leg buckled, and she caught him. Blood soaked his pants leg and colored the sand, welling through his fingers where he clutched the wound.

"Can you make it to the building?" she asked.

Bell's apartment complex rose above the beach, a five-minute walk. Longer if a bullet struck you in the leg.

Grinding his teeth, he nodded and limped over the sand with Bell supporting him. With her free hand, she dialed 9-1-1. An ambulance was on the way.

As Bell glanced over her shoulder, a dark figure disappeared behind a dune along the distant shoreline.

CHAPTER NINETY-ONE

The Florida storm over the Atlantic turned the sunset bloody and flickered lightning like snake tongues.

Christina Wolf sipped a Merlot on her balcony overlooking the ocean as darkness rushed out of the east. The beach house rental was a splurge, a method to unwind and put her work as an information technician specialist aside. She'd survived a messy divorce to Kevin, and Buddy, her Irish Setter of fifteen years, passed in July, leaving Christina alone for the first time since those post-college bachelorette days when her biggest concern was which club to frequent with her friends.

Her job had become a dead end, a compromise. It paid the bills, but she hadn't been excited about work in years. Now at forty, she felt alone in the world. Both parents dead. Her brother, Logan, a fugitive running from the government. The things the media claimed Logan did, the grotesque murders, didn't seem real. She refused to accept her brother was a serial killer. He didn't slaughter men across the United States.

And he didn't murder Renee. He loved his wife. Worshiped the woman. Logan rarely smiled before he met Renee in college. Christina's brother always seemed so serious, so career-driven even as he studied criminal justice. But when Renee entered the room, the corners of Logan's mouth quirked up as though he concealed a joke behind his lips.

She hadn't heard from Logan since Renee's murder. But now and then she returned from work and found differences with her house—someone had tightened the lock on the back door which no longer jiggled, and once someone fed Buddy and left a vase of wildflowers on the kitchen table. She wanted to believe the silent benefactor was Logan, not Randy or Kylie next door, the way a child attributes presents at Christmas to Santa.

And this evening she'd discovered the Merlot wrapped by a red ribbon and waiting on the counter. Kevin hated wine, especially Merlot, and she'd forgotten the pleasures of wine during her suffocating marriage. The only surviving member of her family who appreciated wine was Logan. Still, it was more likely the homeowner left the bottle as a gift and she'd overlooked it on her first day inside the house.

Swirling the wine, she raised the glass against the sky's deepening reds and admired the color. She closed the patio door against the thickening wind. Inside, the house seemed darker than she remembered. Christina flicked on a lamp, disappointed when the light did little to drive back the shadows. Two shopping bags from her day at the Fair Haven Beach shops sat against the door where she'd dropped them after discovering the wine.

As she crossed from the living room into the entryway, a noise came from behind her. The moan of a floorboard. She spun back to the darkened living room, the sectional sofa dividing the floor from the large screen television on the wall. Old houses made scary sounds, she told herself. The wind clamored at the sliding glass door like it wanted to break through.

Snatching the bags, she climbed the staircase to the master bedroom. The floor-to-ceiling window offered a spectacular view of the water, and she contemplated reading a Thomas Harris novel while overlooking the ocean.

First, she determined to change into something more comfortable. Trading the dress shorts and tank for sweatpants and a baggy t-shirt, Christina padded barefoot into the hallway.

The noise came again. A dragged-out groan, like a monstrous beast creeping through the shadows.

This time she was sure it was a floorboard, not the fitful moan of a settling house. She stepped back from the rail. Heart thundering, she believed a prowler had broken into the rental. And her phone lay on the kitchen counter.

Quiet in the gloom, Christina backtracked to the bedroom and edged the door shut. A feeble hook-and-eye latch hung beside the door. Wincing when the lock rattled in her shaking fingers, she connected the pieces and stepped away. There had to be a phone in the room.

Except there wasn't. And the dark view through the window showed the next house several hundred yards down the beach.

She listened at the door. Ear pressed to the wood. Hands curled into fists and eyes clamped shut.

No sound came from downstairs. Had she overreacted to a random noise?

The clink of glass pulled her eyes open. Then the *glug-glug* of poured wine.

Yes, someone was inside the house. A hopeful thought occurred to Christina. Logan was downstairs. He sneaked inside to surprise her and partook in the gift he'd left on the counter.

Terror prevented Christina from calling her brother's name. Instead, she slid the windowpane up, cringing when the wood shrieked and gave her away.

The two-story plunge ended in a pile of sand and scrub grass. Too far to leap, but she'd take a broken leg over rape.

The screen remained the only barrier between Christina and freedom when the bedroom door imploded.

She shrieked as the flimsy lock burst off the jamb in a shower of splinters. It couldn't be Logan. Her brother wouldn't hurt her, would he?

The dark shadow filled the doorway. Christina shoved both hands through the screen and knocked it off its hinges. As she ripped the screen out of the frame and climbed onto the sill, his hands grasped her hair from behind and yanked.

Christina's head slammed against the hardwood. Her vision blurred as two hands clasped around her neck and lifted her off the floor as though she was a child's doll.

Legs kicking and flailing as he walked her across the room, Christina beat at the masked figure's head.

When he reached the wall, he smashed the back of her head against the plaster. Christina went limp. The room turned black.

Then the masked killer swept Christina into his arms. Almost lovingly.

The starlight caught the wicked gleam of his blade as he drew the edge across Christina's throat. Her body convulsed, and he hugged the dying woman, whispering in her ear that it was time to sleep, time to let go of the pain.

He stood over her, grinning.

Admiring the pooling blood.

Plastic wrapped around his shoes and up to his calves. He'd leave no identifying footprints, and the woman's DNA would be at the bottom of a dumpster after he discarded the plastic.

From inside his jacket, he removed a black sack and placed it over Christina Wolf's head.

"Come home, little one. Time to sleep."

CHAPTER NINETY-TWO

The bright lights of the hospital stood in stark contrast to the night when the physician's assistant pulled the last stitch tight on Gardy's thigh.

Bell sat in the corner and waited for the assistant to clear the room. Gardy's legs dangled off the table like a child at his first doctor's exam.

"I hate stitches," he said, gritting his teeth when the man bandaged the wound and secured it with tape.

Bell leaned forward with her elbows on her knees.

"Be thankful the bullet grazed your thigh."

The talk of bullets and snipers won an unsettled look from the physician's assistant. He hurried out of the room as though he suddenly realized there was somewhere he needed to be.

"But I doubt the shooter aimed for your thigh," Bell said, tapping her keys against her leg. "For that matter, I'm unconvinced he targeted you."

"There you go trying to steal the spotlight. You said you saw the guy?"

"Hardly. I saw a shadow on the far side of the beach. No way I could ID the bastard."

Gardy rubbed at his chin.

"So he fired from two hundred yards. Considering the strength of those wind gusts, I'd say he's a damn skilled shooter."

"The wind saved our lives. A light breeze, and the medical examiner would be pulling bullets out of our skulls."

"Nice thought."

The police had responded to the gunshots, and after learning the shooter struck one of their agents, the FBI arrived. With the FBI present, a police detective named Schroeder interviewed the two agents while Gardy awaited stitching. Neither Bell nor Gardy told the investigators anything useful.

"Funny," Bell said, meeting Gardy's eyes. "One second we're discussing a political assassination and Weber's involvement, and the next we're under fire."

"Hold up. *You* discussed Weber's involvement, I listened."

"And did you learn anything?"

"Only that losing a chunk off your thigh hurts like a son-of-a—"

"It's the same sniper, Gardy. The same killer who shot the congresswoman and tried to kill us in the alleyway."

"Must be more than one shooter," he said, picking at the tape. "Unless the guy you shot came back to haunt you."

A dark memory returned to Bell. The night she took down the God's Hand killer and rescued San Giovanni's daughter, a sniper shot at Bell and Logan Wolf on a Virginia hillside. After she killed the sniper, she discovered a pendant around his neck. A pendant worn by special ops. When she directed the FBI to the sniper's coordinates, the body vanished.

Bell peeked down the hallway and closed the door.

"Former special ops soldiers don't come cheap, Gardy. You might not believe my conspiracy theories, but it's convenient the guy disappeared when the FBI investigated the hillside. Not a single bullet found, not even from my gun. How's that possible?"

"How is it possible Don Weber monitored our conversation and called a hit? Paranoia is getting the best of you."

"He's corrupt, and San Giovanni knew."

Gardy opened his mouth to argue and snapped it shut.

Bell's phone hummed inside her pocket. She entered her passcode and found a text from the BAU at the same time the message arrived on Gardy's phone.

Gardy squinted, holding the phone at arm's length as he read. His eyes widened.

"Impossible," Bell said.

The murder scene was still fresh, the body discovered inside a beach house in Fair Haven Beach, Florida, after an anonymous message tipped off the local police.

"That's Wolf's M.O. You still think he only murders male serial killers?"

Bell placed her hand over her mouth.

"Gardy, read the name of the victim."

"What's that have to do with…"

Gardy's mouth hung open. When he glanced at Bell, his eyes seemed to say the name had to be coincidental.

"Christina Wolf is a common name, Bell."

But he knew better. They both did.

"That's his sister's name. And I don't believe in coincidences."

As she read through the case briefing, Gardy eased himself off the table and hissed when his leg met the floor.

"So Wolf murdered his sister, same as he murdered his wife in 2013. I hope you realize Logan Wolf isn't some broken teddy bear you can take home and mend. He's a lunatic, Bell."

"Christina Wolf," Bell said, ignoring Gardy and reading the name aloud as if doing so would make sense of the situation. She swiped the phone over to her contacts list and phoned Harold, the BAU's technical analyst who possessed a knack for gathering background information on suspects and victims. "Harold, it's Bell. I need you to look up Christina Wolf's background and tell me if she's Logan Wolf's sister."

A pause.

"It's her," Harold said. "Christina Wolf, age forty. Younger sister of Logan Wolf. Divorced. Resides in Palm Beach, Florida."

Ending the call, Bell dropped her arm against her side. Had Logan Wolf lied to her and pulled the wool over her eyes? Or had the pressure of being on the run sent him over the edge and turned him against his last remaining family member?

"Harold confirmed it," Bell said, leaning against the wall. Her legs felt like rubber bands. "She's Logan's sister."

"Then it's time I did what I should have done months ago."

He shrugged into his jacket and reattached his holster.

"Oh, no you don't," Bell said, finding her sea legs. "You're injured. Until the FBI clears you for field work, you're on the sidelines."

"That never stopped you."

"The doctor hasn't released you from the hospital yet."

He glared impatiently at his watch.

"Fine. I'll stick around until the doctor springs me, but you're not going anywhere until I get word from Weber on my status."

"Too late, Gardy. The BAU booked my flight out of

Dulles in four hours."

"What?" Gardy checked his phone and scrolled through his messages. "I didn't receive the flight notification."

"That's because Weber isn't sending you."

The truth struck Gardy, and he sank onto a chair and buried his face in his hands.

"This can't be happening. I'm this close to catching Wolf," Gardy said, pinching his fingers together for emphasis. "And they pull me from the case."

Glancing at the time, Bell felt her heartbeat quicken as a flutter of nervous energy moved through her stomach. It was always this way when the BAU called her to a new case and she needed to race against the clock. She did the math in her head—a quick stop at the apartment to grab her travel bag, which she kept packed for these situations, then she'd gas up the car and fight the DC traffic. If she hurried, she'd have time to eat a late dinner and still make her flight.

"You're not leaving me here, are you?"

"Sorry, Gardy. I'll lobby Weber on your behalf."

"That's what I'm afraid of."

Bell twirled the key ring around her finger and threw him a sympathetic glance over her shoulder.

"Get better, Gardy. I hope I see you in Florida."

CHAPTER NINETY-THREE

Too many questions. Not enough time.

During the trip home, Bell couldn't concentrate on the road. Logan Wolf dominated her mind. She'd believed him, though she never trusted the serial killer. Now she felt used, fooled, lied to. After almost causing an accident, she pulled into a gas station and closed her eyes. Around her, the world went about its business as though nothing unusual had occurred today. For Bell, the earth split open and swallowed her.

Her bag lay open on the passenger seat. Buried at the bottom in a hidden compartment, a burner phone hid from prying eyes. One of three Logan Wolf had given her. The fugitive often threw the prepaid phones away after one use, but since he trusted Bell, they often kept a phone for a week or more when they communicated frequently.

Though Bell had been aware Wolf had a sister, he never mentioned her. Bell had assumed he wanted to protect his sister and shield her from the madness surrounding his life. Why would he murder Christina?

After her head cleared, Bell pulled onto the interstate, pushing the accelerator to make up for lost time. Traffic thinned along the Chesapeake Bay, but the late night traffic near DC would be a bear. Stars lit the sky from one horizon to the next. A strange orange glow grew out of the east. For a moment, she worried she'd fallen asleep at the gas station and lost track of time, but the dashboard clock read midnight.

As she turned down the coast road, a smoky scent reached her nose. Something was wrong. Anxious energy fueled her. Pushing harder on the gas, she navigated the black Nissan Rogue around hairpin curves, slowing only when she entered the residential area.

The shock of seeing her apartment complex on fire brought her to a screeching halt. Roadblocks prevented her from advancing, and a man directing traffic raised his hand at her and pointed in the opposite direction. He wanted her to turn around and leave.

She lowered the window and flashed her FBI badge.

"FBI. I need to get in there."

"Not tonight," the man said, turning his eyes toward the two firetrucks outside her apartment complex. "Nobody gets in."

Craning her neck around the man, Bell spied the unmarked black SUV at the back of the parking lot. Agent Flanagan. The FBI routinely positioned an agent at Bell's apartment complex, hoping to catch Logan Wolf. In the past, the fugitive had slipped around the FBI and entered Bell's apartment without drawing attention.

Bell waved to the volunteer and backed the Rogue down the road until she paralleled a flat patch of meadow. Swinging into the meadow, she locked the vehicle with the key fob and walked past the roadblock. The man warned her not to approach the fire, but he let her pass. It didn't hurt that she allowed her jacket to fall away from the Glock-22 on her hip.

From the back of the parking lot, she watched the flames snap along the roof of one apartment on the far right. The fire hadn't spread, but it would if the wind picked up. Behind her, a television news crew raced their van down the road only for the roadblocks to thwart them.

Flanagan, the hawk-nosed junior agent who trailed Bell during the Nicholas Winston serial killer case, leaned against the SUV, arms folded as though he expected her. She had questions for Flanagan. What was he doing in Blackwater, Virginia while Bell and Gardy pursued Winston? She assumed Weber had sent his pet-agent to spy on her. Bell painted on a smile as she strode up to the junior agent.

"How's Agent Gardy?" Flanagan asked.

"The bullet grazed his thigh. He's stitched up, but he'll be in pain for the next week. Did you see how the fire started?"

Flanagan extended his arm toward the ground-floor apartment three buildings over from hers.

"The fire started in the kitchen. A neighbor called it in before I noticed the smoke."

That was the O'Connor's apartment. The seniors were in Oregon visiting their daughter and had asked Bell to keep an eye on the place. How could the fire start in the kitchen with nobody home to cook?

Bell started forward, and Flanagan snatched her by the arm.

"You can't go inside."

"I'll be late for my flight. My bag is in my apartment."

But it was too late. The fire chief filed the neighbors out of her building where they wandered toward their cars like lost souls.

"Well, I guess I'm flying to Florida without a change of clothes," Bell said, placing her hands on her hips. "This should be interesting."

"New case, Agent Bell?"

"Weber didn't tell you?" She cocked an eyebrow, but Flanagan didn't take the bait. "You seem to know my every move. I've been meaning to ask why you drove to Blackwater."

"Blackwater? Oh, you mean the Winston murders."

"That's right."

"I'm sorry, Agent Bell, but you must be mistaken."

"Gardy and I saw you."

Flanagan shook his head and turned to watch the fire.

"I mean no offense, but I wasn't anywhere near Blackwater during the Winston case. Now if you don't mind, I'm heading back to the office since you're on the way to Dulles. Safe travels, Agent Bell."

Flanagan drove off and abandoned her in the parking lot. Liar. She didn't know what the junior agent was up to, but she'd keep eyes in the back of her head on future cases. The conspiracy theorist inside her believed Weber wanted dirt on Bell, a justification for firing her.

Directing hoses at the blaze, the firefighters appeared to have the blaze under control. They might clear her apartment for entry in the next several hours, but by then she'd be in Florida. Bell's neighbors asked her what she knew about the fire. She didn't have answers, only the usual platitudes to have faith. Things would be all right.

She walked back to the meadow, stepping with care through a muddy area which tried to rip her shoes off. When she passed the roadblock, the volunteer firefighter manning the checkpoint waved her down.

"Hey, someone started creeping around your SUV while you were at the fire."

Bell stopped and squinted into the darkness. At the edge of the meadow, a shadow vanished behind a stand of trees.

"Did you see his face?"

"Too dark. I yelled, and he took off in that direction."

The volunteer gestured toward the trees where Bell spotted the shadow. She thanked the man and moved toward the Rogue with her gun drawn.

From her hip, she removed a flashlight and aimed it at her vehicle. No broken windshield, no random graffiti.

Her heart pounded in her ears as she swept the beam across the seats. Nobody hidden inside.

She was about to click the key fob when her instincts screamed something was wrong. Bell backed away and rounded the Rogue, studying the vehicle as she flicked the light over the doors. Then she bent down. An object caught her eye on the undercarriage. Too small for her to discern at night. The little box flashed a green light and turned dark again.

Dropping to her stomach, she swept the light over the undercarriage.

And saw the explosive.

CHAPTER NINETY-FOUR

Bell's breath caught in her throat. She inched backward, watching the bomb as though a cobra coiled and hissed beneath the vehicle.

When she'd scrambled a safe distance from the Rogue, she jumped to her feet and put her hand over her heart. The man at the roadblock glared at her.

The Rogue rested a safe distance from the firefighters, but if the bomb exploded, debris would put the volunteer at risk. Breaking into a jog, she called Harold at the BAU and told him to send the bomb squad. By the time she ended the call, she stood at the curb, the volunteer taking a step away from the roadblock, sensing danger.

After she told him about the explosive, he contacted the fire chief. The man yelled orders over the radio.

"Are you certain you can't identify the man?" Bell asked.

"It's like I told you. It was too dark to get a good look at him, but now that you mention it, he looked under your vehicle."

Flanagan popped into her head.

"A black SUV drove out of the parking lot ten minutes ago. He must have passed your roadblock."

"I saw the SUV. Tinted windows, government plates."

"That's the one. The driver wasn't the man beside my vehicle, was he?"

The volunteer shook his head.

"No. I watched the SUV drive off. If he came back, I would have noticed."

The bomb squad spent a long time removing the explosive from underneath Bell's vehicle. She would miss her flight. Though the circumstances were beyond her control, Bell spent ten minutes on the phone with the angry deputy director who wanted to know why she wasn't in Florida.

"The next flight departs at nine o'clock. I expect you to be on it."

Weber hung up before she replied. The sun would be up soon, and she hadn't slept a wink. At least she was allowed to enter her apartment and grab her travel supplies.

The bomb squad leader, a tall man with a shaved head, glasses, and an ear piece attached to a wire, walked toward Bell as she pocketed her phone. She knew him as Cashman. The squad leader wore a dark blue uniform, making him difficult to see in the dark, and moved with purpose and efficiency as he crossed the meadow.

"You were lucky," Cashman said. "A radio transmitter controlled the explosive. He could have set it off at any time."

Bell's eyes swept the far end of the meadow. The bomber needed to stay close to fire the explosive. He fled after the bomb squad arrived.

"So starting the engine wouldn't have set it off."

"Nope. You attract a lot of bombers, Agent Bell?"

"I have a bad habit of pissing people off."

After the team cleared her Rogue, she drove to the apartment complex, nervous every time the tires hit a bump, worried another bomb lay hidden inside the vehicle.

She slogged up the apartment steps, exhaustion smothering her anxiety as the sun peaked over the Atlantic. Inside, she gathered her belongings and grabbed snacks for the drive to Dulles. Her eyes swept the living room, suspicious, and stopped on the sliding glass door to the deck. From here she discerned the trench beside the ocean, the waves filling the excavation with sand. The trench where Gardy and Bell almost died.

The ride to the airport left her wondering about the bomb and the fire. Too coincidental. The past months' events made it obvious someone wanted her dead, and the attempts on her life had become a weekly occurrence.

As she swerved through highway traffic, her phone rang. Her mother's name appeared on the dash, and she accepted the call, worried her parents had more bad news. They planned to move to a retirement community in Arizona. Bell's research suggested the owner might be unscrupulous. Several retirees claimed the owner cheated them out of their savings.

"Were you in a fire?"

Tammy Bell's question took her daughter by surprise.

"How did you find out about the fire so fast?"

"Your father heard about it on the news. We were so worried."

"The fire didn't reach my building, Mom. I'm fine."

At least her mother hadn't learned about the bomb.

"That's so frightening. I hope nobody got hurt."

"Everyone made it out before the fire got out of hand, but one of my neighbors lost their belongings."

"Oh, that's horrible." Bell imagined her mother touching her heart and fanning her face, a habit she repeated whenever she encountered tragedy and loss. "Let us know if we can help. Your father and I have led a fortunate life."

"Yes, you tell me often. Is everything okay, Mom? It's

only seven in the morning."

"Everything is wonderful. We keep hoping you'll stop by with Agent Wolf again. Your father can't stop talking about him."

Bell's stomach dropped as she remembered Logan Wolf paying a visit to her childhood home. She'd chalked the visit up to one of his mind games, but after his sister's slaughter, the memory sent a shiver down her spine.

"Agent Wolf is out of the country. We're not sure when he'll get back."

"A shame. Such a nice man. We were thinking of inviting him over to meet the—"

"Actually, Agent Wolf wants to transfer to another agency. We won't see much of him from now on."

Bell overheard her mother's disappointment as she told her husband the bad news.

"I almost forgot," Tammy Bell said, rummaging through the closet. "You received a package yesterday afternoon. No idea why they sent it to us, and there's no return address, but you'll need to pick it up when you have the time."

The Rogue swerved out of its lane and drew angry horns from the other drivers.

"Don't touch the package."

"What do you mean? I'm holding the box right now."

Before Bell could stop her, Tammy Bell tore the box open. Heart surging into her throat, Bell prayed the next sound wouldn't be an explosion a split-second before the call cut off.

"Mom? Put the package down and wait for me."

"Well, isn't that odd? The box is empty."

"Empty? Why would anyone send me an empty box?"

"Wait a second. There's something under the paper."

"Are you listening to me?" Bell searched for an opening in the traffic glut. The next exit was less than a mile away. “Don’t touch anything.”

“It’s a note. Strange. What does this mean?”

“What does the note say?”

“It reads, *Come home, little one. Time to sleep.*”

CHAPTER NINETY-FIVE

"I don't care if Weber hasn't cleared you for field work," Bell said, forcing her way through the crowd blocking her gate.

She'd sprinted from the TSA checkpoint to the gate, but the gate attendant hadn't boarded her row yet.

"You're the only person I trust. I want the note and box dusted for prints, hair fibers, anything that tells me who this person is."

"You believe it's the same guy who planted the explosive?" Gardy asked, raising his voice so she could hear him. He was at the office, waiting to meet with Weber.

"And the man who tried to take our heads off last night. Yes, Gardy."

"But why an empty box with a vague note stuffed in the bottom? If this guy wanted to send a message, he'd plant another explosive."

The gate attendant welcomed Bell's row to board. A brunette woman wearing too much makeup budged in front of Bell and clipped another passenger with the edge of her suitcase.

"Maybe he figured the delivery company would detect the explosive." Hearing Bell, the brunette woman swiveled her head around and edged away. "Or he's playing games with me. Hell, I don't know."

"Candice just rang my phone. Time to see Weber. I gotta go. Regardless of what he says, I'll pay your parents a visit as soon as I can."

"You're a lifesaver, Gardy."

Turbulence ruined the trip to Miami. Bell remembered Gardy's penchant for airsickness and thanked the heavens he wasn't on the flight. The elderly woman in the next seat moved to the back of the plane to sit with her family halfway through the trip, and Bell felt comfortable removing her iPad to page through the Fair Haven Beach crime scene photographs.

The slash across Christina Wolf's throat was clean and efficient, executed by a steady hand. This killer had experience. The ominous and familiar sack over the victim's head haunted Bell. She'd reviewed these macabre scenes too many times, and she never got used to them.

Next she paged forward to a recent photograph of Christina Wolf. The resemblance to Logan Wolf struck her. The firm set of the mouth, the high cheekbones, the inquisitiveness of the eyes. All eerily similar.

After she read through the police report, she put the iPad away and leaned back, closing her eyes. What sent Logan Wolf over the edge? If he'd wanted to murder his sister, why wait until now?

The smothering heat of summer had left Virginia for the year, but when Bell stepped through the sliding glass doors to pick up her rental car, she found where summer hid. The wall of sun and tropical maritime air blanketed Bell as she slipped her sunglasses on and dodged the taxis and Uber drivers. She descended a short stairway to the rental lot and found her vehicle, a sporty red Kia with a long scratch across the hood. Placing her bag at her feet, Bell buckled under a wave of paranoia. A businessman talking on his phone eyed Bell curiously as she dropped to her stomach and checked the undercarriage. Clear, though the muffler was on its last legs.

The dashboard clock read noon as she fought highway traffic. Thank goodness for GPS, for she'd never visited the greater Miami area. The synthesized female voice directed her to the Fair Haven Beach police department. Checking her notes, Bell showed her badge at the front desk and asked for Detective Larrabee. As though she was poised at the door waiting for Bell, an African-American woman in a beige skirt suit and heels clicked across the operations area and held out her hand.

"Welcome to Fair Haven Beach, Agent Bell," Detective Larrabee said, her handshake firm. "Just you?"

"My partner is indisposed this afternoon, but I hope to have him with me by tomorrow."

"Good. Do you prefer to ride with me to the crime scene, or would you rather follow?"

Knowing by the time she finished the walk-through she'd need to hustle to the hotel and check in, Bell chose to follow Larrabee in her rental car. The trip took fifteen minutes.

Palms flanked the two-story beach house. A man and his beagle walked the otherwise empty beach as Larrabee pushed aside the yellow crime scene tape and unlocked the door.

"The owner has a house two miles south of here and rents this place during the off season. Our vic paid for a week's stay." The cacophony the sea breeze caused vanished when Larrabee stepped into the foyer and closed the door. "We get our share of violence in the Miami area, but Fair Haven Beach is a vacation town. This time of year, the shops and restaurants close early, and everyone knows their neighbors by name."

Bell gave a non-committal nod and studied the layout. The foyer opened to a dated kitchen, an unusual layout for an older house. A bottle of Merlot rested on the counter beside an empty wine glass.

Slipping on a pair of gloves, Bell lifted the glass to the light and studied the edges.

"Did you test the glass for DNA?"

"We dusted for prints. You think the killer drank from the glass?"

"Just a hunch."

Beyond the kitchen, a living room held a sectional couch, television, and two end tables. The deck beyond the sliding glass door drew Bell's eye. Christina Wolf must have admired the ocean from the deck. God knew Bell would have.

"The killer entered through the deck door," Larrabee said, gesturing at the door. "He broke the latch and came inside, probably while the woman was away. We found two bags from the shopping plaza. No other signs of forced entry. The screen is off its hinges in the master bedroom. Apparently, she broke the screen trying to escape."

Larrabee led Bell up the stairs. The master bedroom lay at the end of the hallway, and one large window set on the eastern wall lent a view of the water. But the blood-soaked carpet held Bell's attention.

"We think the killer grabbed her at the window and pulled her back," the detective said, dropping to one knee beside the gore. "Then he killed her here. What we don't understand is why. Was this a random murder? Revenge?"

"Not vengeance. Not even rage."

"I thought most violent murders were rage-based."

"This murder is cold and calculated. No stab wounds, no strangulation. This almost looks like a contract killing." Bell swept her thumb across her throat. "Whoever our killer is, he kept his control. And he's done this before."

"A serial killer?"

"Perhaps."

After Larrabee finished the briefing, she sat in her car

while Bell walked through the house. Since joining the BAU, Bell preferred to study the house alone, without the distraction of people offering opinions and breaking her concentration.

She began at the patio door. Latches on sliding glass doors are notoriously easy to jostle open. A smart killer would begin here, and Logan Wolf was the most intelligent murderer she'd studied. From the deck, he could have watched Christina. Fantasized the murder before he acted.

Sand speckled the deck, not unusual for a patio overlooking the beach. The door opened to the living room. No hiding places here, but a closet off the foyer intrigued Bell. She pictured Christina at the counter opening the bottle of wine. She might have heard the ceiling groan and gone upstairs to investigate.

No, that didn't feel right.

Sticking to the shadows bleeding down from the walls, following the arc the killer likely would have taken, Bell stepped through the kitchen and pulled the closet door open. More sand dotted the bare wood floor. Backtracking through the living room, she discovered sand in the shadows. The cleanliness of the downstairs suggested the owner tidied up after coming inside and wouldn't leave a speck of sand. Yes, the killer took this path and hid inside the closet.

After stepping into the closet, Bell stood in darkness. Even with the door closed, she peered through the sliver-opening between the door and jamb. She pictured Christina pouring wine at the counter, taking a sip and carrying the glass of Merlot out to the deck. For many serial killers, a voyeuristic viewing of the target offered sexual gratification. He might have fantasized. Christina Wolf was a pretty woman who kept herself in shape.

Except Logan Wolf wouldn't fantasize about his sister.

He might have gifted Christina the Merlot. That

sounded like Wolf. But little else fit beyond the precise sweep of the blade against Christina's neck.

Now she pictured Wolf's sister on the deck, one arm leaned against the rail as she took in the ocean view. A perfect time for the killer to emerge from the closet and climb the stairs toward the bedrooms. Christina could have turned around and looked past the deck door, the killer invisible to her inside the dark living room. He stared at her, Bell thought. The thrill of knowing she was so close yet couldn't see him.

She replayed the murder scene in her head upstairs. Struggled to imagine Wolf in the killer's role. Something didn't fit.

She took pictures of the house on her way out. After suggesting Larrabee dust for prints inside the closet, she left for the hotel.

Wolf didn't murder his sister.

CHAPTER NINETY-SIX

From the parking garage rooftop across the street, he studies the photograph and compares it to the beautiful woman at the hotel check-in desk. Scarlett Bell, an agent with the FBI.

She's alone. Vulnerable.

The man behind the desk hands her the key card, and she lifts the travel bag at her feet. Through the binoculars, he follows her to the corner room on the second floor, 215. The Florida sun scorches the pavement, but he sticks to the cool shadows and slides along the concrete wall until he stands even with her room.

Agent Bell fumbles the key card and kneels to pick it up, and he glimpses bare thigh when her skirt runs up. His heart hammers when she suddenly spins and looks directly at him. Yes, she senses him. Can feel him in the shadows the way a grasshopper does the trapdoor spider.

He edges back, ensures the darkness cloaks his presence. After a tense moment, she opens the door and disappears inside.

The man smiles. He's butchered dozens, though never had he killed for money. For fifteen years, he's traveled the back roads of the United States, stealing the unprotected from their families and claiming them as his own. He's careful. Methodical. And he doesn't make mistakes, which is why he never attracted attention. No buried bodies for a weekend warrior geologist to uncover, no manifestos sent to the nation's largest newspapers. His trophies travel with him.

He touches the black van's sliding door. The four sealed barrels stand on the other side of the door. His butterfly collection.

No mistakes. He's a ghost.

Which makes him wonder how the FBI man wearing the blue suit, ear piece, and sunglasses found him in 2013. The government knew he was a murderer, though he doubted the FBI appreciated how many lives ended at his hands. But they didn't arrest him. They wished to hire him.

On a hot evening in July of 2013, he crept inside the residence of Logan and Renee Wolf. His instructions were clear—slaughter the woman without leaving a trace of his presence and make the murder appear ritualistic. Interesting. He didn't get off on the ritualistic bullshit. Taking a life and keeping it for his own satisfied him. The 2013 murder left him cold and detached. Though he enjoyed slitting the woman's throat, stuffing her head into a black bag felt forced, contrived.

Now the FBI had found him again. He felt certain they would arrest him this time, but the new FBI agent, a thin, young man with a hawk nose, handed him three photographs. Targets. If he murdered all three, the FBI wouldn't pursue him. They'd continue to pretend he didn't exist. A fair deal, though temptation urged him to gut the FBI agent for threatening him.

He followed the first woman for a week before she rented the vacation home along the ocean. The attraction he felt for her mystified him. There was something dangerous about her, something clandestine, as though she clung to a dark secret. He senses she is related to the woman they asked him to eliminate in 2013. Renee Wolf.

He had his own methodologies for killing beautiful women, but the agent insisted he slit the woman's throat and place a bag over her head as he'd done in 2013. He doesn't understand why. Doesn't care. Taking a life excites him and leaves him sleepless for days, and last night he relived the murder as he stared up at the ceiling in his van, the barrels beside him, the scents of metal, death, and rust stewing.

Slipping the photograph of Agent Bell into the envelope, he studies the last picture. A man. He never butchered a man before. Not for pleasure, anyway.

In the cool gloom of the garage, he unlocks the door and slides the pictures under the driver seat. Then the man pockets the keys and crosses the busy thoroughfare, heedless of the Corvette that screeches to a halt and assails him with a horn. He enters the main lobby and passes the front desk without generating interest. The hallway is dark. Voices travel from behind locked doors, unaware death passes on silent footsteps. Eschewing the elevator, he takes the stairs at the end of the corridor. Concrete and echoes.

One flight up, he edges the door open and stands outside room 215. He touches the door and imagines Agent Bell on the other side, placing her hand against the barrier to mirror his. Like lost soul mates.

He will kill her tomorrow.

CHAPTER NINETY-SEVEN

Bell shot awake. Someone was outside the door.

Grabbing her holster off the bed, she placed her eye against the peephole. The balcony lay empty. Her nerves had gotten the better of her again.

An hour remained before she briefed the Fair Haven Beach PD, and she had no idea what to say. The BAU asserted Logan Wolf murdered his sister. She wouldn't lie to a room of law enforcement officers.

A message arrived from Gardy. Her partner left a half-hour ago and would be in Bealton soon. Had they made the right decision by not involving the FBI at her parents' house? To the untrained eye, the note looked like a practical joke. But Bell sensed a more ominous intent.

She showered and changed, and as she grabbed her phone off the nightstand, it rang. Except it didn't. It took her several confused seconds before she realized the ringing came from her bag. Wolf's burner phone.

Bell tossed the bag's contents across the bed and snatched the phone before it stopped ringing.

"Wolf?"

She waited for the serial killer's eerie sing-song voice. When he spoke, he sounded different. Shattered. Furious.

"You were wrong, Scarlett. I warned you not to fail me."

Bell sat on the edge of the bed.

"The profile of Renee's killer is correct. Now, tell me where you were last night."

Laughter.

"Am I a suspect, dear Scarlett? Do you think I..." His voice broke. Wolf lowered the phone against his chest and composed himself. "Since the night that butcher stole Renee, I've tracked this killer. You told me he didn't exist, that someone murdered my wife and set me up. But now this. My only remaining family. Gone because I believed you."

"I just returned from studying the murder scene, but I guess you already knew."

"To prove I killed Christina?"

Bell held her response, searching for the right words. "To prove to myself you didn't."

"I could have saved you the effort."

"But you were there." Quiet followed. "The bottle of Merlot. That's something you would do."

His silence spoke volumes.

"Yes, I left the bottle. Christina always appreciated a fine wine, and I wanted to surprise her and give her happiness. She deserved it after all she'd gone through. But I didn't murder my sister. I wouldn't harm a hair on her head."

"This is a problem, Wolf. Your DNA is inside the house. If the CSI crew found anything to implicate you, there's nothing I can do."

"I was careful. I never touched the bottle without gloves. But I could have protected Christina had I any idea she was in danger."

Bell parted the curtain and looked down upon the hotel grounds. A pool with two children swimming, the father sipping a tropical drink. Palms swaying. A rundown hotel next door with plenty of dark shadows behind its walls.

"Are you in Fair Haven Beach, Wolf?"

"What if I am, Scarlett?"

"Leave. Someone set a trap for you. Don't you see?"

"If you think I'll leave with the man who killed Renee and Christina so close, you're the one who's insane."

"This man didn't kill Renee. That was a professional hit."

"Yes, yes. You keep repeating yourself, but you're wrong. I overestimated your profiling ability, I fear. You've led me to dead ends one too many times. It pains me to blame you, dear Scarlett, but you're responsible for Christina's death. And now you must pay. An eye for an eye."

The call ended. Bell stared at the phone as it trembled in her hand. She dropped it to the bed as though it morphed into a scorpion.

Back at the window, she peeked between the curtains. She opened the door and swept her gaze along the street. A college age girl rode past on a bicycle. Cars motored from one red light to the next.

Her eyes stopped on the three-level parking garage across the street. A black van with tinted windows pulled out of the garage and turned the corner, speeding past the building before she got a look at the license plate.

Then she spied the dark figure at the end of the block. Watching her from behind a stand of palms.

Logan Wolf.

CHAPTER NINETY-EIGHT

"You're sure you can't stay for dinner?"

Gardy didn't want to impose on Tammy Bell, and besides, he'd lied to Weber and claimed he needed to see his doctor for a second opinion on his leg. The deputy director would ask questions if Gardy lingered in Bealton.

Though Mrs Bell had placed her fingers all over the box and note, Gardy wore gloves as he searched for evidence to identify the sender. He found nothing. Whoever sent the box, he was experienced and careful.

Come home, little one. Time to sleep.

Gardy didn't understand the meaning of the message. Mind games from the same man who placed the explosive under Bell's vehicle?

"Smells great, Mrs Bell, but they need me back at work."

"You're limping, Agent Gardy."

"It's nothing. I pulled a muscle at the gym. I guess my back squat isn't what it used to be."

The level look she gave Gardy told him she wasn't buying it.

"Well, you'd think the FBI would grant you time to heal before tossing you into the field. Speaking of which,

Scarlett threw a fit over this little box. I worry she's under too much stress. She's not thinking straight."

"I'll keep an eye on her, Mrs Bell."

"I know you will, Agent Gardy. You're a good man. You'd make a fine husband someday, and I've tried to convince Scarlett to settle down—"

"I need to get back to Quantico," Gardy said, his cheeks blooming.

He tossed the box in the trunk and pondered the note's meaning while he followed Bealton's roads back to the highway. The little town held ghosts. Every street corner reminded him of the God's Hand killer and Logan Wolf, and he wondered how different Bell's life would have been had she grown up elsewhere.

His unease grew. Something about Bell's trip to Florida didn't sit right in his stomach. Why hadn't Weber sent another agent in Gardy's place? Between the multiple attempts on their lives, neither Bell nor Gardy should have been in the field.

He popped four ibuprofen in the parking lot. The stitches stretched and burned when he climbed out of his van, the wound tightening after the long drive. Under the late day sun, it was impossible to see beyond the windows, but Gardy felt Weber watching him as he climbed the steps. Gardy did his best not to limp.

Candice, Weber's administrative assistant, blew into Gardy's office the moment he sat down.

"Deputy Director Weber wishes to see you. Now."

Gardy sighed and straightened the stack of paperwork Candice had left him and slid it to the corner. He felt tempted to sweep the mess into the garbage can.

The wound screamed at him, and he stood in the doorway and took a composing breath as he willed the pain away. Then he continued down the hallway to Weber's office, nodding at passing agents as if he didn't have a worry in the world.

Weber didn't look up when Gardy knocked, only motioned toward a chair as he jotted information on a form.

"How's the leg, Agent Gardy?"

"Better."

"Not good enough for field work. Let it heal and you'll be back in no time."

"Sir, if I may. Agent Bell is alone at Fair Haven Beach. There's no reason I can't catch the next flight to Miami and be there to watch her back."

"You're not fit to work, and Agent Bell is a big girl. She can handle a murder case on her own."

"Two attempts on her life in the last twenty-four hours. Why is she even allowed in the field?"

Weber groaned and leaned his elbows on his desk. After rubbing his eyes, he tapped his pen on the desk.

"Perhaps I was too hasty sending Agent Bell to Florida alone. You understand my desire to act before Logan Wolf pulls another vanishing act."

"You're certain Wolf is in Florida?"

"That can't be a serious question. The killer's M.O. matches Wolf's, and a traffic camera in Fair Haven Beach caught a man who resembled Wolf two hours before the murder."

As much as Gardy wanted to implicate Logan Wolf, Weber's shifting eyes belied him.

"All the more reason to send backup to Florida."

"Agreed. I'll send Agent Flanagan."

"Flanagan?" Gardy sat forward and squinted at Weber. "He's a junior agent. You can't send him to a case this big."

"Agent Flanagan has proved himself and won't be a junior agent for long. You didn't protest when I put Flanagan on duty to watch Agent Bell's apartment, so why complain now?"

"That's different."

"How so? If Logan Wolf appeared, Agent Flanagan would have apprehended him."

Gardy bit his lip. Weber had sent Flanagan to spy on them at Blackwater Lake, and he didn't trust the junior agent. Time for Plan B.

"You're right. Bell can handle the case on her own. With my injury, Agent Flanagan should slide into my role. I have paperwork to catch up on, anyhow."

"That's a sudden change of heart."

"Now that I think about it, Deputy Director Weber, my leg is bothering me. All this sitting around isn't good for the healing process. I'll take you up on your offer and accept the sick leave."

Weber narrowed his eyes.

"Strange the pain increased so suddenly."

"I should take a week off. Rest up and make sure the wound heals. I don't want the injury to linger for months because I rushed back into service."

"All right, Agent Gardy. I'll have Candice give you the paperwork."

Gardy pushed up from his chair, limping to play up the pain.

"I better not find out you flew to Florida, Agent Gardy. Lying about an injury and claiming sick leave could mean your job."

Gardy grabbed his keys and took the elevator down to the ground floor. Throwing looks over his shoulder, he ensured nobody followed as he unlocked his van and pulled himself into the driver seat. As he pointed the vehicle toward the DC suburbs, he dialed Bell. She sounded harried when she answered.

"Someone's following me, Gardy."

At that moment, he checked his mirror and noticed a black SUV trailing him, staying several car lengths back.

"That makes two of us. You get a look at the guy?"

"I've seen Logan Wolf enough times to recognize him."

"Wolf is there? I figured he'd flee by now."

Gardy's pulse quickened. Bell without backup and Logan Wolf stalking her. He needed to get to Florida.

"Wolf didn't kill Christina, Gardy. I know you think he murdered his sister and wife, but it doesn't add up."

"So someone else murdered Christina Wolf? How many serial killers can one village hold?"

"Wolf blames me, but I'm sure the profile I gave him is correct. And what do you mean, someone is following you?"

"Maybe I caught your conspiracy flu," Gardy said, adjusting the mirror. "But there's a black SUV seven cars behind me. He's been there since I hit the interstate."

"Be careful, Gardy. You don't know if it's the sniper."

"Well, he can't line up a shot while driving seventy outside of DC. And I doubt TSA will let him board with a rifle."

"Don't tell me Weber allowed you to fly to Florida."

"Of course not. I'm injured and can't do my job. It's best for everyone I take a week of sick leave."

Bell snickered.

"Nicely played."

Gardy swerved into the passing lane and shot past a pickup truck. A moment later, the black SUV executed a pass and kept pace.

"I thought so, but Weber is on to me. Which explains my tail. But I'm stopping at the San Giovanni estate before I beg, borrow, or steal a ticket at the airport."

"The estate? Why are you stopping there?"

"Something you said. San Giovanni found dirt on a politician but didn't bring it to the committee."

"How would the mother know?"

"She might not, but I bet the mother remembers

where San Giovanni kept her files."

He told Bell he hadn't identified the box's sender in Bealton, but he left out Tammy Bell suggesting he'd make a fine husband for Scarlett. Gardy couldn't deny his heart beat faster when Bell entered the room, but there was no future in pursuing a fellow agent, especially one who didn't show the slightest interest in him.

Gardy frowned.

"I don't get it. A serial killer murders Christina Wolf after a sniper shoots at us and someone places a bomb under your vehicle."

"The events are related, Gardy. I haven't connected the dots, but I will."

When Gardy took the exit ramp, the mysterious SUV disappeared.

CHAPTER NINETY-NINE

Bell didn't recall the last time she felt this lost on a case.

She kept her briefing vague for the Fair Haven Beach PD, and by the time she finished, she hadn't conveyed new knowledge. Now she bristled under the stare of Detective Larrabee.

Seated behind her desk and irritably rocking in her chair, Larrabee ordered Bell to close her office door.

"You're holding out on me, Agent Bell."

"Why do you say that?"

"You danced around that briefing, and you don't buy half the theories you put forth."

Beneath the desk, Bell dug her nails into her thighs. She couldn't lie to Larrabee, nor could she tell her the truth. Before Bell opened her mouth to reply, Larrabee reached inside her desk and slid a photograph in front of Bell. A picture of Logan Wolf.

"Your own people say this man murdered Christina Wolf. Turns out he's my vic's brother, and if that isn't enough, he's a fugitive and the most renown serial killer in the United States. But you don't believe he did it."

"Did someone at the FBI call you?"

"I have my sources. Answer the question."

Bell picked up the picture and studied it. Wolf was younger then, an agent with the BAU. A flicker of hope still burned in those dark chasms for eyes. She could continue to lie to Larrabee, but it wasn't worth the trouble. By this time next week, she'd either be dead or out of a job.

"Yes, Logan Wolf is the victim's brother, but he didn't kill her."

"Explain your reasoning, Agent Bell, and it better be good."

Larrabee's face remained unreadable as Bell detailed Wolf's background and her theories about the serial killer. Why he killed. Her belief he never murdered his wife. It occurred to Bell Larrabee was the first person besides Gardy she'd confided in about Wolf's innocence in 2013. When Bell finished, Larrabee turned a pen over and over on the desk, eyes unblinking.

"Now that's the briefing I expected when I requested FBI assistance. If you'd given me anything half that good, we'd already have the perpetrator behind bars."

"I don't understand the murder, Detective."

Larrabee rocked back in her chair and set her heel on a drawer.

"What's the confusion?"

"This serial killer struck without emotion. The cut across Christina Wolf's throat is too perfect, too precise. It more resembles a contract hit than the act of a deranged murderer. And yet the unknown subject displayed characteristics of typical serial killers."

"Such as?"

"He didn't storm inside at the first opportunity and execute Christina Wolf. Instead, he stalked her. Watched her from the closet, maybe sipped from the wine bottle." Bell shook her head. "It's as if he switched midstream from lunacy to a paint-by-numbers murder."

"It's difficult for me to accept the killer isn't Logan Wolf when the method of killing matches his."

"This sounds crazy, Detective, but the killer wanted us to think Wolf murdered his sister."

The theory hung in the air as silence blanketed the room. Bell expected Larrabee to snatch her phone and dial the BAU to complain about the rogue field agent sitting across from her. Instead, she examined Bell the way she might an interesting piece of art she hadn't figured out.

"Two serial killers in Fair Haven Beach. I hope you're wrong, Agent Bell."

An Internet search returned five liquor stores in the village. One stuck out to Bell. D'Angelo's catered to discerning connoisseurs, people who appreciated fine wines. On her way to D'Angelo's, Bell phoned her mother and suggested her parents visit Helen, their friend in Fredericksburg. Tammy Bell listed all the reasons they shouldn't go, but Bell persisted until she agreed. Good. One less thing to worry about in case another package arrived.

The shopkeeper, an Italian man with black, slicked hair and a pencil-thin mustache, recognized Logan Wolf from the picture Bell showed him.

"An interesting man," the shopkeeper said, smiling. "And he knows his wines. He purchased our finest bottle of Merlot, paid with large bills, and told me to keep the change. It was a generous tip."

He estimated Wolf visited around one o'clock. Wolf's sister hadn't taken the house keys from the realtor until noon, so that meant Wolf already knew her plans. He must have followed her for days.

Calling up a map on her phone, Bell studied the terrain around the beach house. Like Miami, Fair Haven Beach was pancake-flat along the coast. Palms blocked the view from the nearest neighborhood. Nowhere to stake out the beach house without drawing attention.

Bell stopped at a surf shop three blocks from the ocean and purchased a beach hat, a new pair of sunglasses, a lounge chair, and a swim dress. To complete the disguise, she plucked a Dan Brown paperback off the counter. The teen boy working the desk took one look at Bell and agreed when she asked to use the changing room.

Bell cursed herself for not remembering sunscreen as she danced over the hot sand. The beach was empty except for a fisherman casting a line a hundred yards down the coast. Keeping the beach house in view, she walked until the two-story home appeared toy-like. Then she set her chair where the tide clawed at the sand. She raised her binoculars.

Perfect. She had a clear view of the deck door and the flapping crime scene tape. If the killer returned to relive the crime, she'd see.

A man approached from behind. Alone.

Bell opened the book and hid the binoculars inside her bag. She heard him stomp through the shallows, the gulls scattering.

False alarm. A woman shouted from further up the beach, and the man, obviously her husband, rushed to meet her.

The day grew late. Shadows lengthened and played tricks on Bell, fooling her into believing the killer had returned to the beach house.

At six o'clock, she began to feel foolish. She'd lose the sun soon, and the burn across her shoulders would leave her wishing for a sweatshirt.

But as she lowered the binoculars, a man rounded the beach house and ducked beneath the deck.

CHAPTER ONE HUNDRED

How can a mansion be a tomb?

That question rolled around in Gardy's mind as he walked the desolate halls of the San Giovanni estate. Footsteps announced Joelle's presence upstairs, but San Giovanni's daughter hid inside her room and didn't show her face. Pots clanged in the kitchen as the cook prepared dinner, the echoes lonely.

The grandmother, Alessia San Giovanni, looked strikingly similar to her daughter, though the lines in her face dug deeper than when Gardy last saw her a month ago. She wore a black dinner dress to match the pitch of her hair, and her heels tapped the glistening floor as she led Gardy past the dining room and kitchen toward the study.

"Lana kept a laptop in her bedroom, but she did most of her work in the study," Alessia said, hands clasped at her waist.

"As long as you understand this isn't an official visit," said Gardy, his eyes drawn to the impressionist paintings lining the corridor. "Technically, I shouldn't be here."

Alessia glanced at him from the corner of her eye.

"Agent Gardy, you and Agent Bell are the only people

Lana trusted in her final days, so I wouldn't let anyone near her computer but you. I can't promise you'll find anything useful. Lana remained secretive, even with her family, but she shared her access codes with me."

The study was the mansion's most impressive room. Stretching two stories along the back of the house, the glass ceiling offered unobstructed views of the sky. Long windows took up most of the back wall. One could lounge on the sofa and watch the sun rise.

It took a minute for the computer to reboot, then Alessia slipped a note card of passwords in front of Gardy.

"I'll leave you to it, Agent Gardy. Find my daughter's killer."

Alessia shut the door, and Gardy felt tiny inside the cavernous room. He began his search, stepping through file folders and sub-folders, until he discovered the work files for the corruption task force. From his pocket, he removed a list of cases the task force took public. Gardy checked off each case until he found a file that didn't link to any known cases.

Ewing.

Senator Chet Ewing, Gardy thought to himself as he double-clicked the file. Random characters filled the window, eliciting a curse from Gardy. San Giovanni had encrypted the file. This would take longer than expected. Checking the time, he realized he only had ninety minutes to drive to Dulles and catch his flight to Florida.

"What did you have on Ewing?" Gardy muttered, picking up the phone.

He called Harold's direct line at the BAU, relieved the technical analyst hadn't left for the day.

"I'm sending you a file, Harold. How fast can you decrypt a document?"

"Depends on the encryption strength," said Harold, calling up a terminal window on his workstation. "Uh, aren't you on sick leave?"

"As far as Weber knows."

"My lips are sealed."

"Like Belinda Carlisle."

"Who?"

"Never mind, just break the code before I miss my flight."

Harold typed away at his keyboard.

"Going somewhere, Agent Gardy?"

"I'm thinking someplace warm and tropical."

Harold issued a nervous snicker. The technical analyst knew Weber had eyes everywhere inside the BAU.

"Cracked it. Give me a harder challenge next time."

"You're a genius, Harold."

"I trust you'll remember who stuck their neck out for you come Christmas. The decrypted file is headed your way."

Harold's email popped up, and Gardy sent the file to his iPad.

"I'm heading to Dulles now. Thanks a million, Harold."

The list of cancellations didn't affect Gardy's flight to Miami, but a delay at the TSA checkpoint left him hobbling for the gate before the plane took off. He sent Bell a message and promised details on the Ewing file, but she didn't answer.

Night spread toward the runway as the flight crew prepared for takeoff. The cabin lights shut off, and the interior became dark. When the plane climbed to cruising altitude, Gardy removed the iPad from his seat compartment and called up the file.

Halfway through the document, he feared for Bell's life.

CHAPTER ONE HUNDRED ONE

Gun in hand, Bell crept along the tall grass and dunes. She'd read Gardy's message and knew San Giovanni had dirt on Senator Ewing. It must have been big since the information got San Giovanni murdered. But why was Bell in the cross-hairs?

The pitched roof of the beach house jutted above the sand. The rest of the home hid from her sight. Digging the phone out of her pocket, she dialed Larrabee. The detective would be there in fifteen minutes.

But Bell didn't have fifteen minutes. Full dark raced across the ocean and cloaked the intruder. He might be anywhere in the dark. Even right behind her.

She ducked low and ran to the palms, cursing the narrow trunks that did little to conceal her presence as she placed her back against a tree. Then she spun off the tree and sprinted to the wall, keeping her head below the first-floor windows.

When she rounded the house, she squinted her eyes, trying to make out the shadows beneath the deck. Impossible to see. The gun trembled in her hand as she slid along the wall and edged closer to the stairs. Close enough to make out shapes, she discerned footprints beneath the deck.

One hand on the rail, Bell pulled herself onto the deck and stood with her back to the wall. From here, she could see the snapped crime scene tape and the unlocked latch to the sliding glass door. On a silent count of three, Bell reached out and slid the door open, thankful it whispered along the grooves. She spun inside the dark confines.

The hand reached out of the shadows and gripped her by the throat. His other hand knocked the Glock from her hand and covered her mouth. She couldn't see the man's face, only his silhouette as he shoved her against the wall. She brought her elbow against his arm, but he was too strong. As she squirmed along the wall, a glint of moonlight caught Logan Wolf's face.

"Wolf, let go."

"Why should I, Scarlett? Because of you I have no family."

Bell swung her head forward and knocked it against his. His eyes crossed, and his hand sprang off her neck. She sucked air into her lungs, but he dropped down and snagged her gun. Now he took a step backward and aimed the Glock at her chest.

"I knew you'd come," he said, shifting to stand between Bell and the deck door. "You're as predictable as a sunrise. You'll go to your grave believing I murdered Christina and came back to…what is it you profilers call it? …relive the crime."

"No. You didn't kill your sister. But you're walking into a trap, Wolf."

"It appears I laid the trap for you, dear Scarlett."

"Someone wants us dead, Gardy included. It got me thinking about the night the killer took Renee's life."

"Be careful. You're walking a razor's edge mentioning her name."

"Put the gun down, and let's talk this through."

"Not a chance."

Bell rolled her neck. Phantom fingers curled around her throat.

"The sniper who shot at us on the hill, the man who tried to kill Gardy and me, and Congresswoman San Giovanni's assassin. They're all interconnected, and you're at the center."

"A serial killer took my wife, just as he murdered Christina. He's still in the village, Scarlett. I can sense him. And before I leave this little village, I'll feed him his heart."

A sound came from outside. Someone running through the sand.

"We have a visitor," Wolf said, turning his attention toward the windows.

"I called for backup. If I were you, I'd put the gun down and vanish. I doubt Detective Larrabee came alone."

A second set of footsteps circled the house.

"You buy these conspiracy theories. I see it in your eyes. Interesting."

"Think back, Wolf. Did you investigate Senator Ewing?" Stunned, Wolf glared at Bell. The corner of his mouth twitched. "Because San Giovanni started a file on Ewing, and a month later, a sniper put a bullet in her head."

Wolf shook his head.

"No, it can't be. A serial killer murdered Renee."

"That's what he wants you to believe. Tell me what you knew about Ewing."

Wolf flung the sliding glass door open and escaped into the night a split-second before the police burst into the house.

"Freeze, police!"

"Don't shoot, Larrabee. It's Agent Bell."

Bell raised her hands. The lights flicked on, blinding her. Larrabee, dressed as Bell had last seen the detective, rushed into the room beside a male officer a head taller than her.

Bell walked to the staircase and craned her head toward the landing, a diversion to pull Larrabee away from the deck. Though Wolf threatened her, Bell felt an undefinable need to protect him. He was just as much a victim as Renee and Christina.

"Was the killer here?" Larrabee asked, drawing her gun.

"A man broke inside," Bell said, nodding at the torn police tape flapping in the wind. "He must have heard me, because he jumped off the deck and ran toward the neighborhood before I could cut him off."

"I want the CSI team back," Larrabee barked at her partner. "Have them dust the door for prints and go over the downstairs with a fine-tooth comb. Find out who was in this house tonight."

Wolf wore gloves, but Bell worried he'd left a trace of DNA evidence behind.

"The team is on their way," the officer said.

"Thanks, Vargus. Agent Bell, meet Officer Luke Vargus."

Vargus tipped his cap. Bell touched her neck, drawing Larrabee's attention.

"You okay?" Larrabee asked Bell.

"Yeah, I slept wrong on the plane."

Larrabee nodded without taking her eyes off Bell. With her partner on the phone, Larrabee inched closer, her hand brushing the hair off Bell's face.

"It looks like someone grabbed you. Your neck is red."

"I keep rubbing at the pain, trying to loosen it up."

"Stop by my car on the way out. I keep aspirin in the glove compartment."

Bell waited with Larrabee and described the approximate size and age of the intruder. A half-hour later, the CSI team arrived.

As the crew went to work, Bell checked her phone. No news from Gardy.

Did Senator Ewing order the hit on San Giovanni?

CHAPTER ONE HUNDRED TWO

The knock on the hotel room door pulled Bell out of sleep. Night butted against the window. Too early for housekeeping.

Bell crept to the peephole and exhaled at the sight of Gardy, her exhausted partner leaning against the door frame.

She unlatched the bolt and let him wander inside, a carry-on bag tossed over his shoulder.

"What time is it?" Bell asked, squinting when she flipped the light on.

Her nightshirt rode up her hips, and she tugged it down as he pulled his eyes to the wall.

"It's too late to be awake." He tossed the bag in the corner and slumped into the lounge chair in the corner. "Sorry. No vacancies in the village. Do you mind if I crash?"

"No, no. You can stay. It means a lot that you came."

He rubbed his eyes and yawned.

"First things, first. You'll want to see this file."

"Hold on, Gardy. I need to wake up."

Bell pulled a half-full soda bottle from the refrigerator and took a swig while Gardy loaded the Ewing file. She raised a finger and disappeared into the bathroom. Closing the door, she scowled at the mess of hair atop her head and ran a brush through the knots. Testing her breath against her palm, she grabbed her toothbrush and scoured the stench out of her mouth.

By the time she finished, her head cleared of the grogginess. She leaned over Gardy's shoulder and began reading.

After a minute, she sat on the corner of the bed and dropped her face into her hands.

"This can't be true. If it is, Ewing is—"

"A cold-blooded killer." Gardy scrolled to the middle of the document. "San Giovanni asserts Senator Klein's car crash wasn't an accident."

Twelve years ago, Senator Klein held an eight-point advantage in the polls over Ewing before his car shot off the interstate during a rain storm and ended up at the bottom of the Potomac.

"You didn't read all the way to the bottom," Gardy said, handing Bell the tablet.

Gardy spun the chair toward Bell, who skimmed through the congresswoman's findings. Her eyes froze over the last paragraph.

Against the orders of his superiors, one FBI agent investigated Klein's death and suspected foul play. A BAU agent named Logan Wolf.

The new knowledge hung like a sword and kept them silent. When they finally debated the findings, neither could keep their eyes open.

Bell wasn't certain when she fell asleep. She recalled thrashing beneath the covers, the implications of the secret document haunting her every time she closed her eyes. Now the sun beamed through the windows. Gardy lay curled under a sliver of blanket at the foot of the bed.

Bell sighed and folded the covers over him. He made a contented groan and pulled the sheet over his face.

The shower spray steamed the bathroom. Bell leaned one arm against the wall as the water cascaded over her head. According to San Giovanni's findings, Ewing built a network of mercenaries and special ops soldiers. She hadn't uncovered the money trail before she died.

Bell toweled her hair dry, adrenaline keeping her upright when her body wanted to sleep another eight hours. After she dressed, she found Gardy awake and waiting for her on the chair.

His cheeks colored when she turned on the light.

"I don't remember crawling into your bed. That was terrible of me."

"If anyone should have the bed, it's you. That chair must be murder on your leg."

"Pretty damn inappropriate, though."

"Gardy, I trust you," Bell said, wondering what might have happened had she woken before dawn and found Gardy sleeping beside her.

"Anyway, it won't happen again." Bell flicked him with the towel. "What was that for?"

"You snore."

"I don't."

"Really now? You sound like a cow with a tuba stuck up its—"

"Fine. Can we get breakfast and figure out how to handle this Ewing situation?"

"There's a cafe down the block. I hope you brought something besides your work clothes. It's a million degrees outside."

Gardy changed into shorts and the unfortunate *Florida Is Hawt* t-shirt he'd purchased in the airport gift shop. When he pinched the bridge of his nose against the headache-inducing sun, Bell offered him her sunglasses.

After they grabbed croissant breakfast sandwiches, Bell led the way to the village park. Except for a mother and toddler using the swing set, the park was empty when Bell and Gardy grabbed a bench beside a tennis court. Gardy scanned the street, stopping on the parking garage. Too many places for a sniper to hide.

The injured, betrayed look in Gardy's eyes felt like a kick to Bell's stomach. He'd devoted his adult life to serving his country, always playing by the rules, and now he couldn't trust the BAU or his elected officials.

"You know I don't have a weapon," Gardy said. "TSA frowns on that sort of thing."

Gardy needed the FBI to submit an armed travel request allowing him to bring the Glock. No way he could have done so without alerting Weber.

"I have a backup weapon."

"What? Why?"

"Remember I bought another Glock after Weber suspended me?"

Gardy scratched his head.

"Yeah, I remember. If I'm going to break the rules, I might as well go for broke. Tell me why the senator wants Wolf dead."

"Wolf talked to the wrong people about Ewing, and the senator found out," Bell said, watching the mother give the swing a shove.

Gardy picked at a dandelion and tossed the flower into the grass.

"Why not order the hit on Wolf? Take him out and Ewing is free and clear."

"You know the answer, Gardy. A man like Logan Wolf isn't easily killed. Better to frame him, turn Wolf's own people against him."

"So Ewing hires someone to kill Renee and makes it look like Wolf did it."

Bell wrapped the rest of her breakfast and set it aside.

"And he makes the murder appear ritualistic, convincing Wolf a serial killer targeted his wife."

"But we don't have a single witness to corroborate the congresswoman's assertions. And there's no telling how many people this involves."

Bell leveled her eyes with Gardy's.

"We know one person who's involved. Don Weber."

Gardy deliberately set his breakfast down on the park bench.

"This again?"

"His sole focus is Logan Wolf. It's not an obsession. Weber didn't care about bringing Wolf to justice. He wants Wolf out of the way because Wolf has information on him."

"Care to elaborate?"

"I'm still connecting the dots, but I guarantee Weber is protecting Senator Ewing. You said so yourself a thousand times—the government promoted Weber beyond his competency. Could be Ewing agreed to push for Weber's promotion if the deputy director buried Wolf's case against him."

"So why do Ewing and Weber want us dead?"

Bell scrutinized the shrubs bordering the park. She felt eyes on her.

"Because Weber knows Wolf helped me at Blackwater Lake and in New York, and Weber is afraid we'll share information and blow him out of the water. That explains why Agent Flanagan followed us. I think I'll call Harold and have him query the 2013 database for any documents pertaining to Logan and Renee Wolf."

Gardy leaned back and locked his fingers behind his neck. The corners of his mouth tilted upward, suggesting Bell's conspiracy theories had hit a new level of ridiculousness. But his mind worked behind his eyes. Missing puzzle pieces fell into place.

"There's one way to prove Weber and Ewing tried to

kill us," Gardy said, cocking his eyebrow.

"Go on."

Gardy chewed the last of the croissant and tossed the wrapper in the trash.

"Let's catch a sniper."

CHAPTER ONE HUNDRED THREE

Larrabee shot Gardy a perfunctory look. No doubt the special agent's touristy clothes tampered her enthusiasm for Bell's partner. The detective's eyes glistened with intensity. Bell thought she could read Larrabee's doubts as if flipping a magazine open.

Detective Larrabee joined the Fair Haven Beach PD twelve years ago and found the department dominated by white males. They'd confined Larrabee to small cases, a quiet prejudice aimed at keeping her low on the totem pole. But she won the respect of her colleagues and rose through the ranks to detective on talent and steadfast persistence.

Larabee swiveled her gaze between the two agents.

"Tell me why you brought me here."

They sat at a long wooden table with years of scribbles etched into the surface. Bell preferred the neutral ground of the community college library. She didn't want Larrabee's colleagues overhearing what they had to say.

Florescent strip lighting hummed overhead. Two female students strolled among the stacks, and Bell waited until they moved on before she slid the FBI reports to Larrabee detailing the congresswoman's assassination and the attempted murders of Gardy and Bell on the

Chesapeake Bay. Larrabee set the two documents beside each other and moved her eyes between each, comparing.

"The assassination upset me," Larrabee said, turning the documents face-down. "San Giovanni was a beacon of hope for a lot of us. I buy your argument that the same shooter tried to kill you after you aided the congresswoman. But I fail to see what this has to do with my case."

Bell knew bringing Larrabee into the fold was a huge risk. If the detective dismissed the claims, she might contact Weber. But as Bell laid out her argument, the doubt vanished from Larrabee's face. The detective's eyes sharpened at the mention of Senator Ewing. Bell handed Larrabee the iPad.

"Agent Gardy discovered an encrypted document on the congresswoman's home computer. One of her sources claimed Ewing orchestrated Senator Klein's death, and I'm convinced Deputy Director Weber works for Ewing. I already confirmed Logan Wolf was the only BAU agent who pursued the Ewing case. "

Hearing Wolf's name rattled Larrabee. A female librarian pushed a cart of books past the table. When the woman turned the corner, Larrabee leaned forward.

"The FBI report implicates Wolf in his sister's death. Tell me the truth, Agent Bell. Is Wolf in my village?"

"Yes, but I assure you he didn't murder Christina Wolf. She was his only family."

"You must know Logan Wolf well if you can speak to his character. That concerns me."

"Nobody at this table trusts Logan Wolf," Gardy said, breaking in. Bell looked at him in warning. "But I agree with Agent Bell. He didn't murder his sister. Another killer did."

Larrabee dropped her pen on the desk.

"Two serial killers. Any more good news you want to share with me?"

"Look, we aren't asking you to alter your investigation," Bell said. "Continue searching for Christina

Wolf's murderer as you have with full support from the FBI."

"And by *FBI* you mean the two of you, not Deputy Director Weber."

"Yes."

"So what do you want from me?"

"Work with us. If I'm right, we'll catch Christina Wolf's killer and the man who tried to shoot Gardy and me."

"What makes you think the sniper is in Fair Haven Beach?"

"Because the attempt on our lives felt desperate. Weber and Ewing know we're gathering evidence to bring them down, and Wolf is at the center of the conspiracy."

Bell suggested a plan to lure the sniper out of hiding. Larrabee chewed on the idea for a long time before locking eyes with Bell.

"So you want me to turn you in to the FBI. Risky. If this plan blows up in your faces, you'll both go to jail."

As Bell continued, Gardy shifted uncomfortably. Bell hadn't shared her plan with him until now.

"Phone Don Weber and suggest your concerns about the way I'm handling this case, ensuring you mention Gardy is here. In the meantime, I'll plant an idea in his head."

"Explain."

"There's a man who follows my cases. A reporter named Gavin Hayward."

"I've never heard of him. Is he with *The Times* or *The Post*?"

"Neither. He writes for a gossip rag called *The Informer*."

Larrabee's mouth twisted.

"Yes, I'm aware of *The Informer*."

"Hayward begged me for the inside scoop for months. I'll tell him we're meeting with Logan Wolf and give him a location of our choice. As soon as Hayward releases the news, the BAU will find out. Weber and Ewing can't resist an opportunity to kill all three of us."

Larrabee drummed her fingers on the desk and looked up at the lights.

"What a world we live in where a snake like Ewing can elevate himself to the top of the government. But as much as I admired Congresswoman San Giovanni, this document is conjecture and hearsay. I'm going out on a limb for you."

"When this is over, you'll be the detective who captured a government assassin and Christina Wolf's murderer."

"I should bring my partner in on this. Vargus is on the fast track to detective, and he knows how to keep a secret."

"Sorry, I can't take the chance. Keep this plan between the three of us."

Larrabee released a held breath and closed her eyes.

"Okay, Agent Bell. I'm giving you forty-eight hours to prove you aren't insane."

CHAPTER ONE HUNDRED FOUR

He hides inside a study cubicle in the library, one wide and bloodshot eye leering at them between the door and jamb.

Now and then a student passes the cubicle and interrupts his concentration. The males he ignores. His eyes linger on the girls. Young and beautiful, so much like the dozens of girls he's claimed as his own. It would be easy, so easy, to take one today. Follow her across campus and discover where she lives. Dormitory doors are cheaply constructed and flimsy, and the pathways between the dorms and quad are dark and poorly lit compared to large university campuses. This is his hunting ground.

There will be time for the girls after. When he's finished.

Scarlett Bell's legs cross under the table, and she tosses her hair back as he struggles to read the female agent's lips. Something about catching a serial killer. The thought amuses him. He's read about the men she captured, but she's never met one like him. He'll enjoy cutting her open and sealing her inside the container. Keeping her forever.

But the ebony-skinned detective pulls his attention.

She equals Scarlett Bell's beauty. He hadn't banked on the detective's presence, nor the male agent beside Scarlett. They pose new problems he must eliminate. First, the sensual detective. He'll deal with the man later.

Christina Wolf's killer, the ghost who haunts America's plains and its coasts, cities, farms, and forests, remains as patient as a stone on the bottom of a river. He waits until the three stand up from the table and agree to meet later. Except one of them won't be alive by then.

The door whispers open on well-oiled hinges. As the three targets descend the stairs, his shadow passes across the bookcases and leaves a chill in its wake. Merging with a group of students chatting with a professor, he follows the detective through the quad after she splits from the two agents. Curvy hips fill her skirt. Heels click the concrete walkway while she hustles toward the parking lot to escape the heat.

She clicks the key fob while he presses against his van, the baked aluminum searing his flesh. Good. She drove her own car, not a police cruiser. That means she's off the clock. The police won't expect her back at the office.

He whispers her plate number three times and commits it to memory in case he loses her in traffic. When she closes her car door, he lifts himself into the van and follows her onto the thoroughfare, always careful to keep a few vehicles between them.

The chase takes them through the center of the village and away from the ocean. The houses shrink as though they lack the water to sustain them, and the well-manicured lawns give way to bare patches where the grass wilts under the unforgiving sun. Another stroke of luck. Fewer security systems stand in his way.

The woman pulls into a driveway, the blacktop crumbling with disrepair. She locks the car and carries her bag around the back of a small coral-painted two-story, pausing on the steps to glance back at the black van idling curbside. Did she see him in her mirrors?

Without giving the van a second glance, the detective unlocks the door and disappears inside.

Now he waits for dark.

***

Detective Larrabee didn't anticipate the anxiety she experienced when she phoned Don Weber at the FBI's Behavior Analysis Unit. She couldn't recall the last time she deceived another member of the law enforcement community, and Deputy Director Weber had the power to ruin her career if he suspected.

Weber came off as affable. Larrabee surmised he strove to make favorable initial impressions with the police departments his unit assisted, but she sensed a shark swimming beneath the surface. This was a man whose next move always strengthened his position.

He thanked Larrabee for expressing her concerns over Scarlett Bell's profile, and she felt him bristle over the phone when Agent Gardy's name came up. Larrabee only hoped Bell knew what she was doing.

She flipped the television on and kicked off her heels, then seeing nothing good was on, she shut down the TV and returned to the kitchen. Searching through the refrigerator, she settled on a yogurt and padded back to the living room with the snack. Thick drapes shut out the sun and concealed the junk pile marring her neighbor's fenced-in front yard. This had been a nice neighborhood when she inherited the little house from her mother, and now it attracted drug users and a criminal element. Last year, her arms full with grocery bags, she heard a distinct racial slur from across the street. When she turned, she found Mr. Randolph on his front porch rocking chair, beer in hand, stained wife-beater tank drooping off his shoulders. The son-of-a-bitch lifted his middle finger when she stared too long. If he was willing to harass a cop, how would he treat another minority family?

A scratching noise against the siding caught her attention. Yanking the curtains back, she craned her head and searched the driveway. Satisfied nobody was messing with her car, she shut the curtains and checked the back door lock.

Sighing, she set the empty yogurt cup down and climbed the stairs. The bedroom was darker than the living room. She used blackout curtains so she could sleep on overnight shifts. A box fan in the corner buzzed with white noise, a sound she'd grown so accustomed to she never turned the fan off. She kept her bedroom military-neat, no laundry to trip over, the bedspread smooth as calm waters while she fished sweatpants out of the dresser. A gilded photograph of her mother and father, both gone for five years now, stood beside a jewelry box on the dresser. She touched the photo and silently asked them if she was doing the right thing, lying to one of the FBI's most powerful agents.

Eyeing the clock, Larrabee noted she had five hours until she met with Agents Bell and Gardy at her hotel. She set her alarm to go off in three hours and curled beneath the covers, the extra pillow draped over her ear to block out the neighborhood clamor.

Larrabee didn't sleep long.

When she sprang awake, she knew something was wrong. A sound. Someone outside…inside?…the house. Her body went rigid as though she'd fallen back on a sheet of ice.

Larrabee willed her legs to move. She drew down the blanket, the chill of the climate-controlled air coaxing her flesh to rise in goosebumps.

She reached out for her gun and remembered it was downstairs. With her phone.

Shit.

What was it she'd heard? Maybe nothing. Just the slam of a car door or one of her neighbors cursing.

She lay her head back on the pillow and strained to listen as the box fan drowned out the outside world. That's when she knew she wasn't alone in the house.

Larrabee crept down from the bed and slid along the wall, searching for something, anything on her desk that would serve as a weapon. The metal jewelry box had sharp edges. It wasn't enough to kill a man, but if she brought it down at the right angle, the box would excavate a chunk of flesh and make the intruder think twice about fighting.

Lifting the box, she moved on cat's paws to the door. She slid the door open a crack to see if anyone was on the landing.

Empty.

She exhaled a moment before a thumping noise came from behind. Inside the closet.

Larrabee spun around.

And saw the wide, psychotic eye glaring at her through the cracked open door.

She screamed and turned to run when he lunged. His hand grabbed her hair and yanked, snapping her neck back. Her feet flew out from under her, legs splayed as he climbed atop her stomach. She swung the jewelry box and knocked his head sideways. Blood trickled down his forehead as she brought the box back for another swing.

A powerful hand shot down and gripped her neck. Squeezed. Eyes wide and desperate, she slammed the jewelry box against his head and scraped flesh and hair away from his scalp.

Eyes rolling back, the maniac toppled over and collapsed on the floor. Larrabee screamed for help as she squirmed to get out from under him. She still lay beneath his dead weight.

Coughing, she slipped one leg free and slammed her foot into his ribs. He struggled back to his knees as she kicked out again and stung his chin, whipping his head back.

Crawling on all fours, Larrabee struggled toward the closed bedroom door. She reached the threshold, but he grabbed her ankle and dragged her back into the bedroom.

She beat her fists against his face and drove the point of her elbow against his neck. But he didn't flinch.

The backhand slap stunned her. She stumbled backward, the room spinning, floor rising to meet her. Larrabee's head struck the wall. Stars flashed in her eyes as she swung blindly.

Then the maniac wrapped his hands around her throat and lifted. Suspended off the floor, eye-to-eye with the maniac, her legs kicked at him as he squeezed the life out of her.

With one hand, he propped her against the wall like a rag doll. The other hand reached behind him and removed the knife, razor sharp and bloodstained.

She knew who he was now. Christina Wolf's serial killer. Peering into his eyes opened a window to the bodies he'd left behind. He was more than a murderer. He was a dark legend. A whisper told at midnight to frighten children. Nothing could stop him.

He came here to kill Larrabee. After he snuffed out the last remaining light in her body, he'd butcher Scarlett Bell. And Neil Gardy.

And any mortal fool enough to stand against him.

CHAPTER ONE HUNDRED FIVE

The conversation with Gavin Hayward of *The Informer* left Bell queasy as if a thick sheen of brown grease slicked her skin.

But the bait was set. Though she discerned Hayward's doubt—he didn't understand why she'd contact him with classified information—the rat snatched the cheese. Now she only had to wait until the story went live on the tabloid's website.

Outside the hotel room window, the brutal heat waned, and daylight took on orange and red tints. The sun dropped below a line of palms through the west window.

"You sure about this?" Gardy asked, checking his gun.

She wasn't. How could she be certain about a plan she'd cobbled together in a few hours?

A text from Larrabee sat in Bell's phone. As agreed upon, the detective had called Weber and planted the seed that something was wrong in Fair Haven Beach. The instant he found out about *The Informer* article, he'd contact the sniper and order the executions. But Larrabee hadn't answered any of Bell's texts since.

Bell fed Hayward a vague description of the meeting

site so the public wouldn't figure it out. She didn't want a hundred vigilantes to wreck her plan. But Weber would recognize the location a mile from the beach house where the serial killer murdered Christina Wolf.

The location seemed perfect: unless the sniper broke into a populated home along the beach, the only hiding spot with an unobstructed shot was the cluster of palms and scrub on the north end of the beach. That's where Bell would wait.

"I'm calling the police," Bell finally said, taking one last peek through the curtains. She spotted a shadow in the parking garage. It might have been anybody, a shopper searching for his car after closing time. But the dark presence set her on edge as she searched for the black van she'd seen yesterday.

"Larrabee is on her day off," Gardy said, holstering the gun. "Could be she wanted to unwind this evening. Or maybe she got cold feet after calling Weber."

"It doesn't feel right. I'm worried about her."

Bell sneaked another look between the curtains. No sign of the man in the parking garage.

The officer who answered the phone sounded at his wit's end as a man, probably someone the police arrested, yelled about his rights in the background. He huffed as Bell explained her concerns. Despite his reservations, the officer agreed to send a cruiser past Larrabee's house.

After thanking the officer, Bell refreshed the main page of *The Informer* on her phone. The short article headlined the page in bold letters. *FBI's Scarlett Bell Meeting Serial Killer Logan Wolf*. She clicked the article and skimmed the text, catching two typos in the rushed article. Hayward had come through.

"Hayward published the article," Bell said, sliding the phone into her back pocket. "Let's give Weber ten minutes to call his mercenary."

"It won't take him that long."

Gardy's phone rang as they prepared to leave. He mouthed, "It's Harold," while the analyst fed him the information he'd dug up on Weber and Logan Wolf.

"Send me the document, Harold," Gardy said. "And I want you to send a copy to an attorney I know…right… here's his contact information."

Gardy read Harold the information and gave a thumbs-up to Bell.

"We've got Weber," Gardy said when the call ended. "He ordered surveillance on Logan and Renee Wolf in 2013. The bastard knew the wife's daily routine down to the minute."

"Good move sending copies."

"Not that anything bad will happen to Harold."

"Or us?"

Purple gloaming made the village seem alien and otherworldly as Bell and Gardy descended the steps and crossed the vacated thoroughfare. With the shops closed, the village seemed like a ghost town. She half-expected tumbleweed roll across the road.

Entering the parking garage prickled her skin again. Gardy glared at her when she pulled to a stop on the second level.

"What's wrong?"

She swung her eyes through the garage, past the concrete beams to the darkness gathering along the far wall.

"Nothing. Let's go."

Gardy remained silent during the ride across the village. This was how he acted when a case made him nervous. She kept checking the mirrors, expecting to see a trailing vehicle, but the roads remained empty except for a few cars entering parking lots for big box stores and chain restaurants. Bell caught herself gripping the steering wheel and eased off, forcing herself to regulate her breathing. The plan seemed foolhardy as they approached the coast. She feared for Gardy, the senior agent who'd looked after Bell through her first years with the BAU. An unwanted memory flashed in her mind—Gardy bent over the steering wheel, head dripping blood after they crashed in Coral Lake, New York. She didn't know what she'd do without him in her life.

He caught her staring.

"We always find a way," Gardy said, sensing her doubt. "Stay focused on what we need to do. It's a solid plan."

It isn't, she thought. Too many loose ends, too much potential for the case to blow up in their faces. And she couldn't shake the feeling that someone had followed her since she arrived in Fair Haven Beach.

The beach house came into view when she rounded a dogleg curve that deposited them onto the coast road. The steepled roof looked like a shark fin. Yellow crime scene tape glowed in the fading light.

Bell parked along the road, and they walked down to the palm grove, unconcerned about anyone seeing the rental car. She wanted to announce her presence, make sure the sniper knew where to find them.

Guns in hand, they sifted through the trees. Nobody was here. Good. They had time to scope out the area before the sniper arrived.

Dusk turned to dark, and the dark turned black and oily. A brisk wind off the ocean tickled the fronds and hurled breakers against the sand. But still no sign of the shooter.

"Where do you think you're going?" Bell asked when Gardy left their hiding spot and headed toward the beach.

"We're supposed to be meeting Logan Wolf. Somebody needs to play the part, and I'm a more convincing male."

She wanted to say something snarky. Break the tension threatening to tear them in half. She couldn't. The words died on Bell's lips when he abandoned her.

Then she barely saw him anymore as he merged with the night. He holstered his gun and concealed it beneath his t-shirt as he paced the beach. Gardy stopped near the shoreline and waited. Solemn as a statue.

She never heard the footsteps approach from behind.

CHAPTER ONE HUNDRED SIX

The callused hand covered Bell's mouth and yanked her backward. She swung her elbow back at his head, but her assailant ducked the blow and placed a knife against her throat.

"Shh," her abductor said, whispering in her ear.

His forearm clamped against her chest and held her in place. She sank her teeth into his flesh. No effect. The man didn't flinch.

Powerful arms spun her around, and she stared into the black, depthless eyes of Logan Wolf. He placed his forefinger against his lips and pointed past the trees. At first, she didn't see anything. Then stone crackled underfoot as someone approached along the gravel shoulder off the coast road.

The wicked edge of his knife poised beneath her chin. But he made no move to sweep the blade through her flesh. Instead, he tilted his head, an indication he wanted her to circle around the grove.

A shadow drifted among the trees. Deadly and silent. She spotted the rifle a moment before the man ducked out of sight.

Her heart hammered. Gardy stood inside the

shooter's scope. A sitting duck.

"He won't shoot yet," Wolf said, his face close to hers. "He wants all three of us."

Bell nodded. How the hell did Wolf know their plan? He must have followed Bell and Gardy. That would explain the sensation of being watched, but Bell sensed something darker in the night. Pure evil.

Wolf sheathed the knife and pushed her shoulder. "Go."

Bell moved on all fours through the grove. The wind and waves masked her progress, but she couldn't see the sniper anymore. Assuming the assassin set up his shot at the edge of the grove, Bell worked toward the beach. The sea breeze threw sand in her eyes, blurring her vision. Then she spied the barrel poking out from the trees. God, she'd almost crawled into the shooter.

She scurried back, afraid she'd spooked him, when another shadow closed in on the shooter from behind. Wolf.

On the beach, Gardy stood with his hands in his pockets. He kept them there so one hand stayed close to the Glock, but that wouldn't save him if the sniper pulled the trigger.

Wolf was close. Almost on top of the shooter.

The sniper sensed Wolf and spun around, but with his high-powered rifle centered on the beach, he couldn't defend himself. Wolf shoved the sniper to the ground and stuck the point of his blade into the soft flesh below the man's chin. Bell rushed out of hiding with the Glock aimed at the shooter.

"Don't kill him, Wolf."

"Why shouldn't I? He would have cut us down and never lost a minute of sleep."

"Do as I say."

Bell swung the gun at Wolf, and the serial killer shot her a wry smile before he pulled the knife back. Hearing the commotion, Gardy broke his cover and ran toward the grove. Bell turned her flashlight on the sniper.

"You the one who shot at us in Virginia?" she asked, pulling the rifle out of the man's reach. When he didn't answer, she stepped down on his hand, eliciting an angry moan as she pressed the Glock to his head. "Tell me who hired you."

Taking the flashlight from Bell, Gardy swept the beam over the shooter, hissing when he realized how close he came to being shot. He drew the Glock from his holster when he saw Wolf.

"How did Wolf find out about the meeting?"

"Apparently he reads the same websites as Weber," Bell said, grinding her foot down.

The shooter winced, but he refused to speak. Reaching down, Gardy ripped off the black hat and revealed the man's shaved head. Stubble dotted his face, his skin wrinkled and parched from too many years under the sun. Bell placed him in his forties.

"I'll make this easy for you," said Bell, kneeling so she was face-to-face with the shooter. "We're already aware Senator Ewing contracted you to murder us, and Don Weber at the FBI made the call. Give them up, and we'll let you live."

"I don't know what you're talking about."

The man's voice was hoarse and gravely. His smug grin stretched the width of his face.

"The last man who tried to shoot me ended up with a bullet in his forehead. Right here." Bell jammed her finger above the man's eyebrows. "Why protect Ewing and Weber? They'll toss you away after they finish with you. Don't think they won't sell you out to save themselves."

The man spat. The glob landed on her sneaker.

"Nice," she said, wiping her sneaker off in the sand.

"You aren't gonna do shit," he said, grinning. "You're

federal agents. What will the government say if you shoot an unarmed man?"

"Check him," Bell said.

Gardy searched the man's pockets and shook his head. Except for the rifle, the man came unarmed.

"See? What did I tell you? Haul me into jail for aiming a rifle at the surf."

"You aimed at my partner."

"Prove it."

Wolf lurked in the shadows, his gaze fixed on the shooter. He lifted his eyes to Bell, and an unspoken agreement passed between them.

"You'll give us a full confession," Bell said, smiling. "I'm going to enjoy this."

"Stupid bitch. Place me under arrest or let me walk."

"Your benefactors marched you into a meat grinder. Allow me to introduce you to a man Don Weber ordered you to shoot tonight. His name is Logan Wolf. Does that name mean anything to you?"

Gardy glanced at Bell and opened his mouth. She shook her head. The sniper kept grinning, but uncertainty leaked into his eyes.

"Maybe you've heard of him. He's the FBI agent who went rogue in 2013 and became the nation's most wanted serial killer. Does that ring a bell?"

The sniper's eyes moved between Bell and Wolf.

"I don't believe you."

"He slaughtered dozens of men we know of. Who knows how many more? Wolf slit their throats and spilled their blood, then he placed sacks over their heads. Rumor has it he hides their faces so the spirits of the deceased can't look at him anymore."

When the man's stoic expression failed, Wolf snaked a hand into his pocket and removed the sack.

"This is insane, Bell," Gardy said, rounding on her.

"We can't stand by while Wolf murders this guy, no matter how reprehensible he is."

"Then we won't watch," she said, lowering the gun as Wolf slid the knife against the sniper's throat. "Come on, Gardy."

Wolf's eyes smiled back at Bell as she left him alone with the gunman. The man's protests turned to screams as Bell and Gardy walked away.

CHAPTER ONE HUNDRED SEVEN

Whirling lights painted blues and angry reds against Detective Larrabee's house. A throng of neighbors came outside to watch, some holding beers and claiming the bitch got what she had coming, others wide-eyed and covering their mouths with their hands as the crime techs ascended the front steps, little baggies covering their shoes.

Officer Vargus, the policeman who'd accompanied Larrabee to the beach house and found Bell inside, stood in the doorway. His face looked pale and drawn, his eyes unfocused as he checked the credentials of everyone entering the house. The first on the scene, he'd discovered Larrabee in the upstairs bedroom, the walls and carpet soaked with blood. The memory of Larrabee's bloody outline against the wall was one he couldn't exorcise. As though the killer hoisted the detective to the ceiling before he tore her to pieces.

Chief Sahd, gray-haired and harried after the emergency called him away from dinner night with his wife, nodded at the two crime techs passing him.

"She upstairs?" When Vargus only glared at Sahd, the chief touched his shoulder. "Vargus, what happened here?"

"Don't go up there, Chief. You don't want to see what he…Jesus, it doesn't even look like her."

Sahd nodded grimly and pushed past, but the chief would probably clamor down the stairs a minute later. Vargus would give Sahd points if the man didn't vomit in the bushes.

The hulking officer felt as if he'd shrunk several inches since arriving at Larrabee's. He studied the onlookers, most of them looky-loos and rubberneckers who wanted to glimpse a dead cop. They'd have to wait a long time. The CSI team had a helluva mess to sift through.

Vargus bit his tongue over the thought. That *mess* upstairs was his partner, a woman he admired. To Vargus, Larrabee seemed bulletproof, invincible. The murderer who killed her was no ordinary man. He was a demon wearing human skin.

Another squad car arrived as Vargus scanned the crowd. Fair Haven Beach didn't attract serial killers. He recalled a handful of murders during his ten years on the force. But he knew enough to suspect the killer stood among the crowd. Blending in. Watching. He studied the faces, passing over animated expressions of horror and elation and honing in on the rapt and silent. These were the most likely killers among the mob. The faces of death.

A hand grabbed his shoulder, and Vargus swiveled around to Chief Sahd staring at him. Sahd looked as if he'd aged twenty years since viewing the murder scene.

"You have any idea who did this to her, Officer?"

Vargus couldn't focus. His attention kept drifting back to the crowd.

"Vargus, who did this?"

Shaking his head, Vargus guarded the door as the medical examiner's car pulled to the curb.

"Larrabee got in over her head with that FBI agent."

"Agent Bell?" Sahd narrowed his eyes. "Are you saying there's more going on than this serial killer case?"

"Just a feeling. Detective Larrabee held nothing back, but she hid her activities after that agent arrived."

"The killer targeted one of ours, Officer, and I want him caught before sunrise. I'll handle the crime scene. You find this Agent Bell. I want to know what hell she dragged Detective Larrabee into."

CHAPTER ONE HUNDRED EIGHT

Gardy cringed every time the sniper squealed. Bell did her best to block out the horror, to compartmentalize the unthinkable. She couldn't. It sounded like Wolf was carving a live pig inside the grove.

She looked up when the vegetation parted. Two shadowed men shuffled toward the road. Wolf clutched the unknown man by his jacket, keeping the shooter on his feet.

"His name is Grant Schlosser, and he's prepared to make a full confession, including the fire he started at your apartment and the bomb he placed under your SUV."

Wolf tossed Schlosser forward, and he fell against Bell's rental, his hands leaving bloody palm prints on the trunk. He lacked part of one ear, and a long, gory trench cut from Schlosser's cheek toward his eye.

"We can't take his confession like this," Gardy said. "This is torture."

"As long as he implicates Ewing and Weber," Bell said. "I'll sleep like a baby, regardless."

Gardy wore an incredulous look on his face. He didn't want any part of Wolf's confession methods.

"This isn't the man who killed my sister," Wolf said, jabbing the point of the knife against Schlosser's jugular.

"But I bet he knows who did."

Schlosser's Adam's apple bounced as he swallowed hard.

"I know other men are involved, but I don't know names."

"You lie."

"I swear."

"They paid you well, I trust," Bell said, lifting the shooter's chin to examine his wounds. "They better have, because your pain is just beginning if I find out you're lying."

Gardy opened the back door. Bell shoved Schlosser inside. Fixing the gun on Schlosser, Gardy slid into the backseat beside him.

Bell gazed at Wolf in the moonlight. Determination and hate lit a fire in the serial killer's eyes, yet his shoulders slumped with the exhaustion of a man who'd shouldered horror for too many years.

"You'd do well to disappear, Wolf. This time forever. I'll clear your name in Renee's murder, and Ewing and Weber will pay for what they did to us, but I can't protect you."

"This night doesn't end until I find Christina's killer."

"Sorry, Wolf. You're not coming with us. You found your way here, so I assume you have transportation nearby. Get in your car and drive. Don't stop until you find a coast you don't recognize."

"Such a shame our time together must end. We could have made an incredible team, the two of us. Imagine what we could accomplish if we fought on the same side."

"I'll never be like you."

"You already are."

Bell shifted her feet. She sensed Gardy's eyes on her from inside the car.

"Remember what I told you. This is your only chance if you want to remain a free man. I need to go."

Bell turned away. Wolf clutched her shoulder and spun her around. She stared into his eyes, two lost souls peering back at her. Her breath quickened, fingers sliding toward the Glock.

When he pressed his lips to hers, she fell back against the door, head swimming with a million reasons to push him away.

She didn't.

His kiss rippled warmth through her body, sent pins-and-needles down her legs. When he pulled away, she'd lost track of time. He strode into the dark, a low chuckle riding the wind as he disappeared.

"Until we meet again, Agent Bell."

Bell touched the door handle and waited. The silhouettes of Gardy and Schlosser in the backseat barely registered in her mind. Finally, she tugged the door open and slid behind the wheel. As she fired the engine, Gardy's eyes found hers in the mirror. She looked away before the hurt grew unbearable.

Bell pulled onto the road and turned the car around. The sooner she brought Schlosser to the police station, the better. She wanted this nightmare to end. After the courts convicted Weber and Ewing, she'd call it a day. Walk away from law enforcement, corruption, and murderers forever. She was young enough to enter another field. Maybe follow her parents to Arizona and forget the last two years happened.

The village lights glittered in the distance when the van rammed them from the side. Tires screeched. Then the car spun across the median and flipped into the ditch.

Her vision spun. The scent of burned rubber met her nose as she struggled to work the feeling back into her legs.

The spiderweb of fractured windshield caved in toward her face.

"Gardy?"

No answer. She tried to turn her head, but agony stopped her dead.

A door opened and shut. Footsteps.

Bell searched for her gun and found it on her hip, but her body lay wrenched around the steering wheel, preventing her from retrieving the weapon.

"Gardy, wake up!"

The door flew open. Hands groped inside and tugged at her arm. The seat belt, the only reason she was still alive, held her fast. The madman severed the straps with his knife and hauled her from the vehicle. She collapsed against the blacktop, body screaming as he reached for her again.

He hoisted Bell by the neck and threw her into the ditch. Rocks tore at her back. She scrambled to her hands and knees, but he was too fast. Relentless.

His arm clubbed the back of her head and turned the world upside down. A boot caught her under the chin and snapped her neck back with a spray of blood.

As she rolled onto her back, he pocketed the knife and produced a camera with a glowing screen. The brightness seared her eyes, but when she tried to look away, the madman snatched her chin and forced her to look.

And Bell saw Larrabee's butchered body, the detective's blank eyes staring accusingly.

She swung her leg and struck his ankle, tripping him up. His arms pinwheeled before he slammed shoulder-first against the blacktop.

The maneuver bought her enough time to retrieve the Glock before he sprang to his feet. She squeezed the trigger. The bullet punctured the madman's shoulder and knocked him against the van. She recognized the vehicle from the parking garage. Several large bulks stood behind tinted windows. A shiver rolled through Bell as she imagined what lay inside the barrels.

One hand clutching his shoulder, blood spilling between his fingers, the killer battled back to his feet. She squeezed off a second shot. It sailed wide and took out the van's side mirror. He stalked across the dividing line while Bell dragged herself to the shoulder. He kicked the gun from her hand when she tried to center the weapon, and it skidded through the gravel and came to rest in a patch of weed and tall grass growing in a bordering meadow.

Bell scurried after the lost weapon. He grabbed her ankle and dragged her into the road.

The blade caught the starlight as he leered down at her.

"Come home, little one. Time to sleep."

The knife flashed at her face when another gun blast thundered over her head. The killer flew backward and landed on his elbows. A fresh wound bubbled blood from his thigh. Bell twisted her head. Gardy slumped over the ruined car, the undercarriage steadying his grip on the Glock. The next shot sailed past the killer and blew a hole through the van. Losing his balance, Gardy tumbled to the pavement.

The scuff of boot against blacktop was the only warning Bell received as the killer loomed over her. Powerful hands gripped her hair and yanked. She slid across the road, the cruel surface tearing her knees while she fought to spin away.

With one hand he threw the van door open, the other buried in her hair and ripping locks from her scalp. The van trembled as he stepped inside. An overwhelming death scent rolled out of the vehicle. Now inside the van, he dug both hands into her hair and tugged. Her body lifted off the pavement as her neck arced backward.

She landed inside the death van. Eyes glassed over, she stared at the doubled visions of barrels stacked along the walls. This was the end. He was too powerful.

The growl of another motor pulled the killer's eyes to

the road. An SUV skidded to a halt and fishtailed toward the van. Bumpers slammed, and the killer toppled onto the macadam as Bell cleared her head. She prayed the police had arrived, but she knew better. Wolf came back for her.

Knives cut through the air. Bell slumped against a barrel as something shifted inside. While she blocked out the image of what lay inside the barrels, Gardy yelled from across the road. He'd pulled himself onto the overturned car again and aimed the Glock at the two serial killers.

"Move!" Gardy yelled, motioning Bell to get out of the line of fire.

"No, Gardy. You'll shoot Wolf!"

Wolf yelled out and stumbled. A red line formed and soaked his shirt. The maniac swept the knife at Wolf when Gardy's gunshot caught the killer's arm. He spun toward Gardy, an unstoppable force. Before Gardy could fire again, the killer clutched his neck and squeezed. Gardy's eyes bulged, tongue lolled out as the killer lifted him off the ground and the gun tumbled from his hand. The agent beat his fists against the maniac's face. The killer grinned, his teeth stained red.

Though every bone in her body begged her to stop, Bell pushed herself out of the van and across the road. Wolf circled from behind. Together, they closed in on the killer. Gardy's neck appeared on the brink of snapping when Bell leaped atop the killer's back and raked her nails across his eyes. He threw her off, yet she'd freed Gardy, who lay crumpled in the road. Was he breathing?

Bell sprang up and slammed her fist against the killer's face. The maniac's eyes crossed a moment before Wolf drove the knife into his back. As the killer slumped over, Bell leaped and wrapped her thighs around his neck. He landed on his knees and brought his head up. For a split-second they locked eyes. Then Bell twisted her hips and snapped his neck.

The killer twitched once and lay still.

Bell crawled away. She kept imagining the killer's hands around her neck as she touched her throat and glanced over at Gardy. Her partner's chest swelled and receded. Thank God.

She struggled over to Gardy and supported his head in her lap.

"He's dead, Gardy. Everything will be all right. You can open your eyes now."

Gardy remained unresponsive as Bell brushed the hair from his eyes and felt his neck for a pulse.

"He needs help, Wolf. Can you drive?"

When she turned her head, Wolf had disappeared. Her eyes swept across the road and stopped on Christina's killer. Someone had slit his throat and slid a black sack over his head.

Wolf's stolen SUV butted up against the killer's van, the front ends mangled. All around her, night closed in on the lonely roadway. Crickets sang to the stars, and somewhere a cicada buzzed.

"Wolf?"

But he was gone. She wondered if she'd ever see him again.

CHAPTER ONE HUNDRED NINE

Bell clutched her aching head and peeked between the Venetian blinds into the interrogation room.

Throwing their weight around, the Fair Haven Beach police had seized control of the Grant Schlosser case. They wouldn't have control for long. The FBI would rip the case away once they determined Schlosser's violent crimes crossed state lines. And when they discovered he'd murdered Congresswoman San Giovanni, the feds would nab Schlosser and never let go.

Behind the glass, Chief Sahd and Officer Vargus interviewed Schlosser. Bell smirked at the good cop, bad cop routine when Sahd slammed his fists down on the desk and knocked over a chair. Bell knew the sniper saw her through the glass. He wouldn't look her in the eye.

She checked her texts and found nothing new. Gardy had been at the hospital for three hours. The prognosis—four busted ribs, a concussion, and a sprained neck. He was lucky to be alive. They all were.

Another hour passed. Sometimes Sahd questioned Schlosser, other times Vargus drew the short straw. Together, they filled multiple pages of notebook paper with Schlosser's statements. Bell knew the sniper would tell the truth. Wolf was still out there, and he'd find Schlosser if the shooter didn't confess.

A pall hung over the office. Detective Larrabee weighed on the officers' minds, but each cop tilted his cap when he met Bell's eyes. Executing a cop killer won their respect.

The atmosphere grew darker inside the interrogation room. Sahd and Vargus met eyes and glanced back at Bell. After a moment, Sahd strode into the operations area and snatched Bell by the elbow, ushering her into his office. He locked the door. The silence rang in Bell's ears.

"You realize who Schlosser just implicated," Sahd said, standing behind his desk and leaning forward on his arms.

"I do."

"Jesus H…Senator Ewing and the Deputy Director of CIRG. The assassination of a U.S. congresswoman? How did this war converge on my village?"

Vargus, the first police officer to arrive at the coast road, had identified the serial killer. Greg Maxey, a traveling salesman working out of California. The first unlucky CSI tech to pry open a barrel lost her dinner on the blacktop. Their work had just begun. They'd spend a long time identifying the bodies and matching them to missing person cold cases.

"Do yourself a favor, Chief. Put Schlosser in holding and hand the case over to the feds. You know they'll take charge when they arrive."

Sahd scratched his forehead.

"I don't need this shit."

While two officers led Schlosser to the cells at the back of the office, Bell rubbed her eyes and wondered if Gardy was awake. Yet she couldn't stop thinking about Wolf. Though she couldn't justify Wolf stalking and murdering serial killers, she felt empathy. Ewing and Weber took everything from him. His wife, his freedom, his sanity.

And now his last remaining family member. Had Bell been in the same position, she might have sought a similar vengeance on serial killers.

Bell collected her bag, expecting a wrap-up meeting with Sahd before she left for the hospital. The doors flew open. Bell's mouth went dry as Deputy Director Weber and Agent Flanagan strutted into the office.

"I want this woman arrested," Weber said, pointing at Bell.

The police officer Weber charged with arresting Bell was a thin, short man with a handlebar mustache. He glanced uncertainly at Sahd, who'd wandered out of his office to see what the commotion was.

"Did you hear me? Arrest this woman."

"On what grounds?" Sahd asked, moving to block Weber.

"Conspiring with a known fugitive and serial killer."

Sahd removed the cuffs from his hip as Weber grinned. The smile disappeared when Vargus grabbed Weber's arms and Sahd slapped the cuffs on the deputy director.

"Are you insane?"

"Don Weber, you're under arrest for conspiracy to murder a United States congresswoman," Vargus said. "You have the right to remain silent. Anything you say can and will be used against you in a court of law..."

Weber yanked at the cuffs as Vargus read his Miranda rights. As Flanagan edged away, Bell rounded the desk and ensured Weber's little helper didn't run.

"Chief Sahd," Bell said, rounding on Weber. "I'd like two minutes with the deputy director."

Sahd chewed on the idea before he agreed.

The chief led Weber into the interrogation room. Bell ensured no one looked in on them.

"You're in over your head," Weber said, leering at

Bell. “These charges won’t stick.”

“Sit down,” Bell said, pushing on Weber’s shoulder.

The Deputy Director of CIRG stared darts into Bell as she drew up a chair and faced him.

“We uncovered BAU documents from 2013. They list Renee Wolf’s nightly routine, cross-referenced with Logan Wolf’s work schedule. This evidence is in the hands of an attorney firm which specializes in law enforcement corruption. When I’m done here, I’ll make sure Congresswoman San Giovanni’s task force members have their own copies. Should anything happen to Gardy or me, the firm will release the information to the US Attorney, the FBI, and the national media.”

Weber raised his chin in defiance, but he swallowed when they locked eyes.

“You were always a disgrace to the BAU, Agent Bell.”

“Unfortunately, you won’t be in a position to accept my letter of resignation. Say hello to Senator Ewing for Lana when you get to prison.”

The first glint of sunshine warmed the eastern sky when Bell arrived at the hospital.

His ribs bandaged, Gardy slept fitfully on the hospital bed. Bell pulled a chair beside the bed and watched him. The senior agent wore a boyish expression as his eyes swiveled beneath closed lids. Dreaming of a better time and place.

Two orderlies chuckled in the hallway. Bell closed the door and settled into the chair. Checking her phone, she noticed a message from Harold from an hour ago. He wanted to know how Gardy was doing. Bell exhaled. Harold was safe. She returned a quick text and urged Harold to get out of Virginia for a few weeks. Take that vacation he’d put off all year.

Bell didn’t realize she’d fallen asleep until the nurse brushed against her while checking on Gardy. As Bell straightened Gardy’s blanket, her partner assessed her through thin slits for eyes.

"How are you feeling?" she asked, knowing it was a meaningless question. She could imagine the amount of pain he experienced.

"Doctor says the ribs will heal on their own, but it will take months before I'm myself. How about you?"

Bell shrugged. Her body ached as though she'd crashed a car and flipped into a ditch.

"I'll recover, but the rental company will be pissed."

Gardy gave his Muttley the cartoon dog snicker and clutched his ribs.

When they were alone again, Bell filled Gardy in on the night's proceedings. The Fair Haven Beach police arrested Weber and turned him over to the FBI. The rumor of Senator Ewing's impending arrest had leaked to the press.

"What about Wolf?" Gardy groaned.

"He's gone. For good this time, I think."

"Don't count on it."

"The crazy part is the momentum is on his side. The police cleared his name regarding Christina's death, and it's inevitable the FBI will do the same with his wife's murder. In the eyes of the law, he'll be an innocent man."

Gardy looked toward the window. The deep blue sky spoke of optimism and new beginnings.

"Sure, if you don't count the serial killers Wolf murdered."

Bell leaned closer and threw a glance over her shoulder. The door stood closed.

"There's a serious issue with those murders."

"Educate me."

"Wolf never left DNA. The FBI has surveillance footage of Wolf in the area for two murders, but they can't convict him on a couple random sightings. And his modus operandi?" Bell raised an eyebrow. "Turns out a certain serial killer used the same method to kill Wolf's wife and sister."

"And now that serial killer is dead, and the FBI thinks he's responsible for Wolf's murders. Very convenient for your friend."

Bell looked down. Her hands rested on the bed a few inches from his. A silence borne of lost opportunities and regrets passed between them. Sitting this close, Bell couldn't deny her feelings for Gardy. She wished once, just once, he'd shown the same interest in her. In recent months Gardy seemed on the verge of bonding with Bell. Gardy never followed through, and that told Bell he'd never take the next step.

"You're leaving the FBI," he said, dropping his eyes.

It wasn't a question. Bell had reached the end of the road, and Gardy read the lack of direction and purpose in her eyes. She was lost.

"Yes."

He bit his lip and picked at an invisible piece of lint on the blanket. After a moment, he nodded.

"So this is the end. For us, I mean."

A tear tracked down her face. She'd entered the FBI to avenge her childhood best friend, a girl who died young after a serial killer stole her from the world. When the killer resurfaced, Bell ensured he'd never hurt anyone again. Through her brief career with the BAU, she always believed better days awaited her.

With Weber in jail and Ewing's arrest imminent, Bell accepted better days would never arrive while she worked for the FBI.

But she couldn't abandon Gardy now. He looked broken inside and out.

"You aren't getting rid of me that easily. I'll have plenty of free time. Who better to check on you while you rehabilitate your injuries?"

"No, you should go on with your life, Bell. Don't wait around for me. I'll only slow you down."

She stared down at her hands, wishing he'd asked her to stay. For him, she would have. Then she set her hands against the bed and stood.

"If you're certain."

"I'm certain I want you to be happy."

She turned and opened the door. Once she stepped outside of this room, there would be no turning back. They'd see each other at the criminal proceedings and the case debriefing, but the gap between them would be too large to bridge.

When she looked over her shoulder, Gardy's chin dropped to his chest.

"What if happiness means having you in my life?" Gardy asked.

Bell smiled. Maybe she'd stick around a little longer.

***

Thank you for being a loyal reader!
If you love dark psychological thrillers, read my new serial killer series, Darkwater Cove.

Check Darkwater Cove out on Amazon

Let the Party Begin!

I'm a pretty nice guy once you look past the grisly images in my head. Most of all, I love connecting with kickass readers like you.

Join the party and be part of my exclusive VIP Readers Group at:

WWW.DANPADAVONA.COM

Show Your Support for Indie Thriller Authors

Did you enjoy this book? If so, please let other thriller fans know by leaving a short review. Positive reviews help spread the word about independent authors and their novels. Thank you.

Author's Acknowledgment

Mind of a Killer would not be possible without the encouragement, support, and efforts from my patrons.

Tim Feely
Lisa Forlow
Steve Gracin
Dawn Spengler

I value each one of you more than I can express. Thank you for believing in me.

Why Novellas?

The world of entertainment has changed. While I enjoy movies, I watch Netflix series and comparable programming more frequently. Movies are too short to match the story and character arcs of a well-written series, and that's why I favor a long series of novellas over a few novels.

I prefer a long series which I can lose myself in, but broken up into smaller, manageable episodes that don't take up my entire evening.

In short, I'm writing the types of stories I enjoy and composing them into forms I find preferable.

I sincerely hope you enjoy the Scarlett Bell series as much as I love writing it.

How many episodes can you expect? Provided the series is well-received by readers, I don't foresee a definite end and would prefer to expand on the characters and plot lines for the foreseeable future. I still have plenty of devious ideas for upcoming stories.

Stay tuned!

About the Author

Dan Padavona is the author of the The Scarlett Bell thriller series, Severity, The Dark Vanishings series, Camp Slasher, Quilt, Crawlspace, The Face of Midnight, Storberry, Shadow Witch, and the horror anthology, The Island. He lives in upstate New York with his beautiful wife, Terri, and their children, Joe, and Julia. Dan is a meteorologist with NOAA's National Weather Service. Besides writing, he enjoys visiting amusement parks, beach vacations, Renaissance fairs, gardening, playing with the family dogs, and eating ice cream.

Visit Dan at: www.danpadavona.com

Made in the USA
Las Vegas, NV
09 May 2022